Finding Love in Friday Harbor, Washington

Washington Island Romance Series

Finding Love in Friday Harbor
Finding Love on Bainbridge Island
Finding Love on Whidbey Island

Finding Love in Friday Harbor, Washington

Washington Island Romance Series

by

Annette M. Irby

The Team: Miralee Ferrell, Judy Vandiver, Nikki Wright, Cindy Jackson
Cover Design: Indie Cover Design, Lynnette Bonner Designer

Mountain Brook Ink is an inspirational publisher offering fiction you can believe in.
Printed in the United States of America

ENDORSEMENTS

Annette M. Irby has done it again, this time within the pages of *Finding Love in Friday Harbor, Washington.* Broken promises, secrets, and loss combine to test the mettle of the story's main characters. Irby reaches deep, and delivers an emotionally-satisfying gift to her readers. With picturesque landscapes and charming secondary characters, Irby will earn new fans with this one. My advice? Make room on your "keepers" shelf!

Loree Lough, bestselling author of 115 award-winning novels, including newly-released 5-star reader-favorite, *50 Hours*

Romantic Times Review

The author deploys beautiful metaphors in the first few pages of this book, effectively drawing the reader into this sweet story. Vivid descriptions, perfect pacing and clever dialogue make this tale come alive on the page. The characters are likable from the start. The way that Hunter cares for Mikaela is heartwarming. No story is believable without conflict, and this one has plenty. The author knows how to reveal just enough about her characters to keep the reader engaged. When the reader meets Hunter Cahill, he is recovering from the loss of his dad and still reeling from his breakup with his ex-fiancée Mikaela Rhoades. He is delighted but also conflicted when she returns to Friday Harbor to launch a new marine biology program that is directly involved with his family business, Cahill Touring. Mikaela hopes that she will not reunite with Hunter, but her heart longs to rekindle their love. Together, they struggle to navigate the choppy waters of what could have been and what may be. (MOUNTAIN BROOK INK, Aug., 290 pp., $11.99)

Dedication

This book is dedicated to my parents, Douglas and Virginia Monroe, whose support and love have encouraged me to work hard and dream big. Thank you for your example of faith, commitment, and integrity. I love you.

Acknowledgments

I'm so grateful to many people in my life who've offered support, encouragement, even prophetic input. My heartfelt thanks to the following folks:

Paul, my dear husband, co-dreamer, and biggest supporter, thank you for helping brainstorm, for believing in me, and for being my first reader. Your excitement and encouragement, as I chase these dreams, mean so much to me. I'm so grateful for our twenty-six years (and counting) of marriage. I love you.

My beautiful family, thank you for your support and sacrifices, especially during NaNoWriMo. This book series is a victory for all of us. I've enjoyed our research trips—beachy days (as often as possible!), the whale watching tour, and ferry rides for up-close encounters with sea life. To my oldest daughters, I love watching you discover your dreams and be rewarded for doing what you love. And to my youngest—I always told you we'd go out for ice cream when I got this contract. Then, last year I got to keep that promise. Go for your dreams, my daughters! I'll be here cheering you on. I believe in you and love you with all my heart!

Karen Gleason, Angela Premoe, and Virginia Monroe, my sisters and mom, are the best supporters and some of my first readers. Thank you for sharing my excitement on this journey. You're all a big part of these dreams coming true. And to my brother, Patrick Monroe, thank you for your support behind the scenes. Much love to all of you!

My critique group, the McCritters: Ocieanna Fleiss, Dawn Kinzer, and Veronica McCann. This novel has been many years in the making, and my dear critique partners have seen many incarnations of this story. Dear, dear writing buddies—I'm so thankful for you and for our friendship over the past decade plus. Write on, friends!

To Linda Smith, though you won't see this, thank you for letting me use your typewriter to pour out my stories as a teen. I have fond memories of you and those visits. Your joy was contagious, and you set a caring example of welcoming friends and family. You are missed, my friend.

Friend and mentor, Karen Ball, for your input on this story and my writing journey. I'm so blessed by your friendship all these years!

Cheryl Wyatt, you've been such an encourager ever since we met. I appreciate your Christ-like heart. Thank you for welcoming me into your writing life, my friend. Hugs.

I've learned so much from Rachel Hauck and Susan May Warren. Thank you for mentoring, writing how-tos, and teaching workshops. I sincerely appreciate you!

ACFW (American Christian Fiction Writers) has been such a helpful organization for me as a writer, providing friendships, mentoring, workshops, conferences, and networking. If you're a Christian writer, I highly recommend connecting with this organization!

Thanks to my father-in-law, Dr. David Irby, former Vice Dean for Education, University of California San Francisco School of Medicine and professor of medicine, for answering my questions about the hierarchy of universities. I've really appreciated your gracious support over the years as I've pursued my dreams, and your readiness to help with this project was such a gift. Thank you! And to Janet and Leah, thank you for your interest in my writerly world all these years.

Cahill Touring is loosely based on a real whale-touring outfit located in Friday Harbor, Washington. The folks at San Juan Excursions are fantastic (watchwhales.com). Captain Pete and his wife Erin answered many questions for me. They were very welcoming and gracious, both during the tour our family enjoyed with them, and later in our e-mailed conversations. I situated my fictional whale touring office a little differently in Friday Harbor and changed many things to fit my story. If you get a chance to tour Washington's Salish Sea with them, do it!

Whenever we visit the Pacific Coast, we love to pick up a

sampling of fudge at Granny Hazel's Candy and Gift Shop in Westport. I loosely based my Granny Belle's shop on theirs because I was so inspired by their chocolate-peanut butter fudge and cute shop. Check it out if you get a chance. Oh, and they ship orders as well! (grannyhazels.com)

All that said about my experts, let's chalk any "mistakes" up to artistic license.

To my church friends over the years, thank you for your support. George and Wendi Miller, thank you for your friendship and support. And to George, for your prophetic input. Sean and Stacia Walker you've been such encouragers. I'm grateful for you both. Butterflies, Sean!

Yeshua, the Bridegroom, you are the One who both placed this dream in me and the One who is bringing it to fruition. Thank You for calling me and fulfilling my dreams as I delight in You. You are my Beloved, and I adore You.

Return to the stronghold,
You prisoners of hope.
Even today I declare
That I will restore double to you.
Zech. 9:12 NKJV

CHAPTER ONE

Rain drizzled over the empty parking lot at Lime Kiln Point State Park, well north of Seattle. This close to the Salish Sea, the mercury floated near fifty degrees, despite the calendar's June date. Only one other vehicle—a scuffed pickup—sat abandoned near the trails this early. Professor Mikaela Rhoades could have the place to herself. But it wouldn't have mattered if there were hordes of people. She'd find a spot to pray, contend for peace.

Her lungs squeezed in her chest. Did Hunter know yet?

Cold wind pitched mist at her face. She ducked under her raincoat's hood, scooting across the parking lot, past the closed gift shop/interpretive center and orca sculpture. The scent of salty air reminded her of why she loved the water, her career path.

Was it a mistake to be here?

Oh, Lord, help. You brought me here. Please make this work.

She must remember to breathe. There were three reactions to fearful things—fight, flight, or freeze. Her reflex, almost every time, was to freeze. If she held her breath, the proverbial monster wouldn't find her. She could hide. Evade. But always, she had to then face whatever the fearsome situation was and overcome. Otherwise, she'd never have gotten this far. Never have suggested this plan.

Never come this close to a collision with her past.

I'm going to see him again. Something she'd been avoiding for over a decade.

Her phone buzzed against her leg. She'd just talked with her family, updating them, sending Dad love on his special day. He'd called her Kayla, making her remember how Hunter had always called her Miki, after the first part of her name, while her dad preferred the latter part.

Maybe this was her boss calling.

She scurried under the slight overhang of the map wall and

pulled out her vibrating phone. Dr. Amelia Wren's photo gazed up at her. Mikaela corralled her thoughts and connected the call. Wind buffeted her from behind, rousing a shiver while her eyes reviewed the image of her favorite place on earth—the Salish Sea all dotted with islands.

"Hello, Dr. Rhoades." Amelia was using her "all-business" voice. She sounded strong today. Mikaela pictured her salt-and-pepper curls, intelligent eyes, and laugh lines. The years hadn't diminished her zest for life, or authority. Too bad zeal hadn't healed her—another thing for Mikaela to pray about. "All settled in?"

Tucking her phone against her ear inside her hood, Mikaela rounded the map area and started down the evergreen-surrounded path between her and Haro Strait. Hopefully, the rain would let up soon. "Yes, thank you."

"And the accommodations?"

"I found a rental overlooking Griffin Bay." The department chairwoman wouldn't like this. The university had offered housing, but Mikaela couldn't see herself in dorm-like accommodations all summer. She didn't mention her beach cottage was one she'd always had in mind if she ever returned. Amelia needn't worry. Mikaela would be nearby and could easily access the grounds and faculty at the labs. Plus, Mikaela's not living in the dorms meant more room for students.

The other option had been to move in with her grandmother, but Granny rented rooms to several students, and Mikaela preferred downtime at day's end. She should, however, get over to see her soon. Granny Belle might have some wisdom to help Mikaela through the summer. Maybe she'd recite a verse, like *"Cast all your cares on Him because He cares for you."*

Yes, that one.

He cares for me. He cares.

"If I'm able," Amelia was saying, "I plan to visit in a few weeks, and perhaps bring the funding representative with me." Mikaela heard snipping and pictured her boss navigating the balcony of her Seattle condo tending her plants, broomstick skirt fluttering around her ankles. Must not be raining there.

2

"I'd be happy to have you." So long as she found her footing first. Best to look competent when they visited. The funding rep? She didn't look forward to welcoming him. Theirs was an arrangement that kept the rep at arm's length, for at least a little while. One saving grace in this endeavor. He could just stay in Seattle for now.

"Have you been to Cahill Touring since you've been back?"

"Not yet. I'll be there Tuesday." Too soon to come face-to-face with Hunter.

Coward? Probably.

Ironically, this brainchild had been Mikaela's. After learning from Hunter's mom how much they could use the help, Mikaela had nudged the department's chairwoman into supporting her crazy notion, touting how the program would benefit both the University of Seattle and its students, as well as Cahill Touring. Then, she'd found funding. Since this was an extra program, the students paid for the privilege of being here during summer term. But ongoing, Mikaela still had to appease the funding representative, Dr. Denver Smythe. His family's foundation would fund the research in the pilot program, the new lab in Hawaii. This summer's project proved the next one was viable.

"Oh, that's right. It's Sunday." Silence rolled along between them like slow-moving water down a rocky creek bed—familiar territory, but nonetheless rife with sharp obstacles. Dr. Wren had no room in her life for church or God or taking a Sabbath, though Mikaela had spoken to Amelia of her relationship with God. "Well, Tuesday is soon enough. I know you realize all that is at stake."

Mikaela knew once a person gained Amelia's support, she'd cheer them to the finish, like she'd faithfully done in Mikaela's life and short career so far. Amelia had once been friends with Reid Cahill, so when Mikaela pitched the idea, Amelia had appreciated the opportunity to help. But Dr. Wren had never known everything about the connection.

Mikaela broke free from the madrone trees right as the wind kicked up. The sight of Haro Strait arrested her. Even oppressed by clouds like today, the view of rushing gray water between here and

3

Vancouver Island captured her like few other locales. The lighthouse lay in the distance, a bit more of a hike. "Now that I'm onsite, I'm more convinced than ever this will be one of our best endeavors, hopefully continuing for years." Of course, she'd be gone by fall. But that's what Hunter preferred, according to their last conversation twelve years ago. By autumn, the benefits would be obvious for the Cahills. Mikaela could walk away knowing she'd tried, and hopefully helped. Then someone else could step in here while she took what she'd learned over to Hawaii.

"One more accomplishment before the Big Island, right?" Amelia's voice sounded wistful. Maybe she'd rather be the one spearheading the Hawaii pilot. "Still, I'd love for you to settle down someday."

Ah, it had only taken ten minutes to arrive here again— Amelia's favorite topic lately. Sure, Mikaela longed for a husband to share her life. But she wouldn't divulge that to her boss and give her more ammunition. "There's too much yet to do."

Several secrets pressed for release to her mentor, including candidness about the conflict of interest between her and Captain Hunter. She stuffed those thoughts and put a smile into her voice. "Maybe one day, when I meet *the one.*" Dr. Wren didn't need to know Mikaela had stopped looking years ago. Back to this summer's project. "Don't worry. I won't let you down."

Or the Cahills, for that matter.

Hunter Cahill dug his oar into the strait. Biting wind threw water at his face, burrowing into his street clothes. No wetsuit or even a lifejacket today. He'd been in too much of a rush to get here. Out of habit, he scanned the waters for signs of life. A short, dark gray dorsal surfaced a couple hundred yards toward the center of the channel. Harbor porpoise usually traveled in pods of three to six animals. Dall's porpoise the same. Not that he was on duty right now.

He paddled north, toward Lime Kiln Lighthouse. As he predicted, the churning tossed him like a cork today, and the current dragged on his boat.

If his dad knew he was kayaking alone in these conditions, he'd have said, *"What are you thinking, Son? Always take a partner in choppy weather. Where's your life jacket? I raised you to have more water smarts than that."* But then Dad would ease up, seeing the way Hunter wrestled. He'd know exactly how to help, what advice to offer.

Too bad he couldn't advise him anymore.

This time Hunter wasn't imagining the presence of harbor porpoise. Their grayish dorsals pierced the surface in a pod of five just off to his left as they raced north.

A mottled Pacific harbor seal twisted up to the surface next to his kayak before dashing back under. Sea otters poked their velvet noses out, watching him. Dad would have loved this, despite the mist. If he were here, he'd talk about the wind velocity and predict orca activity.

Then he'd tell Hunter what he'd told him since that summer— that he'd made a mistake all those years ago when he let Mikaela go.

A huge mistake.

Hunter's chest ached. Relinquishing his dad was hard enough. Death hadn't given Hunter a choice. But Hunter was the one who'd chosen to release Miki.

And he was drowning because of it.

His abs burned and sweat broke out on his face, mixing with the mist. He considered shedding a layer but didn't want to lose his momentum. Stroke right, then left, right, then left. Pause.

How often had his dad challenged him about giving up on Miki? The last time they'd been together on the water, they'd discussed her . . .

Wind bullied the clouds across the early autumn sky that day. Dad breathed deep, working his kayak closer. "You've never cared for anybody like you care for her." Present tense because Dad knew Hunter had never gotten over her. They proceeded along in tandem, talking above the wind.

"True." His gut clenched just thinking about her. "But it's been over ten years. She's probably married with six kids by now, all of them non-fish eating and not a landlubber among them." He grinned as the image of Miki with an imaginary gaggle of blond offspring finding green shore crabs under every rock, worked him over.

"And I loved her like a daughter." Aw, Dad. "I understand why you went on with your life, Son." His dad stilled his oar and rested a fisted hand on his thigh. "But if she ever comes back to the island single, if you ever get another chance, promise me you'll pursue her—romance her. Promise me you'll give it one more try."

Maybe Hunter had sensed it was the last time they'd talk like that. Maybe he realized how much it meant to his father for him to agree. Whatever the reason, fool that he was, Hunter caved. "I will, Dad."

Of course Miki had never returned.

So here he was, alone and off the hook, trying to keep his dad's business afloat. Maybe the new arrangement with the University of Seattle's marine bio department would help. Professor Matthews, or Michaels, or whatever his name was—Mom hadn't given Hunter all the details—was due to arrive this week. Hunter would have to tolerate college students on his bridge, asking questions, trying his patience. But he'd do it. Anything to keep Cahill Touring open. For Dad.

Hunter watched two black dorsals slice through the water dead ahead about ten yards—one higher and straighter than the other. Never got old. He held his breath and stilled his oar. A smaller, curved fin joined them, surfacing momentarily before arcing back into the strait. Their offspring. Dad would have talked nonstop about the pod, but he'd always been so hyped about marine life. So much like Miki.

There was one more thing Hunter had to do before he pulled his kayak from the channel. For the rest of his life, his hero would no longer be here to offer advice or direction or affirmation. Hunter's throat burned, and he tightened his jaw against the quivering in his chin.

A wet gust of wind blew at him, and he faced it, arms still for a moment. Waves tossed him side to side. He sucked in a ragged breath, sighted a mighty eagle soaring over the water, hovering near the tall Douglas firs.

"Happy Father's Day, Dad."

He gave himself one moment...to picture Dad, see his smiling face as he captained the *Millennium*. His eyes always shone with light and warmth, but you wouldn't want to cross him. He was a good captain.

Hunter shook off the memories rolling through his mind, worked the kayak forward. Something caught his attention on shore. One person stood alone on the rocks, peering out, binocs raised. The on-again, off-again rains had glazed every surface. Not even tourists had ventured out this morning. Only that lone figure up there, too close to the edge. A single slip and he'd be a goner.

Yellow slicker. Long legs, lean build. Escaping strands of dark blonde hair flipped in the wind. Hang on.

Hunter had grown up here. The island's residents were mostly familiar—even at a distance. No local would stand there in this weather. They'd choose a better time. Tourists might, but today's conditions must've chased them away because he hadn't seen a single soul until now. Only one person he knew would brave it. Someone so crazy about whale sightings she'd risk climbing slippery boulders and reject the buddy system, just to get close to the water. His heart thumped.

Miki.

CHAPTER TWO

So, Jesus, I'm in over my head here. But I couldn't ignore Lauren Cahill's predicament with all the financial trouble for their family business. And I know Hunter would never have asked me himself. Even thinking of him, that she'd see him in two short days, made her tremble. *I need Your help.* She waited a few moments, but peace didn't follow her words. What was she missing? *Lord, show me.*

Mikaela narrowed her eyes, studying the water. No dorsal fins peppered the strait up close. But, there was a kayaker out there. Someone brave enough to endure forty-degree waters should his boat tip. She tugged her hood tighter to keep out the wind and climbed the boulders to get closer to the sea. Out in the channel, the kayaker stroked, right, left, right, left, pause. Two more sets, rest and scan.

The sight whisked away her oxygen. Only one person she knew paddled like that.

Hunter.

She reached for the round pendant around her neck and pressed it against her chest. The metal felt hot on her skin. Of all the places on the island to run into each other, and after her day and a half on location already, she spied him *here*? She'd avoided the docks in town, the touring office, and she'd shopped for supplies in the middle of the afternoon when he'd have been out on tours just to avoid him.

He rowed parallel to the shore, glancing around, probably spotting that circling bald eagle she'd photographed with her phone. She raised the binoculars to her eyes, zoomed in on the kayak. Her breath puffed out, fogging the chilly air. Yes. Hunter.

When he turned his head her direction, she shifted so perhaps he'd think she was studying the waterways. Then, she slowly panned back to him. The whiskery shadow on his jaw gave him a rugged look, and he'd filled out more since high school. Muscled, capable, still loving the water. Taking advantage of a few hours before the day's tour began, oar in the sea, taming the choppy waves.

He wore a ball cap over his short brown hair. Thanks to the zoom, she caught his mesmerizing gray eyes taking in everything around him. He tipped his head up far enough to catch her standing there. She yanked the binocs from her face, taking one slippery step back. His gaze seemed to lock on her, and she couldn't tear her attention away.

A huge black-and-white animal shot out of the water barely off land. Another joined the first one. Breaching orcas! She jolted, her foot slipping on the slick boulder. *Oh Jesus, help!* Her arms pinwheeling, she screamed and skidded down to land hard on the rock, sliding fast. Her heart thrashed in her chest. Pain shot to her brain, blinding her.

Instantly, icy water chased from her feet to her neck, up and over her head as she joined the orcas, wolf eels, giant Pacific octopus, and everything else living in the Salish Sea.

Shoulders tight, Hunter sucked in a breath as the woman disappeared under water. He cut his kayak toward shore, stroking hard, arms burning.

Dear God.

God didn't hear his prayers for himself, or the family business if their books were any indication, but he hoped God would hear this time. Could it really have been Miki? *Help her surface!* What if she'd hit her head on the way in? If she involuntarily inhaled, she'd drown. And any time in the water today would mean hypothermia.

He sliced across the insistent current toward the water's edge. A vice gripped his ribs as he searched the park for a researcher, anyone who could throw a life ring or call for help.

No one.

And she hadn't surfaced.

He maneuvered as close to the rocks as he could, to where he'd seen her go under. Waves harassed his kayak. There! A wavy yellow windbreaker under the water. He held his breath. The woman's head broke the surface, and she sucked in oxygen. Hunter's lungs expanded in unison.

His heart pitched. *Miki.*

Jesus, we need you.

Why was she out here alone? Where was her husband or boyfriend?

Thankfully she'd always been a strong swimmer. She was treading water. He held his oar in one hand and reached for her, automatically flexing to pull her up with him. Wait. She couldn't join him on this one-person kayak. If they tried to finagle something, they'd capsize it, and she'd go back under.

Sputtering, she grabbed his arm. He held on tight, curling her fingers around the kayak. Then he jumped out and joined her in the strait. He checked a wince as the water rushed in to needle his skin, crush his chest.

He tucked himself next to her and circled her body with one arm. *Oh, Miki.* Her glazed hazel eyes didn't focus on him; her teeth chattered violently.

"Hold on to me."

She let go of the bobbing kayak. Her arm lightly circled him as he hauled her toward a good place to climb out. Shaking violently, she groaned.

Jesus, I know I haven't prayed much lately, but, for her sake, I will. Please . . . don't take her again. Not like this.

The boulders lined up like tyrants bearing knives. There. A gap. He pushed up, gulped air, tightened his grip on her. Her kicking had slowed, but he didn't mind doing most of the work. "Stay with me!"

Hunter's feet connected with solid ground. He dragged them both out of the water, turning to get his arms under Miki and lift her. A trail of red snaked down her denim-clad leg beneath a gash that might need stitches. Good thing the six-gills avoided the bright surface, though any longer in the water and blood might have brought the sharks out of hiding. If he hadn't been there . . .

10

Biting wind blasted them, and he tucked her closer, willing strength into his numb legs as he hiked. She seemed to revive, clinging to his chest with more strength, shivering as he rushed her to his truck.

Thank You, God. Now he could go back to not talking to Him.

"Thank y-y-you, Hunter." She *did* recognize him. He shuddered with the realization. "Still a h-h-hero." She'd called him that the first time he'd shown her orcas. The time they'd kayaked together, and she overturned. He'd helped her right her craft, and they came up sputtering, hot sun blazing on wet shoulders while they laughed.

But he wasn't any kind of hero.

He deposited her on the bench seat of his truck. She trembled against him. The wind's chill tunneled in through the open passenger door, so he pressed toward her, filling the doorway. He reached around her for the blanket behind the seat, eager to warm her up, calm her violent shaking.

His frozen fingers landed on an extra coat. She didn't resist as he pulled her soaked windbreaker over her head. Hmm. No ring on her left hand, though there was a flash of gold chain against her neck. He tugged his dry jacket around her quaking shoulders.

"I've m-m-missed you."

He swallowed, tucking in the blanket he'd found. His hands shook, and he fumbled for her seatbelt. As he reached around her, she gripped his soggy T-shirt, drew him close. Her breath sent a shiver up his spine. He went still.

A decade plus faded away. He didn't breathe as he pulled back enough to meet her eyes. She tugged him closer, chilled hands finding the back of his neck, gaze aiming for his lips. He'd seen that look a thousand times. Knew her intentions.

Wouldn't cooperate.

She closed her eyes, hauling him nearer. He ground his jaw and turned his head, letting her kiss land on his face instead. He winced. If she was in her right mind, she wouldn't act like this. Shock made her vulnerable.

She made *him* vulnerable.

He shut her door, then jogged around and climbed in, flipped

11

the heat on high, and threw the truck into gear to get her to the clinic. His first mate would have to take today's tour. He'd understand. Only on the island for a short visit, and Miki would spend it in urgent care.

Halfway back to town, she unbuckled and scooted over to him, curling in toward his shoulder. He wrapped an arm around her— merely to help her get warm. She still fit against his side. Memories flashed in his mind of so many rides in the family truck, cuddling together.

Dad's challenge played through his mind, but he knew she'd only be on the island a few days. What good would his promise to Dad be then? She'd check back out of his life, and he'd never see her again. No doubt when the shock wore off, she'd forget how she'd reacted to seeing him today. Plus, she probably had somebody in her life—ring or not.

A life that no longer included him.

CHAPTER THREE

Sunshine glittered off Friday Harbor, casting a misleading brightness over the day. Late Tuesday morning had warmed to sixty-eight degrees, which allowed Mikaela to wear a breezy skirt and keep the pressure off her bandaged leg. Cahill Touring's office loomed larger as she approached it on the right, here on Front Street. So familiar. Hunter could be anywhere nearby now, though hopefully, he was on the dock, or better, on the boat.

Mercy, Lord.

Her fingers tingled, so she shook her arms. *Keep breathing.* It wasn't as if she were about to face an enemy or that she'd done something shameful, but anxiety taunted her.

Lauren Cahill held open the office door as Mikaela approached. Her blonde hair had gone grayer. She wore it layered around her face, right at shoulder length. She still seemed fit, judging by her trim figure. Or maybe grief suppressed her appetite. "Hi, Mikaela. I'm so glad you're here."

Embracing Hunter's mother again felt like time travel back to Mikaela's teen years. Her heart shifted, her own anxieties forgotten. "I'm so sorry about Reid." Captain Reid Cahill—Lauren's husband, Hunter's father—had died less than a year ago.

When Lauren pulled back, she cupped her hands under Mikaela's forearms. "Thank you."

Mikaela met the other woman's light blue gaze, let quiet surround them for a second. "How are you?"

After a deep sigh, paired with shining eyes, Lauren said, "I've been better. But we're hanging on." She mustered a smile. "Having you here gives me hope." She glanced toward the huge windows and back again. "I haven't told Hunter, but things are worse than I've let on to him. He's taken his father's death pretty hard."

Mikaela's throat tightened over her protectiveness. Beyond Lauren, who had been there for him? Did he have someone special in his life, and if so, did she know of his strong bond with his dad? "We all loved him dearly." And Mikaela owed Reid a lot. They'd shared meals with Dr. Wren, so Lauren knew Reid had introduced Mikaela to Amelia all those years ago. From there, Mikaela had chosen Amelia's department at the university and now worked with her, serving as assistant professor. But no one in Friday Harbor knew all Amelia had done for Mikaela. If Reid had never introduced them, Mikaela wouldn't be standing here.

Lauren eyed Mikaela up and down. "How are you feeling? Hunter mentioned your dip."

She wrinkled her nose. So humiliating. "Besides the bruises, I'm fine." If you didn't count the nerves in her stomach over hearing his name and standing in his family's shop. Gearing up to watch him in this new capacity, while working side by side.

Sure, he'd already seen her—only two days before. Neither had mentioned their summer assignment. She'd been so loopy with shock and hypothermia. When she'd brought up Cahill Touring, Hunter had shushed her and adjusted the heated blankets around her shoulders. Funny to see him in scrubs. But of course he'd been soaked through like her, and that was all the clinic could offer. She'd met a lot of people since she'd left here twelve years ago, but she didn't know many who would dive into Haro Strait's freezing waters to rescue someone. After the doc's assurances she was fine, he'd bailed to recruit a friend to bring her car back from the park. Maybe they'd retrieved his kayak too.

After the humiliation of Sunday morning, she'd prefer not to have to face him now. But she was scheduled to join the day's tour, line things up for the students to assemble tomorrow—all part of her professorial duties.

"He said you didn't need stitches." As subdued as Lauren seemed, her blue eyes glinted in the overhead lighting. Hopefully she didn't feel she needed to put on a "happy face" for Mikaela.

"Thankfully I didn't." She peeked around the place. No one else in the shop or the office. Her stomach fluttered.

Lauren cocked her head. "He's out on the boat."

Whew . . . Except. "How did he take the news?" She let her lungs expand a smidge. *"Cast all your cares." Don't freeze.*

Hunter's mother bit her lip, adjusted the tubed posters of marine life and maps of the Salish Sea in a nearby bin. "Umm . . ."

Mikaela's stomach knotted, fears confirmed. *Uh-oh.* "He thinks he's getting a stodgy old coot, doesn't he?" Of course, since Sunday he may have put it together. "It's not as if 'Professor Rhoades' is anonymous."

"Ah, but 'Professor M.' is." The phone rang, and Lauren rushed behind the counter. "Cahill Touring, how may I help you?" She gave Mikaela a sheepish smile and then turned to her computer. "Certainly. Let me check on that date."

Hunter didn't know she was the one he was expecting. Great. No warning. Just, "Here I am. Mind if we work in close quarters for the season?" He'd kill her. She closed her eyes and focused on inhaling deeply. Now *she* had to be the one to tell him.

She waved to Lauren, not feeling angry with her. Then, she pushed through the office door and started down the dock, praying every step. When she'd arranged for this collaboration, keeping the news from Hunter made sense. She and Lauren were running a secret mission, of sorts, for his own good. No doubt, he wouldn't have agreed otherwise. But that decision made today harder. Surely he would see the merit in her proposal. But what if he objected, maybe due to pride or his own humiliation? She'd have to head back to Seattle and figure out another way to prove the Hawaii pilot was viable.

Suddenly her plans depended on him in a way she never imagined they could. Especially since the cords between them had only grayed over time; they'd never broken.

Hunter busied himself on the bridge, prepping the *Millennium* for the tour. His dad had been so proud when he bought this ship. Originally, the *Millennium* was used as a Navy search and rescue vessel. The stories she could tell. Since then, she had been adapted for use as a private yacht. The drone of the engine sounded strong—no hiccups so far. They'd be good to go for the tour.

"*Hellooo.*"

Early passengers lingered yards away, behind the locked gate near the building where they'd get the rundown from a staff member before boarding. So why was someone calling from the dock? He peeked out but couldn't manage a good angle for looking straight down, so he started for the stairs.

How was Miki after Sunday's spill? His hand went to his face where she'd kissed him, but he willed it to his side. Hopefully the injury hadn't wrecked her getaway time with her grandmother. Yesterday, he'd had the day off and not seen any sign of her around town. She must have gone back to whatever it was she did now. Her grandmother mentioned Seattle, and she might have mentioned her job now, but he'd tried to forget it. He never asked about her— didn't need the reminders of her life without him.

No issue, then, of wrestling with the promise he'd made to his father. Miki would fade back out. He'd forget how she'd clung to him after he pulled her from the water, or how she'd peered up at him with admiration in her eyes. Called him heroic. Kissed his face.

Made him feel like twice the fool—once for each time he'd let her go.

He trotted down from the bridge, glanced at the dock, and nearly ran into—"Miki?"

"Permission to come aboard, Captain?" She wore a feminine skirt, all layered around her long legs down to strappy sandals. Her blonde hair draped in wide curls, decorating her shoulders where a girly top hugged her lean curves.

What was she *doing* here, and why hadn't his staff stopped her? Not only did they lock the gate, they kept a close watch at this hour. No passengers were allowed yet. She knew that. Had she come to thank him again? Update him on her injury?

"You're already on board." Okay, so he sounded surly. But, seriously. A two-sided war raged inside, alternating *go away* with *never leave me again.* He crossed his arms over his chest. He'd put on a hostile front because she wouldn't be here long, and showing signs of weakness never served him well. What did she want? To take the day's tour for old-time's sake?

She offered a sheepish—and intoxicating—grin, her hazel eyes hooking him against his will. "I am, aren't I?" She straightened and gave him a sharp salute. His pulse flashed. "Professor Rhoades, reporting for duty, sir."

He blinked. "What?"

"Professor *M.* Rhoades, at your service." Her eyes shone as if she knew that's how Mom had referred to her, and he had to look away. *She* was the stuffy prof they'd promised him?

His mom had set him up.

He rubbed the back of his neck. To top it off, this harebrained last-ditch program lasted through the entire season. He was doomed.

And humiliated.

Mom told him the University of Seattle was their lifeline, their rescue from the looming financial shipwreck. She'd let it slip that in order to solidify the deal, she may have divulged their need. That meant Miki knew his role in sinking this ship. Knew he'd failed. If this program didn't work—and it couldn't once he canceled it—they'd finish this season and find a buyer for the *Millennium.*

Then Hunter would try to live with the fact he'd failed his dad.

But he would cancel. Then, Miki could head south, out of range of his new and unimproved self, and hopefully, forget the ornery man he'd become.

She blinked up at him, waiting him out, something like hope in her eyes. Such foolishness. She couldn't be surprised at his reaction.

Her chipper expression slacked. "You going to say anything, Captain?" Her voice sounded too cheery, like she was trying hard to overcome her insecurity as he stared her down. "Should I disembark and return when the others board?" She spun and marched back outside, leaving the cordon dangling as she hopped off the ship and onto the wooden slats of the dock. Then, she faced him and waited. From the looks of it, she was walking fine. No trouble with her injury.

"I'm glad you're okay." He hadn't meant to sound so . . . quiet.

That got her attention.

"Thanks to you." She drew in a long breath, all false cheer gone, replaced by something far more threatening—sincerity. "That's why I'm here, Hunter." She spoke softly. "To help *you*."

Waves slapped the hull of the ship and gulls cried overhead as other vessels pulled into and out of the harbor.

"Please let me."

Hands at his waist, he hung his head. He couldn't bear the shame of his failure or that raw hope in her eyes—couldn't pretend it didn't wrench his insides, turn them wrong side out.

Hang on.

His head snapped up. "This was your idea?"

She pressed her lips together and went still. The *Millennium* bobbed a bit, even given its mass, and he widened his stance. He hadn't invited her here. He dragged his gaze from her, studying the sailing class out in the bay—the boats' white sails clustering in a group.

A million questions lined up, but he wouldn't blurt them.

She peered up at him as if still wanting acceptance. But what was he supposed to do? Admit he liked this superhero gesture? Tell her that the idea of a summer side by side with her sounded peachy?

Still, as much as he wanted to send her away, he couldn't. Whether they carried on with this foolishness or not, she'd sail with them today. Then, he'd talk to Mom—come up with something else.

Because no way would he play the fool again.

But he didn't have to be a beast. He reached across the distance and offered a hand. "Come aboard, Professor."

She grinned before letting him help her reboard the boat.

Her faceted eyes glinted—were they green, or brown? He once thought he'd spend a lifetime trying to solve that mystery. "Listen," her voice went all sincere and gentle again, reeling him in with kindness. He recrossed his arms. "I believe we can make this work." Could she hear the double meaning in her own words? They nearly killed him. Her gaze flitted back and forth between his eyes, as if she was studying him too.

Steps pounding down the dock—determined, authoritative—made Hunter turn. Mom. He softened his face, though he wanted to quiz her. Not in front of Miki.

She stopped next to the *professor* and eyed him with her Mom Face. "Everything all right here?" Something about the fact she drilled her gaze through him with a pointed glance at Miki had him checking a sigh, glad he'd already invited the professor aboard.

"Mom."

"Cap'n." She gestured toward Miki again, and he finally caught on.

"Welcome," he said to her. Then, he speared his mother with a look. "Let's talk later."

She gave a satisfied smile before she returned to the dock.

With that, he shifted toward the stairs and called over his shoulder toward their visitor. "Last minute checklist on the bridge. Make yourself...comfortable." Because heaven knew he wouldn't be comfortable until she returned to her own life and let him return to his, broken as it was.

CHAPTER FOUR

Not exactly what she'd expected, but not horrible. Of course, he seemed to prefer she evaporate or go overboard, but he hadn't canceled the whole program. Yet.

Welcome. Moments ago he'd stood right there, dressed in khaki slacks and the company issue turquoise polo, like the navy one his father used to wear, with the Cahill orca logo. His gray eyes seemed to glow, as if playing with the aqua color under the bill of his captain's hat. Such an official—and austere—reminder he was now captain here in place of gentle, welcoming Reid Cahill. And the man she'd known as Hunter—the romantic, optimistic, kind person—was now absent as well.

Sunlight slanted through the window, splashing heat on her legs while she watched boats bob in the marina, their shining hulls brilliant against the startling blue of sea and sky. Somewhere in the last twelve years, Hunter had gone churlish. On Sunday, in crisis, he'd been kind. The way he'd carried her into the clinic, tucking her close. She'd insisted on a wheelchair, rather than expect him to keep carrying her. He'd insisted she shut up. But he'd winked. No sign of that caring side today.

She had some work to do. Anyone within range of them would perceive their tension. If Dr. Wren and Dr. Smythe did come to observe, they'd rethink everything.

Sam Kerry, Hunter's first officer, boarded leading a ten-year-old girl, if Mikaela had to guess her age.

His eyebrows hiked. "Mikaela, is that you?"

"Hi, Sam," she said, reaching to shake his hand. He'd been around for probably thirty years. Same red beard, though it'd gone a little grayer around the edges. She'd always thought he looked like an old sea captain himself. He'd been content to support the Cahills all these years. He'd probably covered for Hunter during his mission of mercy at the clinic with her over the weekend. "Good to see you."

His brown eyes twinkled. "Hey, meet my granddaughter, Cheyenne."

The pretty redhead stared up at her with deep green eyes and dimples. She stuck out her hand. "Nice to meet you."

Mikaela liked her go-get-'em spirit right away. Would her own children have been strong like Cheyenne? Long ago, Hunter and she had dreamed of having four kids—the perfect balance of playmates. But imagining them as ten-year-olds—that she'd never done. She'd always pictured babies, toddlers. And then, the breakup. She'd never wanted a family with anyone else.

Not that it mattered now. That familiar ache punched deep. She shook it off. At this moment, she was on duty. "What brings you on board, Cheyenne?"

"Captain Hunter promised I could visit the bridge."

"That was nice of him." More proof that despite his currently gruff disposition, Hunter obviously hadn't become the troll he wanted people—or maybe only her?—to believe he was.

"Her parents are taking an Alaskan cruise for their anniversary." He gave Cheyenne a side hug. "So, the wife and I are on grandparent duty this week."

Sam stepped to the stairs. "Hey, Cap'n." He used a pirate voice. "Permission to bring Cheyenne up there?" He winked back at his granddaughter.

"Sam, I need to see you alone for a minute." Hunter sounded stern, as if he'd changed his mind. No doubt Mikaela would hear that off-putting tone a lot this summer from *the captain*, especially if he kept up the crankiness. She'd have to warn her students.

"I'll entertain Cheyenne, Sam. Go ahead."

"Thanks." He smiled at his granddaughter then turned toward the stairs, his eyebrows furrowed.

Would Hunter let Cheyenne down? He'd always been enamored with kids. Was he still? Years ago, when his toddler cousins came over, he'd been the first to engage with them.

Mikaela led Cheyenne to the snack bar between the front and rear salons. Obviously the pre-teen had been on the boat before.

She seemed to know the layout. This cabin, or salon, offered nearly 360-degree views—perfect for whale watching. All around them, windows provided a visual of the bustling dock and other boats in the harbor. Flashes of blue and sunlight glinted off the water. A Washington State ferry offloaded its recent passengers two docks down.

Naturalists were due to arrive any minute, as was the snack bar barista who would set out the food for the tour. They didn't offer much in the way of real sustenance, but they could keep folks going for the four-hour tours with granola, candy bars, chips, bottled waters, and soda.

"Want a snack?"

Cheyenne nodded.

Mikaela ducked behind the familiar counter and grabbed a bag of trail mix and a water bottle for Cheyenne. The boat showed its age—the scuffed paint, the worn pleather covering the benched seating. Perhaps this summer's program would bring enough income to afford renovations. Mikaela tossed cash into the jar hidden from view. Up the stairs, Sam and Hunter carried on a muffled conversation, so Mikaela pointed out the marine life poster to distract Cheyenne.

Ten minutes later, Sam returned. "Okay, Cheyenne, let's go on up." She cleared her trash and followed her grandfather toward the stairs. Sam let her precede him. "By the way, Professor, welcome aboard." He tipped an imaginary hat.

Mikaela offered a playful salute. "Thank you, Sam. Glad to be here." They exchanged a glance. He seemed happy she was with them, but she had a feeling Hunter had given him an earful.

Still, Hunter deserved credit for inviting Cheyenne up. Hopefully, he'd put his grouchy evil twin away. She'd love to peek up the stairs and watch him interact with her.

For now, she would keep her distance. Maybe once they were underway, she'd join them. There were rules about how many people could gather on the bridge at once. That and she didn't relish taking those stairs. Her leg was still stiff, which only reminded her of his heroic side. Why couldn't he accept help himself?

Pacing the salon, she fished out her new cell phone to check e-mail. There were responses from three out of five of her students. She'd have to track Destinee down and make sure she didn't blow off this opportunity. The group would come aboard tomorrow for the regular tour. She'd scheduled a dive for them next week.

Half an hour later, she stood on the bridge as the staff welcomed passengers downstairs. Out in the harbor, a California sea lion thermoregulated, floating on her back with her fore and hind flippers open to the sunshine like a wide hug so she could adjust her temperature. If only Mikaela could adjust the emotional thermostat up here, where Hunter fumed as he went about preparations.

She could have forewarned him months ago with a simple phone call or checked to make sure Lauren had told him. She shouldn't have procrastinated telling him until the day she showed up. So, what? Was he going to brood all day? From the corner of her eye, she caught a glimpse of his granite expression. So far, yes.

She was here now, and they had work to do. For starters, today was about preparation for the kick-off. They hadn't discussed how the summer would run, or exactly what he expected from her students. Or—

"So, Prof"—he cleared his throat—"we're going to need a few ground rules."

Ground rules. Did that mean she could stay? Hope flared. But they'd never needed guidelines before. Relating had always come easily for them when she'd been a teen barista during summers here, and he'd been running back and forth on errands for his father, Captain Reid.

Prof. She quenched a sigh.

His voice sounded gritty, as if he weren't much of a talker anymore. Little chance, then, of discussing the elephant on the boat—how he'd rejected her all those years ago. Of course bringing that up would mean divulging her own reasons for staying away all this time. Maybe he was ready to simply leave the past alone. Fine. Good, actually. She'd prefer to avoid it. They'd start over—as coworkers.

"That is *if* I decide you can stay."

CHAPTER FIVE

Dad couldn't have known how seeing her again would hurt—make Hunter want to keep his distance. A film reel of memories seared his mind just seeing her. Close proximity amped the effect. His phone buzzed. A text: *BE NICE.* For some reason, Mom didn't believe he could be polite to their new "guest."

After Cheyenne left the bridge earlier, he'd called his mother. She'd admitted disturbing news in two parts—one, Dad's life insurance policy hadn't been enough to pay off their debts and mortgage loan. So, not only was Hunter's promise to his father on the line—to keep the business running—but also his charge of providing for Mom. Hunter couldn't let this program fail. And two, Miki was headed to Hawaii after this summer's stint.

Of course she was. Hawaii had been her goal since they were seventeen. She wanted to swim with the humpbacks or some such nonsense.

Over the years, he'd imagined their reunion. What he'd say. How she'd respond. He wouldn't have expected it to happen in a work setting.

After Mom's warnings about their situation, he couldn't see a way out of this. But agreeing to cooperate felt like announcing: *Look at me, the failure.* That thought burrowed deep and then burned.

If they had to do this, professionalism might give them each a life ring. The old Hunter would have snagged Miki close for a long hug full of apologies and promises before the tour began. He'd try to ease those fears he read in her expression. But these days, Hunter kept his old self suppressed—head barely under the water where he could pretend life didn't hurt.

Back to your own raft, Hunter. Put on your captain's face.

"Students tomorrow. Are they briefed?" He kept his tone clipped. Chilled. He peered at gauges, avoiding her eyes. He'd already double-checked everything, but she didn't know that.

"Yes. They are." Her tone matched his with a hint more ice.

Okay. So implying she didn't have her scholars in order hadn't gone over well.

She huffed. "We're really not going to talk about it, not going to clear the air?"

Is that what she wanted? Okay. "You didn't have to come this summer." *Hear what I'm not saying.*

Her brows crunched up. "What?"

If this ship sinks, I don't want you here to witness it. Hero, indeed. He stayed silent. Let her figure it out.

"I'm talking about our past." She jerked a thumb between them. "You know, the pain you inflicted?"

How exactly did she interpret their breakup? They'd never had a chance to talk about it since. He shook his head, peering around for escape routes, except this was his ship, and his *life*, and he couldn't escape. No. They were *not* having this conversation right now. Not ten minutes before sailing time. He straightened his hat and took his place behind the wheel.

"The kids know about not crowding the bridge? No paper in the head? What time to arrive and that we're expecting them to play host, be professional?"

From the corner of his eye, he saw her angle her head as if scowling at him. He peeked, and sure enough—the death glare. "My *students* are briefed."

"I know they're not employees, and they're paying for the right to be on board, but we've got a business to run." *For as long as we can.*

She shook her head. "I don't believe you." She faced the harbor, arms crossed, shoulders stiff. The *Millennium* rocked beneath them.

Keeping his distance, he moved around the bridge, monitoring the progress of the day's passengers outside. Only a few more families. A much smaller group than when Dad ran things. About seventy patrons, beyond crew. To keep things comfortable, they never filled to the official capacity of one hundred. Everyone paused for a photograph of their particular group ahead of boarding and that took more time, but the photographer paid him a percentage of her take, so it'd been good for at least a little income.

Suddenly Mikaela was right there. In his space. Crowding. He couldn't get around her in this half-circle-shaped room. She scowled up at him, and he remembered the nine-year-old in pigtails. He'd yank one if she sported them today.

He bit the inside of his cheek before offering a gruff, "What?"

"How are we going to work together if you won't discuss it?" Her eyes shone. No fun for her, this little reunion. She walked into it. Should *he* feel badly about that? What did she expect?

With a lot of effort, he willed his expression to remain neutral, though he'd barely contained his wince. All that pain he wished he hadn't caused. A hundred memories of how she felt in his arms, head against his shoulder, clinging to him from fear or heartache. Not that he'd ever minded. And not pain he'd ever caused, until . . .

There'd never been another woman for him except her.

Yeah, they had a lot to talk about. *Um, Miki, you left and never came back. Remember that part?* But going there meant having a conversation twelve years overdue, and even he didn't have the courage for that, which was why he hadn't pushed it after her refusal to return his calls. Hunter saw their relationship as either on or off, together or—

"You knew about my dreams." Her hazel eyes sparked, contradicting the aching pain in her voice. "School was always my plan. Why did that throw you off?"

He stared at her. Is that what she thought? "You really wanna go there, now?" He gestured around them. The clock had ticked past sailing time, and the last passengers were straggling aboard.

She probably had no idea of his restraint. As captain, he could delay their departure, put everything on hold, help her see. Let his heart out of its cage, and dive into this overdue chat. Or he could send her away. For good.

She only blinked at him, breathing fast.

Be nice. Mom's words echoed in his mind.

"We're ready, Cap'n," Sam called from below.

The usual welcome announcement broadcasted over the PA as

Jace, one of the younger naturalists, recited it from the base of the stairs.

Hunter moved into position behind the wheel and adjusted his captain's hat. A breeze carried cool air into the bridge through open windows, and he inhaled food smells from the wood-fired pizza oven restaurant across the street. But even the aroma of sausage and roasted peppers couldn't distract him for long.

Miki found a spot nearby, no longer jabbering. He preferred the silence to her accusations. Still, he'd rather brood without her standing there—Professor Mikaela Rhoades, forever Miki.

How was he going to keep that straight all summer?

A sharp pain harpooned his chest. They couldn't go back. And rehashing wouldn't help. She'd just said, given the chance, she'd do the same thing again—leave. The realization sunk into his gut and pressed into the sediment like a rough cement block. This was a confirmation he'd have preferred to avoid for a lifetime.

Except . . . she was here now.

He zeroed in on his job as captain, the role that kept his dad's business—and Hunter—alive. He worked the lever to guide them away from the dock, and soon they were steering northwest out of Friday Harbor. They'd monitor intel from other whale-watching groups in the Salish Sea about current marine animal activity, and all the touring outfits would flock to that location. Until then, he'd guide them out past Brown Island, eastward into the San Juan Channel, toward Shaw Island, and then westward toward Haro Strait, while always studying the waterways.

"You know, Hunter—" Her tone showed her lingering hurt.

"Captain." He took his eyes off the water long enough to catch her pained expression. A cringe surfaced, trailed by stinging regret. He'd never been a monster with her. But so he didn't forget himself, she could use his official title. Even if it killed him.

After several moments she snapped to attention and saluted him again, only this time with no humor in her eyes. "Aye-aye, *Captain.*"

He clenched his jaw, and the ropes around his heart wound tighter. If they didn't seriously need this program to work, he'd cancel the arrangement right now. Maybe there was still a way.

If there were any room to pace, she would, but short of the leap of faith required to walk on water, the boat was overflowing with tourists, and she was stuck. Without privacy, she couldn't even call her best friend, Jenna-Shea Brown. So, she'd text her.

Back in the crowded salon, a mom bounced her fussing baby on her knee. He'd probably sleep soon, given the boat's increasing speed. Teens thumbed their phones and dads pointed out sights beyond the windows to fidgeting six-year-olds clad in life jackets, while Jace made announcements to the passengers. A few patrons stood on the outer deck, riding the motion with springy knees and hands clutching the railing.

From a corner chair, Mikaela swiped letters, glad for no current responsibilities.

Shea's words popped up on her phone's screen. *HE'S PROBABLY STILL HURTING.*

AND I'M NOT? SEEING HIM AGAIN IS MAKING ME CRAZY. HE STILL SMELLS THE SAME!

OF COURSE HE DOES. AND I GET IT, BUT YOU'VE GOT TO FIND A WAY TO WORK TOGETHER THIS SUMMER, EVEN IF HE WON'T TALK.

HE'S MAKING ME CALL HIM CAPTAIN!

HA!

This wasn't the help she'd hoped for.

YOU WENT QUIET.

She bit the inside of her lip. *I THOUGHT I WAS PAST THIS. I'M A WIMP.*

NOPE, YOU'RE ALL HEART.

I'M SURE HUNTER WOULDN'T AGREE. TO HIM, I'M A HEARTLESS OGRE.

UNH-UH, HE'S JUST ON GUARD. YOU SHOULD THINK OF A WAY TO OVERCOME HIS WALLS. OTHERWISE, THE STUDENTS AND THE DEPT CHAIR WILL ONLY SEE TENSION. NOT A GOOD WAY TO BEGIN THE PROGRAM.

I CAN'T FIX US IN ONE DAY.

TRUE.

BUT YOU'RE RIGHT ABOUT THE VIBE HERE: H O S T I L E
I BELIEVE IT.

"Excuse me, Professor," Jace—the naturalist who made the announcements—stood over her table, his brown biceps stretching the short sleeves of his navy company polo shirt. "The captain asked for you upstairs."

"Thanks." She swiped a quick TTYL to Shea and sucked in a deep breath. *Give me strength.* Which reminded her, she could use more prayer time.

When she'd chosen this mission of mercy as a potential project, she'd hoped Hunter would be grateful, that he'd see she was only trying to help. That loyalty motivated her—loyalty toward Reid and Lauren Cahill. And Hunter too, for crying out loud.

Jace unlatched the cordon barrier and let her through to climb the stairs.

Maybe, secretly, she'd wanted something else, though she hadn't admitted it to herself until right then. Maybe she'd also wanted . . . closure.

At the top of the stairs, she felt woozy. *I have to stop holding my breath on stairs. Or when approaching my doom.* She almost chuckled, but then caught sight of Hunter's back.

She moved around him, stepping left into his peripheral vision. Though he didn't look at her, she knew his turquoise shirt set off his eyes. She must stop noticing that, or how the fabric stretched around his shoulders, broad chest, and biceps. He still wore the captain's hat, the brim of which he pinched when he gave her a curt nod.

His first mate was nowhere in sight, like earlier.

Oh, good. Alone again.

She took a position near the left windows. Wouldn't do to block his view since he held all their lives in his hands. He stayed silent, and she determined not to be the first to speak. He'd called her up here. Instead, she stared forward now, watching the blues of the sky and the channel meet the greens and browns of the islands. They sailed at a swift clip, bounding over the water, passing smaller vessels.

"We never set the ground rules." His voice sounded gravely. He didn't want her here. Her heart ached. Of all his potential responses to seeing her again, she hadn't expected enmity. Why couldn't they be civil to each other?

If Hunter were one of her students, she'd lecture him—force him to see why he should choose gratitude. But she wasn't dealing with a nineteen-year-old. She wasn't even dealing with a friend, apparently. An old wound stung inside at that thought.

"No comment?"

Fine. "Sure. Since this is your boat, what did you have in mind?" Was it too late to change course? Get Dr. Wren on speaker, list her objections, and come clean? Convince Amelia to let Mikaela abandon ship?

"Professional titles at all times." He still didn't look at her.

"Got it." She hadn't exactly been healed before this summer's get-together—hadn't fully come to terms with his rejection, though she had moved on. She hadn't been angry, either. Until now. She crossed her arms.

His brows hiked, and his mouth quirked as if he'd noticed her posture.

Glad she could still entertain him.

"As far as the students, do you have a plan to keep them busy?"

Why did he have to continually imply she couldn't handle her responsibilities? "Of course."

He grunted. "Can you answer with more than two words?"

"No. But I do have a question for you. What shall we do about all this tension, huh, *Captain*? What's your plan for that, oh man in charge?"

He winced. She'd gone too far.

She shouldn't stoop to petulance, but somehow he brought out the bratty side of her. She'd learned compassion over the years. Why was it so hard to access that right now? Maybe because he'd snubbed her attempts at compassion in action. But that shouldn't be a reason to withdraw. Right?

His turn to go silent. The radio came to life with a sighting, and Mikaela scanned the waters. Nothing visible here.

"I need to send an e-mail," she muttered while he focused on the information about J-pod west of Spieden Island—resident orcas.

She studied him in his full-on captain mode. His own interpretation—stoic. Unyielding. Why had she thought this could work? She'd contact Amelia and find an alternate solution. Perhaps one of the other marine bio profs could replace her. That way the Cahills still got their help, the students got their hands-on experience, and Mikaela got out of here.

Hunter finished his response to the other captain and went still. "Wait."

She stood at the top of the stairs, but didn't turn, didn't give him the satisfaction of seeing her. Stupid burning in her eyes.

Idiotic mission.

"I don't like being one of your marine mammal rescues." This time the gruffness in his tone sounded emotional, not irritated. She'd missed that intimate inflection—a sound he didn't let most people hear. A timbre he used to save for her.

His words meant he'd figured it out, why she'd come. *Rescue.*

"I don't like it, but I know Dad would be glad you're here." He blew out a ragged sigh, and she almost turned. The reflection in the window showed them back to back—him facing the channel to steer them toward whales. Her facing the stairs—the escape hatch.

Each facing the truth.

"For what you're doing for him"—the reflected image clenched his teeth—"thank you."

She nodded toward the reflection. Then, with blurred vision, she took the steps, to where, she didn't know. Drat, how small this boat felt today. How small would it feel all summer while they sailed together? Because she wouldn't e-mail Dr. Wren. She'd make this work. For Reid. For Lauren.

For Hunter.

CHAPTER SIX

Strolling the long, forest-lined road, Mikaela closed her eyes for a moment and pulled the salty air deep into her lungs. The usual sense of calm that settled over her this near the sea didn't arrive and she resumed her walk, sandals crunching over the pebble-strewn road. Once every several steps, she'd catch a glimpse of the bay—diamonds shooting off cobalt waters. Then, more trees, a house here and there. Finally, Granny's cottage came into view beyond a grove, brushed by dappled sunlight. She'd want to know all of Mikaela's plans, how things had gone with Hunter their first day, what God was saying to her lately.

Mikaela slowed her steps. Sure, she'd shot a few prayers heavenward since arriving, but were she and God on open-as-a-book terms? Not exactly. Not since she avoided asking Him certain questions. She certainly couldn't explain to Granny that sometimes she didn't want to learn what God desired. Anyway, this wasn't a good-or-bad, right-or-wrong situation. This was ... well, a confusing mess. But it wasn't like Mikaela had chosen an evil path.

All she wanted to do was help the Cahills, and get through this summer to the next assignment, heart intact.

The challenge with Granny was her ability to see past façades and use compassion against her guests. Well, against their hard-built walls. And what compassion didn't best, wisdom did.

At the end of the long driveway, Granny Belle stood on her porch, holding a spouted watering can over her head to nourish her fuchsias. A hummingbird dive-bombed past Mikaela, and she ducked, squealing.

"Mikaela, you're here!"

She swatted the air near her ear, still shuddering, the thrum of hummingbird wings strong in her memory. "Hi, Granny."

Isabelle Calhoun trotted down the steps. She'd always been light on her feet. Even with snowy hair now, she seemed young and spry, the stark white only bringing out her bright eyes. "I'm glad you're back!"

Stepping into her arms, inhaling the aroma of chocolate, and Mikaela was back at age seven, visiting Granny Belle's Fudge Shoppe, sampling whatever she could snatch. "I've missed you."

"Welcome."

A lump crowded Mikaela's throat. The acceptance, the warmth—both had been missing from her life for too long. Sure, she tried to create a hospitable atmosphere in her classroom, but that warmth wasn't always returned and a woman's reserves could run low. Maybe this . . .haven was exactly what she needed. Though she wasn't staying in her grandmother's house, this place, so familiar from her summers on the island as a child, felt like home.

"C'mon in." Granny bounded up the stairs. "I have barbecued chicken and potato salad."

At the table, she took Mikaela's hand and they bowed their heads. "Lord, thank You for bringing Mikaela back this summer. I know You're working in all our lives, and I thank You for that too. Please show us Your will. And bless this food. In Jesus's name, amen." They opened their eyes, and Granny Belle held the tongs toward Mikaela so she could grab a chicken leg from the heaping platter.

"There's enough food here for all your tenants," Mikaela noted.

"Yeah, I keep extras in the fridge." But something didn't add up. Mikaela glanced around. "Quiet house tonight?"

"For now. So tell me, how are things with Hunter?"

Months ago, Mikaela shared the summer's plan with Granny, but had asked her to keep the news to herself. Perhaps she should have given her permission to tell. Maybe arming Hunter would have worked better. But she wouldn't start there. "You mean before or after he rescued me from Haro Strait?"

Granny Belle's hand stopped mid-scoop over the glass bowl of potato salad. "What?"

Mikaela told her the rescue story. "You should have seen him—all concerned. Of course, I was out of it from the trauma." After shuddering for effect, she dropped mixed fruit onto her plate and handed the dish to her grandmother. A scent of sweet cantaloupe mingled with the tang of barbecue sauce and made Mikaela's stomach growl. "He took the day off from tours to help me."

"Of course he did." Granny nodded. "He's a good man, Hunter." She tipped her head and met Mikaela's eyes. "And you're okay?"

"Yes. Healing." In fact, she'd removed the bandage last night. Mikaela gazed through the windows at Griffin Bay where sunshine glinted off foamy blue waves. Wind chimes jangled on the back deck in a melodic tune.

Spicy sauce awakened her taste buds, and she mentally scheduled more walks. If she dropped by for meals too often this summer, she'd need a lot more exercise to burn all the calories. Her cottage was a good distance. That should help.

"You're rather quiet." Granny reached for her forearm, and Mikaela made herself meet her gaze. Why had she thought she could keep anything from her, when everything here made her feel safe? Made it easy to lower her guards?

"He's different." Mikaela sighed and glanced outside, then back. "Still noble, but . . . grumpy now. Unfriendly. *Not* likable."

"He's been through a lot. Probably figures he only has to be civil to his customers."

She chewed a juicy bite of peach and swallowed. "I'm hoping he won't eat my students for lunch."

Granny Belle chuckled, but then sobered. "I know you're here on a mission of mercy." At Mikaela's grimace, her grandmother patted her hand. Such thoughtfulness sank deep, prodding more tears. "Did you think it'd be easy?"

Same question she'd been asking herself since Sunday. She hadn't anticipated that Hunter might be wholly different. Their thoughts no longer synced. She wrapped her arms against her front as if she could block out the memories flashing through her mind— beach walks, fingers linked with Hunter's; bonfires at low tide; both their families on overnight boating trips. Hunter's teary eyes when she'd told him her dreams. Him walking away. No explanation. Her own sobs in a lonely nook of the ferry that took her home.

"He sent me away." Her voice cracked.

Granny Belle tilted her head. "Are you sure about that?"

She leaned back in her chair, gaze wandering to the hydrangeas blooming outdoors. Each lime green ball of buds biding their time for more hours of sun and warmer temperatures. "So, it's too much to ask for him to be kind this summer? We have a history together."

"Question for you, dear: have you two ever talked through the past?"

"That would require him to speak. And right now, he's hiding behind 'ground rules'." She used her fingers to make air quotes.

"So, how will you work together?"

Good question. One thing she did know is she couldn't let Hunter, or this situation, paralyze her. At some point, over the years, she'd come to a place of not letting others tug her down into the boiling crab pot. The method had worked well for her, allowing her to accomplish her goals. Determination rose in her now, and she reached for the butter. "I have no idea, but we will."

Two things stood in the way of her leaving this topic alone: One, Shea's suggestion Mikaela find a way past his walls. And two, how her heart kicked against the thought of truly letting him go for good. Because, apparently, she never had.

Granny's fork scraped her plate and brought Mikaela back to the table. "So, I know you kept me updated on him," Mikaela said, "but it's been a while. I guess part of me thought he'd be taken by now." A complication that would have made things both easier and harder this summer.

Her grandmother shook her head. "There's no woman in his life, that I've seen. He strikes me as rather . . . lonely—focused on his dad's company, providing for his mom. Which is why it's so noble what you're doing. And, perfect timing, if you ask me." She lifted her lemonade glass in a gentle toast before taking a swig.

Granny Belle knew Mikaela wasn't attached either, which left the door wide open for shenanigans. There'd always been an assumption between the families, a notion that one day Hunter and Mikaela would end up married. Best to nip that right now. "You and Lauren aren't planning any matchmaking mischief, are you?"

CHAPTER SEVEN

"Oh, I almost forgot." Her grandmother jumped up and retrieved a pie from the kitchen's bay window. "Blueberries from last year's garden."

"You didn't answer my question." The last thing skittish Hunter needed, especially considering their unstable professional collaboration, was for his mother or Mikaela's grandmother to attempt to get them together.

One more half turn of the pie at the table's center and Granny Belle finally looked up. "Reid always said you two were perfect for each other . . . I happen to agree."

"*Were.* Exactly. Not anymore."

The room went quiet as they each returned to their meals, though Mikaela could feel her grandmother's gaze on her.

"There is one more thing about Hunt I wanted to mention."

Hunt . . . She hadn't thought of him like that in a long time. Something about her grandmother's tone stalled Mikaela's hand in mid-air. "What is it?" She set down her fork and rested her elbows on Granny's informal table before linking her fingers and trying to look calm, as if her stomach wasn't clenched.

"Lauren's worried about him. He hasn't grieved yet. I mean, he is grieving, of course. But she said he hasn't really let down his guard, let himself *feel* the loss."

Her heart twisted. She studied Granny's face. "I want to help him." Her appetite faded.

Granny's hand covered hers. "I know. I believe you will." She breathed deeply and sighed as if shaking off the heaviness in the room. "So, tell me more about your program."

Ah, a topic she could discuss without emotional weight. She reached for her fork. While Mikaela explained, she heard the crunch of tires over gravel through the open front windows. Probably one of the students Granny rented to. Something dark flashed through the window sheers billowing on a breeze, and Mikaela nodded toward Granny. "Company."

The quick rap of two knocks on the door sent her grandmother bolting from the table to answer, her rush punctuated with flustered blouse smoothing.

"Isabelle?" Hunter's voice outside. "I got your message."

Oh, no. What had she done?

Granny swung open the door. "Welcome, Hunter."

He turned from greeting her, still smiling as he met Mikaela's eyes. She gulped lemonade to drown her anxiety. Hunter at work, on the boat, was safe. Formal. His stubborn determination to remain professional was a safety net, even for her, though she'd never tell him that. His presence here, in this familiar setting where they'd run up and down the stairs and kissed on the porch swing— Not. Harmless. Especially when he smiled.

His expression faded to cool as he registered her presence. "Oh."

Did he have to sound so disappointed to see her? So much for her emotional resolutions. She gritted her teeth. If only it were truly up to her whether she let something bother her. Forget the freeze response. Right now, she simply wanted to flee.

"Hunter, how are you this evening?" Granny sounded too cheery as she moved toward Mikaela. He didn't follow.

Suddenly the extra food made sense. She'd planned this all along. "Join us?" Granny pointed toward the table in the open room. "I've got warm blueberry pie for dessert."

Hunter swallowed, hands in his denim shorts pockets, gaze darting between them. At this hour of the day, his face was outlined in scruffy whiskers. He'd changed since the tour and now wore a black T-shirt, which showcased his light brown hair and gray eyes.

Oh, help.

His attention swung back to Granny. "You mentioned something about your washer?"

"Well, wouldn't you know it? One of my tenants got it back into place a while ago." She toyed with her rings—one for every finger. "I made your favorite."

Panic shot Mikaela to her feet. "This isn't what it looks like. You're welcome to stay for dinner." Her words came fast. "I wanted to check something out back." She darted outside before he could respond.

Coward.

Sure, running was overreacting. Tell that to her feet as they sprinted away from the house, urged on by her heart. In all the years of college, grad school, and teaching, she'd avoided romantic relationships, blaming Hunter the whole time. Clarity flipped a switch sending blazing light into a corner of her heart. Targeting him seemed easier than accepting the truth. Seeing him changed the intangible to material. No more hiding. Or blaming.

Yes, she had to deal with the truth. But she didn't have to do it immediately.

She slowed her steps and guzzled oxygen, blinking fast. *Focus on something else.* She tipped back her head. The Douglas fir and old-growth cedars threw their green canopies against an azure sky, while deep blue Steller's jays pitched from branch to branch. If Hunter left Granny Belle's now, it'd be because Mikaela was there. The adult in her mind pointed at the house and commanded she march back inside and finish her evening. Standing out here was rude, especially to her grandmother.

But the woman in her heart couldn't do it.

If she analyzed this situation, she could hold herself together, act like the grownup she'd become—free from the past and the pain. Denial was the ferry from the ache of reality to the island of functionality. Heaven help her if she ever stopped crossing that channel.

Plus, what was the alternative? That he confess undying love? Say he hadn't meant to reject her? Their time had passed.

The memory of Hunter's fading smile moments ago made her cringe. In fact, all of Hunter's reactions today stung. Until tonight, she hadn't realized why. His clipped words and cool tone only confirmed that the years hadn't brought him to a change of heart, phone calls aside. He still chose to reject her. Which could only mean he didn't want her in his life, and maybe he never had. Their history together didn't mean as much to him as it did to her.

She didn't mean as much.

She swallowed against the burn in her throat and glanced at her surroundings. *Focus on something else.* Anything *else.* What did it matter now?

Ugh. It mattered. Rejection dredged a channel through her heart.

Did you think this would be easy?

Docks lined the waterfront on both sides of Granny's, spaced along the shore several yards apart. The blues of the bay and the sky vied for her attention. The rocky shoreline sported stones and sandy patches with broken shells. Drying seaweed tossed the scent of briny decay into the air.

Granny was right. Mikaela hadn't thought through the emotional cost of returning. This was supposed to be a stopover. Not a trip down memory lane with a shovel for digging up heartache. What had she been hoping for? Had part of her wanted to renew a relationship with Hunter?

No. Of course not. Right?

She pressed the hidden pendant against her chest, its chain so familiar around her neck.

Waves battered the sandy beachfront as the tide clambered up the sandy slope. Quick steps carried her to the dock. The boards could use some work. Without Granddad here to keep things up, the whole place needed repairs—fresh paint for the house and shed. Ground clearing of all those wiry brambles on the northwest side of the property. New planks here on the dock.

Granddad . . .

"Isabelle wanted you to know she's sorry for interfering."

Mikaela gasped and turned at the sound of Hunter's voice, meeting his eyes.

"She made me promise to play nice." His stoic face broke into a fleeting grin before he lowered his head and wiped it away. Wind off the bay pressed his T-shirt to his chest, and Mikaela averted her gaze, hugging herself.

The past crept into the silence between them, making demands.

"Listen," Hunter said, shifting his weight. "I think it's best if we . . . leave our history alone." His voice wavered. "You know . . . go from here, like nothing ever happened."

Go from here. The same resolve she'd been talking herself into, but coming from him the words sliced her heart. Now he'd confirmed her guess. If he wanted to essentially erase their history, she *had* never meant anything to him. *Like nothing ever—* She gulped and angled herself away from him. How could he say that?

Maybe she'd misunderstood. She blinked fast again, tried to school her voice to request he clarify. "You want to pretend we never knew each other?" Her voice didn't hold up. *Shoot.*

He rubbed the back of his neck, one hand at his waist, eyes squinting toward the water. "The way I see it"—his voice sounded scratchy too—"we only need to convince your grandmother, your boss, and your students we can get along. That shouldn't be too hard for two adults like us, right?"

She pressed her lips together. He really didn't get it.

"Anyway, it's only for the summer." His gray eyes reflected the bay while the sunlight glinted off his light brown hair, no doubt planning to bleach it blonder this season while tanning his skin. "Then, I hear you're off on another adventure."

"Yes, I am." She bit her lower lip. *Counting the days. Starting now.* If she survived.

As much as she hated to run—again—she scurried past him. "Let Granny know I had to get home and plan for tomorrow," she said, her knees threatening to fail on her.

If only her duties didn't take her right back to his boat come morning.

Great. Now he'd really blown it. *Like nothing ever happened?*

Idiot!

Where had that even come from? He watched her march around the side of the house, out of sight.

It was as if seeing her was too much for him. His heart wanted to take over, was used to calling the shots when he was with her, but his grown-up mind always stepped in.

And said stupid things. Especially after all her vulnerability since she got back. Isabelle had sent him out here to apologize on her behalf, maybe coax Miki back inside where Granny could do so in person, and he'd messed things up.

Moments later, he clumped his sandals over the house's wooden deck boards toward the slider.

"She wouldn't come back with you, huh?" Isabelle stood at the open kitchen window. "C'mon in." She faced him as he closed the screen door.

After she slid a plateful of food across to him, she pointed to a barstool. "Sit, please. Have some dinner."

The memory of how he'd just wounded Miki ate at his stomach, but for this honorary grandmother, he'd try. "Thanks, Isabelle." Barbecue-scented steam washed toward him from the reheated plate. He never ate during tours and didn't usually have time until later in the day.

"You used to call me Granny Belle, like all the other kids. Remember?" She wiped down the countertop.

"I remember a lot of things." He bent over the plate, rounding his shoulders, tucking in his elbows, avoiding Granny Belle's eyes. The first bite of potato salad burst on his tongue with mayonnaise, mustard, and spices. Maybe he could eat.

She rinsed another plate and set it in the dishwasher. "How hard is the program this summer?"

"Not hard." He shrugged. "Touring with repeat passengers—students—on board."

"Then, what's the problem?"

Could he tell her? Should he? He'd never confessed this to his mother or his buddy, Dan. But perhaps Isabelle was safe. Plus, maybe she could help him. "I don't trust myself with her." And rightfully so after his stellar performance outside.

Granny leaned against the counter, towel clenched in one hand, listening. Waiting him out.

41

"I'm not the same person she left." His voice went all gravely, and he chugged iced tea. That catch in his throat was happening too often lately. *She left.* His own words echoed off the sunlit eastern wall as the westward sun angled in. Miki had gone and then Dad. Oh, and God. Hunter blew out a loud breath and busied his hands and mouth with chicken. He'd said enough, thought too much. Hated the whole thing. Especially the water in his eyes and the gut-wrenching pain.

"She told me you saved her from drowning."

He grunted. Of course he had. He'd have done that for anyone.

"Sounds noble to me." Granny Belle leaned against the sink, facing him, giving him space.

Huh. Noble. Right.

Her sigh carried from across the bar. "You get that she's trying to help."

He nodded, blinking, but not looking up. Granny had a way past any bravado he'd fooled himself into thinking he had.

"Did you tell her thanks?"

"Sort of." On behalf of Dad. His own foolish pride kept him from admitting he needed her help. A braver man would've said it already.

Granny Belle reached over and covered his resting hand with her own while his eyes burned. "I know this is difficult, this whole season has been painful, but ... what if this is the part where God turns it around?"

Wind chimes clanged outside, and a breeze rustled the curtain over the sink as her words swirled around in the air.

That would require God's attention, and He'd already proven His lack of concern.

Hunter drained his glass, and she refilled it. The next breeze carried a gull's cry into the house.

"For what it's worth, you're doing the right thing, by going ahead with this program, I mean. You've got a good heart, Hunt. You need to remember that about yourself. And what you're doing for your dad?" He glanced up then. Granny's blue eyes filled. "He'd be proud," she whispered.

42

Hunter gulped against the stab in his chest and shoved off the barstool. "Sorry—" He darted toward the door. "Thanks—" He'd meant to add more but couldn't manage it.

After slipping into his truck, he backed around to face the road. Headed this direction, he could let the tears run. He took the long driveway toward the street but stopped several feet back. He needed to think, collect himself. And he'd drive better if he could see.

He'd promised Dad to keep the tours going. But Dad being proud of him? No. Not with how the business was failing. One thing was certain, he had to clear things up with Miki, which involved swallowing some—okay, most—of his pride.

Starting with an apology.

Right now.

CHAPTER EIGHT

Mikaela sat on her back deck, laptop open on the round table, hot tea warding off the chill as the sun lowered in the June sky. Granny had promised blueberry pie. Mikaela would have to settle for fruity tea instead.

Beyond the grassy lawn a few yards away, the bay splashed incoming waves beckoning her to walk, but she truly did need to finish preparations for tomorrow. She'd have to face Hunter again, merely several hours from now. Had he really meant—

Lord, this hurts. I know I was foolish, thinking I could simply sail in, act the heroine, save his business, and then sail away. Conviction dug deep. She'd been borne along by pride. Great. The floral aroma of pansies carried on the breeze. *Forgive me? And I know I haven't prayed about my role here, outside of my job. Please show me how to help the people around me.* She studied a boat out in the bay, watched it drift on the calm water. *I hadn't realized I needed healing for how things ended back then. But either way, I have a job to do. A boss to please. And a future to ascend to. Please guide me.*

No, she wouldn't ask Him what she'd avoided questioning all these months. Wouldn't broach the subject of her and Hunter. Just because God had brought her to the island, didn't mean He had any intentions for Hunter and her to be anything more than co-workers.

Of course, she couldn't hide from God. He saw her avoidance, knew her heart. But in this one area, she'd rather not hear His thoughts.

Her phone rang on the glass tabletop, and Dr. Wren's face appeared on the screen. She answered. "Hi, Amelia." The department chair represented friendship and even comradery, yet as Mikaela's boss, she was the one to please. Plus, Mikaela was walking a tightrope keeping certain things from her.

"Hi, Professor. Seems we've hit a little trouble."

Had Hunter contacted the U and tried to back out? Would he do that?

"What's happened?" Mikaela bounced her heel on the deck boards as her stomach clenched. *Breathe.*

"One of our students withdrew from the quarter—a family situation. We'll need to send someone else so we can cover our costs and keep our agreement with the Cahills. Know of anyone?"

This was why Mikaela hadn't heard back from each of her students. She grabbed a notebook and fanned herself, suddenly warm. They'd offered the opportunity to the eligible people, and everyone who could be here was planning to arrive by tomorrow morning. She pushed back in her chair and scanned the nearby evergreen trees. Their sweeping branches appeared black against the sky's fading light. A motorboat sped toward land, no doubt unequipped for night-time sails.

The funding she'd secured paid her salary, but didn't cover the privilege of sailing daily with the Cahills. The students were paying that share. Missing one student meant they couldn't keep their agreement. All the other funds were designated for other purposes.

Lord, help.

"Let me see." After putting the chairwoman on speaker, Mikaela pulled up a roster on her computer and scrolled the lists. "We may have to expand the parameters for qualification. Most potential students are at their summer destinations, either breaking from school or on assignment elsewhere."

"Otherwise, how are things going?"

Good question. "Lauren has been so gracious. I know I can count on her whenever a need arises." She leaned toward her monitor, mentally reaching for something complimentary to say about the captain. "Oh, look." A name jumped out from the screen. Perfect timing. "What about Pierce Carter? He's new to the department this year, I believe."

"You haven't met him?"

"Not yet." Mikaela clicked through to find his profile.

Dr. Wren was quiet for several moments.

"Is there something I should know?" Whenever Amelia had

concerns, she generally shared them. Why clam up now? "Seems to me he may be our only option."

"I believe you're correct," Amelia finally said. "Why don't you contact him?"

Still wondering about the strange reaction, Mikaela clicked his name to send him an e-mail. "I will." He was closer to her age and yet unmarried, which might mean he could be flexible—perhaps even relocate to the island with little notice. "We'll have to overlook the rules to let him participate, since he may not have the pre-reqs out of the way. Think the chair will be okay with that?" Mikaela teased her boss as she typed a quick note to Pierce.

"Hmm . . . I think, for the sake of this program, we can make an exception. Perhaps give him a creative assignment." The chairwoman's smile was evident in her voice. But then she went silent, and Mikaela wondered what she would say next.

Mikaela invented a usable paragraph, knowing she'd rework it once this phone call ended and she could fully concentrate. "So . . ." she said, mindful of their connection, and wanting to let her mentor know she was refocused on their conversation.

"So, we've known each other a long time, right Mikaela?" Gone was the reference to her accomplishments, her degree, and position. This couldn't be good.

"Yes . . ." Her hands abandoned the keyboard and now hugged her teacup.

"When were you going to tell me about the extent of your previous relationship with the captain?"

The cup slipped, slamming against the table and spilling tea through the grid that made up the tabletop. She snatched her laptop and phone away from the danger. Shaking, she set her computer in a dry spot and pressed off the speaker option on her cell. Her stomach clenched as she spun toward the bay. As much tension and heartache as her visit here were already causing, she couldn't let the Cahills down now. What if the department chair—

"Were you afraid I'd nix the entire program?" Dr. Wren asked.

Exactly. Even now, Amelia could pull Mikaela off the team.

Except . . .

If reassigned, she could save face while leaving and effectively push Hunter from her life for good. She pressed against the ache that thought brought. It'd help if she knew her own mind. *Focus.* "I wasn't sure . . ." Was she speaking to her friend and mentor, or her boss? "How did you find out?" A huge blue heron swooped in and landed in a madrone tree right down the beach.

"When I first spoke with Lauren about this summer, she mentioned a few things. I've been waiting for you to tell me."

Mikaela stood at the end of the lawn, gazing at the waves from a boat's wake. For two years, she'd been trying to prove herself professionally to her mentor, and to the other powers-that-be at the U. Mikaela pursed her lips and sighed, her shoulders dropping. She'd hoped to keep this from her boss. What if Amelia couldn't overlook this lapse in judgment, this blaring conflict of interest? "I apologize for not being up front with you. I'll understand if you decide to make... changes."

Amelia sighed over the connection. "I'm disappointed you didn't trust me." Ah, that tone belonged to her friend. "But, I can understand your choice."

The bomb teetered close to dropping.

"However, because you weren't up front with me, I'll be keeping a closer watch."

And there it went. Mikaela's stomach cramped. A large part of the mission this summer was about proving herself. Now, she'd proven herself untrustworthy.

"Because of your conscientiousness, I assumed you'd require less supervision, but now I think I'll schedule a few drop-ins after all." She sighed. "Still, I believe it would be best if we kept this information from Dr. Smythe."

Relief offered her a full breath. "Thank you." For now, this would keep her failures from the one holding the purse strings. She straightened her shoulders. She wouldn't blow this second chance. "I agree." Though Amelia would never say it, and Mikaela would never remind her—Hawaii was Mikaela's way of showing her appreciation to the chairwoman. She had to come through, had to prove herself. No matter what. Mikaela kicked a pebble into the incoming tide.

"I'm certain you will tread carefully." Dr. Wren gave each of them a minute. "Now that we've covered all that," she said, compassion influencing her voice. "How are things going, really?"

How much to share? Secrets had gotten her in trouble. But transparency could get her fired. "Challenging." He *had* broken her heart. Twice. The latest about half an hour ago. "We'll find our way." Should she tell Dr. Wren that Hunter hadn't known who was coming as the U's rep? The story was a little comical now, so she did. And Amelia's laughter felt like a reward.

Someone slammed a car door nearby. Her neighbors were arriving later than usual tonight.

Their conversation was silent a moment. For several weeks, they hadn't discussed Amelia's condition. "How are you feeling?" Mikaela asked.

"Oh, you know, good days and bad."

Knocking carried from the front of the house. Mikaela spun toward the cottage. "Excuse me, Amelia, I think someone's here. May I call you back?" Had Granny come to make sure Mikaela was fine?

"Certainly. Update me Friday on how this week went and what Mr. Carter decides."

Mikaela scooped up her laptop and scooted inside. "Of course," she answered her mentor, and they disconnected the call.

The visitor tapped the door once again.

"Just a sec," she called. Then, she settled the laptop on the breakfast bar and moved toward the living room. Enough drama today. She needed a long soak in the hot tub out back—an opportunity to pray and brainstorm how she and Hunter could find a way to work together.

And before she reported to the ship tomorrow, she needed to shore up her guards. Because that man was all kinds of dangerous to her heart. He always had been.

CHAPTER NINE

Mikaela glanced through the window flanking the left side of the door, catching a glimpse of . . . a black T-shirt?

What was Hunter doing here?

How did he know where she was staying? Lauren or Granny must have told him.

He stood there, pockets stuffed with his fists, shoulders hunched. He tipped up his head and offered a sober—less guarded—expression. Her breath hitched. Gone was the scowl of earlier, replaced by a softer brow. And a wetness in his reddened eyes as if he'd come from a painful meeting. But hadn't he been at Granny's, with her? *That* meeting hadn't been all roses and rainbows for her either.

Her heart contracted, and for a second, she wanted to hug him—ease the pain she saw there. Except for what he'd said less than an hour ago—

"Can I talk to you?" His voice sounded muffled through the window. "Please?"

Had he come to cancel the program after all? Was he willing to let his dad's business fail, without even trying, simply because she was at the helm of this experiment?

She reached for the knob, willing her thoughts to settle, the ache in her shoulders to ease. They kept finding themselves here, on the edge of civility and answers. She knew the old Hunter would have cleared the air their first encounter. But, even with him standing here now, the door open between them, she couldn't picture *him* opening up.

Rather than let him into the house, she closed the door and gestured toward the pair of Adirondack chairs, away from the too-cozy swing on the opposite side of the porch. "Have a seat."

The sun tucked itself behind the row of poplars, washing the sky in pastels of an inverted rainbow.

He leaned against the porch railing, facing the chairs she'd referred to, ankles crossed. The shadow of a grin materialized. "You scored the Herschfields' cottage."

She'd once shared with him how she'd love to live here one day. He'd teased her about her dreams. Now, she was living more than one of them.

Too bad that wasn't enough.

From her leadership training she recalled she shouldn't place herself in a lower position, and sit while he stood, but the aqua chairs beckoned her, and she dropped into one. Scrounging for objectivity in the face of his well-past-five-o'clock shadow and tender eyes, she crossed her arms over her chest and waited. At some point, she'd need to bring up this latest glitch and the department chair's news. But that would all be moot if he came to "fire" her.

Once again, her past and present hinged on him.

"About tonight..." He paused and glanced toward the side yard. She took the opportunity to study him. *What weight he must carry on his shoulders—his dad's business, the pain of losing him.* They'd been close. The financial needs. She'd felt dependent on his decisions only moments ago. But how dependent was he on new passengers or her students coming through? And what did that do to a man's pride?

Since arriving a few days ago, she'd been so consumed with the university's goals here, her desire to help Cahill Touring, she hadn't truly considered Hunter's state. She'd approached this whole summer assignment... selfishly.

Maybe this was where she could start to change. "Hunter, I'm sorry." She uncrossed her arms.

His head jerked up. "Wha—?"

"I've been self-absorbed." Granny was right, not only had Mikaela not thought this through, she'd blown it. *She* hadn't valued their past.

"Are you kidding?" His voice sounded raw. "You're back here to help. *I'm* the idiot."

She'd seen this summer in Friday Harbor as a stepping stone.

"Nah, I was . . . I'm ashamed to say this, but I was using this quarter as a means to an end." And by extension, she'd been using the Cahills as the same. Conviction yanked her heart, and she stood. "Can you forgive me?"

He scoffed, but without scorn. "I don't—"

She offered her hand as if he were a colleague, and their handshake was a sign of good will. That *was* what he'd said he wanted—a professional rapport.

But instead of shaking her hand, he shook his head. "*I* came to apologize for being a jerk." He pointed up the road. "At Granny's."

She dropped her arm and took up a position at the other railing, so they stood angled toward each other—not head-on, but somewhat facing each other. A start. "Maybe we're even?" she offered, not wanting to humiliate him by making him explain. He'd suffered a lot in the last couple of years, and that was based on what she knew had happened. Certainly there was more she didn't know about, more that Lauren hadn't shared. Either way, Mikaela wanted to let him off the hook. "You don't have to—"

"No, let me get this out." He gripped the railing on either side of himself, his body coiled, biceps twitching as his attention bounced around the porch. "I–I wasn't expecting to see you again. It's been twelve years." His gaze collided with hers, but he dislodged the connection right away, head tipping down. "I mean, on a regular basis." His head came back up. "You surprised me."

She cringed. "Yeah, apologies for that too. I assumed Lauren would have told you before I arrived."

His grunt broke some of the tension circling the porch. "Before you dunked yourself in the strait."

"Well, there's that." She grinned at him, enjoying this fragile connection.

He entertained his grin for long moments this time. The fine crinkles at the corners of his eyes drew her. Those lines hadn't been there all those years ago, but they lent him a wise appearance. Electricity zinged between them. Bold, this current. Familiar. Delicious. And oh so dangerous.

That reminded her. She still had his jacket. "Hang on?"

He nodded. "I'm not going anywhere."

She wouldn't stop to read into that semi promise or his gentle tone. "I'll be right back." She'd carry on. Maintain her guard. Do the next thing. She darted inside, found the jacket hanging in her laundry room, and squeezed one sleeve in her hand. Yes, dry. She brought the coat out to him. "Here you go."

His fingers brushed hers, and she remembered how gently he'd held her, carrying her into the clinic. Her recollection of the actual rescue was fuzzy until they drove up to urgent care. He'd been so concerned, stretching out of his new comfort zone to check in with her, press his face to her head—trying to warm her up? If she remembered correctly, he'd been shivering too.

She dislodged those guard-rending thoughts and went for something light. "You've rescued me a few times over the years."

He draped the jacket over the railing, not responding. But that was one more way he was heroic. He wouldn't take credit, wouldn't grandstand. No, he'd stand there, all humble and irresistible, and test her resolve without saying a word.

She placed a hand against her fluttering stomach. "I—I'm glad we've found this amiable place."

Another grunt.

"What?"

"'Amiable?' You came back sounding all professorial."

"Ha! 'Professorial?'"

"I'm not used to it." The way he tilted his head, though, indicated he didn't hate this change in her. Then he sobered. "But I never meant to imply we had no history together." His words seemed scraped over sharp rocks.

She swallowed hard and studied the evergreens in the front yard. He hadn't meant those words. He *did* care. Once. Healing whispered over a deep place inside. Still, no way was she fishing for his status right now.

He rubbed a hand over his scruffy face, and the scratching noise carried toward her. A crazy memory of running her fingertips over his five o'clock shadow skittered through her mind. *Stop it.* She tore her gaze from his downturned face and pressed her lips together.

"I'm an idiot. Forgive me?"

She swung her focus back to him and allowed a grin. "I'll try." Her teasing response earned a half-smile on his handsome face.

He seemed to want to say something, but he looked away, face tipped toward the yard. Was he about to send her away? Did he still want her to leave?

She had to know. "So, am I fired?"

His squint spoke before his words came out. "No." His intense gaze opened up. "Of course not."

Relief swelled on her next breath. They could make this work. Unless the chairwoman's update wrecked everything.

"I have news," she dragged out the word *news*, dreading the possibility of upsetting their fragile common ground. "I've just heard from Dr. Wren. We've had a little setback."

"What happened?" His brow creased, but he didn't seem panicky. If only she could bottle courage and guzzle some when anxiety overtook her.

For now, she'd try to hide her own worries. "One of our students had to back out of the program, last minute. So, we're scrambling to find someone else." They'd find someone. They had to.

"Oh." His chest rose and fell with a deep breath. Knowing Hunter, she guessed many thoughts spun through his mind. Would the U cancel the program for lack of funds? Was he wondering if she'd leave as quickly as she arrived?

Would she?

But the immediate concern was holding up her end of the agreement. "We promised a certain amount to Cahill, and I'll do my best to see that we don't flake on that."

He reached for her, but dropped his hand before he could touch her. All this current between them and he hadn't even touched her yet tonight. Heaven help her if he did. Because he challenged her convictions, made her reconsider every single one.

"I don't doubt you will."

She scrambled for his meaning. "I'm sorry?"

"Find a way."

Right, the funding. "I do have one possible candidate. He's closer to our age, and hopefully he's reliable." Though, since he hadn't had to earn the right to be here, who knew how he'd do? "Serious about his education." Again, hopefully.

Those fingers reached toward her again. Made contact with the back of her hand. *Whoo.* Sparks. She shivered.

"Don't worry, Miki. It'll work out."

She held her breath. Against his own ground rules, he'd used her old nickname. His gray eyes offered a dose of courage, and she drank it in.

"I believe in you."

She gave him her "I'm not buying it face," and he scrambled for ways to convince her. But she'd have to see for herself. Except, he could add, "You got here, didn't you, Professor?"

Ah, that grin was quite a reward. "Thanks, Hunter." See that? She didn't call him Captain but seemed to absorb his words. He could almost see the tension leaving her shoulders as her posture relaxed. When had she gotten so uptight?

Yeah, maybe the two of them could do "amiable" after all. Apologies had a way of smoothing things over, though he hadn't expected *her* to apologize. He was the one who'd blown it. "So, we're okay?"

She gave him a genuine smile, and he lapped it up. "Sure."

There was plenty they hadn't talked about, and he wasn't volunteering to go there now. A bat swooped low in the yard, diving between evergreens. Had she seen it? If so, she'd duck inside any second and they'd lose this moment. He had to keep her talking. "So, if this new student you're considering doesn't work out, what's next?" He gulped and tried to appear indifferent. "Skip ahead to the next thing?" Who was he kidding? He could never be indifferent about her being here.

She hugged herself, the tension returning. A breeze tossed

loose strands of blonde hair around her shoulders. She faced the wind and closed her eyes, letting her locks blow behind her, as if she stood on the bow of a ship. "You know, I haven't considered what's next if this thing . . . uh, sinks. This project is a pilot to prove the next one can succeed."

He was surprised by her anxiety. She used to be all about "let God carry your burdens" and "if it's meant to be, it'll happen." Gone were her carefree platitudes. What had happened to change her? And why wasn't she mentioning God with this latest glitch? Should he? Except what was he going to say, "Hey, pray about it" when he'd never do that?

An inner nudge reminded him God had answered when Miki needed Him that first day.

If God would answer for her sake, would He answer for his? Stupid question. If God cared, He would have spared Dad for at least a couple more decades. Their business wouldn't be on the verge of bankruptcy, and their homes' mortgages would be paid. Miki's program wouldn't be in danger of falling apart. So, obviously, He didn't care.

Hunter reached for Miki's shoulder, let his hand touch down on her light sweater. Caught his breath at the current between them, even now, then watched her go still. He wanted to offer her courage, help lift the burden she readily accepted these days. "It'll work out."

She met his eyes and he left his hand there when she didn't pull away, caressing her shoulder with his thumb a moment before lowering his arm.

"Anyway, I'm not letting you off the hook yet." He was going for teasing, but the jolt up her spine and the resulting shiver testified against him. He'd blown it. "That's not what I meant." Oh, to be able to ease her fears. "I'm not worried about the income, Mik—Mikaela." Her expression softened. "I'm not."

"Well, we had a deal." She licked her lips as if nervous.

He nodded. "We did and I hope it works out, for your sake." He'd always wanted her to succeed, to thrive. Even when her success meant she'd leave.

"That's kind." Her shoulders lowered, and he battled the urge to offer a neck rub. "But I'm here for Cahill as much as for the program and my students."

"Who makes the call? How big of a say do you get?"

"Here's the thing—not much. And I'd feel like a failure for letting everyone down if this program sank." Her brow wrinkled. "But if I can't find someone . . ." She didn't have to say it. He knew.

"Then, here's hoping the new guy comes through."

Hunter hadn't meant to sound so . . . hopeful. Not in front of her. Not yet. Hadn't meant to long for more time together. But . . . He met her eyes. *I want you to stay.*

I want to stay.

Some things hadn't changed. They could still chat without talking.

Maybe he could help. He'd make a call himself, check in with the department chairwoman. Maybe they could work something out. Rework the contract they'd all signed—well, Mom signed on Cahill's behalf. Find some other way to keep the program alive.

Later, he climbed into his truck, still feeling her hand on his arm when she thanked him for coming over to apologize. No one had ever made him feel like Miki did. But it was more than their chemistry. She dove into life. She overcame challenges, as if the only outcome she'd tolerate was victory. And, of course, part of his attraction was their history. But chasing her, pursuing her? He wasn't that brave. Or stupid. No. They would work together. They'd see the project through, but he'd be careful. *Sorry, Dad.*

Letting her in, even a little, made him feel weak—exposed. And in for more pain *when* she left again. Because she would.

She always did.

CHAPTER TEN

Breathe. No way should Mikaela let on that this new student—the one Dr. Wren went silent about—was their slim hope for a future on the island. Her fingers tingled. Holding her breath wouldn't solve this problem, and a lot of good she'd do if she fainted before the new guy answered his phone. What was that, five rings now?

"Go for Carter!" he answered. Oh, he sounded young—immature. Hadn't his records shown he was only two years younger than she?

"Hello, Pierce?" Mikaela paced her tiny living area, then grabbed her keys and stepped out onto the back deck of her temporary beach cottage.

Music blared in the background on his end. "Atcher service. Who's this?"

She willed steel into her tone and her nerves. "This is Dr. Mikaela Rhoades. We've been exchanging e-mails about the marine biology program's satellite project this summer."

"Oh! Hi, Doc." His tone shifted a bit toward formal. Some scrambling on his end and then blessed quiet through their connection.

She paced the length of the deck boards, back toward the hot tub. "Is this a good time?"

"Sure."

"I'd like to discuss the program and see about your interest and availability." *And convince you to come.* But she wouldn't say that aloud. She couldn't get Amelia's strange silence out of her mind. What was Mikaela missing about this guy? "Do you have any questions?"

"I received the PDF, but I haven't, uh, looked at it yet." Clicks filtered through from his end. "I'll pull it up now."

He hadn't even reviewed the information? Her feet pounded around the side of the house, eager to move in light of Pierce's disinterest. Made sense. Of the two of them, the biggest stakes were hers.

At the end of her driveway, she turned south onto the peaceful island road. "Perhaps it would help if I covered the bullet points?" She'd have to recall them from memory, but anything to convince him to join them.

He mumbled a string of words as if he were reading aloud. "Thank you. I've got it in front of me." He paused, and she gave him several moments. Desperate as she was, she wouldn't push. For now, she'd indicate where she was going so he could follow.

"What it boils down to, Mr. Carter, is an opportunity we'd like to extend to you. I understand you're new to the marine bio field, so we wouldn't expect scholarly research. Rather, I'd find another role for you."

"Thank you, Prof," he said. "Problem is I can't. I mean, I'm busy. *If* I could break free, it probably wouldn't be until maybe mid-July."

Mid-July? His words halted her halfway to Granny's house. "Well, unfortunately, that doesn't fit with our schedule." She clenched and unclenched her free hand in an attempt to recirculate oxygen. "I realize this is very short notice, but we'd prefer for you to arrive this week, if possible." She cringed. Good thing he couldn't see her. Of course they were asking the impossible. Not many people could move with so little notice.

"Well, that's the best I can do. I know my uncle wants me to find a way, but I'm locked into this job in Seattle."

She withheld her sigh. "I understand. I won't take up any more of your time."

They disconnected. Her nails dug into her palm. *Relax.* But her fist didn't unclench.

Now what?

The phone rang three times before connecting with an invitation to leave a message.

"Hello, Dr. Wren, this is Captain Hunter Cahill." Hunter's fingers shook, but he couldn't let nerves stop him. He might, however, cut back on his morning coffee tomorrow. And he thought Miki was the anxious one. "I wonder if you remember me."

His living room seemed smaller than normal as he paced the worn hardwoods to the window and gathered his thoughts. He shoved back the dusty curtains and watched light pinpoint the floating specks as they swirled. "I realize you've been mainly working with my mother, but I'd like a chance to talk with you. My best call-back times are Tuesday through Sunday before noon. Tours begin at one. Monday is our day off, so anytime that day is fine. Thank you." He left his number and hung up.

Restless after disconnecting, he pocketed his phone and left the house. He'd jog up and down the miles-long island road, see if he could burn through his fears. No question, Dr. Wren would ask him what he wanted.

What did he want?

He'd wrestled all night with that one. As risky as this was, now that Miki was back, he wanted her to stay. He stretched at the porch steps. She'd brought hope into his life and not just because she was here to help Cahill. He envied how she faced life—expectant. Probably wasn't healthy to draw hope from another person—what would Granny Belle say? She'd open her Bible, offer him a Sunday school lesson about finding hope on his own. And he'd listen because he respected her. But he couldn't "turn to God" right now. Wouldn't—didn't—couldn't—trust Him.

So, he'd take hope where he could get it. Especially when it came packaged in the familiar, beautiful, and kind person who was Mikaela Rhoades. But a big part of him wanted to keep his distance, fortify his walls.

His promise elbowed him. *Dad.* He'd seen these traits in her, as they all probably had. Dad figured Miki was the perfect match for Hunter—enough sanguine to overcome his melancholic leanings, Mom had said.

But neither of his parents would want him to be selfish, and he'd agree. What was Miki's goal? Was Hawaii what she really wanted? It's what she'd wanted as a teen—some glam position in the tropics. Of course, he could never move there with her. His life was here with Cahill Touring, for as long as they kept it running. And there was nothing selfish in keeping that promise.

Hunter wasn't proud of how he ping-ponged between wanting to support her—a noble motive—and wanting her to settle here—a selfish one. *If she ever comes back to the island, promise me you'll pursue her.* Dad must have known there'd be two sides to that crazy promise, including a lifetime's worth of potential for a future together, or a lonely one apart.

He jogged north. Sunshine glinted through the trees, but the temps at this early hour kept him cool as his feet pounded the street. Evergreens lined the road on both sides, with gaps for long driveways winding into the woods or back to homes on the waterfront.

His phone buzzed against his leg and he scrambled to grab it, slowing his pace to a walk. The chairwoman's name appeared. He inhaled deeply to catch his breath, and swiped the screen. "Hello, Dr. Wren?"

"Yes, Captain. Good to hear from you." She sounded older than Hunter remembered. He'd met her as a teen. Dad had her over a few times. All she did was talk to Miki about marine biology, picking up on Miki's drive to have a career in rescuing marine animals—at the time, her goal in life. Amelia had motivated Miki so much back then that his girlfriend had applied to the U of Sea as a junior in high school.

"I'm so sorry for your loss. I've always admired your father's drive to build his business there on the island. He was a true inspiration, a kind and honorable man."

He hadn't expected the chairwoman to go in this direction. It was a moment before he could speak. Then, all he had was a simple, "Thanks."

"Your mother has been a great help in coordinating our efforts there." She paused for a moment. "How are things going? How is Professor Rhoades?"

Sounded like the department head thought of people in terms

of their titles—captain, chairwoman, professor, doctor. For a moment, as he marched the sun-dappled road, he was glad for his own. Just so, for once, he measured up.

"Things are . . . progressing." Using formal speech was annoying. He'd never been one for posing. "I want to help the professor succeed here." Amelia didn't need to know his motivation, right? Or that he was afraid Miki would have to leave soon. "She mentioned a student canceled at the last minute." His breath hitched, and he gulped. *Chill.* Coming off unhinged wouldn't help Miki's cause.

"Oh yes, that. We're working on it. We're set to make some special arrangements, provided our choice can come on short notice."

Hunter rubbed the back of his neck. "If he can't, does that mean the program is suspended?"

"Captain, I realize we're contractually obligated to uphold our agreement." She sounded confident things would work out. "We will find a way to pay you, even if the summer's program must be canceled or reworked."

Is that what she thought? That Hunter only wanted the funds? He slowed his stride and came to a halt. Perhaps he should help the chairwoman see his motives here. But how much should he tell her? And how much did she know? He couldn't remember if he and Miki were open about their dating relationship when she visited. If she knew of their full romantic history, she'd probably consider this a huge conflict of interest.

If he was going to be selfless, he'd have to see to Miki's success. Strive for it. Like she did. Dad would pat him on the back—wouldn't he?—for wanting the best for her. Hunter studied the treetops as the wind harassed them sixty feet up. "I'm not worried about the funds. Maybe we could brainstorm a backup plan."

"I'm working on it." She paused. "But there is one thing you could help me with."

"Sure." Whatever it took to keep Miki here, because as torn as he was, he was not ready to see her leave yet. "Name it."

"I want the best for our professor." Sounded exactly like

Hunter's thoughts. She went quiet for a moment.

Our professor? Maybe the chairwoman did know their history—more than what she'd witnessed during those summer visits.

"Professionally and personally," she continued. "I'd like her to see there's more to life than a career."

Had he heard that right?

"I realize that might surprise you. I'm guessing you thought I was part of why she's so driven."

He snorted, but cleared his throat to cover it. "Yes, actually." If she wasn't prodding Miki to work so hard, who was? The other faculty? The benefactors?

"She did mention this summer's pilot was her idea, didn't she?"

"Yes." A humbling moment for him. One that still stung.

The conversation paused, and he considered the ferns clumped together near the Herschfields' cottage driveway. Miki's place. How had he gotten here? He didn't want to bring her in on this conversation. He pivoted and strode away. Hopefully the trees would hide him if she stood outside right now.

"I green-lighted this trial because I saw the potential benefits, how it could help you and your family. But as far as pushing forward, that's all her. Surely she was as determined as a youth. At least, that's how I remember her when we met that summer." She paused. "I fondly recall my time with your family, Captain. I'm hopeful this summer is advantageous for all of us."

"Thank you."

"I have a request for you. I haven't discussed this with Lauren or Dr. Rhoades, but in the interest of helping this program succeed, I'd appreciate a weekly report from you. Of course Mikaela keeps me updated, but from your perspective, you see? And this is assuming all continues as originally planned."

Weekly reports? This was new. But what if . . .? "That might mean Dr. Rhoades"—oh, he hated calling her that, but he would, for the chairwoman's sake—"and I would need to meet after hours to check in. There isn't much time for lengthy discussions during the tours." Was that what she meant? Was the doctor prescribing he spend one-on-one time with Miki?

"That is exactly what I propose—the two of you meeting, if not daily, then three or four times a week, during off hours, away from the tours and students. I'm glad you see this my way." She took a breath. "Of course the meetings don't all have to be structured. Take the ferry to Vancouver. Sail to Bellingham. Remind her there is joy to be had on the water, besides research."

His pulse ratcheted up. He'd like that too. And now, she'd given him permission. "I assumed our professor"—he grinned to himself knowing she couldn't see him—"wouldn't have free time this season." Or he'd feared she wouldn't spend any off hours with him.

"She'll make time for these meetings because they directly affect the program. Listen, I need to run. Please update me via e-mail on Monday evenings, or call if there are problems. I'll inform our professor of this request, so you won't have to. Thank you, Captain."

And she disconnected the call before he could respond.

What had just happened? Had Amelia really directed him to . . . *date* her number one prof?

Sounded like something Dad would have ordered, if he were still here.

Was everyone in on a conspiracy to bring them together? His mom keeping the secret that it was Miki coming up to the island. Dad's insistence only she would make him happy. Before their breakup, Granny was convinced they belonged together too. She'd even said it went beyond their families to how much they had in common and how deeply they cared about each other. Couldn't argue with that.

Sometimes, and he wouldn't tell anyone this—he even wondered if God might be in favor of them being together. But that was crazy. He didn't care about Hunter's happiness.

Hunter took his long driveway back toward his house. What would Miki say when her boss told her? He tripped into a pothole and grimaced. He should order a load of gravel, level this driveway out, but he couldn't afford it.

That reminded him. He needed to get over to Granny Belle's and replace those dock boards before one of her boarders broke a limb. Maybe he could see Miki while he was there and avoid "Professor Rhoades," since, if the professor had heard from Dr. Wren, the *captain* might be in for it.

He heard a scuffle behind him, from several meters back, toward the road, so he turned. There was Miki, striding past his house. She seemed wrapped in her own world, oblivious that he stood within sight of her. Even from here, he could see an earbud cord dangling from her closest ear as she marched. So natural to spot her here on the island—his favorite person in his favorite location.

A part of him snapped into place.

She belonged here, near him. His heart thumped, and his feet stilled as it hit him. He wanted her in his life, and not only for a few weeks. In fact, if she weren't in such a hurry, with a phone to her ear all of a sudden, he'd call out to her, make up an excuse to hang out until sailing time.

What had gotten into him? Who dove in a second time to a known hazard?

She peered over and caught a glimpse of him, startled, and shot forward, but not before he waved. Timid like a fawn sometimes, that one. And anxious—more than ever. He'd have to help her overcome that, get her to relax. Ah, dates to sail around the Salish Sea. Maybe Dr. Wren knew her better than he thought she did.

The same way Dad knew him. Hunter wasn't one to let a miracle sighting get past him. She was within range. And like when he toured, he'd chase her down. Only this marine mammal he wouldn't observe from afar. He'd capture her.

Okay, Dad. I'm in.

Even if it cost him his heart. Again.

CHAPTER ELEVEN

"I'm sorry, what?" Amelia couldn't mean it. Mikaela had called to update the chairwoman on the fact Pierce Carter couldn't come after all. They needed to brainstorm a solution, or Mikaela would need to start packing and call off her students. Except, maybe they could carry on with the program, one person shy, drag funds from somewhere . . .? This was why she needed her mentor's input and direction.

Not this sea mine Amelia had dropped. "I know the Cahills are important to you," Amelia continued. "What's more, we're in contract. I'm going to talk with a few more contacts here. You focus on getting off to a strong launch there, which includes these meetings between you and Captain Hunter."

Right. *Sure it did.*

Following Mikaela's silence, Amelia continued. "I've recently spoken with him, and he willingly agreed."

He had? And since when were they chatty? "I'd be happy to meet with Lauren."

"Mikaela, honestly." The rebuke hit Mikaela deep inside. Yes, she was being petty. And now that the chairwoman knew their history, there'd be no more hiding. "For one thing, Lauren isn't the one captaining the boat, sailing through the islands daily. She works behind the scenes. The captain—"

"Yes. You're right, of course." The gulp of pride scratched on its way down. Maybe it wouldn't be so bad? Hunter and she had found a less hostile place . . . That look in his eyes as he'd all but told her *I want you to stay.* Her response: *I want to.*

But this directive to meet more regularly, away from the students? Since she'd returned, he'd had this guarded vibe about him—in the creases at the corners of his eyes. A vulnerability that testified of his grief for his father. She had the sense he'd rather not be open, would rather keep his distance. That worked for her—

protected her too. Except, then he'd sought her out to apologize. Maybe he didn't prefer she evaporate anymore.

These mandatory meetings could wreck everything—well . . . not the program. Extra attention would likely help there. But her plan to keep her distance, to not let him get close again. To not give in to this wooed feeling he conjured in her from the first time she saw him as more than an annoying brother all those years ago . . .

She strode down the quiet road, passing driveways, when movement caught her attention to the right. Ah! How had she arrived at Hunter's place? She jolted, he waved, and she sprinted forward. So much for discussing it the next time she saw him. That little chat could wait.

"Mikaela, are you there?" Dr. Wren sounded impatient.

She shook herself free of her thoughts. "Yes. I apologize. You were saying?" She tried to calm her thumping heart. Seeing Hunter stirred too much inside her, so much she'd let grow dormant over the years. A side of her she couldn't let live again. For both their sakes.

"Thought I'd lost the connection. Anyway, I recommend you be proactive and suggest meeting times to him the next time you see or speak to him."

No problem. She'd jump right on that. She blew the loose hairs from her forehead.

" . . . there's more to life than a career."

She must have missed more of Amelia's speech than she'd thought. "I'm sorry?"

"I've been trying to help you see it." A gull cried over the connection. Amelia must be outside her condo in Seattle—maybe sitting on her balcony or tending her potted flowers. "Take in summer there at the island. Slow down. Enjoy your life . . . now."

Mikaela slowed her steps, since she was free of worrying Hunter might chase her down the street. Her winded breaths blasted her phone until she shifted her wrist.

"Dr. Smythe is very anxious."

Hmm, a turn of conversation. "I hadn't realized Mr. Carter was his nephew."

"Well, since he didn't work out, that won't matter now. A complication we didn't need." That last part came out quietly, and Mikaela wondered if she'd heard correctly.

"I'm curious—what do you mean?"

"Nothing. Doesn't matter now. Let me know how things go there with your students' arrival and your meetings. I'll update you after our meeting here. And . . . relax Dr. Rhoades."

Sure. Right after she scheduled her several meetings a week alone with Hunter.

A truck pulled in behind him. Dan. His buddy parked and climbed out. "Hey, don't tell me you've already run this morning."

"Not exactly." Hunter had planned to shower, but he had a couple more hours before he was due at the dock. "Let's go."

Dan pocketed his keys. "Let me stretch first, dude." Dan kept fit, like Hunter. But stretching was just smart.

Hunter pressed his heel to the ground and lunged forward on his other leg before bending to work his back muscles. "I talked with Dr. Wren. Interesting conversation."

Dan used his truck's running board to work his hamstrings. "What's the old guy like?"

"Dr. *Amelia* Wren. And honestly, I thought I'd have to talk her into letting up on Miki—you know, stop putting all that pressure on her. But it sounds like Miki's putting the pressure on herself."

"Knowing what I do of Mikaela, I'm not surprised." Dan straightened. "C'mon."

They headed north. Would they run into Miki? A few cars passed, now that the hour was later, but generally the road was quiet, save all the birds carrying on. An eagle cried overhead, but Hunter didn't have to look up to identify it. He wouldn't be surprised if a swirl of drifting feathers fell next.

"Where are you with your promise to your dad?"

Hunter pounded faster. Confessing this to his buddy would

mean razzing. But also support, which he could use. "I'm ... committed."

"Yeah?" Dan had that I'm-wearing-a-dopey-grin sound in his voice, and Hunter glanced over. Yup.

"Good. I can't imagine my life without Beth. And as far as I'm concerned, you and Mikaela are long overdue for a coupla wedding bands."

Hunter scoffed, but a fierce longing opened up in his gut, one he'd kept clamped down for about twelve years. Could he help it if he pictured a wedding canopy on the beach, Miki's white dress tossed in the same wind that toyed with her blonde hair? *Please, God.*

Wait, he didn't pray anymore.

"Go for it," Dan repeated.

"You sound like the department chair now."

"What, she wants you to marry Miki, and maybe jeopardize the U's plans for the future—which I'm guessing don't include this little island." They thudded past another driveway.

"She didn't say that, but she did say Miki needs a personal life. And she wants us to meet after hours."

"Hmm ..."

"Might not matter." He puffed. "If they don't get another student in to cover their bases, they may have to close the whole thing down, cut their losses, and drag Miki back to Seattle." His lungs squeezed at that thought.

Dan glanced over and squinted. "You can't let that happen."

"That's why I called the chairwoman."

"Who'da thought you'd have an ally in her?"

"Right?" Hunter was ready for a topic shift. Considering what he was about to risk sent his stomach churning like a stormy sea. "Hey, how's Beth? Did you guys find out what you're having?"

Dan's steps slowed. Hunter matched him. "It's not good news, man."

"What happened?" They came to a winded stop.

Dan rolled his neck, hands on his waist. "The ultrasound showed some complications. I don't even understand it all."

Hunter eyed him. "Can they fix it?"

Dan shook his head. "No." He stared up toward the sky while he caught his breath. "Beth's at risk for preterm labor, but Baby's not due until early November."

Knowing he had so little to offer, Hunter wished he could point Dan toward someone who could help. Dad would have brought up God. Too bad Hunter couldn't—or wouldn't—do that. Wind threw an errant cedar branch deeper into the forest, ruffling the ferns. Dan could use some power on his side. "We don't really have the medical resources to help here on the island, do we?"

Dan shook his head, raw pain in his eyes. "She might have to go live with her parents in Seattle for the next several months. Beth's local OB said we shouldn't panic, but she recommended Beth get close monitoring." Dan blew out a hard breath. "I'm scared, man."

Hunter hadn't seen him like this in all their years of friendship. "Is Beth safe?"

Dan met his eyes. "I don't know."

Well, Hunter couldn't talk to God, but Dan's pastor could. Given Dan was a praying man himself, maybe God would have mercy. "Have you told Ted?"

Dan studied Hunter, probably remembering that Hunter didn't bring up church much. His friend had tried to talk him into attending again after Dad's death. Too many unanswered questions. And not only about Dad either, but his buddy knew that.

"I did. They're praying. Pastor Ted and his wife have been over to the house a few times. Beth's on bed rest until we get more answers."

"If she moves south, do you go with her?"

"No way I can leave now." Dan tightened his jaw. "We got a new contract for a three-house build over the next several months. We need the money."

Hunter clasped his shoulder. "Dude, this sucks. What can I do? Need anything done at your place? What about a job in Seattle?" Hunter mentally searched his contacts. "I can't help in contracting, but I know a couple Port of Seattle guys." Dan had started in maritime work years ago, then switched to general contracting when he married Beth so he could be on the island and not working on the water.

"I don't wanna bail on Hank. But I can't live without Beth." Dan shoved his fists into his windbreaker's pockets. "There is one thing you can do."

"Name it."

Redness rimmed Dan's eyes. Hunter understood that. Not that her life was in danger, but Hunter was finally admitting to himself he didn't want to live without Miki.

"Pray for us?"

CHAPTER TWELVE

Hunter wanted to shake his head, refuse. But knowing what it had cost Dan to blurt out the request stopped him. Dan knew Hunter didn't pray anymore. And it wasn't as if Dan had demanded Hunter pray aloud—try to drum up a few words to God—right then. Smart guy.

He clenched his jaw. He'd much rather have dug a foundation for a new outbuilding or roofed Dan's sprawling house. "I'll see what I can do."

After Dan left, Hunter showered, and, once he'd found a bottled water in the worn fridge, he made his way to the deck on the beach side of the house. The yard could use a trim soon. His deck needed a new coat of stain, if he could swing it. He stood at the railing, watching a blue heron swoop toward the bay.

A few days ago, Hunter had prayed for Miki without stopping to think first—like the reflex that shot him into the strait after her. Now, Dan's wife and baby were at risk. God heard other people's prayers. Stuck in the same jam, even if he wasn't on speaking terms with God much lately, Hunter would want everyone praying.

Nutcase. Hypocrite.

But where else could he go? Where else could Dan and Beth go? That reminded him, Dan hadn't mentioned the gender. Maybe they couldn't tell yet. Or maybe news of the baby's sex was secondary to worrying about the baby's life.

Tough business—going in to learn whether to paint a room pink or blue only to find trouble.

He tugged out his phone, texted Dan. OK IF I GET OTHERS PRAYING? Mom and Granny Belle would pray, maybe Miki as well.

Minutes went by while he waited for a response, then: ONLY IF YOU DO TOO.

Hunter grunted and chugged his water. Yeah, Dan had seen through him. And he wasn't letting Hunter dodge this one—or push the responsibility off onto others.

Something prodded his chest. A tug drew him. Familiar. Distant, as if on the other side of Hunter's walls. Yet welcoming, somehow. How long since he'd felt that?

He'd missed it.

He worked his jaw, checked right and left. No neighbors around. Maybe God would hear, since He favored the Thorntons. Plus, if Hunter prayed now, he'd have done his part since Dan hadn't asked for anything else. Hunter could tell him he'd followed through, sidestep any probing questions, and walk around with a clear conscience. Mostly. But he'd still make a few calls to Seattle.

That same nudge again.

"God, it's their baby ..." Reflex drew the whispered prayer out of him. He worked a fist open, then closed. Any more words dried up at hearing his own rough voice, knowing Who he was talking to. The water bottle crinkled in his tight fingers. He leaned on the deck's railing.

Before putting up those internal barricades, before all the disappointments that cracked his heart open, he'd fantasized about marrying Miki and running Cahill alongside Dad for thirty or forty years. On that side of the barriers, he'd believed good things would happen in his life. He had daydreamed up a brood of Cahill kids terrorizing the island, making Dad proud. A son or daughter to take over the family biz when Hunter and Miki retired.

The years had proven he couldn't have those things, no matter how much he'd once hoped. But Dan didn't deserve this new stress. Over the last seven years, he'd confessed to Hunter their struggles to have kids. Pregnant ... no longer pregnant.

"They've made it this far." A few months this time.

That same soul-deep knock. What did it mean? God wanted him to face the thoughts behind those walls? Or God wanted him to see something he wasn't seeing, feel something he wasn't feeling? He grunted again. *Not feeling* kept him going. Studying the world behind his walls might reduce him to uselessness. Find him sitting in a kayak without an oar in the middle of the Strait of Georgia, spinning in the currents and easily picked off by a freighter. And worse, uncaring that he saw it coming.

But then he wouldn't be here for Mom.

He crushed the now empty water bottle in his hand and turned back toward the slider. He didn't need this little counseling session. *Wonderful, Counselor*... The trouble with God was He'd always known Hunter so well—too well.

Ask for a token.

His feet stopped. What in the wor—? That phrase felt foreign. It hadn't come from him.

A *token*... Some kind of sign that God cared. Pieces of a memory verse crossed his mind, and he scoffed. *"Show me a token for good..."* From the Psalms. Sure. Because evidence of His goodness was everywhere in Hunter's mess of a life.

Mikaela is back.

His jaw clicked from the pressure. *Mikaela is back.* And he'd never thought that would happen.

"What if this is the part where God turns it all around?" Granny Belle's words.

Hunter tipped his head so the graying sky filled his view. "You want me to ask for a sign that You ...?" He turned toward the water and squinted against burning eyes. The bay churned in the next gust.

The same drawing, stronger this time. Insistent. Irresistible. Pushing hope toward him.

Fine.

Where to start? He groaned, elbowing pride aside. "You wanna make a way for Miki to stay here?" Forever. Except God wouldn't make that decision for her. And neither could Hunter. She had to choose it. So, he'd ask about the short-term. "For the summer?"

Pretending not to watch the dock from the wheelhouse, Hunter fiddled with the radio settings aboard the *Millennium*. Sam carried on with prep work, no doubt aware of Hunter's tinkering. From the sounds down the dock, Miki's crowd of students was here. Apparently, they'd at least go ahead with today. He sighed deep, and Sam glanced over, a grin twitching his scruffy mustache.

"Haven't seen this side of you for a long time, Cap'n." Leave it to Sam—who'd known Hunter since birth—to read him like a chart.

"Yeah, you focus on getting us ready to launch."

Sam offered a goofy salute. "Aye-aye, Cap'n."

Hunter chuckled as he skimmed down the steps. When he hadn't been able to sleep the night before, he'd ended up back out on the deck, stargazing. Still wondering if God cared about his future, or about the things that worried him.

Had the U found a solution? Was Miki going to be able to stay for the season? Almost as big was the question of how she'd reacted to the chairwoman's new requirement. *He* loved the idea of one-on-ones. He stuffed a grin as he considered that she probably wouldn't.

Drawn to her, he strode through the main salon, toward the dock. From here, surrounded by her students, she seemed cheerful. Maybe that was her leadership face. Jacket in hand, she wore jeans and a flowing shirt. Her blonde hair glistened in the sunlight like spun gold. Every now and then, she'd peek over at the ship as she led the group, her hazel eyes glinting in the light. His heart caught.

Yeah, he wasn't just hooked, he was reeling toward her, out of his control.

He stepped into the doorway, unclicking the cordon.

"Good afternoon, Captain." She met his eyes, so much passing between them. His heart lurched as she held her smile during their moment of eye contact. All this chemistry and she had no idea of his new resolve, his intention. His determination to woo her no matter how long she stayed.

Easy, Cahill.

"Permission to bring my students aboard?" she asked.

He stepped aside, extending his arm to the salon. "Permission granted, Professor." This time the title felt good, like mutual respect. Still, he fought a grin as her troops jumped aboard.

Moments later the group of four students filled the salon,

especially the big guy, who dwarfed everyone else in both height and girth. Next to him, there was the nerdy-looking kid; a tall, blonde woman who had dressed in bright colors; and the spirited gal who eyed him up and down and gave knowing looks to the others.

"Captain Hunter," Miki said, her voice formal. Let her impress her students. Miki pointed to the tall, mocha-skinned woman. "This is Destinee Fulbright. She's a grad student and has been in the marine bio program for over a year."

Hunter shook the woman's strong hand. "Nice to meet you."

"You too." She seemed to stifle a giggle, as if she knew some private joke. But there was no way Miki would tell her students of their history. Not if he knew her like he thought he did. Which of course he did.

A sense of satisfaction settled inside with that realization. Maybe that's how he'd start—using what he knew about her to woo her.

Miki pointed out the tall, thin woman. "This is Anya Grigori. She's from Russia, also a second year."

They shook hands. "Iz nice to meet you, Captain." Her accent influenced her words.

He nodded at her.

"This 'linebacker' is Kristopher Townsend," Miki continued, a hint of teasing in her voice. Charming, watching her interact with her students. The big guy stepped forward and engulfed Hunter's hand in his paw. Miki pointed to the final kid, the nerd who seemed content to hang in the background. "And this is Seth Foley. They're both third years and might join me in Hawaii this fall."

Hunter shook Seth's hand, ignoring the dig about Hawaii that Miki probably hadn't intended.

He addressed the group. "Did the professor explain the rules on board the *Millennium*?" They all nodded. No one spoke, as if they were intimidated by him. Might be the captain's hat he'd donned. "Great. Go grab sodas, on the house. We'll join you in a minute."

"Oooh, 'we'." Destinee cooed while the others exchanged glances before all of them ambled off toward the snack stand.

Yeah, they'd have to keep an eye on her.

Several feet from the others, he faced Miki. "Any word from your student?" Hunter kept his voice low. She had no idea how much hinged on her answer. How hope hung, gasping for news.

Miki turned her back to her crew, her expression dimming. She spun her thumb ring. The news couldn't be good. "He had a prior commitment."

Hunter's gut sank, but he didn't need to add to her stress. "Okay, well, we'll find something else."

"You're good with things moving forward?"

He fought a full-on smile, tucked his fists into his pockets, and nodded. "Yeah."

She leaned closer. "I wish I had the resources to cover it myself, but I don't."

He breathed deeply, drawing in as much of her vanilla scent as he could, making up for lost years. Muscle memories triggered, but he fought against bringing her close. *Hands off.* For now. Hopefully. "I know you would." Another side of her that made her heroic.

Her student couldn't come . . . See? This was how Hunter expected God to answer him—by not answering. What was new about that? So much for His *token.* Miki would be back in Seattle by Friday. May as well have asked for the moon.

"We need to schedule some—"

"Meetings?"

The look on her face told him she was unsure, but was that due to the program or the idea of alone time with him? They'd managed just fine the other evening on her porch. He wouldn't scare her. He'd take things easy. Let her set the pace.

If she stayed.

Destinee reappeared. "Hey Prof, did you hear back from Pierce?"

Miki spun and eyed her. "How did you know I'd been in contact with him?"

"He called me, bragging how he might skip pre-reqs and climb aboard anyway." She turned toward Hunter. "And if he does come, watch out. He's closer to yer age, and every bit as ho—"

"*Ms.* Fulbright." Miki glared at her student. "Excuse us," she said to Hunter, then steered Destinee away.

"Aw, Prof, you need ta loosen up." Destinee's words carried back toward Hunter.

He stifled a grunt—part amusement, part concern. He would never mock Miki, but Destinee had a point.

He stepped onto the dock, waved for his staff to join him. Right now, they had a sail time to make. When his crew had gathered, he called over the students for intros. He'd already briefed them on his expectations for how they'd interact. But, watching Jace meet Destinee raised new flags. Of all the participants, Destinee seemed the most unpredictable. Good thing Hunter could trust Jace to follow the rules. When the guy drew Destinee over to the stairs to show her his station, Hunter followed, cutting their interaction short, sending Jace on an errand up on the bridge.

He'd better warn Miki. No matter how long the students were here, he couldn't allow flirting on board. Cahill's reputation was at stake. They weren't the only whale tour business around. When Dad ran the biz, he'd kept tight reins on employee fraternization. Since Hunter would be up in the wheelhouse most of the time, Miki would have to keep watch down in the salon. "Professor Rhoades, another word?"

She joined him, and once again they stepped away from the group for privacy. Already passengers lined up way down the boarded walkway, ready for a photo and a trip out to see the whales. He'd keep his voice low. "Listen, I noticed Destinee and Jace flirting. I've told him what I expect, and I'm sure you've addressed the same thing with your group. But could you keep an eye out?"

"Absolutely. Of all my students"—she shot a glance toward the ship behind Hunter—"she's the loose cannon." He wished he could capture that hint of warmth in her eyes as she gazed up at him.

Near the offices, the first mate raised his voice to give the passengers the usual spiel. Time was short.

"Listen, I wanted to apologize for Destinee's outburst." She peeked around him, but the students were all involved on board somewhere. "All that nonsense about how hot you and Pierce both are—" She clamped a hand over her mouth.

He should resist, he really should. But— "What was that?" He kept his voice quiet as color took over her face. A smile toyed with her mouth. He'd missed that almost-grin, the way she tipped down her head as if shy around him. No sign of Professor Rhoades in sight, only beautiful Miki.

She peered up at him. "Captain . . ." Humor swam in her bright eyes.

"No, I really think I need to hear that again." He cupped his ear. "Something about the temperature or something . . ."

He watched her, standing there, the hem of her blouse tossed about in the breeze off the water. No walls between them. This was a golden moment—the kind he wanted to create and memorize this summer. As teens, they'd worked together and practiced hands-off during the tours. Then, in the evenings they could run down to the beach, holding hands, take the kayak out, spend hours together. He could hold *her*. He'd touched her arm last night on the porch, felt the jolt. But what he really wanted was to hold her. A yawning ache opened in his chest, and he almost reached over.

"Hey, Prof, you wanna remind me what our goals are here?" Destinee. Surprise.

Miki held up a hand, silencing her student. She studied Hunter as if realizing what they'd shared—all these unguarded moments. Then, she smoothed her top and straightened her spine. Professor Rhoades reporting for duty. He had the crazy urge to salute her.

"Is that everything, Captain?"

"For now, yes. Thank you." He kept his posture and expression neutral, but he hoped she read his thoughts. All those years ago, he had cherished his time with her. They'd had such an intimacy between them. He missed it.

The women boarded the *Millennium,* and he followed them.

What had his dad said? To romance her? That would take strategizing and serious restraint. He couldn't let on at work how he felt about her, couldn't let her students see this side of him. And Destinee was rather aware.

Were keeping the business alive and romancing Mikaela two

exclusive plans? No. He'd just have to woo her after hours.

How convenient, then, that personal time away from work was what Dr. Wren had prescribed. Now to see if Dr. Rhoades would cooperate. Because even if they didn't have the whole summer, they had today. And he'd make the most of it.

CHAPTER THIRTEEN

The microwave clock read 10:11 as Mikaela paced Granny's sunny kitchen. The students' share of the money was due to Cahill this week, which meant they had forty-eight hours.

After their tour the previous day, Hunter had said he wanted to meet, but she'd excused herself, not really acknowledging her boss's directive. Why spend time together and bring another layer of complications to this situation if she were destined to leave?

Granny Belle shifted behind the counter. "You're going to wear a hole in the floor."

She stopped. "Sorry, am I making you nervous?"

Granny sliced another apple into quarters. "No, but you are anxious enough for two people." She pointed her knife at the barstool across the counter. "Have a seat."

Mikaela sat, propped her foot on the footrest, then jiggled her leg. "I need to problem solve and fast." She wouldn't think of asking her grandmother for the funds. But maybe Granny Belle would have some advice. *C'mon, God. Show me.*

Granny dropped the fruit pieces into the bowl, adding to the ones she'd already cored and quartered. Her crisp was coming together. "I understand. So, what is God saying?"

"I haven't asked Him exactly. I've been too busy begging for His help."

The teaspoonful of fragrant cinnamon went still over the bowl. "Begging?"

She shrugged. "It's an anxious thing I do. I'm working on it." *Keep breathing.*

"You haven't asked Him?"

She grimaced at her grandmother who had succinctly diagnosed Mikaela's knot. "What if I don't like what He says?"

"You think you got here without Him?" Her voice was gentle despite her directness.

"Of course not." If God hadn't opened doors, she wouldn't be here. So, why did she feel like she had to beg for answers and His help?

Granny set down her measuring spoons and wiped her hands on a towel. "Who does this program benefit the most?"

"Students, my mentor, the Cahills, the research foundation." A thought struck that she hadn't ever considered. "Do you think the program has to save lives or souls to be valid, to gain God's blessing?" Perhaps that was why she didn't have peace lately.

Granny shook her head and selected a large plastic spoon from her caddy. "What if God has you here on the island for another reason?" She stirred the apple, cinnamon, and sugar mixture, scenting the air. "Or, what if Hawaii is a short-sighted vision?"

How could it be when it'd been her goal for so long now? And recently, the elements came together making her more certain God was in this. Plus, if she were meant to be on this island, why pull her out early? Was whatever God had in mind already completed, her time here about over? "I wish I knew."

"I recommend asking Him and listening." Granny glanced toward the bay. "If you're free right now, there aren't any boarders by the water."

"Good idea." She'd zero in on one question, not all the others she'd avoided asking Him. No problem.

Prayer hadn't been a chore for years, but praying about directives didn't come easily. And dread? That was new in regards to prayer too.

She sighed, stepping out onto the bright back deck, breathing in the salty breeze. When was the last time she'd had intimate communion with Him? A deep, long conversation that went both ways? Where she listened without fear of what He might say?

Sometime around the day she had pitched Friday Harbor to Amelia. Long ago, Mikaela decided the best proximity to Hunter was distance—except for this summer. What if God had something to say about that?

The grassy yard gave way under her sandaled feet. Dark-eyed juncos flew past between the rhododendron bushes, their white tail

81

feathers flashing as they chirped and dove. Several American goldfinches flitted to the feeder Granny always kept stocked with seeds, perching to eat. Mikaela was due at the harbor soon for the day's sail, because for today at least she'd carry on here.

Sunlight glistened off the boulders out in the bay as she drew toward the edge of the sloped lawn with its low bulkhead lining the shore. She dropped onto the pebbly beach and brushed sand from the wooden pilings so she could sit. Long ago, Granddad Ben had placed these wide, flat-topped posts side by side to provide a barrier that would prevent erosion at the edge of their property. This far from the waves' reach at high tide, the pylons only stood about three-and-a-half feet tall—a great place to alight and pray. Judging by the white smears drizzling here and there, the herons and gulls enjoyed these posts too.

There'd been a time she could merely breathe His name, and peace would envelop her. She inhaled. "Jesus . . ." Anxiety withdrew like the low waves receding a few yards in front of her as peace pushed in. Calm reassurance. How long since she'd basked in that?

Apparently resisting the Prince of Peace kept a sense of well-being at bay too.

Near her feet, a tiny green shore crab came out of hiding, skittering over the pebbles, maybe searching for another place to hide—a large enough rock. A salamander materialized and darted toward the largest stone nearby where it settled on top to sun itself. The crab burrowed under the same one. For one, a hiding place; for another, a warm and comforting surface. Would an eagle find the top creature and gobble it up?

"I admit that I need You. We all do."

All these years and through the trial even Hunter didn't know about, she'd had no problem admitting her dependence on Him. But that incident had shaken her faith, and she'd never recovered a belief that didn't waver.

Hmm . . . another reason she'd pulled back from Him.

Now uncertainties lurked, springing up to distract her. Like Granny's questions in the house. Should Mikaela have chosen some missions-based career? One that saved souls or lives? The Hawaii project would honor her mentor, so that was noble, right? *Right, Lord?* It wasn't as if Mikaela pursued this launch in her own name. But nobility wasn't always the only requisite for God's favor or blessing.

Plus, she could *fill* her days with nobility and not touch God's plan for her.

Originally, she'd wanted to go into marine animal rescue, but that dream faded while at the U as competing opportunities opened up. Would rescue be a more noble direction for her to take now, since it was mercy based? Would God like that better? Or bless that more? If only she knew what He knew about this situation, could see the view He had like those bald eagles soaring over the bay.

All these questions about her career unnerved her. She'd thought them answered long ago. Settled. Coming back to this island churned up the past. She picked up a nearby pebble and threw it into the water. The splash didn't satisfy, and she sought a larger rock to toss. This one gave a gratifying *sploosh*.

Did You bring me here to test my resolve? To make me second-guess myself? My career?

Silence.

She longed for the prayer times that had felt like communion—hearing His voice, sharing her life in intimacy. Why did she suddenly feel disqualified?

Most of her questions about work were moot because she had commitments, both to the U and the Cahills, not to mention her students. No changing course now.

She settled on the bulkhead again and tipped her head back to gaze at the clear blue sky. No signs. No skywriting. No answers.

If this were God's idea, why was He so quiet? Her heart ached. Feeling disqualified chased away that elusive peace too.

"Mikaela, dear, could you come up here?" Granny called from the deck.

She stood and brushed herself clear of sand, then hiked toward the house. As she climbed onto the deck, Granny led a twenty-something man toward her. She'd seen him before, but couldn't quite place him. He towered over Granny and stood a bit taller than

Mikaela. He wore skinny jeans, so he looked thin. His tight polo shirt, with a scarf and jacket, made him seem rather out of place here on the island—urban. Foreign. He wore his wavy dark blond hair short, coupled with a well-trimmed beard. Granny didn't usually introduce her boarders to Mikaela, so why bring them together?

"May I help you?" she asked as they stood amidst the deck furniture.

"Oh, I'm sorry," Granny said. "This is Pierce Carter." She turned to Mikaela. "This is the professor, Pierce." Pride shone in her eyes as she introduced them. Maybe Granny *was* proud of Mikaela's career choice.

Pierce? But, he'd said he wasn't coming.

His handshake was strong. "Hey, Prof. Remember that commitment I mentioned? Well, it ended. So"—he shrugged—"I decided, why not head up here? I mean I'm guessing you still need me." Something about his stance—the slight lean and the way he slowly crossed his arms—Mikaela read conceit and entitlement, and it irked her.

When he'd changed his mind, why hadn't he called to inform her? Ask if the position was still open? The audacity. Was she supposed to just permit him to assume the role now? What if she'd found a replacement?

"You presume the opportunity still exists." This might be God answering her prayers, but she did not need a flaky, immature narcissist in her program. Sunlight glinted into her eyes and she shifted to let the evergreens block the direct light, but quickly regained eye contact. "I apologize for any expense you've incurred traveling here, but when you said you weren't going to be able to come, I deduced you meant it."

"Oh, I shoulda called." He straightened his posture, his expression veering toward arrogant, especially given that he offered no apology. "You see, when I talked this post over with my uncle, he insisted I drop everything."

Dr. Denver Smythe. Right. The cranky funding rep who'd been fretting all over Amelia's office lately, but keeping his distance from

Mikaela—thankfully.

"I'd hate to disappoint him." Pierce uncrossed his arms and grabbed each end of his scarf with his hands, casting glances between Granny and Mikaela. He appeared ready to add a shrug as if the decision made no difference to him because Mikaela would face all the consequences. "My uncle mentioned that he'd spoken at length with Chairperson Wren this morning before I boarded the seaplane in Kenmore." He eyed her. Was that enjoyment on his face? "I'm guessing she hasn't had a chance to call you yet about it."

As if on cue, her cell rang and Amelia's face showed on the screen. She swiped to answer. "Good morning, Dr. Wren. Would you mind holding for a moment?"

"Sure, Mikaela." Amelia didn't sound as formal as Mikaela chose to right now.

Somehow this department first year had decided he was in charge. She needed to regain control. "I will discuss this with the department chair," she said after covering the phone's mouthpiece. "But first, how did you know where to find me?"

"I called Destinee, and she told me to check either the little cottage down the shore or this quaint little house." He gave Granny a smirk. "I hope that doesn't offend you."

Granny Belle retained as much grace as ever. Mikaela knew she could handle him. "Granny, would you occupy our guest for a bit? I'll only be a few minutes."

"Sure thing." Her grandmother nodded and ushered Pierce back into the house. If anyone could tame him, she could. "I've got hot apple crisp."

Once again Mikaela walked toward the beach, out of earshot of the kitchen's open windows. She squeezed her phone before pressing it to her ear. "Good morning, Amelia. I've met Pierce."

"Sorry I couldn't reach you sooner. I've had back-to-back appointments since my conversation with Dr. Smythe."

"I understand." She rubbed the back of her neck. *Stay calm.*

"At first, I wasn't certain having Pierce involved was such a good idea. I've some concerns about his professionalism, and I wanted to honor the Cahills by including only competent folks."

Mikaela couldn't agree more. She tipped the phone away from her mouth and sighed, then tipped it back. "What makes you think he isn't competent?" She had her own concerns—his self-entitled demeanor, lack of professionalism—like Amelia had mentioned—unwillingness to apologize, etc. Her minor in psychology pointed toward narcissism with maybe a touch of resentment aimed at his uncle. But she'd appreciate hearing her mentor's opinion.

"Between you and me, his uncle has tried—somewhat unsuccessfully, according to my colleagues—to pawn him off on several different departments, hoping he'd find something he liked and would commit to it. Pierce is a career student, always changing majors, hiding at the university to avoid life. Dr. Smythe sees Pierce as his responsibility since his parents are out of the country." Amelia offered a short chuckle. "I knew our time would come."

Delightful. Now, he was her problem. "So there's no way to reverse this?"

"No, but on the upside, you'll find the funds are ready for payment to the Cahills. Ahead of deadline."

Mikaela let the news sink in as her shoulders relaxed a bit. One of her first reasons for organizing this trial was to help Lauren and Hunter. Now, they'd have the money the U promised. She couldn't wait to tell them.

"Thank you. They'll be relieved to hear that. And I'm glad to meet that part of our agreement." But were they bringing challenges to Hunter and the business by including Pierce? The ache at the back of her neck had moved to her forehead.

"Of course, we'll have to work well with Mr. Carter, given his uncle is the funding representative."

"Thanks for appeasing Dr. Smythe. I know he's been haunting your office."

"He's simply anxious. He's accountable to his family's foundation. And if things don't go well, this could reflect badly on him."

"The foundation's board chose this direction." Which Mikaela appreciated since as the paid admin she could ease up on her own endless research for a short season. *I'm thankful for that, Lord.*

"Yes, I'm sure they weighed the risks. And so far, they're relaxed about it, giving you the time you need to get things running."

"I'm glad we made the agreement with Dr. Smythe, to hold him off until several weeks in." *Thanks for that too, God.*

She rubbed her temples. She'd have to tolerate Pierce's entitlement, one of her least favorite personality traits—or disorders. Perhaps she should dunk herself into her hot tub for the next hour and a half.

"Have you and the captain spoken about our new arrangement? Now that the program will continue, it's time to get started."

"Yes, I—I mean, we will meet soon. After the tour yesterday, I needed to get in touch with some other leads on filling the vacancy on my team." She pressed a molehill down with her foot, thumping the mud flat. More Hunter time. Except, he had proven helpful. They could brainstorm solutions as issues came up. Keep things professional.

"Well, that's all resolved now," Amelia said as if there were no concerns for her in Mikaela and Hunter meeting regularly. No tension, conflict, or history. "Update me in a couple of days?"

"Yes."

"Good luck," her mentor said in a gentle tone before clicking off.

She'd need more than luck. *Lord, is this Your answer?*

One of the elements Mikaela loved about teaching college students was their relative maturity and their commitment to this field. Only the determined were here. And she'd take the most promising and qualified to the Big Island. So, after this summer, she'd hand Pierce back to his uncle and be free. She could look forward to that.

For now, she had to figure out what role he'd play. She'd find him something not-so-glamorous. Something humbling. Did Hunter need anyone to clean barnacles off his ship's hull? She grinned as she returned to the house. Time to face the newbie.

CHAPTER FOURTEEN

Fifteen Years Ago

"Knock it off, Micah."

"C'mon, Hunt. She's a girl!" Apparently the kid wouldn't have mercy on his own sister.

Hunter's biceps tightened as he straightened his spine. Hard to look tough sitting in a kayak, but he would still intimidate Miki's kid brother. Or get splashed trying. "Dude, I'm warning you."

Micah scowled hard at Hunter, then used his oar to spin his kayak and paddle away.

Hunter glanced over at Miki. "You okay?"

Her wet hair glistened in the sunlight, little rivulets running from the long blonde ends down her tanned arms. Her hazel eyes glinted in the brightness. The tank she wore with shorts made her look slim and healthy. Strong. She'd always been pretty, but when had she gotten so beautiful? Something about being fifteen really worked for her.

Today he'd ask her the question he'd considered bringing up all summer so far. If she didn't still treat him like a brother, he would've done it already. He had to show her he'd changed. She may see him the same as she always had, but he sure didn't feel the same about her.

They had a few things to overcome–distance for one. The fact she lived in Seattle, and he lived way up here in Friday Harbor. The fact they only saw each other at holidays, school breaks, summers. But no one at his school could compare with her. He brought his kayak closer.

"I'll be fine. Thanks." She started to row away. Yeah. Independent. Did she think he'd splash her next?

He gripped her kayak and nodded toward her brother. "What's the rush? You wanna catch up with him?"

She peered into his eyes. He smiled so she'd know he wasn't a threat like her brother. "No, you're right. I don't," she said.

"Let's go this way." He pointed in the opposite direction.

At a private beach several yards down the shoreline, Hunter gestured toward the sand. "Wanna hang out here?"

"Sure." She steered toward the beach, and he followed. Sunshine bore down on them, and Hunter liked how it warmed his back. He'd already stripped off his tee.

As they beached and stepped free of their kayaks, he reached for hers and dragged both of them farther up the slope, away from the stretching waves. Usually, she insisted on doing it herself, but she let him this time.

They found a large log, battered by the weather, now bleached and waiting for visitors. For the moment, the cliffside hid them from view of the house and no one occupied the stairs. If the owners came down to their dock, they were toast. "We'll have to make a run for it if the Clarks show up," he said, clearing dirt from the top of the log and pointing for her to have a seat.

"True." She sat, a hand on each side of her gripping the log. "I'm up for it."

One more thing he liked about her.

"Little brothers are annoying." She worked her damp hair into a long braid and swung it behind her back. He liked the wisps that breezed against her face. Should he tell her that?

He took a spot next to her on the log and nudged her shoulder. For now, he'd keep things light. "Agreed." Jonah, his own kid brother, made him nuts too. A piece of driftwood shifted toward them on the tidewaters. A seal bobbed to the surface, and Hunter pointed it out.

She grinned. "Sometimes you're so much like your dad."

A sincere compliment. "Thank you."

"See yourself running his business one day, pointing out seals and whales for a living?"

"Maybe. But college first, Dad's orders."

"Right? Me too." Her long, tanned legs stretched in front of her toward the sand.

"Miki?" He shifted on the tree trunk, angling himself so he could see her.

"Yeah?" That gentle gaze had always gotten to him. The same tenderness she kept from her brother and saved for injured animals. That she used it with him? Made his heart tilt.

Pushed him to ask his question. "You can say no, but I wanted to ask you something." *It'd probably be too much to reach for her hand. Right?*

She drew in a shallow breath. "Okay . . ."

"I love you coming up to the island every summer, and the holiday visits when you guys can." Her family's cottage gave the Rhoades a getaway spot, far from the city.

She gasped and her gaze locked on his, and it was as if they each held their breath. Wait. Had he really just said, "I love you"?

So much for keeping things light.

"I mean, I—I love seeing you." *C'mon, Cahill. Get it together.*

She relaxed a little. Was she afraid to mess with their friendship? Afraid to risk losing it for the possibility of having something more? Should he wait? Cuz, really, he didn't want to risk their friendship either. His life wouldn't mean as much if she disappeared from it.

"Me too, Hunt. I like that we're friends. We can, you know, talk to each other." She nudged him this time, as if to say, *Lighten up, dude. Friends don't freak out.*

He chuckled, and it sounded weak to him.

Friends. That's what he wanted to change.

"We've known each other forever."

"Hunt. Spit it out."

He snorted. "Right. Even though we live hundreds of miles apart, I want to . . . I mean, I wondered if you'd be my . . . uh . . ."

Her eyebrows hiked. "Girlfriend?"

He sighed in relief. "Yes." He studied her now. Because in the next couple of seconds she'd determine whether they could be happy or whether he'd just lost everything. How did she see him now?

Her tanned fingers tightened on the log under them. She went quiet, and his fears were confirmed. She didn't want this—wasn't willing to risk their friendship for what could be.

He started to stand. "Sorry, I—"

She snagged his arm this time. "Hunt, wait."

"Yeah?"

"I thought you saw me as a . . . a sister."

He drew shallow breaths. Swallowed. Cleared his throat. "Not anymore."

Hunter shook off the recollection. It'd been ages since he'd entertained memories of their history. But since she'd reappeared, she invaded both his thoughts and his dreams.

This morning, she'd called him saying she had news and wanted to meet with him before the sail. Was she about to tell him she was leaving? Her voice hadn't let on either way.

His heart thumped as he strode to his office. He felt fifteen again. Her news would change their future.

Lord, if You're still listening . . . help her stay?

That long-ago day on the Clark's beach, she'd told him she didn't want to hurt him, especially since she'd return to Seattle in late August. So, no deepening relationship. But by mid-summer, he'd convinced her.

And it all started with a kiss.

The key to working with Pierce this summer would be to help him see she was the boss. For that reason, she'd insisted on driving him to the university's labs to collect the others and then head to the marina. He'd left his expensive convertible at his rental house.

Focusing on Pierce kept her from thinking about Hunter and those mandatory meetings. Now that Pierce would stay, those meetings were unavoidable.

Still, she couldn't wait to tell Hunter the good news. Cahill Touring would have the income boost, as promised. Before today's tour, she'd send the students for coffee so she could find him. Never mind those butterflies inside. He deserved to know the student had come through.

Somewhere along the quiet roads, she'd landed on an idea. Pierce would spend the summer as her assistant. At her first opportunity, she'd pencil down a list of duties to keep him busy. She'd begin by tasking him to log their activities every day. Maybe she shouldn't see him as a filler, but he hadn't proven himself trustworthy yet. Best to occupy him, but not rely on him.

The U provided a minivan for faculty use for ferrying students. None of the others expected to see Pierce today. The crew erupted as they pulled out of the lab's parking lot. When the hubbub died down, Mikaela spoke to Pierce in the front seat. "I need to give you your duties. Right before sailing time, let's meet for a few minutes."

"Aye-aye, Chief."

Destinee scoffed behind him as Mikaela pulled onto Front Street. "Mr. Carter, I'd prefer you call me Professor or Dr. Rhoades."

"Sure thing, Prof."

Close enough for now.

At the docks, she sent the students across the street to the coffee stand. So far, no sign of Hunter. She'd prefer he not see the new student until she talked with him. Better make this quick.

Still seated in the driver's seat, she faced Pierce on the passenger side of the van. "I expect respect from you as long as you're here." For the sake of the U's rep, but also Cahill's.

He hunched over his cell, thumb-scrolling. Could she look forward to him acting like a teenager all summer?

Where was the aspirin?

"Put the phone away."

"Sure thing." That phrase again, but he cooperated by tucking his cell in his back jeans' pocket. Here's hoping the thing fell into the harbor.

Bad professor, bad.

She produced a legal pad and pen from her bag. "I'd like you to log the activities on board—the areas we sail to, marine life, etc. I expect a detailed report at the end of each sail."

He crossed his arms. "I could use my iPad for that."

"Sure. Where is it?" The guy didn't carry a backpack. He seemed the type to be paired with a messenger bag.

"In my car." He smirked. The vehicle she'd required he leave behind.

"Tomorrow then. For today"—she pushed the pad of paper toward him—"the old-fashioned way will work."

He accepted the notebook with a scowl. "The other students— what are they doing?"

"Researching, but they're all well into the program, so they have legitimate projects this season."

He squinted at her. Gulls shrieked over the bay, gathering near a boulder.

"I'm due to touch base with your uncle, Dr. Smythe, soon. I'd like to give him a good report, providing things go smoothly. Think we can work that out?" She'd stooped to the threat of tattling. Yeah, he brought out the best in her.

He glanced outside, shifting in his seat. Apparently his attention span didn't last longer than a few minutes.

"One more thing. I'll expect professionalism on the tours. You'll be punctual. We are here supporting Cahill Touring, which means we show respect and work hard."

He saluted her. "Yes, sir, ma'am."

She refused to let him irk her. Instead, she drew a long breath. "Okay, please join the others across the street. I'll see you all back in half an hour."

He climbed out of the van, and she snatched up the strap of her bag and headed into the office. Hunter's truck wasn't here yet, but Lauren's car was. She'd start with her.

"Good morning, dear," Lauren said.

She approached the counter where Lauren typed busily on the computer. "I have good news for you," she sang.

Lauren's face brightened, and her fingers stopped. "You do? Oh, hang on." She focused behind Mikaela who turned toward the entrance. A UPS driver rolled a stack of boxes on a hand truck along the dock to another nearby business. No sign of Hunter.

"He might have parked far and hiked in." Lauren always seemed to know when Mikaela was searching for her son. "He does that sometimes, when he wants to think."

"I remember." She'd kept recalling his little habits lately, which also conspired to draw her toward him.

Lauren stepped from behind the counter. "What's happened?" Oh, this lovely woman needed this news. Mikaela's heart warmed even more.

"We found another student to fill the slot. We're all set for the season."

"Oh, fantastic!" Lauren hugged her tight. "I knew He'd come through. I just knew it."

The lock jangled behind her, and Mikaela pulled back to see Hunter step into the shop.

"I've got to tidy up the restrooms before we kick off the day's tours. I'll see you both in a bit," Lauren said right before leaving them alone.

Hunter, wearing tan Dockers and his Cahill-issue aqua polo shirt under a navy jacket studied her. "What happened?"

He smelled good. She hadn't forgotten, and neither had her heart apparently. Images flashed of times when she'd been close enough to feel the scruff of his whiskers on her own face, whisper a secret in his ear, hear him do the same in hers. Her breath caught with the stab of an ache she hadn't felt in years.

Hunter stepped closer, bringing his sandalwood aroma with him. "What is it?" Concern crowded around his gray eyes.

Snap out of it, Mikaela. She shook her head and stepped back. "I have good news. That . . . student came through. We're on for the summer."

His eyebrows rose. He'd placed his hands on his waist, elbows fanned when she'd stepped back. Now his jaw slacked as if he couldn't believe her. "Really?" His eyes went tender, shiny.

Why—

"This means," she went on when he stayed silent, "I can make the payment to your mom today. And all is well. What a turnaround, right?" *Thank You, God.* Maybe He condoned her work, even though she hadn't chosen missions. Funny that she'd never questioned that so much as during the last day.

Hunter rubbed his scruffy chin, and she watched him, mesmerized. Thing was, he didn't usually go all quiet unless he was deep in thought. Something else was happening here.

Curiosity ate her up, and though she shouldn't push him, she had to know. "What is it?"

"I can't believe... I mean I wondered..." His Adam's apple worked up and down, and this time she waited him out. Finally, he drew a long breath. "This means, you're staying."

She nodded. This once, she wouldn't quantify her time here, wouldn't remind him she'd be leaving in a few short weeks. She'd simply rest in this moment.

His scruffy face shifted into a tender smile. "I'm glad."

"Me too." And for the first time, she was.

She could stay.

Hunter let that thought settle deep into the sediment of his gut. She'd gone off to get her students, but he'd found a sunny spot on the top deck of the *Millennium* and grabbed the railing. Head tipped toward the warm sun, he closed his eyes. A sharp breeze made him glad for his jacket. Mornings would soon warm here, but the breeze off the water could demand a windbreaker. Let the crew carry on preparations inside. He needed a sec. *"The student came through."* He'd almost lost it.

That meant... Wow. That meant God came through on His token.

"What if this is the part where He turns it all around?"

Not only was Miki back, but somehow—miraculously?—she'd be here all summer. Last night, all seemed hopeless. This morning? Hope.

Did that mean all was fixed between Hunter and God? No. What if all this was only a coincidence?

Another breeze washed over his face.

I miss you.

Hunter gulped, searched the harbor. God's voice? Admitting how much Hunter missed Him meant letting down his guards and diving headfirst into the well of pain and questions from the last year—agony he'd rather avoid.

God and he would have to pick this up later. For now, he had a summer of romancing Mikaela ahead of him. He yanked out his phone, sent her a text: SO, ABOUT THOSE MEETINGS.

CHAPTER FIFTEEN

Miki hovered around the new guy so much, Hunter would be surprised if he didn't change his mind. Get off the island as soon as possible. She'd quickly introduced Hunter to him as the students arrived earlier. Now, she stuck by his side, or kept him next to hers. And whenever Hunter passed, she'd conveniently lean toward the new kid—Carter Pierce? Pierce Carter? Two last names in a row. Hunter better pick one—he'd go with the guy's last name. She'd lean toward *Carter* and carry on a long monologue, shuffling papers on the notebook he carried. Yeah, every detail seemed super important.

Could he help a small grin when he thought about what Dr. Wren had told him? *Help her see there's more to life.* Hidden in her agenda were the words *She's lonely. Do something.* Hunter remembered his teenage impression of Amelia when she would visit his father. She was much less formal then—more personable. He'd wondered why she always visited alone, staying in a local B&B for a few days during the summer. But never a husband or even a boyfriend. And always a little bit frail. Was her loneliness the reason she pushed for Miki to find more in life?

Did Miki think she was fooling him? He knew her too well. As much as she'd changed, and she had—she'd found strength and determination and courage to chase her dreams and make them happen—she was still the same at heart. And she couldn't hide that from him.

He'd help her see he was still the same too. Granny seemed to think he wasn't a threat to her. Sometimes he felt up to this challenge from his dad. Sometimes . . . He only hoped he wouldn't break her heart this time.

He stood in the wheelhouse, eyes trained on the seascape as their tour got underway, taking in the blues of both sky and sea. Other boats dotted the harbor, including other touring vessels. For years, the touring businesses had all coexisted, all based out of Friday Harbor. There'd been enough tourism for all of them. The key was a good reputation.

As much as he'd rather avoid it, there was a topic he needed to bring up with Miki, and eventually Granny.

Dan's boss, Hank, had called early that morning. He'd asked to borrow Cahill's larger pleasure boat, but Hunter needed the Cahill vessel with the students this week. The other possibility was using Ben Calvin's. Hunter hadn't discussed that vessel with Granny Belle Calvin or Miki for about . . . fifteen years. Did Granny still have her late husband's boat?

Footsteps thumped behind him, and he turned for a quick glance. Carter and Miki approached up the stairs. He squinted forward again at the view. She'd brought her buffer. They moved into his vision on the right. He tucked away his grin.

"Captain, I wondered if you might have any tasks that Pierce can help with on the daily tours?" She was still trying to find a spot for the new guy.

"What are your strengths?" Hunter glanced in his direction. He stood there in skin-tight jeans and a form-fitting button-up shirt and scarf as if he were a feminine hybrid, but he carried himself as masculine.

"I like computers, programming, graphics, web design, HTML language." He shrugged. "Stuff like that."

So, what was he doing on board this ship and not in some computer gig somewhere?

"Not a huge use for that up here." He pulled them around the western tip of Brown Island, heard Jace give the naturalist's spiel below.

Miki shot Hunter a look. *Help me.*

How could he ignore that? But perhaps he could split this little twosome up, remove Miki's buffer. "I'll give it some thought. Listen, could you excuse the professor and me for a moment?"

"Sure." Carter spun toward the stairs.

"Please send Sam Kerry up," Hunter called after him. His first mate could take over the wheel for a few minutes.

"Okay." Carter thudded down as if he'd been waiting for permission to escape.

Miki started to follow him, but Hunter hooked her with his gaze. "Can I have a minute?" He kept his hands at the wheel and returned his attention forward. "There's something I need to ask you." He flashed to that conversation all those years ago, on the Clark's beach, his heart diving into the deep water. Did she ever think of that day too? Of his question that sunny afternoon?

"I got your text. If this is about Amelia's required meetings, it can wait." She tried to brush past him.

"Miki, please."

She froze, and then came back into view, a question on her face. And for once, no comment.

Ahem. Sam's throat clearing—Hunter knew that sound. "Right behind you, Cap'n."

Hunter relinquished the wheel. "If you wouldn't mind, Sam."

"You got it."

Seth, the nerdy student who sometimes haunted the bridge, joined Sam. Good. The kid had an eagle eye for spotting wildlife. Hunter gave him a nod of welcome, and Seth grinned back.

"Oh, and when are you going to bring Cheyenne in again?" Hunter said to Sam.

His first mate's sun-wrinkled face creased. "She had a great time that morning."

"Tell her she's welcome anytime." Hunter had always loved kids. Maybe one day he'd have his own running around. Miki and he had talked about that years ago. Maybe having three or four when they married. That dream died when she left. Now, though . . . Did Miki still want to be a mom? What would life look like one year from now? Two years? *Getting ahead of yourself, Cahill.*

"Will do, Cap'n."

Hunter faced Miki and nodded toward the door leading to the *Millennium's* somewhat private upper deck. "Professor, a word?"

She gave Sam a small smile and then preceded Hunter outside.

No passengers allowed here. So, if they kept their voices low, they could chat without being overheard. Plus, the engine and wind noises blocked a lot of sound. Because of the wind, most passengers were indoors down below until the whales appeared as they maneuvered out to prime orca pod locales. Out of habit, and okay maybe nerves, he scanned the waters. Given the day's intel, it shouldn't be too long now before whale activity.

At the railing of this private spot, she faced him. "Listen, I know Dr. Wren said we need to meet"—she crossed her arms over her chest, guards goin' up—"but we see each other all day every day— except Mondays. I'm sure we can cover what we need to in a brief recap before or after the tours. Don't you think?" Her body language told him she attempted to hide her nerves. Why was she so afraid to be alone with him? She hadn't seemed afraid the other night.

All day every day. Was that so awful?

Wait. That look—all walled off and squinting at him. She didn't trust him. Why? Hmm. A mystery he'd have to solve. Until she let down her guard, they wouldn't get anywhere.

"Did I do something to . . ." God forbid. "Hurt you?"

"Ha," she scoffed.

Ohh-kay . . .

"But you didn't want to talk about it, remember? The first day?"

Oh yeah. The past. So somehow, though *she'd* left him, she blamed him? Great.

Noises came from down below. Passengers were getting restless, willing to tolerate the wind of their fast travel out to Haro Strait. Better speed this convo up.

He stepped closer, though her barbs dared him. He gestured to the air. "Windy." *Just hear me out.* "I'm sorry I hurt you." Oh, was he. "And I promise we'll talk about that, air it all out."

She pressed her lips together. *Yeah, sure.*

"We will. But right now, I need to talk something else over with you." Emotions barreled in on every side. Her grandfather. Her interpretation of what had happened that summer. His fault.

Like it or not, they were going there.

"I need to ask you about something, and I'm afraid you may like this less than the thought of those meetings." They'd never talked about everything that happened that day with her granddad.

What? Was God—or someone—determined to make them dig up all the buried, sandy shrapnel of their past? Make them face all the questions and pain? Deal with it finally?

The wind blew her hair around, and she grabbed a handful and started braiding it. His breath hitched. The reminders. Did she have flashbacks too? He dipped his head to regain eye contact. But she peered away. Hiding.

He shrugged out of his zippered windbreaker and didn't wait for permission before wrapping it around her sweater-covered shoulders. Then drew in a deep breath. Now or never. "It's about the *Isabelle*."

Her gaze finally darted up. She took a break from her braiding and slipped her arms into his jacket. "Granddad's boat?" Her pretty brow crinkled. "Why bring that up?" Her fingers went back to twining her hair.

Should he just pitch his question or soften the impact?

She tossed her new braid behind her, but the wind still targeted blonde wisps and splayed them around her face. He wanted to brush them back, touch her skin. She gathered his jacket close around her neck.

"Remember Hank, Dan's boss?" She nodded. "He needs a larger vessel for this season. I can lend him ours, but only if I can then borrow someone else's." He'd considered suggesting Hank talk to Granny, but in her shoes, he'd rather a close family friend use the boat, *if* Granny still owned it and *if* she were willing to lend it out. So, he'd loan Hank the Cahill craft and borrow hers, provided things worked out. "Does Granny still have it? And what do you think she'd say if I asked her to borrow it?" Hands in his pockets, he hunched his shoulders against the chill, loving how she looked tucked into his oversized windbreaker.

Miki stepped to the rail. Was she scanning for marine life? Or was she trying to avoid this conversation?

He approached the rail beside her, gripping the metal bar with his left hand. "Forget it." *We'll find another way. Maybe Dan's parents' boat.* Except that they used their family boat every weekend, which would be the peak time for private charter demand. And theirs wasn't as luxurious. Not for the first time,

Hunter wished for a business partner who could run charters anytime, even overnighters, without the restrictions of Cahill's currently scheduled afternoon tours.

She pivoted then and he could see her face, wearing all kinds of misery. She needed a hug. If only he could oblige.

He reached for her shoulder. "I'm sorry I brought it up."

She gave him a glance before facing the bay again. "It's silly." Her voice came out scratchy, and she swiped a finger under her eye. "I mean it's been so long now. I thought I was . . . past it."

Tell me about it. He thought he was too. Ever since Hank had asked, Hunter had been reliving his own failures that day. "We'll find another way."

She eyed him, and as if finding strength somewhere, she straightened her spine. "Honestly, I don't know if Granny still has it. We haven't talked about it in over a decade. I haven't even seen it since that summer."

Neither had he.

This was another reason they could use regular meetings. Add their unfinished business to the itinerary. "So, about getting together tonight . . ." he tried.

The hint of a grin, one raised blonde eyebrow, the slightest nod. Isabelle's house was neutral. "You going to be at Granny's later?"

"Yes, for dinner. Maybe hang out afterward. Why, you looking for a meal invite?" Her grin was back. A pressure lifted from his shoulders.

"Actually, that sounds good . . ." He smiled at her. "Nah, I was hoping to fix the dock for her."

"Yeah, the property could use a bit of attention these days."

Neither of them mentioned Granddad. Didn't need to.

"Think she'd mind?"

"Nope." She hugged herself, and he wished again that he could. "If you drop by, you could mention the boat to her. See what she says."

"Right. I might do that." That settled things for now. His turn to scan the bay. Sure enough, dorsals. He stepped toward the window and tapped the hard plastic. When Seth glanced back, Hunter gestured toward the pod of Dall's porpoise. Sam was already nodding and easing up so the vessel slowed. They'd give their customers something to see today. Downstairs, Jace announced the sighting—the speakers mounted outdoors blaring his words.

Miki snatched her phone from her small backpack and tapped photos, snapping shot after shot. He'd almost forgotten how often she used to seize opportunities to get pictures. But the marine life show didn't interest him half as much as her excitement. He still couldn't believe she was here, with him. Close enough to touch, close enough her scent wafted toward him with the salty breeze.

She stepped right up next to him, bumping his arm with hers. Out of the corner of his eye, he caught his own reflection next to hers in the front-facing camera on her phone. Orcas breached in the background. "Selfie!" she squealed.

He gulped with the sensation of being so close to her, then breathed deeply of the vanilla aroma of her hair. He'd missed that. The phone's camera clicked, and he realized he'd been smelling her hair. *Oops.*

Dope. "Let's try that again," he said, smiling into the screen. He leaned down closer to her face. Real close and she didn't seem to mind. Selfies got them near each other, but he wanted her trust, her heart again.

Could he risk giving her his?

Another click.

His private seconds with Miki seemed over as people scrambled for the decks, shrieking directly below them. This part of their tours always concerned him. What if someone went overboard? The staff was watching closely, and every child under the age of twelve wore a life jacket as a general practice. Still, he worried for people's safety. That and Cahill didn't need any bad press right now.

"I'll see you at Granny's tonight. But about tomorrow night—how about my place, six? I'll feed you," he coaxed. He'd put off the meetings an extra day to give the skittish professor a chance to feel safe around him once again.

She raised one eyebrow and gave him *the look* as if to say, *Yeah, I saw what you did there.*

Please?

She offered a slight nod, humphed, and darted inside.

"It's a date," he murmured before following her and catching his breath.

CHAPTER SIXTEEN

Mikaela carried the steaming platter of corn on the cob over to the table while Granny poured iced tea. The aroma of grilling burgers filled the kitchen. Sunlight slanted in the windows from the western side of the house, visible in streaming yellow rays from where she stood.

"Is the captain free tonight?" Granny Belle asked, the sparkle in her eye not quite hidden from Mikaela.

The captain. That phrase shouldn't get to her. All those years ago she'd known he'd be captain one day. Now he carried himself with authority and strength. With enough confidence to disarm her. But Hunter was . . . Off. Limits. For his own sake. "He mentioned coming by tonight. I'm not sure when."

"Well, I made extra—you know, for boarders or him."

"Right, Granny." As if she were fooling anybody.

"How are things going with the new student? He's not giving you trouble, is he?"

"Why?" What had Granny seen when he was here?

"He struck me as . . . as if he's not exactly trustworthy." Granny shook her head. "Probably shouldn't say that. I don't know him."

"Well, he's still new. I've got all summer to try to bring out his strengths."

Granny set the plate of oatmeal chocolate chip cookies on the bar for later. Hunter's favorite.

Mikaela busied herself with place settings. "Have you had a chance to spend time with Lauren lately?"

"No, and I was hoping she could come to dinner tonight, but like last time I invited her, she said she's busy. I worry she may be isolating herself. She's sort of pulled back since Reid's passing. Maybe I'll try to connect for lunch on a Monday when she's off for the afternoon."

They took their seats at the table. "I can't imagine losing a husband," Mikaela said. "Did you feel like hiding when Granddad died?" Would Granny mind her bringing up Ben?

"Some days." Granny's blue eyes went wistful. "But you were all still here that summer. What kind of hostess would I have been to go hide in my room?"

Mikaela pressed a hand over her grandmother's. "I was so young then. Didn't really know what to do. I hope we weren't in your way." She wouldn't bring up the actual trip. Never had and didn't want to tonight.

"No, quite the opposite. Your mom told me about all the extra chores you and Hunter did that summer. I'd ask who did the dishes or who weeded the garden or mowed the lawn. Always you or Hunter, she'd say." Granny squeezed her hand this time. "That meant more than you knew."

They did all those extra chores because they felt responsible. Or at least, Mikaela did. Still did. "I'm sorry he died so young." She gulped. She'd never said those words aloud.

Granny's eyes misted, but she didn't turn away. "Me too."

The burgers didn't seem appetizing now. That day, Granny had stayed here at the house, but Hunter had gone with Mikaela, Granddad, and Reid. If anyone knew what she'd done—or failed to do—Hunter did. The shame of her mistakes could engulf her if she let it.

She'd submerged those thoughts all these years, buried the pain. Now hurt pushed toward daylight. She needed to distract herself. The whole time she layered tomato and lettuce onto her blurring hamburger bun she could feel Granny's eyes on her.

"You know, I never talked about that day with you." Granny's voice was soothing, and Mikaela took courage. "I'm sorry you had to witness it."

She lifted her gaze to Granny's. "I'm sorry it happened." Even though she was now thirty, this conversation took her back fifteen years, complete with a trembling jaw.

"Well, I don't know why it did, but I trust God had a plan. He's been a strong Husband for me since." The lines around Granny's eyes crinkled. "The best."

The front screen door rattled with someone's knock. All the boarders knew they could come right in. So, who . . .?

"Hello?" Hunter's voice came through the screen. "Granny Belle?"

A sense of déjà vu swept into the room. Mikaela used her napkin to swipe under her eyes, while she loosed a long exhale. Granny squeezed her free hand and gave her a look meant to buoy her.

"Dinner's on, Hunt. C'mon in," Granny said as she stood.

Mikaela sniffed. Having Hunter here at this moment, with the past strewn all over the table, might fully undo her. She rose to fetch the pitcher of iced tea, one hand on her clenched stomach muscles. He would probably bring up the *Isabelle*.

Lord, give me courage.

Fifteen Years Ago

"So, there's someone down in Seattle, then?" Hunter paced to the end of the dock and turned.

"No. It's not like that." She crossed her arms over her chest, Walls going up.

He scuffed closer. "You can't see me as anything other than a brother?"

She pressed her lips together, then drew a deep breath. "No, not that."

Good. Hope.

He softened his stance, focused on making his expression kinder. "So, what is it? I'm not good enough?" The question burned.

"That's not fair. You know that's not how I think."

"Well, your parents are really well-off. We're merely touring business owners."

She shook her head. "I don't care. I love what your family does. And you know my family doesn't judge anyone."

Longing covered him, and he reached for her arm. "Can't you tell there's something different this year?"

"Yeah, you're acting weird." She jumped down from the dock onto the sandy waterfront of her grandparents' beach. "C'mon, let's collect sea glass."

Okay, he'd humor her.

Head down, she combed the beach, every now and then bending to pick up opaque scoured glass pieces. A tiny crab darted near Hunter's feet. The creature seemed desperate to find cover and return to familiar safety. Yeah, Hunter could relate.

Was that why Miki was avoiding him? Safety?

She carried over a rainbow of shells and glass. "Can you hold these? I want to find more."

He opened a palm to her. As their skin touched, electricity shot up his arm. He sought her eyes. *Can you feel that?*

But she was already shifting away, leaving her treasures with him.

He stepped into her path. "What are you afraid of?"

"Tripping on these rocks, Hunt. Move."

He stood his ground. "Mik. Talk to me."

She spun and went the other direction.

There was one way he could think of to prove things had changed between them this summer. But she'd have to stand still for him to test his theory.

They said girls matured faster, so why was he standing here holding shells and sea glass while she scoured the beach for more like a hyper child?

At the family bonfire later that night, he brought her a hotdog and settled next to her on the end of a log.

"Thanks, Hunt. I've been thinking about what you said."

Gulp. She had? "And . . .?"

The others in the circle seemed caught up in conversations. So, he kept his voice low. "Want to walk?"

She finished her dog and then stood to brush her shorts clean. "Sure."

This beach provided the privacy of a place to stroll and not be overheard. Both their families stayed back at the fire.

Several paces down the shore she took his hand, and he checked his startled reaction. This was new. He might never let go.

"I'm glad we're friends," she said.

He caressed her skin with his thumb. Mm-hmm. Friends.

Moonlight reflected on the still bay, full and bright, creating a trail of white light moving toward them on the surface. Water lapped the sandy rocks as they picked their way along. Yeah, a great backdrop for this conversation. Hopefully, he wouldn't say something stupid.

"Me too."

"And I never want to lose that."

"Me neither." His ribs felt tight. Everything was on the line.

She stopped, faced him. Moonlight glinted off her hair, her eyes. "But I'd hate myself if we missed out on something *just* because I was afraid."

He reached for her other hand. Now he held both. "You're not alone, Mik."

"I know."

"I'm taking the risk with you." Would that give her courage?

Her shoulders rose and fell with her breathing.

"But how do we know if it's going to work?" Like him, she wanted assurance. He had none.

"We don't . . ."

"You're willing to take that risk?"

"For you? For us? Yeah. Yes, I am." He'd never been more convinced of anything. Even before she'd arrived this summer, he knew he felt something more toward her. Something bigger than both of them.

She shook her head, drew away.

He clenched his fists at his sides, wanting more than anything to reach for her. "The only thing I can give you is a promise."

She turned back toward him, went still and met his eyes.

"I will never break your heart." He reached for her hand. *Please. Trust me.*

She stepped closer, taking his hand. His heart skipped a beat.

"I'm scared," she said.

"Me too. But what's bigger than that is how I feel about you, Miki."

The ghost of a grin toyed with her mouth. "Yeah, and how's that?"

"I'm guessing it's the same way you feel about me."

"Well, you already know I love you."

He choked. "You do?"

She elbowed his gut, catching him off guard. "Of course. We've been best friends for years!"

He tugged her arm so that she bumped into him. "You . . ."

Her impish smile lit a fire deep inside him.

He wrapped both arms behind her, and she didn't resist. "Say it again?" He swallowed, watching her mouth.

"No, you say it."

"What? Are you still unsure how you feel about me, Miki? Because I can prove to you how you feel."

She scoffed. "Oh, you can?"

"Yup, in thirty seconds or less."

"Yeah, right."

He reached toward her face, his thumb grazing her chin. She gulped this time, suddenly sober. "So, I want to kiss you." His breath caught on the words. "But it's your call." This would prove his point. Convince her she felt the same way. Step onto a boat together that would never dock again.

She swallowed. "My call?"

"Mm-hmm." He searched her eyes. "So . . ."

"So, Hunt, how'd the tour go today?" Granny brought his attention back to the table, and he shook off the memories.

His temperature had risen with the flashback, and he moved to open the slider. "Do you mind, Granny?"

"Of course not."

Miki stood at the table, placing a glass of iced tea at his spot. He watched her settle, glad she didn't bolt this time. But her eyes were wet. Did that mean she'd already brought up the boat?

He relished the breeze pushing in as he yanked back the glass door, leaving the screen in place. "The tour was good. Had some Dall's and transient orcas."

"Great." She dished a burger and bun onto his plate.

"Thanks for having me." Often the house was crawling with students. "Where is everybody?"

"All out, busy. I don't see much of my boarders during the summer. They're usually either working, studying, or partying—none of that ruckus here."

Hunter glanced around after smearing mayo on the toasted hamburger bun. No sign of Carter. "What about the new guy?" he kept his voice low.

"Haven't seen him since today's sail. He's got other accommodations."

Sure he did. The urbanite would never lower himself to live here.

Miki seemed to come to life. She crunched into a pickle spear. "Did he look a little green to you out on the water?"

"I thought I noticed something. Have him bring motion sickness meds next tour. The vessel's large enough, most folks don't have a problem." They might need to keep anti-emetics on hand for him. The slice of beefsteak tomato landed with a satisfying slap, and Hunter layered on a leaf of lettuce. "So, Granny, would you mind if I worked on your dock?" He met her blue eyes.

She smiled at him. "That would be great, Hunt. I've been meaning to hire someone—you know a teenager or somebody. But I'd appreciate knowing you fixed it." Her voice cracked.

Miki reached for her hand. "Granny?"

Hunter grimaced. What had he said? "I'm sorry. Did I upset you?"

"No, no." She turned watery eyes on each of them. "I'm fine. The reminder hurts, you know . . .? My Ben always took care of those things."

Hunter's throat burned now. If he hadn't failed all those years ago . . . But this wasn't the time to discuss that, or even think about it. He'd never talked that over with anyone. Not his dad. Not Miki. And definitely not Granny, which might make his request—when he finally had the courage to spill it—all the harder to bring up. Unless she didn't see Ben's death like he did.

Isabelle straightened. "Yes, and please help yourself to any of the tools in the garage." She turned to Miki. "You could help him, dear. You were always good with your hands and woodworking."

True. Miki had often joined in, building plenty of docks and decks throughout their childhood summers together. "What do you say?" he asked her.

"Sure." She looked over at him, mischief in her half-grin. "Maybe we could have our 'meeting' while we're at it." Was that playfulness? Delicious. His gaze locked on her.

"What meeting?" Granny asked, snagging a handful of baby carrots before passing the bowl.

"Chairperson Wren feels it would benefit the program if we were to meet regularly"—Miki's smooth voice was full of sarcasm as she imitated a radio personality—"outside of the tours." The exaggerated irritation in her voice made him chuckle.

Isabelle looked between them. "Why?"

Hunter's appetite had returned, and he took a big bite of his burger—the grilled meat firing his taste buds. Let Miki handle it. He withheld a grin while she spooned veggie dip onto her plate, taking her time to answer.

Finally she shrugged. "Ask Hunter."

Well. He couldn't very well spill the chairwoman's reasoning—that Miki needed to relax more. He wasn't tasked to bring more work, but to create relaxing moments—Amelia had clarified in a later e-mail. *We both care for her, want her happiness and ultimate joy. So, how do you feel about showing her there's more to life than work? Are you game?*

Oh, yes. He was.

But the guise for these meetings was program check-in.

Think fast.

"Dr. Wren's looking for several voices on this project. I'm one of them." He pinched three ruffled chips and shoved them into his mouth. There. Honest, though not necessarily the whole truth. He had to keep his grin under water.

"Sounds fair." Granny sipped her iced tea, as if she weren't smiling behind her cup but Hunter saw it anyway. "So, what are you both doing for the Fourth?" She turned toward him. "I wondered if you and your mom would like to come over after the parade."

"I'll ask her. We have that private charter with Jenna-Shea and her family in the afternoon. No tours, since it's Monday." He studied Miki. "Excited to see Shea?"

"Yes. Can't wait." She paused for a moment. "How is your mom?" Her brow wrinkled, and he read compassion there. She nibbled on an apple slice.

Hunter swallowed his bite. "Things have been hard for her lately." How much to share? Except these two already knew some of the financial stuff, and they knew about Dad, of course. "The bills are piling up."

"The tuition should help, right, Hunt?" Granny Belle sounded hopeful, which only showed she hadn't faced the financial demons he and Mom had recently. Getting slammed, again and again, right when you started to reach the surface, only made you feel like you really might drown this time. And one breakthrough didn't solve everything, usually. What Cahill needed was a sudden reversal— not just a full stop—but a change in direction from financial ruin to stability. He didn't need riches, never had. Only security for himself and his mom and the future.

But he didn't want to dump all that on these two women.

"Yes, it helps." He made eye contact with Miki. "Thanks to you."

She met his eyes, but something about her squint told him she knew more than he'd told her. Had his mother divulged details?

She raised an eyebrow. *Do you need more help?*

Eat your burger.

She smirked at him but dropped the silent topic. The zing of intimacy that allowed them to read each other's thoughts raced around in his chest.

"See there?" Granny eyed each of them. "Hope. God is the God of hope. He'll show us."

Hope. For his family's finances, his relationship with Miki. He really didn't have a choice about cooperating with it. Did he? He worked long hours and never saw the rewards. But he couldn't give up, not with Mom depending on him. Like a prisoner of hope, he moved forward, fearing hope. Avoiding it. Expectation led to disappointment. So, why bother?

His promise to Dad meant he *had* to hope. Darn it. Hope that Miki would come around. Hope that she'd somehow be able to stay. For good.

Unless the business failed. He cringed, but kept his face pointed down at his plate where his pile of chips had vanished. If his business did fail—and he failed Dad—he still wouldn't be free. He'd also promised to take care of Mom. Maybe Hank would take him on. Or he could go work at the Port of Seattle—send checks home to the island. But none of that would bring him closer to Miki since she'd be in Hawaii.

If he failed, he'd have nothing to offer her.

He couldn't blow this.

Somehow sitting here made all his angst churn, and he needed out. "Thanks for dinner. I'm gonna get to work on the dock." He excused himself and escaped the kitchen.

CHAPTER SEVENTEEN

What wasn't he telling her? Not that she was entitled to an explanation, of course. Not after all these years. But as a fellow colleague, she cared.

Fellow colleague. Sure.

When Hunter had arrived tonight, Mikaela assumed he still wanted to bring up Granddad's boat. But he hadn't. What happened to that? Although, honestly, Mikaela was a bit relieved. Granny seemed especially emotional tonight.

"Go after him." Granny nodded toward the slider. Mikaela was already standing from the table.

She found him at Granny's dock minutes later. He'd set up sawhorses and fresh planks of wood on the grassy lawn. Apparently Granddad had kept a few treated boards on hand for repairs to the dock. From her guess, they'd need about three fresh planks. But she hadn't peeked underneath to see if repairs were needed there too.

The way Hunter slammed the wood onto the sawhorse showed his irritation. If he didn't respond well to her appearance, she'd give him space.

"Hunter, what's up?"

He wore a tool belt she hadn't seen in years, slung low on his hips over his jeans, his black tee covering his long torso. As out of line as Destinee had been, she'd been right about Hunter being hot. Mikaela's skin flamed thinking about how he'd teased her, wanting to hear her repeat it. Her gaze shifted up. Right now, Hunter's expression held no playfulness as he focused on his work. She needed to focus too.

He repositioned the hammer and shot her a glance. "We're going to need the power saw." He spun toward the garage, but stopped as if second-guessing. "Wanna help?" he said over his shoulder, his bark a little gentler.

"Yup."

He headed for the garage, and she slowly moved in his direction, determined not to scurry after him as if he intimidated her and she must hurry to appease him. Jumping at his bark would only reinforce it. "I'll carry the extension cord."

They hiked over the lawn, back toward the garage. "Let's find a claw hammer too. You can remove the old boards while I cut the new ones, unless you want to do the sawing."

"Not this time." They entered the garage where he'd left the door up. This two-stall building was attached to a large RV space, with a wall between. When they'd been kids, the boat was stored in the RV stall. Her grandparents had always kept the whole place clean. Now, it housed Granny's Camry on one side, leaving the second stall open on this side. Organized shelves lined the walls. Hunter found the power saw on the tool bench, and she located the orange extension cord on a hook.

Back at the beach, she attacked the old boards. No use trying to get Hunter to talk now. She searched her memory of their dinner conversation. What had triggered the flip of his broody switch? Talk of their finances? It wasn't his fault gas prices had almost driven them out of business a few short years ago, or that they hadn't recovered.

Did he blame himself?

If she guessed correctly, Hunter still planned to approach her grandmother about the boat soon. Was he worried about that conversation?

He skulked toward the end of the dock, far from where she worked, then crouched, and measured one of the sturdy planks near the lawn.

"You going to brood all night?" She hadn't missed his crabbiness.

He ground his jaw, scribbled a number on the board with a wide carpenter pencil from the belt.

She watched a war behind his expression, which made her think he didn't like this dark and cranky side of himself any more than she did. So, why not stop? Why alienate her and maybe even

Granny?

"You want to be alone?"

He stood and tipped back his head, sighing, hands on his hips. His Adam's apple rose and fell a few times. Her guess? He was fighting some serious emotion. Why, though?

Oh.

What if he *did* blame himself? What he needed was a friend—someone who knew him, who could reassure him, help lift the weight off his shoulders. "You know it's not your fault, right?" She used a gentle voice, as if she were trying to encourage a student. "If the business closes? You've done everything you could. Your mom knows that. I know that. No one in this community could fault you." Hopefully God had something else lined up if that were to happen. *You do, right, God?*

Another hard swallow as she edged closer.

"Hunter?"

He pivoted toward the sawhorses, and she sincerely hoped he wouldn't turn on that power tool yet. For safety's sake, she slipped past him and unplugged the extension cord where it met the saw's power supply.

"Talk to me."

An anguished glance from him—that wrinkled brow, those wet eyes—and a shallow couple of breaths before he swiveled toward the garage again, his long-legged strides carrying him away from her. Yeah, a man at war inside.

She didn't follow this time. Would he come back? Wait until she'd given up and finish after dark? Should she finish alone?

She returned to the end of the dock and worked at loosening a nail that stuck up from an old board at an angle.

Back when Granddad died, Hunter had retreated into an emotional cave. She'd never understood why. He'd gone from trying to convince her to date him to almost acting . . . disqualified to date her. That night on the beach they'd almost kissed. Then, the accident, and suddenly they were tiptoeing around each other as if they couldn't even find friendship again.

His brooding lately reminded her of that. Was this how he

117

coped with his father's death? Poor guy. If they were at least friends again, she could wrap him up, maybe soothe his heart a little—even apologize for not being there for him that wintry day after his father died. Instead, she'd been in Hawaii, ironically.

She yanked another nail out of the rotting board. Back to Granddad. If Hunter did blame himself for Granddad's death, she needed to tell him it was *her* fault. Not his.

She'd pried one of the boards from the dock, standing in the ankle-deep water by the time he reappeared. At this rate of incoming tide, she may have to tread water to get the other two boards off if she didn't hurry. She'd work from the top, but someone—one of Granny's boarders, perhaps—had tried to repair these in a way you could only reach the final nails from the water. Maybe Hunter could use a couple of good whacks on this dock to help him purge the pain inside.

"Hunter? Wanna help with these last two boards? Tide's coming."

Without words, he tossed aside his tennies and socks, folded up his pant legs, and waded into the bay on the left side of the four-foot wide dock. She worked on the right side. Together they had the two boards off in a couple of minutes. While he cut the new planks, she strode indoors for towels. Granny had plated some of her oatmeal chocolate chip cookies and prepped a pitcher of lemonade, which she helped carry down to the dock.

"Great progress, you two." If Granny Belle sensed tension, she didn't mention it. "Keep up the good work." She waved, then trekked back toward the house, wrapping her long flowy sweater tight against her.

"Thanks," Hunter called, standing the second cut board against the end of the sawhorse and accepting a plastic tumbler of lemonade while seizing a thick cookie with his other hand. He faced the bay, seemed fascinated with the view.

Mm-hmm. He was avoiding eye contact with her. She knew him so well. And he knew it. "You can't hide all night."

He was silent for a long while. So long, she started looking around for things she could pack up. "You're right. I don't want to fail him." That intimate, quiet voice. So familiar. She welcomed it, and it drew her. Perhaps he didn't like staying in his dark cave alone.

She'd missed his confiding in her. Missed confiding in him. Though she planned to never share her biggest secret. One situation at a time. "Fail whom?"

"Dad." A long, breathless silence followed his words. "I've already failed Granny." His chin trembled, but he guzzled lemonade, and she gave him a moment before responding. What did he mean?

"You haven't failed your dad." He met her gaze, his face a mask of agony. After several seconds, she shifted on her feet. "And how have you failed Granny?" She gestured toward the disassembled dock. "You're helping her."

"Not tonight." His voice sounded broken as he squinted at the bay.

Oh. "You're talking about July Fourth when we were fifteen?" Gulp. That awful, awful day.

He finished a cookie and reached for the pitcher and another glassful of lemonade. Then he grabbed a second treat, keeping his hands and mouth busy.

Yeah. She'd guessed correctly. But hold up. "You can't blame yourself for Granddad." Could she say it? A fortifying breath and a splash of courage. "Not when I'm to blame." Her voice cracked.

His brow furrowed. "What?"

"If I'd known how to operate the radio, I could have called for help."

"The radio? I was in the water with him." Hunter shook his head. "I couldn't reach him. I blew it."

"You weren't the only one in the water." Oh, no. Why had she said that? "Not that I blame you *or* your dad," she added quickly after he flinched. "You guys did the best you could."

He finished his cookie, his right hand squeezing his lemonade glass. His left hand looked empty. Lonely. Almost sad, like the atmosphere. He tipped up his head, misery in his watery eyes, and grimaced. She caught a glimpse before he looked away.

The Hunter she knew received love best through touch. She cared for him, even now. Always had. Probably always would. Right now, she'd show him he wasn't alone. She reached for his free hand, and his head jerked up. But his fingers easily twined with hers, as if from memory. He held tight. His eyes crinkled, and she read confusion in their softening.

"Friends hold hands, right?" she squeaked and then hummed a note as if trying to cover. *I care about you.*

You know I care about you too.

She let that message sink into her heart, hoping she'd read him correctly. His kindness touched her. They'd always be like family to each other.

He gave a nod. "Yes, they do," he finally said, trapping her gaze for a long moment. Such depths. Shared history. A *knowing* like Mikaela hadn't experienced since and probably never would again. More than knowing. Accepting. And more than a hint of longing. That unnerved her. But she wouldn't let go of his hand.

All these years, she'd had no idea they shared this scar. They'd finally brought it up. Maybe she wasn't completely to blame. But neither were Reid nor Hunter. The pain eased a bit with the pressure of Hunter's palm against hers. Did he feel the same comfort? She hoped so. Something to replace—even heal—all that agony.

Waves splashed louder in quick succession and drew their attention. Like the waves that claimed Granddad. No one expected Ben to fall into the water that day. And they certainly hadn't planned to return without him. Well, without him cracking jokes and planning their next boat trip, or demanding the teens hose down the vessel before calling it a night.

Her throat burned, and Hunter squeezed her hand, like he knew. But she couldn't look at him. This pain was why she hadn't wanted to bring this up, why they'd avoided the topic at work that day. But somehow she had to help him see that since that day when she couldn't help, she'd gone into protective mode for her parents, Granny Belle, him. And she'd protected them since, when she could.

Which was why she and Hunter could never be close again.

Only friends.

Friends who held hands.

While Miki watched the water, he watched her face. Such torment there. She truly did blame herself. When she squinted, he squeezed her hand.

Her hand, which *she'd* offered.

Their fingers fit together like they'd never been apart.

She wouldn't look at him now. But she didn't pull back, and he sure wouldn't.

Friends.

Right. Friends who knew each other well. Cared deeply. He brushed his thumb against her skin. She cared for others. She obviously cared for him. But something held her back. She hid behind this "friendship" banner. But who was she protecting? Herself? They hadn't discussed their relationships since their breakup. Had some doofus in Seattle broken her heart?

She glanced back at him then, pain in her eyes. She was serious about taking the blame for Ben's death. She not only didn't blame Hunter—which might mean she never had—but she blamed herself. The only reason he'd known how to operate the radio was because he'd learned very young. Back in their tween years, she'd been more of a tagalong on the boat trips with her granddad, his dad, and him. Of the four of them, Ben or Dad handled the controls. Hunter didn't even stand behind the wheel very often. And Miki hung out on the deck. She'd never had a reason to use the radio.

But even at fifteen he knew how to swim and how to help someone in trouble. The choppy waves shoved him back that day and kept him from reaching Ben. Kept his dad from reaching the older man too. And kept Hunter from peace all these years.

Whenever he and Dad talked about the tragedy afterward— never in front of Miki or Granny Belle—Dad assured Hunter it hadn't been his fault. Always, a haunting look passed over his eyes like a gray cloud in a blue sky, as if Dad blamed himself.

Ben would probably say none of them were at fault. It wasn't as if Ben wasn't a strong swimmer, but what if he'd had some type of episode that kept him from swimming after he fell in? Hunter had never considered that.

He shook his head, physically trying to dislodge the thoughts. That day had changed his life. Sounds like it had changed Miki's too, in ways she'd never explained.

"You can see that, right, Hunter?" She swung their hands between them, standing there on the lawn with him as a breeze picked up. He tugged her a little closer, not wanting her to get cold. "I watched from the boat. I saw you try so hard to help," she whispered. "You *and* Captain Reid."

See, this was why he shouldn't have brought up using Ben's boat, should've found another way. All that pain in Miki's eyes, in her voice. And Granny had put on a strong front with reminders of Ben at the table, but no question Hunter's request would hurt her. He'd have to rethink how to help Hank.

Miki didn't blame him. Too bad her perspective wasn't true.

"What you need," she said, as her mouth twitched from sadness to the slightest grin, "is a friend to set you straight." She nudged his arm, jostling him, knocking loose the memories and heaviness that hung over them.

She'd been so careful about keeping her distance lately. He'd missed her playful side. "I do, huh?" His voice came out strained.

"Yup."

A familiar start for the two of them. But a start. At this rate, he might just win back her trust.

"Plus, I like this Hunter better than Captain Crabby, any day." She smiled up at him, innocent and mischievous at once.

"'Captain Crabby?'" he scoffed, though inside he winced at the truth in her words. Somewhere tonight he'd lost his determination to woo in favor of brooding. Oh, the risks of opening up again. Dad knew that. Knew Hunter hadn't been quite the same since that fateful boat ride. Knew what it would mean to pursue Miki if she ever returned—the risk and pain and surrender. Three things he hadn't required of himself for over a decade.

Three things more difficult after Dad's . . . passing.

Oh, and hope. His mother still kept a typed Scripture from Zechariah about people being prisoners of hope on her fridge. He felt like that right now. Hope had become his warden.

CHAPTER EIGHTEEN

Fifteen Years Ago

Hunter arrived earlier than the rest of his family, knowing Miki and her family would be at the church early. Birds sang outdoors as if the community wasn't gathering for a funeral today. At this hour on a Saturday morning, the church was almost empty. Flowers waited in clusters, especially up by the altar where huge pictures of Ben graced the raised platform. Granny Belle was surrounded by her adult children—Miki's mom and uncles and all their spouses murmuring in low tones. No sign of Micah anywhere.

Where was Miki? He scanned the sanctuary and found her standing in the light of a stained-glass window where sunshine poured through, painting her in soft pastels. She gripped the sill and closed her eyes. No matter what she needed, he'd be that for her today. No ulterior motives. Only support. He'd hold her hand, if she let him. If she didn't mind being seen with him beside her the entire day, he'd stick close.

He owed her that.

He walked up beside her and whispered near her ear. "Hey, Mik. You okay?"

She startled and opened her teary eyes, but she didn't say anything. Didn't need to. Should he hug her? As a rule, they didn't hug much either. Especially since he'd announced he wanted more than friendship. He opened his arms. Maybe she'd come. She crossed her arms over her chest. Perhaps he should put her at ease. "As a friend?"

She walked into his hug, and he felt her tremble against him as if she barely held her emotions in check. He couldn't blame her. His heart burning, he stroked her hair and whispered that they'd get through this.

For some reason, maybe because the adults knew Hunter and

Miki had both witnessed Ben's death, Miki's family welcomed him on their pew for the funeral. And, wonder of wonders, Miki reached for his hand during the service. He gladly held it, caressing her skin, wishing he could take her pain.

He said as much later that night as things wound down at Granny's place. But she only said, "You helped more than you know, Hunt. Thank you for today."

Then she eyed him, studying him until he almost wanted to turn away. "What?"

"You said you wanted to be more than friends, but you acted like a true friend today."

She had no idea of his restraint.

He shrugged to cover his longing to wrap her up again.

She walked right up to his chest, startling him. He enclosed her. "Thank you." Her whisper warmed his neck. He closed his eyes, breathing her in. She pulled back an inch and kissed his face, robbing his breath, but he tried not to gasp aloud and scare her, though she'd surprised him.

She pulled back and met his eyes. He reached up and stroked the hair back from her eye. "Of course."

Their relationship had never been the same.

Someone had taken Hunter's parking spot. He stopped his truck behind the offending vehicle, tempted to honk until the culprit appeared from the neighboring businesses—except that'd tick off his neighbors. Maybe he should park directly behind it. Leave his truck there the rest of the day, through the dive and the tour. Block the idiot in. No local towing company would move Hunter's rig. They knew the routine.

Hunter had posted warnings and *Reserved* signs so he'd always have a stall. He picked up his phone and pressed the listing for Bruce. Tightness burned in his stomach.

"Hey, Hunt."

"Got another one. Any chance you're free?" He fisted his left hand.

"You betcha. Make and model?"

He described the convertible, and they hung up.

Already running late, he didn't have time for this today. They'd head out on their dive in a few, and he needed to prep his dad's smaller boat, *Cahill's Prize*. He tapped his hands on the steering wheel, debated honking again. He still thought of it as Dad's. It'd take time. That's what everyone said. *Give yourself time. Let yourself grieve.*

Yeah, or keep trying to hold it together.

Crowds mobbed Front Street. If they'd had room, Dad would have designated a fourth parking stall for Cahill Touring. Hunter could block the dumpsters—not a good idea with the garbage trucks due this afternoon.

He could almost feel steam rising from his ears. *Focus on something else.*

Miki. He hadn't slept thinking about her and all the recently resurrected memories. The first time their relationship shifted from friendship to romance. The memorial service and the first time she'd kissed his face.

Holding her hand at Granny's beach last night.

She'd loosened up a bit since returning to the island, reminding him of her youth.

He jolted as the tow truck rumbled into the small parking lot. He swung his truck to the right to give the driver room.

His heart thumped thinking of Miki. He'd looked forward to coming to work today, knowing she'd be here and they'd take her crew out for a dive. Maybe get a moment alone together. Start with friendship and build from there, like all those years ago.

Bruce jumped down from the tow truck, clipboard in his hands. He reminded Hunter of an aging football player—tough, tall, wide, several years older than Hunter, and balding.

Hunter climbed out of his own rig and pointed to the tiny convertible. "This one, Bruce. Thanks."

He shook his head, scribbling information on the top sheet of paper on that clipboard. "They never learn."

"Right?"

Pigeons pecked at something on the dock. Hunter looked up. Miki and the new guy rushed from the office, and *Professor Rhoades* directed her student toward him, like a teacher pointing out the principal. Carter looked . . . over-dressed. He wore skinny jeans and some sort of short boots. Another scarf around his neck. Ridiculous hat. And those glasses—they probably weren't even prescription. Kristopher had called him a metrosexual. More urban than island. Couldn't argue with that.

"Wait!" The new guy pranced over. "That's my car. I'll move it."

Hunter scowled at him. "There are three signs."

"Yup. Got it." He dove into the driver's seat and backed out, waving a peace sign with two fingers to both Bruce and Hunter as he squeezed between their trucks.

Entitled city dweller. Hunter clenched a fist, but then turned to Bruce who was already voiding that top sheet. "What do we owe you for coming down?" Hunter would exact the payment from Carter himself and not necessarily in monetary form.

Cool it, Captain.

"Aw, nothin', Hunt." Bruce waved him off. "Don't worry about it."

"You made the trek." And Hunter wanted Carter to pay.

"Makes ya feel better, send him over to our offices. Might have some shrubs that need trimmin' out front." Bruce laughed and climbed up into his truck. "See ya next time."

Miki stood off to the side, probably knowing Hunter needed to pull his vehicle in. When the tow truck was clear of the tight lot, Hunter backed into his stall and cut the engine. Great start to Carter's time at Cahill. Of all the selfish, self-absorbed—

"Hey, Hunter." Miki moved closer. "Sorry about that. I don't think he'll do it again."

He rolled up his window and climbed from his truck for the second time that morning. Miki didn't deserve his irritation. Remembering that should bring his temperature down. "You don't have to apologize for him." He hooked a thumb over his shoulder, toward the hill. Carter might be gone a while trying to find a spot up there. Tourists filled the parking stalls after every ferry load of trucks, cars, and people arrived.

They marched to the office, and Hunter tried to shake off his mood. Why did Miki have to keep seeing him at his most annoyed? Why all the reasons to lose his cool the past few days?

And Miki got to be here to witness all of it. Lucky her.

He opened the door, and she strolled first into the shop. His mother stood behind the counter, this side of the office. "Hey, Mom," he said, and she offered a guarded smile. No doubt she read the annoyance on his face.

"Everything all right?" she asked.

Miki explained the situation.

He turned toward Miki. "I need to do a couple things in my office. Send Carter in here when he gets back?" Hunter knew the kid would have to jog down from one of the farthest streets. Hopefully. Or he'd park illegally. Again. Dude needed a lesson in sacrifice and respect. Hunter could oblige.

From the shop, Miki and Mom chatted for a minute in hushed tones. In a little over an hour, the students, Miki, and Hunter would head out on their first dive. He had a few minutes to tackle the pile on his desk before seeing to the boat.

A card waited for him, propped against his computer monitor. "Mom, what's this?" he called around the open doorway toward the store's counter. He didn't recognize the handwriting.

"One of our passengers handed it to me on her way out yesterday."

He picked it up, turned it over, saw the words: *To the Captain of the Millennium* written in a swirly scrawl. The envelope was sealed, so no one else had read it. He pulled out the card.

Dear Captain,

I wanted to bring something to your attention. My three-year-old daughter and I were passengers on your boat this week and though we enjoyed the sail, and the whales!, I was embarrassed by the behavior of two of your employees. During one of our many trips down to the restroom—my daughter drinks a lot of juice—we saw your announcer and a gal wearing a badge making out in the kitchen. I felt you should know about it because if I were in charge, I'd want to know. Anyway, if that kind of stuff is happening, we probably won't be back. I have a young daughter to protect.

Sincerely,

A customer

Hunter clenched his free fist. What in the—? He reread the note. His naturalist, Jace, and a *student*—they were the only ones who wore badges. Hunter had debated having the students wear company shirts and had decided to give them badges instead.

"Doctor Rhoades, could you come in here, please?" he called, using her formal name in case there were students in the shop now. Why did working with these kids feel like working with middle schoolers? He closed his eyes, rubbing his forehead.

Miki entered the room. "'Doctor Rhoades,' seriously?"

"Close the door."

She did and then raised her brows at him, all signs of humor gone. "What happened?"

He thrust the card into her hands and let her discover what he had. After she scanned the page, she met his eyes. "Destinee and Jace?"

He nodded.

"It's escalating."

"Mm-hmm." When had Jace Jones found time to fool around in the galley? The only time he wasn't announcing was during a lull in wildlife sightings. But those were rare, even during transit. He was supposed to stay at his post at the base of the stairs—standing guard so no one headed up to the bridge, but also ready to relay info they called down to him. Cahill's reputation ... Anger boiled inside Hunter. He gestured toward the page in her hands. "What else have they done on board, in front of passengers?" He'd kill him. "Sam mentioned something the other day. I haven't had time to check on it." He'd *check on it* now. Maybe fire someone.

Hadn't Hunter made it clear this type of foolishness wasn't allowed?

She studied him. "We have to be careful not to overreact. Destinee, and maybe Jace, might counter in the opposite way we direct. So we need to use wisdom. Start by verifying it really was the two of them. Plus, we don't know if other passengers have seen anything."

"If she's such a loose cannon—your words—why is she here?" Didn't Miki understand the stakes?

She scowled at him, no doubt due to the accusation he hadn't even tried to hide. But if he lost this business, he may as well walk away from Miki too, because he'd have no future. No security to offer a wife and family.

"Remember that explanation about how few people qualified?" Her tone sounded as tight as his, as if she too were trying to hold back her emotions. Their newfound peace seemed at risk.

He pressed his jaw together, studying her eyes. He didn't want to say something he'd regret. Best to shut up. *She* wasn't the problem.

She tilted her head. *We're here because we're trying to help you.*

I know. But what if you sink us instead?

She studied him. "You okay today?" Code for: *would you just lighten up, Captain Crabby*?

"I need to fire Jones. And you need to let Destinee know she's no longer welcome aboard either."

He could see her mental wheels turning as she processed his words. "You're going to fire Jace and essentially Destinee too, based on one note from a passenger we don't even know?"

He stilled. She had a point.

Her eyes met his as if trying to communicate more. But he'd lost the connection. All he could think was, *I can't fail this time.*

Their silence lingered a minute. He closed his eyes, his temples pounding harder. "You're right. I'll have another chat with Jones. Do you want to talk to Destinee, or do you think she'll hear it better from me?"

"Hear what?" She crossed her arms. The more he fretted, the more she freaked. "And what are you implying, that I can't handle my students?"

"Only that she's still acting like a high schooler. We need to help her see how serious this is." He straightened, not that he wanted to intimidate Miki. He was simply gearing up for battle with the fools trying to drown him.

"I'll ask her about this." She perched her hands on her hips. "And I've already warned her."

"Well, she's not listening."

"Why are we assuming it's all on her? He's acting like a predator."

"What?" News to Hunter. He *would* fire him. "Are you sure about that?"

"How well do you know him?" She huffed. "I spent a tour next to Destinee at a nearby table. He looked at her like he'd risk more than his job to be with her. He kept getting too close. Leering."

"He wouldn't betray Cahill Touring." Hunter had known Jones a long time. As far as Hunter knew, the guy liked his job and was loyal to the family, even if he didn't always use his head. "Plus, it seems Destinee doesn't mind his attention."

Her shoulders sagged. "Well, what shall we do, Captain?"

Did she mean that in a mocking, you-deserved-that way? Or was she just referring to his role? "I'll talk to Jones. You talk to Destinee. One more incident involving passengers, and they're both out. They sabotage Cahill and *we're* out more than one student's tuition, though I'm hoping she'd forfeit that. Did they sign an agreement or contract for professional behavior?"

Miki lowered her head, but raised her chin a moment later. "That's a solid idea for future programs."

He pressed his lips together.

"I honestly felt they were too old for that sort of 'field trip behavior agreement' treatment. Either way, the U would eat the cost."

He'd give her that one. "Fair enough."

If he fired Jones, he'd find another naturalist, or maybe promote his newer hire. Considering how good he was with people, Jones was ideal for his job, which was why Hunter liked having him on board, in that role. But everyone was expendable if the business was in danger.

"I'll take care of it." Her face showed few signs of the openness of last night. But his probably didn't either.

"Thank you." He tried to soften his voice. This colleague-friendship gig proved harder than he'd thought, and it required an accountability he didn't like, especially with so much at stake. Was this what God asked of him? Was it the cost of fulfilling his promise to Dad?

The world went still around him. Gideon's fleece—Hunter had looked it up since he'd put his own request out to God—followed God calling Gideon on an adventure. Would God call Hunter, and if he accepted, how much would it cost him?

She stepped back out of his office as Carter came into the shop. Hunter seethed as he pitched flyers in the recycling bin to clear his desk. If he wasn't careful, he'd take his frustrations and fears out on this new guy. And after helping his dad run the business for years, Hunter knew that if he wanted to keep employees and not develop a reputation for being a monster, he had to handle this kind of thing well—with a cool head.

Given the circumstances, that might take a miracle.

In some ways, Hunter was more of a grump this morning than when she'd first arrived. He'd better count to ten, because she was bringing Pierce Carter in and the newbie had already apologized and moved his car. Though his swagger made *Mikaela* want to fire him, if she could. Pierce wasn't trying to sabotage him, so the captain had better be nice. He'd only taken his parking spot, not his livelihood.

She straightened her spine after ushering Pierce into the lion's den. "Captain Hunter, you wanted to see my assistant."

"Carter, tell me. Do you have a sight problem? Was the sun blinding you as you parked this morning?"

He shifted on his feet, but he didn't look down. "No, running late was all. Didn't want to keep the doc—uh, Dr. Rhoades—waiting."

Behind Pierce, Mikaela allowed herself a grimace. Maybe she didn't have a solid handle on her students. She'd be more diligent, try harder. Running a program was new to her, and like Hunter had pointed out, she had more to learn. But every lesson she learned now would help prepare her for the Hawaii launch.

She could begin right now with her new resolve to confront her students and help them change, when necessary—a conversation she'd have with Destinee in a short while. She stepped forward, into Pierce's line of sight. "So, you'd rather get your car towed? Or keep the captain waiting?"

Pierce shifted on his feet, but straightened. "I've already apologized. Anyway, I figured no one needed the spot until this afternoon."

"Didn't you notice there are no time limits for parking there?"

He held his ground and peered up at Hunter. "It will not happen again."

"Good. You've already had a rocky start here." Hunter retrieved the towing service's address and held the business card out toward Pierce. "Drop a check in the mail to them for the inconvenience you caused Bruce this morning." Hunter stood straighter. She almost expected him to produce his captain's hat and don it while he spoke. His bearing presented authority without the hat. "You reflect Cahill Touring while you're here. Please rise to that challenge."

Pierce nodded. "Got it."

Mikaela waited for him to add "sir," but he didn't. She checked a sigh because if he had it may have been sarcastic. She had some work to do with him.

Hunter and Mikaela exchanged a look. One confrontation down. Two to go. She gestured toward the main shop and let the new guy precede her. But at the door, she stopped. "I'll tell Destinee she has an appointment with you as soon as she gets here."

Hunter nodded once. Mikaela caught the slightest crinkle at the corner of his eyes, the hint of a curl at the edge of his mouth, right before she closed the glass door behind her. Perhaps he'd guessed that he'd impressed her with how he handled Carter. So, maybe he could get Destinee to cooperate.

CHAPTER NINETEEN

After the upset the other night at Granny's, and not bringing up Ben's boat, Hunter had put off returning Hank's call. He couldn't much longer, though. Right now, he was glad for his family's boat. He knew *Cahill's Prize* like he knew the *Millennium*. He tied off the family's yacht at a buoy off of Turn Island State Park and prepared to help Miki's team get into the water for their first dive of the season. Everyone milled around the cabin of the thirty-nine-foot boat, keeping clear of the captain's chair.

His heart thumped hard in his chest. Tonight, he and Miki could talk alone. Unlike today, where Carter would remain on board while the others dove. But given how queasy the guy looked, Hunter might find him a Dramamine and send him below with a bucket.

The students clustered around, digging out their scuba gear. Carter lingered on the perimeter, shivering and scowling.

Before the dive, Hunter needed to take care of one small thing. "Destinee, could I see you for a minute?"

Her brown eyes peered up at him. She held her wetsuit in her hands. "I need to get into my gear."

"This shouldn't take long." He gestured with an open arm to the boat's small cabin. "The professor won't mind, right, Doctor?"

"Not at all, Captain." When Destinee turned, Miki gave him a look of gratitude. "We'll hold the team for you, Destinee," Miki said.

Mikaela was glad Hunter didn't mind talking to Destinee. When she'd pulled her aside earlier, Destinee had denied everything. Maybe Hunter could get somewhere. Or, maybe she was innocent. Mikaela couldn't tell.

Meanwhile, she'd coach the team and verify Pierce was taking notes. Poor guy. He'd looked peaked for the last half hour. *Cahill's Prize* rocked more than the *Millennium.* Would the department chair and Dr. Smythe really send a landlubber who couldn't handle riding the waves? Right then, he settled on the bench seat against the side of the boat, clutching his stomach.

Mikaela fielded a question from Anya about the oxygen tank settings and watched the cabin. She could clearly see Hunter and Destinee through the boat's transparent plexiglass walls/windows. From his expression, he was trying to appeal to Destinee—the way he dipped his head to see her face. His hands at his waist almost in a relaxed stance. That approach might work. But then Destinee responded. Raised her voice, which meant the rest of the team might overhear.

Mikaela would speak over their voices. "Is everyone clear on their responsibilities?" The sun shone brightly, but the air temperature was probably only about sixty-one, if that, given the winds. A purplish marine layer lingered along the horizon in the distance. The boat bobbed, and gulls floated in the bay. "Seth, do you have the waterproof camera?"

He raised it in his hands. "Yes."

"You guys have fifteen minutes. I don't want us to go beyond that for this first dive. Focus on familiarizing yourselves with this site. I'll expect detailed accounts from each of you, including a generalized map of the layout by the beginning of next week." She'd seen the research of this site, had dived here herself several times. She'd know if anyone brought her incorrect information. "And no hugging wolf eels, Kristopher." That earned a chuckle around the group as Seth slapped the linebacker's shoulder.

Generally, her students each had a research project this summer. Like with the undergrads at the labs, each had a specific area of study. Beyond research, which the students would conduct, Mikaela hoped to later offer more services through Cahill in an effort to perpetuate the U's involvement with Cahill over time. She had yet to pitch that idea to Hunter. Maybe tonight during their dinner meeting? That was one way she could keep things work-related.

Destinee reappeared, but she didn't look contrite. She wore a grin as if she carried a secret.

Mikaela suppressed a sigh. "Welcome back, Ms. Fulbright. While you get into your suit, I have a question for the group." Not knowing what Hunter had already covered, and not wanting to embarrass the woman, Mikaela left her comments at that. She'd get details from Hunter later. Right now, she faced the others. "Anyone recall what the hazards are at this dive site?"

Pierce sat gripping the bench front as the boat rocked up and down. His skin pale, his eyes wide. He wouldn't be answering any questions today.

Seth nodded. "Strong currents."

"Yez, and downdrafts," Anya added while Destinee zipped herself into her wetsuit.

Mikaela nodded. "Good." She addressed the group again. "We'll monitor everything from here. Remember your training, and keep your fellow divers in mind."

Nods and yeses from everyone.

"Okay, help each other double-check your gear."

The students moved about checking oxygen gauges, tanks, and masks.

Hunter went around unzipping the "walls" of the cabin, giving them more room. "Carter—Pierce," Hunter said, his voice gentled no doubt by Pierce's green complexion and what Hunter must know that meant. He reached into a cubby and brought out a small box. "Here, chew one of these." He thrust the package at Pierce who accepted it, gulped hard, and tore open the package.

"Thanks," he murmured.

If today were any indication, Pierce might not offer much help on these trips. Except, he could participate in shore dives since the team would walk in from land. They'd scheduled one at Smallpox Bay in a few days.

The divers went in minutes later, and Mikaela kept her eyes on the water as they faded under rising bubbles.

Behind her, she heard shifting. She turned. Pierce suddenly

stood and chucked his breakfast over the side of the boat. Mikaela grimaced and balanced with bent knees to ride the rocking waves from a low wake. Hunter steadied her student. Hopefully the guy wouldn't fall in.

Fresh wind blew in from behind Mikaela, and she shivered. She stepped into the cabin, searching for something warm to wear. Meanwhile, Hunter tended Pierce, offering him another chewable tablet, from what Mikaela could hear, since the first had surely just been ejected. If he could keep it down, it would have a chance to work. Maybe she'd research getting him a patch. The upside was that seasickness seemed to tame Pierce's self-entitled attitude.

Seeing Hunter had things under control, Mikaela wrapped herself tightly into a Cahill Touring jacket she'd found in the cabin and stood again at the railing at the back of the boat, far from Pierce and his stomachache. She scanned for any signs her divers needed her. Obstacles aside, she loved being out here, watching the eagles circle and the ospreys dive, hearing the gulls screech as they fought over marine morsels. Sea otters bobbed to the surface, and one seemed to wave a front paw before ducking back under in a smooth rolling motion.

This place had never worked its way out of Mikaela's system. Never would. Suddenly she hated the idea of leaving—giving this up and walking away from the Cahills again.

Especially when all of Hunter's best traits had only gotten stronger.

Her BFF Shea planned to visit over the weekend of the Fourth. Mikaela anticipated being grilled by her bestie, but maybe Shea could help. Shea knew her well.

From the corner of her eye, and the scuffing sound, Hunter was behind her. She drew a deep breath. How had she forgotten how much she loved working with him, being near him?

One peek over her shoulder. "How's he feeling now?" Pierce sat on the floor with his head against the side of the boat, agony written on his face. But he wasn't throwing up. If he were well, she'd have him taking notes on the wildlife around them or documenting the dive information they could chart so far—

location, number of students, and other busy work—but he was in no condition to do anything except keep his medicine down.

"So far okay," Hunter murmured. "The med might knock him out. Your kid brother always used to sleep for about two hours after taking it." He paused and then nodded at the jacket she'd borrowed. "Looks good."

"Yours?" Not that she wondered, since it smelled like him—that sandalwood scent she remembered from their youth. Masculine. Earthy. Another delicious element drawing her toward him, like that expression on his face.

"Mm-hmm." He reached over and adjusted the collar, tugging one corner loose, smoothing it out. Nothing unprofessional, only one colleague helping another. Except her breath caught as his fingertips brushed her shoulder. *I have questions for you.*

I know.

In his gray eyes, she read their history and their present. The hint of a possible future. Long ago, he'd shared his dreams—they'd discussed family, settling here on San Juan Island, running the touring business alongside Reid and Lauren. Mikaela becoming a Cahill.

All before she'd gotten the news that changed everything.

"I have a question for you." He glanced over toward Pierce and then back, keeping his voice low.

Oh, she'd rather avoid a deep conversation while they were on duty, but curiosity ate at her. "Okay . . ." Gulp. She scanned the water. No sign of her divers returning.

His expression went tender—such a contrast with the annoyed Hunter countenance of late. An endearing contrast. Her gaze returned to the sea. "Why didn't you come back?" he asked.

Secrets he didn't know. Resulting decisions he'd try to talk her out of because he knew her so well. Which made one-on-one moments like this threatening.

Perhaps it wasn't too late to get out of tonight. Maybe if they covered what they needed to now, she could. "I wanted to pitch an idea to you." If she spoke fast, they could cover the topic and make their upcoming meeting unnecessary. And she could distract him from getting personal. Because as much as she wanted answers, she *needed* her walls. She braved a glance at his face.

One eyebrow up. *You're changing the subject.*

You better believe it.

She gathered her courage. "Maybe we could save time, not have to meet toni—"

Pierce stirred behind them, leaning over the side of the rocking boat again, but he didn't throw up this time. Instead, when he turned back, he pointed to the bench seat near the captain's chair and raised his brows. "Mind if I lie down?" His voice came out more of a groan, and his eyes seemed determined to close.

"Go ahead." She walked closer. "Need a blanket or anything?"

"Ohh . . ." he moaned, and she looked toward Hunter.

"Do you have anything we can cover him with?"

Hunter produced a blanket from under a bench and settled it over their patient.

She stood from bending near Pierce and met Hunter's gaze. He zipped the wall back together to shield the cabin from the wind and tipped his head toward the opposite end of the boat's open area. She led the way over there.

"Landlubber. City kid," Hunter muttered.

She faced the bay. No sign of trouble.

"So, you were saying . . . ?" The humor in his voice showed he saw through her attempt at getting out of their dinner date. He raised his watch into her line of sight as if to add to the list of reasons her suggestion was ridiculous.

The divers were due up momentarily.

She pursed her lips and rolled her eyes—a gesture she hadn't done in about fifteen years. "Never mind."

Hunter chuckled, and she socked him—a reflex, probably, from all their years of flirting. He caught her wrist in his hand—his own reflex—and she grinned at him, raising one of her eyebrows. A deep tenderness washed over his features, drew her, and she stepped closer as his gentle grip loosened. In slow motion, he shifted his hand and threaded his fingers through hers.

His eyes traced her face. *We need to talk about some stuff.*

A splashing noise jolted her, and she dropped his hand, stepped back, found Kris surfacing in the water, and waved. "They're up," she said without looking at Hunter.

"Yup. We'll talk later."

During their meeting.

CHAPTER TWENTY

Twelve Years Ago

"So"—Miki was barely off the boat before she started in. She'd walked off the ferry, left her parents to drive toward the cottage. Every June, she met Hunter on Front Street. From the landing, he'd watched the ferry pull in, as usual, meeting her as she joined the foot traffic. His heart thumped with anxiety, but he'd put off telling her what he needed to tell her, for a while at least. Her eyes sparkled as she glanced up at him. Together, they marched along with the other travelers arriving at the island. Destination: the touring office. "Did you get the ring?"

He grabbed her hand. "Hey! I'm supposed to be the one to bring that up."

"Oh, oops," she said, swinging his hand. "Are you on duty today?"

"Nah, Dad knew you guys were coming. What do you wanna do?"

"Let's go kayaking." The touring office came into view on the right. "Where are you parked?"

He nodded toward Dad's old truck. People milled around them, stopping in for pizza at one of the cafes or searching for the whale tour offices. Hunter wasn't wearing his work polo shirt, so he blended in. He tugged her hand, drawing her closer, smiling down at her. "I'm glad you're finally here."

"Me too." She didn't hold his gaze long. *What had her all distracted?* "Hey, can we buzz by the lab? Dr. Wren left me some paperwork there."

"Paperwork?"

"Shoot," she said, then bit her lower lip. "I was going to wait and tell you later."

"Tell me what?" If he knew they wouldn't get trampled, they'd stop here on the sidewalk. As it was, they stayed one step ahead of the crowds. Soon the people would thin out, but for now, if you stopped, you were toast.

She must have sensed they couldn't pause there too, because she didn't even try to explain. But he wouldn't drop it. Ever since Dr. Wren planted the idea of Miki going to school in Seattle, and not Bellingham, Miki had been slipping away. The best he could hope for, for himself, was to get into Bellingham U. But he hadn't even applied because his grades had fallen. Dad seemed to need him more lately. Plus, who could afford to go to school in Seattle? The cost of living alone would kill him.

All she could talk about in their phone calls and e-mails lately had been *U of Sea* this and *U of Sea* that. Miki's family lived in Seattle. She'd live with them, or nearby—they could afford it. She'd get a job, go to school. What if she forgot about him?

It'd probably be smarter not to propose this summer.

They climbed into the truck, and he backed out. "So, the labs, huh?"

Seat belt on, Miki pivoted, angling herself toward him in the big cab of Dad's old pickup. "I know you and I talked about Bellingham for college." She reached for his hand, as if that would help with whatever bomb she'd drop next. "But I'm pretty sure I'm supposed to go to the U of Sea."

And there it was. "Which means . . ." He cleared his throat. "Which means," he pushed out, watching the road, working his jaw, "we won't see each other for the next four or more years."

"No, it doesn't. You always say that. But it doesn't have to. What about holiday vacations?"

"You won't have a job that keeps you down there near Puget Sound?"

"Oh . . ."

He peeked over and caught sight of her biting her lower lip again.

"I will be interning here and there, all part of the program. They might ask me to work during school breaks."

Yeah, proposing was a mistake. She didn't even know what she wanted. Or, scratch that. She *did* and it didn't include him. At least not for the next few years.

His ribs tightened. He'd been afraid of this. Afraid she'd find a life somewhere else. Without him.

She squeezed his hand in the silence as he pulled down the long gravel road leading to the lab. "Don't worry. Nothing has to change. We've carried on a long-distance relationship for years. Nothing new about that. Right? We're pros." So much hope in her voice. Or was that naïveté? Sounded like she was trying to convince herself.

He should cancel his plan for tomorrow night. Call off the surprise.

This wasn't how their reunion this summer was supposed to begin—her jumping out of his truck at the lab, all gung-ho on launching into her college years without him. She was supposed to tell him she planned to move here, to the island. Live with Granny Belle. Take online classes. Be near for once. Maybe get married soon, and then they could live with his parents until they got their feet under them.

Except for Dad needing him lately, and Mom leaning a bit more, he'd hoped they could get married sooner rather than later. Plenty of married people went to school, right?

She stood at the open truck door, leaning in. "Want to come in with me?"

"Nah, you go ahead."

A cool breeze rustled around her, pushing her blonde hair into her face, but not before he saw the disappointment. "Okay, I'll hurry."

He'd been saving up for a year. He'd planned the perfect proposal—Miki would never guess what he had in mind. Something they'd never done. A place he'd never taken her. Good thing she didn't know, because when he canceled she wouldn't be hurt.

Only fools got engaged before one person left. Okay, not always. Plenty of military heroes and heroines left fiancées or fiancés behind, right?

But he wasn't a hero.

At the building, Miki stepped back outside, clutching a manila envelope, a big grin on her face as she approached the truck once more. He wanted to see her happy. He wanted the best for her. Sure, the best education and opportunities, but he didn't have those same open doors. He was tied here.

Dad had seemed tired lately. Weary. Older, somehow. But whenever Hunter asked about it, he'd always say it was nothing. He'd be fine. Not to worry. But hey, could you help with this or that? Mind doing such-and-such for a while?

Last night, he'd asked Hunter to consider foregoing college and instead get his 100-ton master's license. He'd worried about disappointing Miki—reneging on their Bellingham college plans, at least for now. But Dad seemed anxious for him to prepare to take on the responsibilities of sailing sooner than they'd planned. Sure, he'd handled the wheel a few times, but nothing like he'd watched his father do during storms, close calls with other vessels, or trips to dry dock in Anacortes for repair.

With Miki planning to stay in Seattle, it looked like he wouldn't have to choose between her and his dad's request. Good for him.

She climbed back into the truck, setting the envelope between them so she could buckle up. "Let's go have fun!"

Sure. Forget all that stood between them now. Forget their future apart.

Except . . . maybe it wasn't too late. "Have you actually applied to the U yet?"

"Dr. Wren said to wait until this fall, when my senior year is underway."

So, there was still time.

"I've heard Bellingham U has a great oceanography program," he said as he turned the truck toward the road. "They've started offering online courses you could do . . . from anywhere."

"I want marine biology. And I need to be there in person." She said *person* as if Hunter had suggested she grow a third arm.

Oceanography, marine bio, close enough. "You sound determined."

"Anyway, I don't have an in at Bellingham U. I can't network with the influential people in the field, like I can in Seattle."

He reached across the middle seat and threaded his fingers through hers, their hands resting on that envelope. He wanted to shove it to the floor, but he suppressed the urge. "Nothing's in stone yet. Will you at least consider the fact that we've waited all these years to finally live near each other—year round? We've planned to get married." He pulled the truck to the side of the road, knowing few cars would be out this way. The island was rather calm this far from the hustle of the harbor. And the lab was quiet during the summer season with only a few students and staff onsite. "I need to talk to you about something."

She unbuckled and faced him. He clicked out of his seat belt as well, shifting toward her, resting an arm across the back of the truck's long seat. Her smile, so sweet, open. She radiated love, whether toward him or her parents or grandparents. Or even those marine animals she was always bent on saving. "What's up?" She searched his hands. "I don't see any ring boxes." She winked, and he allowed a smile.

"Yeah, not—not here." Though he did keep the ring in the glove compartment. She didn't need to know that. "My dad wants me to get my master's license, help with the tours."

"That will be great! You'll have so much more to offer with that in place."

Yeah, a lengthy program, especially with all the sailing time they required. But he did love the water and didn't want to be anywhere else. Besides, Dad could sign off on his sailing hours, so Hunter could get the time in. He'd take first aid and submit to the physical exam and drug testing. Then, he'd follow in his dad's footsteps.

She shook her head as if realization had dawned. "But that means you won't be going to college next fall."

"Yeah, I'm going to put it off a little while. Dad's concerned I move forward and become a captain, like him. And really, I've never had aspirations"—he waved his free hand, fluttering his fingers over the frilly word—"beyond that."

She tipped her head. "That's noble. But are you disappointed?"

He studied the huge cedars alongside the road while the sun shot rays between their branches. "I'm only disappointed that you won't be here." His voice dropped to a discouraged whisper.

She pressed her lips together and then relaxed them. "I never planned to move here right after high school, Hunt. You knew that. I always figured I'd be at school somewhere—with you." When she bit her lip, he smoothed her mouth with a thumb. "But to be fair, I didn't expect to stay in Seattle."

"It's killing me to wait." His whisper came out hoarse.

"I know what you're thinking, and you can stop it right now. I still want to get engaged. So we wait to get married. So what?"

He winced.

"You get your captain's license. I'll get my degree. We'll figure things out as we go. We didn't see this coming. We don't know what else is coming, but we can face it together."

See that? Foolishness.

A car whooshed past, rattling the truck. Life was doing that lately—zooming out of control, shaking things up for both of them.

Her gaze went intense. "We can still get engaged."

He didn't answer, didn't know how to.

"Right, Hunt?"

Present Day

Out on his back deck, Hunter fired up his lawn mower. Miki would arrive in about an hour. He wanted the yard to look fresh. He tracked back and forth across the lawn. What had ever happened to the ring he'd given her? She'd never given it back.

Twelve Years Ago

Taking advice from Dad, Hunter hadn't canceled his surprise. So, here they were, high over the islands, getting the aerial tour. He'd told Miki to dress up a little and he'd done the same, pocketing the ring box. But how could he go through with it?

The pilot swung them back toward Orcas Island—the recognizable saddle shape. He'd started off announcing the islands and sights, but Hunter had told him after the initial tour guide spiel, to tone it down, let him and Miki talk. Simply keep flying for a while. Hunter held Miki's hand and watched her face as she studied the view. The sun cast the clouds in pinks and oranges as it set, spilling warm colors into the channels below them.

"I've seen this in pictures, but this is so much better." Her smile splashed joy in his direction when she turned, and he almost forgot his problems. They'd settled into a bit of a routine, though their uncertain future hung over him, pressing him down. She'd seemed glad to be near him lately, as usual, but more excited about college than anything else.

But when she turned that smile on him, he wanted to give her the world. Or at least the ring.

Dad said lately maybe he shouldn't think so often in terms of yes or no, on or off, but in terms of possibilities. Engaged wasn't married. They had time to figure things out. For two years, he'd dreamed of having this chance—ring in hand, Miki's face so close, gazing at him with adoration and hope. Optimism about life. They'd gotten here. He wouldn't squander it now.

He took her hand. "Miki, I've loved you for years, first as a friend and now as a girlfriend. And I want to spend the rest of my life with you." Somehow. He produced the ring box to her quiet squeal and opened it for her to see. It was modest, but it carried his heart with it. A small diamond—what had they said? Point two, or something for carats, in yellow gold. He found her eyes. "Marry me, Miki?" His breath left him at the tears in her eyes.

"Yes!" She squealed and hugged him, the ring crushed between them. She pulled back, and he blinked against the burning in his own eyes as he pulled the ring out and she held out her hand for the finishing touch. The ring went on smoothly, the perfect size. Maybe things would work out after all.

CHAPTER TWENTY-ONE

"It bothers me that Hunter's house is so close." Cell phone to her ear, Mikaela marched along the sun-dappled road toward his home. No need to bring a car when he lived this close.

"What's your plan for tonight?" Shea asked.

"All business."

"Yeah?" Shea sighed over the connection. "Any heart-to-hearts yet? Have you told him?"

Mikaela walked up his long drive, ancient red cedars and western hemlocks on either side with tufts of native ferns at their bases. "No. I haven't. And there will be no heart-to-heart chats, thank you." Shade almost covered his house. Apparently, he liked living as a hermit crab. She'd razz him about it if she hadn't determined, again, that she must keep her distance. No flirting, not even playfulness. Only friendship. Especially after her call to her boss.

"You should tell him."

"Why?"

"Because you've never had closure. And you both deserve that."

Mikaela slowed her steps. She'd be on his doorstep too soon if she didn't. "I'm here," she said quietly, lest Hunter appear on his front lawn where she now stood. "Thanks for the chat."

"Tell him." Shea gave her one second to think, then, "Consider this: you're there, together on the island, and you have the evening alone. Relax for once."

"Gotta go, 'bye," she sang into the phone as Shea grunted on the other end before they disconnected. Sunshine filtered through waving evergreen branches. Birds called to each other. In the serenity of this island, and the safety Hunter kept creating, maybe she could. Maybe she could trust him with her reasons. It wasn't like he still wanted to marry her, right? He'd accepted they could only be friends, and she was leaving.

Except... there'd been that selfie from the upper deck of the *Millennium*.

The photo she'd taken of the two of them before he was ready, where he spun and stopped short to sniff her hair. He'd leaned close, eyelids almost fluttering in the still shot, an expression of... well, longing and pleasure mixed. She hadn't noticed in the moment. But the raw desire on his face in the image took her back to when that zing of attraction was a usual occurrence. Part of her wanted to relish it, even as she strolled down the driveway to see him.

He'd seemed different since that chat. Softer around his sharp edges. Why? There were so many unanswered questions between them.

That photo! If there were no chance he'd be watching, she'd pull out her phone, study it. Maybe assign the image to his contact info, so whenever he texted or called, that pic would flash at her.

Crazy thoughts.

And crazy actions. Like wearing the chain around her neck. Ironically, through the years, the pendant had encouraged her to go for her dreams. Like she carried a small piece of Hunter with her. Feeling the weight of the chain gave her courage. Maybe it was the reminder of all she'd given up to go after her degree and now her career. A sobering reminder.

Maybe it'd felt like the last shred of their final summer together. Unlike his long-forgotten sweatshirt, which she'd somehow taken back to Seattle with her, and which she'd packed away in her closet in a box, she held onto this chain.

See that? Crazy.

She should take it off. Hide it. Stow it in her bag. Except, she hadn't brought one tonight. Did she have time to run home, deposit it on her nightstand? No. So, she'd keep it hidden. She wrapped her sweater tighter around herself, leaving the chain and pendant out of sight, the feel of the gold warm against her skin. He'd never notice.

As formal as she acted, deep inside, she was still Miki. For Hunter's sake, she had to keep him from regaining access to that place.

A serious challenge since part of her—the irresponsible, juvenile part—wanted to go back to the upper deck, call, "Selfie!" and experience him breathing near her hair. Maybe turn into his face . . .

A flash of an encounter slipped through her mind from that day in the strait—a moment she hadn't recalled until now. He'd carried her back to the parking lot, to his truck. She searched her memory, grasping for the sense that she'd been near his face. Why? She'd rested her head on his shoulder as he carried her. But in the truck, after he set her inside? Or maybe later, at the clinic? Something close. Something personal. Something . . . sweet.

She had to push those fuzzy thoughts aside—couldn't let herself toy with them. Not when she'd see him in a minute. This meeting was purely out of obligation to the department chair, and the only warmth would be friendship. Standing away from the windows, she tugged the chain off her neck and shoved the wad of metal links into her sundress pocket. *Foolishness. You can't have it both ways!*

Even Granny Belle didn't know she still wore it. Shea would lecture her for a few hours if she knew.

A breeze ruffled the hydrangea leaves in a nearby bush, bringing Mikaela back to the present. She had only a couple of minutes to subdue her crazy, adolescent notions, which would be easier if he hadn't already hinted he wanted more.

What if, like Shea suggested, for only one evening, she let go of all of her objections and simply enjoyed herself? Relished time with him? Relaxed?

Right then, Hunter rounded the side of the house wearing jeans and a smudged gray T-shirt with grass-stained sneakers. "Oh, hey." He halted but a smile broke out on his face. Did he have to look so . . . *good* . . . all messy and masculine and strong?

"I'm a little early."

His expression went from surprise to pleasure as he met her gaze. She should capture his pic right now and use *that* as his contact photo. All that unguarded delight in his eyes directed right at her. He extended an arm and she moved toward him, debated taking his hand. Who would fault her if she did? Did he expect her to? Friends held hands, right? But as she approached, he dropped his arm. "I was mowing. Do you mind if I get cleaned up?" He pinched the front of his tee and flapped it against his chest as if warning her of the sweat and grass he wanted to hose off. "Here, let me show you the back deck. I've got refreshments. After I shower, I can give you a tour of the house. Sound good?"

"Sure." She followed him around to the "front yard"—the water side. Fragrant cut grass and lilies perfumed the atmosphere. The view exploded before her—all the blues and greens of the bay, Dinner Island, and the sky. The water rested like a sea of glass today, no whitecaps in sight. She gazed at the emerald green of his yard. He had perhaps a quarter acre between here and the water's edge down an embankment. "Beautiful." She glanced over to see him watching her. "Peaceful."

"I agree." His eyes crinkled with a genuine smile, as if glad she liked it. "I'll be right back," he said, and he jogged up to the deck. "Help yourself to a drink. Though I imagine you'll explore the beach first."

"Ha!" He knew her too well.

He grinned and disappeared, and she strolled toward the water's edge. Briny air. Shiny green leaves fluttering on the nearby madrones and rhododendrons. Balmy breezes and a blue bay. Receding tide. Wet rocks. The waves rustled pebbles on the beach. She had to get closer. A couple of crabs scurried out of sight. She'd worn a sundress and carried a sweater, which she now tied over her shoulders to protect it from the saltwater. Thankfully, the weather cooperated with warm temps, but at this hour, the sun slanted from the west. This eastern side of the island missed out on the sunsets. While she was here on San Juan, she should make time to go to Westside and catch a sunset or twenty. She'd missed them.

Sure enough, Hunter returned within minutes, looking fresh in rolled up low-rise jeans and a snug-fitting, clean, black T-shirt. He must favor black now. The color made his eyes flash, even at this distance. His wet, light brown hair drew her attention too. She stood near the waves. He had bare feet as if he didn't plan to walk the rocky shoreline with her, but rather to stay up on the lawn.

Time to interact—like friends. "Hey," she nodded toward his toes. "You can't come down here without shoes."

He chuckled. "Who says I'm coming down there?" She'd forgotten how deep his voice could sound. And how much that timbre affected her.

Covering that attraction—she hoped—she perched her hands on her hips and gave him her one-eyebrow-up look. Like Granny's waterfront, the bulkhead posts here were about four feet off the ground, lined up in a row. If he jumped, he might land on the stones and broken shells that littered the beach. She shrugged. "Suit yourself. I'm on a mission." She focused on the next rock—large enough to harbor creatures, small enough for her to lift one side and watch what scurried.

More chortling. "All right, all right. Anyway, I have tough soles," he said before he dropped off the wooden bulkhead and onto the rocks. "Ouch!" Two steps to catch his balance and then he teetered toward the wooden posts where he plopped down, pulling his feet up. "New plan. You explore. I'll watch." He rubbed one of those tough soles.

She laughed. "Surely you own aqua socks or old tennis shoes." She hoisted up the corner of a large rock, careful of the sharp acorn barnacles, and spied a tiny green shore crab in the indentation the rock had made in the moist sand. She snatched him up before he could escape. Pinching the crab from behind, she carried it to Hunter. "Here, hold this."

He held out his hand, a grin on his handsome face. The daylight shone in his gray eyes—and what that black tee did for those eyes and his unshaven jaw. She shushed the inner voice urging caution and moved one pace closer, balancing on the rocks.

He tipped his head toward her hands. "The crab?"

"Oh, right." She dropped it into his palm. "Don't lose him."

"I won't. You still need to kiss him and put him back when you're done bringing me all his friends."

She chuckled, peering at him. His Adam's apple bobbed with a swallow, and his eyes dipped to her mouth and back to her eyes. "You remembered," she murmured, surprised at his thoughtfulness and how much it meant to her. She'd spent years keeping people at a distance. Here was a man who "got" her. That thought could undo her if she entertained it too long. That truth could hold loneliness underwater until it drowned.

"Of course." His voice came out soft. "Now, bring me his buddies."

She shook off the thoughts and explored the beach, turning her back to him for a moment to gather herself. For several minutes, she peeked under more rocks, found crabs, and added them to his collection. They were too small for their pinch to hurt Hunter's palms.

"These things tickle like mad. When do we let the poor victims loose?"

She stood a ways down the beach. "Are you sure you don't want to join me out here?" she called over her shoulder. Then she watched him.

He slid off the bulkhead and stood. One step. "Ow, shoot! Ee-ya!" He hop-scotched to the one open portion of beach—a raised circle of wet, deep brown sand maybe four feet in diameter. His long toes curled into the dirt.

She shook her head, laughing. She'd forgotten how silly he could be. And how stubborn. All for lack of the beach wear he surely owned. A thought occurred to her: had he been in too much of a hurry to get back to her to stop for shoes? He'd risked barnacles without shoes and hopped to this space, closer to her. His unspoken messages were clear tonight. Heaven help her, she liked what he wasn't saying.

She joined him on the little sandy island, putting them in a small diameter together. His expression went sober as he studied her, both hands cupped together with a bit of light between. She felt like he held more than crabs in his grasp.

"Well, let 'em go." Her voice squeaked, and she fidgeted.

"Nope. You have to do it." He held his "finger cage" toward her.

As a child, she used to kiss all her captives. But she was an adult now. She hadn't kissed sea life in a very long time. Besides, no reason to bring up kissing anything. "For crying out loud. All you have to do is put them on the ground." She studied his fun, teasing eyes. How often had they done this? Her making beach collections, him humoring her?

Perhaps he didn't mean to communicate so much with a gaze, like he could read her hopes or fears, diagnose her hang-ups. Or maybe create a new spot for himself in that familiar part of her heart he'd vacated twelve years ago. A Hunt-shaped vacancy in Miki's heart.

He waited, his Adam's apple shifting again. Then, he lightly shook his hands toward her as if to say, *So . . . you gonna get these guys outta here or not?*

She took hold of his wrists and bent at her knees, bringing him down toward the sand too, while trying to ignore the shooting electrical currents between them. Their faces were mere inches apart now. He smelled like soap, and she made herself avoid his eyes. He cooperated, balancing and crouching with her, and then she slowly pulled back his fingers until the scrambling crabs were once again visible. After pressing his arms toward the sand, she held them there, and he tipped his palms until the creatures half-slid, half-skittered off, bolting for cover.

"They'll find rocks to hide under," she said, still crouching with him.

He rubbed his palms on the thighs of his jeans as if to erase the ticklish feeling. "You forgot to kiss them." His voice came out husky, his breath against her cheek.

Her nerves tingled with the familiarity of his being so close and his choice of words. *Keep things light.* "It's been a long time since I've kissed a crab."

The moment seemed to freeze between them, or perhaps it melted. *He'd* been a crab lately. She'd called him that in her unkinder thoughts. This setting, their proximity, the smell of salt and the grill, and the cry of gulls, plus this time with him—unguarded. And ironically, safe in a way. So much working against her new resolve. She could feel his gaze on her. He didn't move, didn't push for more. Simply waited.

A wave splashed toward them, and she jumped up before it could douse her dress. Hunter shot to standing too, but his calves got splashed. She giggled at him as he scampered back toward the bulkhead like those scurrying crabs. He squawked all the way over to a safe spot. Her laughter mixed with the new waves. So much for a receding tide. Or maybe a boat had produced a wake. She moved toward the bulkhead too, holding her dress hem at knee level.

"Oh, yeah, you laugh." He sat there rolling up his jeans even higher. "Not funny." But he wore a grin.

"It's the risk we take, playing next to the water."

A foamy wave brought fresh bull kelp farther up the beach. She glanced back at him. He sat there, feet on the bulkhead in front of him, arms around his bent knees, glistening skin, seemingly content to wait her out, let her relax. He probably didn't realize his lovesickness was tangible from here. Or the way it drew her heart.

Wait. Lovesickness?

But that open expression she'd missed for twelve years didn't lie. And it still had wooing power.

He'd broken things off back then. Why? Granny Belle had asked her if she was certain he'd sent her away. Could Mikaela have misunderstood him? What was confusing about him walking away and "letting her go?"

Right now he studied her with an expression she feared meant more than she could handle. Even with the light blocked behind him by the tree line near the road, he made quite a picture. Masculine. Peaceful. Attentive. Affectionate?

Refocus. "What's cooking? Smells amazing."

"Steak for you. I knew I'd better not serve you fish."

Ick. "Heh. You remembered."

He tipped his head, hands lightly clasped at his hairy shins. "Of course. Though I threw on some salmon for me."

She grimaced. "Oh, goodie." Marine life was for study, or rescue, not for ingestion. Who wanted to eat something that smelled like seaweed rotting in the sun?

Another chuckle as if he read her thoughts. "C'mon. Let's go."

He stood up and leaned forward, holding out a hand for her to climb to where he was, using the lower wooden circles for steps.

She let him help her. "Thanks." She released his hand as soon as she reached the lawn.

"I'll show you the house after we eat."

"Sounds good. Thanks for having me over, by the way." Of course, they'd yet to have their formal "meeting." They had a lot to talk about tonight—past stuff. If she were brave enough. Who relished the question, "Hey, so tell me, why did you decide I wasn't worth waiting for?" She didn't need the reminder of his rejection.

Lord, that's still an open wound. Only recently reopened. Asking God to heal it might mean more pain. Was she up for that? No, thanks. Though He may not give her a choice.

Hunter nodded. "My pleasure."

His words rang between them as they crossed the lush green yard toward the deck. She envied him his shoeless state and slipped off her sandals. The thick grass carpeted her footfalls in luscious cool comfort and that summery fresh-cut scent. "Ah, this is amazing." She turned in a circle, letting herself enjoy the moment.

"Don't get this in the city." He paused to watch her, then busied himself lowering his pant legs a bit, though he still left them cuffed at the bottom.

She waited for him. "True. I like your property."

"Thanks." They climbed the stairs to the table laden with plates, glasses, iced tea, and lemonade. The closer they got to the grill the more the smell of the seared meat overpowered her. "You really live in a condo without a yard now?" he asked.

"Yup. Right near campus. I have a house sitter for the summer." He didn't need to know she rented an expensive—and teensy—studio.

"View?"

"You know it."

"Figured if you could afford it, you would." He inspected one of the brown rocking deck chairs before turning it to face her. "Have a seat." A habit that hadn't died, his checking for spiders for her. Another reminder of their past that made their get-together tonight

. . . comfortable. But his thoughtfulness yielded keys for unlocking her guards.

He busied himself pouring lemonade for her and iced tea for himself, then dumping a bag of baby carrots into a bowl.

"So," at the grill now, he spoke over his shoulder, "how is Carter after everything?"

She'd debated giving her assistant the afternoon tour off, but he'd bounced back once they were on the larger boat. "I'll need to figure out something else for the dives from now on. He admitted to motion sickness since childhood."

"Figured."

"Right? He could have told me." She stretched back in her chair, feeling tension ease from her shoulders. Their meeting was underway, and it wasn't so scary after all. "What about Destinee? She seemed . . . smug when she came out of the *Prize's* cabin earlier."

"She, uh, accused me of 'crushing on you'." He tilted his metal spatula her way, his eyes crinkling. He shrugged, but didn't admit— or deny—anything. "I reminded her: professionalism at all times. Tried to get her to understand our family's livelihood was at stake, but that didn't seem to click. She did, however, commit to trying harder to keep her distance from Jones at work."

Hmm . . . small boat. Well, larger than *Cahill's Prize*, but not by enough to prevent Destinee and Jace from one-on-one interactions. "You believe her?"

"Nope."

"Jace seemed full of apologies, at least to me." She spread the cloth napkin over her lap. She hadn't ever seen Hunter as a cloth napkin kind of guy. Did he think she expected linens and steaks? Because she was still a simple woman at heart. The same person who'd left this island all those years ago and vowed not to return to stay.

"How did Jace react when you two chatted?" she asked him.

Hunter adjusted the salmon filet and grilling meat aromas mingled—fish and steak—carrying her direction. Was that a hint of lemon? Her stomach rumbled, joining the noises of the birdsong, sizzles, and distant, rhythmic waves.

"He seemed cooperative to me too. I don't think he can afford to lose this job. Especially if he wants to stay on this island and work in the same field. No one else would hire him knowing I'd fired him for a mistake that reflected badly on our rep."

"It won't come to that."

He sighed, his broad shoulders rising then falling on a long exhale. "I hope not." He paused a second, lifting a steak onto a platter. "Any news from Amelia?"

That sounded rather familiar. He hadn't called her the chairwoman, or Dr. Wren. Mikaela's palms started to itch. How often had they spoken? Time to go fishing. "Sounds like you've developed a rapport already."

He slid a salmon filet onto a different platter, and she schooled her features so she wouldn't grimace.

"We've talked a couple of times." His gaze intensified. "I get the feeling she cares a lot about you."

She glanced away. "Yeah." Scary, the implications. Would Amelia tell him something Mikaela never had? She sipped her lemonade, the cubes clanking in the glass too loudly in the serene setting.

He stood next to the table now. "Seems she and I have the same goal."

Mikaela sputtered on her drink and used her napkin to wipe her mouth. "You do?" Had she guessed right? Were Amelia and Hunter in cahoots?

"Yes." He tilted his head. "We both want the best future for you." His voice came out soft, intimate, even a little broken, like his own words moved him.

She fiddled with her napkin, avoiding his eyes. Dare she ask? "In what way?"

He seemed to sense her discomfort and slowly returned to the grill where he used tongs to plate grilled asparagus spears and baked potatoes. "Oh, you know, success. Happiness."

Love.

He didn't say it. But somehow, she heard it.

"A fulfilled life." He sat at the table, smiling. "Shall we eat?"

"Absolutely." Before she learned more uncomfortable facts about Hunter's chats with her boss.

And their wanting her best future. Because there was no way they would agree on what that was.

CHAPTER TWENTY-TWO

So they wouldn't talk about her boss anymore. No problem. They'd finally gotten here. He didn't want to scare her off now.

She pressed her meat with her fork, and its juices ran red. "Might need a minute longer."

"Sure thing." He jumped up and whisked away her plate.

Standing at the grill, he drew a long breath of summer—the searing meat, the salty sea air, the hint of vanilla from Miki's direction. And longing hit him. That they'd spend a lot more evenings together like this one—playing on the beach, the scent of charred meat rising as waves crashed in. That she'd look at him the way she used to.

Right now, she stared off toward the bay as if she were dreaming too. Sure. About Hawaii and turquoise waters instead of slate blue waves.

He shook his head. No use hoping.

Ask Me.

He shot a look heavenward. Squinting. Huh. *Someone* had taken on a new habit and gotten a lot more talkative lately.

"What's up, Hunt?" Miki must have noticed his sudden skyward focus.

"Nothing." He grabbed his iced tea and gulped about a third of the glass's contents.

The last time God had spoken to Hunter, He'd come through. He'd made a way for Miki to remain on the island. And, for the moment, Cahill's finances were looking up. Hope . . .

Just ask.

Could he?

He'd give almost anything to see Miki look at him with acceptance again. Trust. For her to love him again.

"You sure?" She'd tilted her head his direction, like she did care. That look could burn off the thick marine layer suffocating his heart.

Okay. Fine. He gave her a gentle smile. "I'm sure." *Lord, You win. I'll try this again.* Deep breath. *Please heal our relationship.*

There. Hunter would leave his request at that. He brought her steak back. "That should do it."

"Thanks." She smiled at him.

He joined her at the table, resting his elbows on either side of his plate, waiting. Did she still pray before she ate?

She picked up her fork and knife, answering his unspoken question, and sawed off a piece of meat. Medium well, exactly how she liked it. He preferred a bit more pink, but tonight he'd feast on grilled salmon.

She swallowed a bite. "This is delicious, Hunter."

"Thanks." He twisted loose a tender morsel of lemony fish with his fork. "Sure you don't want a taste?"

"Aw, I can't believe you would eat that in front of me."

He grinned. "Mmm . . . so good." He chewed, savoring the citrusy, charred fish. That hint of dill. "And it's not the first time." She socked his arm, and he faked a wince. "I can't believe you won't even try one bite," he said, mimicking her.

Humor glinted in her eyes. "What if I were allergic? Then would you leave me alone?"

He snorted. "Probably not."

She scoffed too. "I believe it." She spooned a scoop of baked potato. "This is a great night for eating out."

Yeah, with you here. Moments like this fed hope, when everything felt right. When it seemed God might be smiling.

Time for a bit of a risk. "So, another question for you." He swallowed his bite of asparagus, reached for his iced tea.

"Shoot."

"Do you ever have flashbacks of our childhood?" He'd start there. What he really wanted to do was clear up their breakup, but he'd go slow.

"Sure . . ." She drew out the word, maybe uncertain what he was asking.

Let her see your heart.

There it was again, His voice. And what a directive. Like Gideon, the fleece accompanied a call. Did Hunter have Gideon's courage? Even Hunter didn't like milling around in his heart for long.

"Especially being here this summer." She looked around the yard, perhaps the view, then back to him. "Like that time we made a fort in the shed."

He refocused. They'd start with the kiddie memories, push off from there. "The bees!" A shudder slithered up his back merely remembering the swarms.

"Not the right spot for a fort."

"Under the deck wasn't so good either. Remember the snakes?"

She shivered. "Yes. And spiders. Thank you for that." Her grin told him he wasn't in too much trouble. She unwrapped her sweater from around her neck and slipped her arms into the cardigan, hiding perfectly beautiful shoulders.

He swallowed. Could she feel the draw too? And if she did, why didn't she go with it? What exactly held her back? Would Amelia tell him if he asked? Did Amelia know?

He cleared his throat. "Any other flashbacks?"

She'd nearly finished her meal now. "A few." Her skin went darker as she bent over her plate. Was that the fading sunlight? Or . . .?

"Like what?" He prompted, leaning forward.

Finally, she met his eyes. "Remember that day at Haro Strait?"

Hmm . . . "You mean recently, or back in the day?"

"This month. And, obviously, that's happened two times too many," she joked, but she wore a grimace like her meal wasn't settling well.

"Yeah," he said quietly, his heart hammering in his chest. His own flashback of her kissing his face.

"On the walk here," she began, running her delicate fingers over the condensation on her glass, "I remembered something about being . . . face-to-face?" She glanced into his eyes, and his world stopped.

He took a shallow breath. How much did she remember? And would she admit to anything—any kind of attraction? "I carried you to the truck. We were"—swallow—"face-to-face then." He kept his voice calm as he if were dealing with a frightened fawn, and he barely breathed.

Her skin darkened even more. So unlike Miki to blush. What did she think happened? Nothing alarming. "You were injured, hypothermic, and I was a perfect gentleman, I assure you."

She grabbed his hand on the table between them, squeezed, probably had no idea the havoc she wreaked on him. "Of course you were. I didn't mean anything . . . happened. I just wondered . . . What happened?" Her grin was as delicious as his salmon, which he gladly neglected in favor of this conversation.

He shouldn't, but he couldn't help it. She'd kill him. "You mean before or after you kissed me?" With his free hand, he reached for his drink and looked off toward the tree line bordering the property as if he were innocent.

She released him. Shoot. "I what?"

She didn't remember. How he loved pushing her buttons.

She went still. That fawn again. "You let me kiss you?"

He tried not to grin. "Well, you don't have to sound so disgusted."

"It's not . . . offensive." She choked and had to reach for her drink. After a couple of swallows, she eyed him. "It's simply not professional."

There was that word again. "I can assure you that my first thoughts after dragging you from the icy strait were far from professional." There. Did she feel that? Suddenly it mattered.

"Rescuing is something friends do." She shrugged, though he didn't buy her indifference. "I get it."

No she didn't.

"But kissing you?" She shook her head. "Not okay."

He reached for her this time—hey, she'd set the limits by grabbing his hand moments ago—but she pulled back her arm.

Great. Now he'd scared her. *Take it easy, little fawn.* "Listen, you didn't kiss me. Well, technically you did."

She groaned, rocking back and covering her face with her hands.

"But not like you think. And anyway, you were in shock."

She stilled. Had she figured it out? "You mean, I tried to kiss you and . . . you turned your head?"

"Mm-hmm." He grabbed his plate and reached for hers. "Help me clean up?"

He heard her right behind him as he entered the house and bit the inside of his cheek to keep from grinning ear to ear. He'd never been one for playing games, but this game was too much fun. "Now that we're in here, let me show you around."

"Hold on," she said, hooking his arm. He stopped walking, spun to face her, glad she felt comfortable enough to grab his attention. "I'm sorry, Hunter. I'm embarrassed, I guess." She stood so close her vanilla scent filled his senses. He couldn't get enough.

He tilted his head and went still. "Don't be."

"Well, thanks for being a gentleman." She made to let go of his arm, but he closed a hand over hers and held on.

"Miki listen, you should know something." He gave them each a moment to breathe, let his gaze dip to her mouth. Could she feel the pull? Their faces weren't far apart, only their several inches in height difference. "Next time, I won't turn my face. You start it; we'll finish it."

She swallowed loud enough he heard it, but she didn't speak.

"Okay?" Could she read all he tried to tell her without words? *I still really care for you.*

She shook her head as if denying his unspoken sentence. He let her pull back her hand this time. But she faced him once more. "There won't be a next time."

He tucked his grin away. *Whatever you say.* She didn't have to know he planned to make every attempt to change her mind this summer.

Time to switch gears, help her feel comfortable again. They moved farther into the house. "So, here's the kitchen." The scarred butcher-block counters. And the old appliances. He wouldn't apologize. At least he had a house. If the bank had any say, he may not soon. But he wouldn't think of that tonight. Tonight, he had a home and Miki was here to share it. He nodded toward the living area visible beyond the breakfast bar. "Living room. Still a work in progress."

She walked out there, putting distance between them. She stared upward. "I love those beams and this cathedral ceiling. It fits you."

Seeing her in his house fit *him.*

Suddenly she spun and came back toward the bar, keeping it between them. And he didn't mind if that's what she needed to feel safe. "Oh, I can't believe I forgot." Her eyes went bright. "I talked to Granny about the *Isabelle.*"

He'd meant to let her know he planned to think of something else, but he'd forgotten. He winced. "I hope it didn't upset her."

"Not at all, that I could tell."

"Did you mention I was interested?"

"No, I thought I'd leave that for you to do. Hope you don't mind I started the conversation."

Hunter pictured her grandfather Ben—the wreaths his face made when he smiled, which he did a lot. The twinkle in his eyes. "That's cool. Thank you." He watched her for signs she might be uncomfortable, but she pulled up a barstool and got settled. If he had to guess, her legs were swinging under the bar. "Does she still have it?"

"Yup. It's in the large bay of the garage."

He'd wondered but hadn't been brave enough to check.

"Did she mention if anyone has used it lately? It might need repairs or maintenance."

"True." She rested her chin on her folded fingers. "I know Reid worked on it after the storm."

Dad. Sometimes the grief hit like two boats off course—the truth colliding with the present. Like her grandfather, his dad was gone too. Hunter grabbed the countertop with each hand and squeezed, lowering his head. She didn't need to witness all the agony that thoughts of Dad brought him. He felt her gaze on him, though.

"Do you think," she began in a soft voice, "that was his way of . . . dealing with Granddad's death, like he was trying . . . Oh, no."

She was almost rambling now. "You don't think he also blamed himself, do you?"

Dad had spent a lot of time at Granny Belle's after Ben's death, like he had been trying to atone.

Hunter locked his elbows and rocked back and forth, pushing against the growing burn in his throat. "Makes sense," he rasped.

Silence filled the house, drifting in on the dusty slanting sunbeams from the high western windows of the living room. Everything blurred.

Across from him, she drew a breath. "I'm sorry I couldn't make the funeral," she said, barely above a whisper.

The refrigerator hummed to life, loud in the still space. A Steller's jay squawked right outside the window.

And Hunter's heart cracked open.

I'm sorry I couldn't make the funeral. He spun for the freezer door and yanked out a tray of ice cubes. Then he pulled down two glasses, blinking fast. He'd get them fresh drinks, something to wash down the pain expanding in his throat, in his chest. He flicked on the sink to cold water and filled both glasses, splashing and hurting and trying not to lose it.

See? All his guards came down with her. Lucky her to see the crab and the crybaby.

Suddenly, she was at his side. She took the glass he offered, peering into his eyes, her own watery. Her chin trembled. "He meant a lot to me. And of course, he was everything to you, to Lauren."

He swallowed, nodding. Couldn't speak. Tears burned. He crossed an arm over his chest and rested his other on top, chasing the ache with the ice water. Scrambling to wall off as much as he could.

Let her see into your heart.

Was that what it would take to heal their relationship? *I can't.*

She reached for his arm, laid her hand on his skin. It felt like a singe. "If there'd been any way I could have made it, you know I'd have been here."

Tropical storms were out of her control, and he'd tell her that if he could speak. Truly he'd never held her absence against her.

"By the time they gave us the all-clear from Hawaii, the funeral had ended." She hung her head as if ashamed. He studied the top of her head, all those natural blonde highlights. "I figured it'd be worse to show up late—not very respectful. So, I chickened out and didn't come at all."

Her regret for not making the funeral undid a part of him he hadn't realized was still in one piece.

To comfort her, he'd find his voice. "I know you loved him." A sob checked his stomach, but he tightened his muscles around it and coughed instead.

"Aw, Hunter."

Enough. He reached for the square white box on the counter. Blinked. *Redirect.* "Realize," he said, sniffing hard, "you get lots of this, but ..." He lifted open the box, shut his mouth.

"Granny's fudge," she murmured. "Actually, I haven't had any yet this summer."

He gave a hard nod and reached for two napkins.

"It's kind of you to remember to check my chair for spiders and to have fudge waiting." She nudged his shoulder as he opened the silverware drawer.

That's what friends did. *Friends with a history.* He'd remember every detail about her the rest of his life. Was she starting to trust him again? He could hope. Still, he hadn't expected friendship to undo him.

He was calmer now. He peeled back the tissue paper, and the aroma of deep, rich chocolate wafted up. Have mercy, he loved Granny's fudge. Would Miki notice if he picked up the whole slab and gnawed off a sizeable bite?

He jerked his head toward the fridge. "Want milk with this?"

"You remembered that too?"

"'Course."

She tugged open the fridge door, and it squeaked on its hinges. After grabbing the quart of milk, she elbowed the fridge closed again, set the carton on the counter, then seemed to debate what to do next. "Sorry for bringing up painful subjects tonight."

He shrugged, considered how to cut this thick block. *Focus on the food, Cahill. Keep it together.*

She touched his arm again. Heartache aside, he could get used to her touching him. "Wait, Hunter?"

He faced her, butter knife in hand. He tipped it away. "Yeah?" What would she ask of him now? He had so little left tonight, and one false move he'd be a puddle on the floor.

"Remember what I said about us being friends?"

"Yup."

"How friends hold hands."

"Sure." He held his breath and caught a glimpse of where her hand still grasped his arm.

She licked her lips. "Do they hug too?"

His heart slipped to his feet, and he set the knife on the counter. She'd let him hold her? She'd hold him? "I hope so." His voice broke again.

Except, did she mean a harmless side hug or . . .

She opened her arms and he mirrored her, still unsure, until she walked right into his chest and pressed her cheek to his T-shirt. Her arms went behind him, tight. He wrapped her up and closed his eyes, his breaths coming shallow again. She had a front-row seat for the race his heart now galloped.

Oh, she smelled good. And she still fit. Right here. Close. *Miki.*

"I'm glad," she said. "I'm really glad we're friends."

CHAPTER TWENTY-THREE

Friends. Okay. Well, friends cleared the air. He eased back, grabbed the milk carton, and caught her hand. "C'mere."

She followed him out to the back deck, fudge in hand.

He pointed. "Have a seat."

They hadn't addressed her comment about them breaking up that summer. It was time.

Twelve Years Ago

He'd never dreaded the end of summer more. Never dreaded seeing Miki before. But today he had to let her go. And she probably had no idea. She'd gleefully worn the ring all summer.

He'd already procrastinated all week, and all day. Now, her ferry left in twenty minutes. He sat in her car with her, in the parking/loading area, wishing he could hold her because he knew this was going to hurt. Both of them.

"I can't believe it"—her face shone like the ring on her left hand—"I'm going to U of Sea! Or at least Dr. Wren assured me I'd get in. She's got some volunteer opps in marine animal rescue that I can do during my off hours, when I'm not working or studying or in classes. And I can observe and work up to actual hands-on rescue—"

"Miki." Ugh. His voice already sounded strained, like sandpaper over the hull of a wooden boat in dry dock.

She stilled. "What happened?"

Sometimes love set you free. But not yet. He took her hand. "I want you to know I support you." He tried to smile, but his throat felt raw and his face didn't feel right.

"I hate that we'll be apart, even summer quarter. That's when the U does most of the research trips." She spoke fast. Had she guessed? Was she trying to keep him from finishing his thoughts?

He nodded. "I know." *Just say it, Cahill.*

"But it's comforting to know you'll wait for me, Hunt. Having your support—"

He gently squeezed her hand. "Miki."

"Yeah?"

"I can't . . . I mean, I won't 'wait'." Tears burned his eyes and he didn't want to make eye contact with her, let her see that pain. But he wouldn't avoid her gaze. Not now. Because for the moment, she was still here. These were their last seconds, and he wouldn't miss this chance for a connection.

Her brow wrinkled. "What?" She tried to pull back her hand, but he held on gently.

Oncoming cars zipped up the hill adjacent to them, offloading from the boat. Soon, the ferry workers would direct these waiting vehicles to load on the outgoing vessel. Only a few moments more.

"What do you mean, you won't wait? It's not like I'll never see you. And I won't be in college forever—a few years." She paused. Did she hear herself? "Okay, that sounds like forever. I can see that. But . . . we're engaged." She held up her left hand as if he could forget.

Foolishness since neither of them knew the future. He should speak now. But no words formed. He rubbed her knuckles. "I'm sorry."

Tears pooled in her eyes as she glanced between him and the ferry workers who directed traffic. They'd call for her lane soon.

Courage, Cahill. He was doing this for her, and there was nothing he wouldn't give her. "Listen," he said, trying to smile, though he felt like there were knives in his stomach. "You'll meet tons of new people. You'll be gone for who knows how long, especially if you go on for your doctorate." He gulped oxygen. "I couldn't ask you to wait."

She covered his lips with her finger. "Hunt, of course I'll wait. This is my dream. But you're my future."

He shook his head. "I'm sorry," he repeated, hating hurting

her—that tremble in her lips, the scrunched brow. The ache he felt from here. "Really sorry."

The night before, as he'd kissed her when he'd dropped her off at her family's cottage, he'd savored those seconds more than any other time with her. He would always remember her fingers in the hair at the back of his neck. The way she tasted of chocolate and marshmallows from the fire pit s'mores.

He couldn't kiss her now, and it killed him. He was releasing her to her future. No ties. That way, if she decided she needed to move to Timbuktu to be happy, she could. He'd never leave this island, but that didn't mean she had to be tied here. He wouldn't hold her to a promise she'd made before this college thing came up.

"I want to stay friends, though." He squeezed her hand again, opening his door with his other hand. "I'll miss you." Hopefully, after college, she'd be back. *Please, God.*

Her chin trembled. "I can't believe this. Was I selfish? Self-absorbed? I love you, Hunt."

The ferry workers started on the left-most lanes. Miki's car sat dead center. She'd have to start her engine soon, prepare to follow the stream of vehicles aboard.

Hunter kissed the back of her hand. "Goodbye, Miki." The knives gouged deeper. He stood from the car and forced his feet away, though she called his name. She couldn't abandon her vehicle and leave the ferry lanes. Moments later, her little car became part of the stream. He faced away again. *Don't look back. Set her free.* She had four to eight years of school ahead of her. He wouldn't stand in the way. But had he said that? Had he explained well enough? Probably not. Not with all the gravel in his throat and those knives in his gut.

She'd meet new people. But for him, there'd never be anyone else.

Present Day

What was Hunter gearing up for? He'd told her to have a seat and then went all pensive while he built a small fire in the fire pit on his deck. She gave up waiting for him to say something and worked to clear the rest of their dinner mess while she nibbled on the fudge. At one point, she found a sweatshirt on the back of his dining room chair and gestured to him through the glass slider about whether he minded if she grabbed it for herself. He nodded, that tender look in his eyes she'd missed. A look she could get used to seeing. A look that said he'd give her anything she wanted.

As she passed by, she held a square of fudge out to him, but both of his hands were busy in the wood and dirt of building the fire. He eyed her hand and her face again. Oops. She'd have to feed it to him, or risk teasing him. Did friends feed each other? *Don't think about it.* When he opened his mouth, she held the chunk to his lips. He bit off a piece, his mouth closing around it as his eyes fluttered shut. Her heart thumped.

That expression remained as he swallowed. "Thanks." He met her gaze once again and then went back to work. She popped the rest of the square into her mouth. Ugh! Could she send any more mixed signals? May as well put her necklace back on and showcase it over his sweatshirt with a spotlight and hand gestures.

She made herself sit in one of the Adirondack chairs and calm her pounding heart. His scent rose around her from the shirt she wore, which she hugged. If she'd been uncertain before, he'd made himself clear—next time he wouldn't turn his face. Whoo . . .

Once the fire was going, he fidgeted. When he shifted back toward the slider, she reached for his hand. "Sit." *Friends.* She let go. "What's up?"

"I was going to grab you a blanket. Want one?"

Her legs were chilled in this summer dress, but her layered core—her thin sweater covered in his sweatshirt—helped. Plus, she didn't want him to go anywhere else. "No, thanks."

He settled in the adjacent chair. "Whatcha thinking about, Miki?" His eyes shone from their earlier moments inside, the lashes still damp.

She didn't mind the nickname tonight. Tonight, it felt right. "A few things." Friends didn't discuss how much they liked the other person's scent. "You first." She curled toward the side, tucking her legs under her, leaning on the chair's left arm. "You have my attention."

"You look good in that."

She smiled. She felt good in it. "Spill it, Cahill."

He chuckled. "I was remembering when we broke up." His voice sounded gentle.

She gulped. This is what he wanted to talk about?

"You look good *here*." He gestured around them at the deck, the bay, the house.

She started to stand, to refuse this topic.

He tilted his head and locked eyes with her. *Don't you want answers?*

Should she simply blurt out her honest thoughts? If not then, when? "If you wanted me here, you wouldn't have sent me away." Hurt, like disturbed sediment, rose to the surface, swirling into muddy eddies. But she wouldn't ask for an explanation. For some reason, she couldn't bury her pride enough to come out and say, "Why did you reject me?" Even forming that question in her spinning thoughts made her wince. She turned her face away so he wouldn't see.

He leaned toward her. "I did not send you away."

Her gaze shot back. "Of course you did!"

That same head tilt as he settled his forearms on his thighs. *Are you sure?*

Fine. "You didn't try to stop me." She crossed her arms over her chest.

"You wanted me to try and stop you? From chasing your dreams? Getting your degree?"

"Of course not." Wood smoke swirled upward, carrying tiny, short-lived sparks toward the sky. Apparently, petulance could still override her other determinations. The biggest question, since he obviously didn't see things the same way, was: had she been wrong all these years?

No. "You weren't willing to wait!" She hadn't managed to keep the hurt from her voice.

"Twelve years? And back then I hoped it might be half that long." He grabbed a huffed breath. "You're all about science, *Dr. Rhoades*. Where is the logic in waiting twelve years?"

All those words but all she heard was: *You're not worth the wait.* Her heart clenched tight. She stood and paced to the farthest part of the deck. Hadn't she gotten past this? How could a decade-old rejection still torment her this much? Her throat burned. Crazy, because she couldn't reverse course now and start planning their wedding.

His footsteps tapped behind her, the wooden deck boards jostling as the sky turned navy blue. He stopped close, but didn't touch her. "I'm sorry if you felt like I rejected you."

No words lined up, so she stayed silent. He'd figured it out. Her eyes burned now, like her throat.

"I wasn't rejecting you." His warm hand landed on her chilled shoulder. "I was trying to give you your freedom."

"We were engaged." Right now, she knew they couldn't go back. But digging into this murky tide pool made her second-guess her past, her decisions, her perspective.

His hands closed over her upper arms. She didn't move away. Now that they were having this conversation, may as well get it all out. Maybe closure would clear up her mixed feelings. Help her move on. She'd put away her necklace and move to Hawaii without always wondering.

"I loved you, Miki." His breath fanned the back of her neck.

Her lungs locked tight, but her heart thumped.

"I didn't mean to hurt you. But who knew if there'd be other guys? Some Captain Stupid out there on the high seas."

Digging deep, she found a drop of courage and straightened her shoulders. Their breakup had, ironically, protected him best. Acting all lovesick and hurt now would only confuse him. She stuffed her pain and grasped her dignity. Pulling away from his touch, she turned toward him and leaned against the deck railing. A few feet separated them again. Good. "Captain Stupid?"

He went still. "It killed me there might be other guys."

Seeing all that vulnerable honesty in his open expression, she couldn't coldly disregard his obvious question. She'd put him at ease. "There weren't." *Nope, only lonely years of me pursuing my dreams . . . alone.*

He seemed to sigh in relief. How long had he worried about that? Maybe Granny hadn't kept him updated. But she would figure out how to forgive him. And she'd leave it at that. For good.

Except, did he mean . . . ? "You saw yourself as doing a noble thing." That changed things.

He grunted, rubbed the back of his neck. "A noble, heart-wrenching, foolish thing."

What's this? He didn't agree with his teenaged self? "Why foolish?"

"Because I wanted us married, Miki." He took one step forward. "In case you didn't notice, I *did* wait. Twelve years."

She gulped at his implications. So he hadn't been serious with anyone else all this time. Firelight glinted off his gray eyes and she wanted to dive in, just for tonight.

He studied her intently. Was he afraid she'd bolt? She should. "I wanted us married then," he said and his vocal words went silent. But his unspoken words . . .

No. No, no, no. They couldn't go in that direction. Not again.

Perhaps he was okay with her letting that news settle in, because he drew a deep breath to continue. "I want to know why you never came back."

"I did. But I . . . hid from you. Like you guessed." *I'm sorry.*

"Why?" Such pain in his eyes, his voice.

"Pride. Fear. Secrets." Oh, she shouldn't have said that. "I need to go." Hugging his sweatshirt around herself, she marched off the deck and into the yard where she could retrace her steps around the house and slog back to her solitary life.

Business meeting adjourned.

CHAPTER TWENTY-FOUR

All weekend, Miki couldn't sleep thinking about Hunter's words—what he'd said about her kissing him, after her swim in the strait, and in the future. Just that thought, and all the tension during the evening . . . Whoo. He'd wrapped her up so tightly in his arms, and she'd slipped back to those days so long ago. So much acceptance, as if all her why-nots wouldn't—couldn't—hold him back. Not that he knew what all those were, of course.

But Shea knew some of them, and she'd be here today.

When Mikaela thought about Hunter, she sensed God might be working in some way, but she couldn't see through the fog to understand. Her mind kept circling back to her secrets. Whole conversations ran through her head: Granny telling her Hunter wanted her for her. Shea telling her to *tell him* already. Hunter opening his arms . . .

No wonder she couldn't sleep.

Today, Hunter and she would have off-the-clock time together at Granny's with Lauren and Shea in attendance. All of them matchmakers, including Hunter now. She was outnumbered and surrounded, and the way her resolve—to keep her secrets and keep her distance—kept wavering, half of *her* had joined them too!

Originally, her best friend, Jenna-Shea, was due the previous Friday, but she'd had to work. So here it was the Fourth of July and Shea would soon arrive. The ferry had pulled in moments ago, the workers tying it off and preparing to let vehicle traffic exit. But first, the pedestrians.

Mikaela waved at Shea amid the sea of walk-off passengers marching onto Front Street. Her friend's long, light-brown hair cascaded down her shoulders. Nearby, two twenty-something guys watched her as they tripped up the road. Of course they did. Shea was gorgeous. And gracious. She wore a navy-blue jumper with a flowing white sleeveless sweater and simple accessories on her wrist and around her neck. Her tanned legs went on forever, given her height, and she wore an anklet above her left sandal. She carried an overnight bag and rushed up to Mikaela. "Hey, Miks! I made it."

"I'm so glad you're here." Mikaela gave her a hug. "I've missed you." Maybe Shea could help her figure out her life. Affirm her choice to protect everyone at her own expense. Who was she kidding? Her psychologist friend would shred her choices, explaining the consequences as she peeled away the reasons.

Shea pulled back, but grabbed Mikaela's shoulders, studying her. People marched toward the shops and marina around them, but Shea didn't let that stop her from taking her time with her inspection. "Something's up."

Mikaela squirmed under her BFF's scrutiny. "I'm certain you can analyze it out of me." With Shea, Mikaela could simply be Miks. She didn't have to be Dr. Rhoades, or Professor, or leader, or program administrator. Or Miki. She could be a gal out with her best friend. How she needed this.

Shea grinned and nodded, taking her place beside Mikaela. "I'll have you fixed up in no time." She hooked an arm through Mikaela's. "Lead on."

"My car's parked up the hill, behind Granny's Fudge Shoppe."

"Our first stop!" She had the tiniest of figures, but Shea knew how to enjoy her fudge.

"We can put your stuff in my trunk and then we're right there for the parade."

They moved toward Spring Street. Shea peeked behind them, as if she could see Cahill's offices from here. "No sign of Hunter this morning?"

Mikaela shook her head, but she couldn't dislodge the teasing in her friend's voice. "We have the day off from tours because it's Monday. That is until your family's private charter this afternoon. We need to be back at the marina after brunch for the sail up to Bellingham to pick up your family."

"My brother and his wife are really excited. They're bringing Jaxon—he's thrilled. And, of course, my parents."

Mikaela hadn't seen Shea's family in a long while. She looked forward to spending the afternoon and evening with them. Shea's clan had been to the Rhoades down in Seattle what the Cahills had been for the Rhoades during their summer trips up here.

After hoofing it up Spring Street, they approached Granny's gourmet candy store. "But first, some happenings at Granny's house. And a parade."

The shop was overrun with customers searching for treats. All the staff members were helping patrons and more lined up. Mikaela led the way into the shop's kitchen. "Granny, Jenna-Shea's here!" Everyone knew her by her first name, not as commonly by her hyphenated name. And only Shea's Seattle friends tended to call her Shea.

"Hi, Jenna! I've missed you." Granny Belle welcomed her.

Shea hugged her. "We only need a sample, and then we'll get out of your way."

Granny spun and reached for the white box on the butcher-block table. She'd known they were coming. "Here, this should fortify you for the parade."

"We'd better go find a spot. Your place for brunch afterward?" Mikaela asked her.

"You don't want to go to the Pig War Picnic this year?" Her grandmother's eyes sparkled with mischief. She knew Mikaela preferred fewer people and less chaos.

Mikaela shook her head. "Maybe next time." Not that she'd be here next year.

"I'm with Miks," Shea said. "Looking forward to visiting your place."

Granny's smile was warm. "Glad to have you."

At the doorway out of the kitchen, Mikaela studied the onslaught of fudge lovers. "Are you coming outside for the parade?" she asked her grandmother.

"Yes, if I can break away from here. I'll see you out there."

Would Hunter make it? He preferred less noisy places too. Some of the local touring businesses sponsored floats, but this year Cahill had decided against it due to cost. Mikaela had been ready to task her students to design and build it. As it turned out, they were going to ride the U of Sea lab's float.

Outside, Mikaela and Shea found a shady spot to hide away from the sun and settled on a towel on the ground. When more folks arrived, they'd probably have to stand to see, but for now, they had a good view of the street and a breezy place for a fudgy snack.

Shea reached for the box. "Hand it over."

"Hey! You don't trust me to slice it up fairly?" She winked, relinquishing the box.

"You know you get stingy with the goods." Shea set to work, very focused on the plastic knife. "What time is it?"

"Fifteen minutes to show time."

"Where's your fiancé?"

Mikaela gasped but tried to cover her reaction by clearing her throat. Shea knew they weren't together—hadn't been together for over a decade. And of course she was only teasing, but her words were a startling reminder of all Mikaela had lost all those years ago with her doctor's words. A diagnosis even Shea didn't know about.

Shea's hand appeared in Mikaela's line of blurring vision. She grabbed her knee. "Kidding, honey. Kid-ding."

Breathe. "Right. I know." She blinked fast. Normally the pain of her sacrifice, of the regrets of her decisions, didn't interfere with Mikaela's plans. She carried on, determined to build as good a future as she could. But with Hunter back in her life, holding her. Tempting her. Yeah, those sacrifices were harsher than ever.

The memory of his positive traits, the ones she loved about him, had faded during her years away. His chivalry, thoughtfulness, kindness. His heroic measures to help others and sacrifice his comforts for their good. Like, how he was working so hard to help his mom, to honor his dad. Mikaela had seen Cahill's schedule, and Hunter was gearing up to offer back-to-back charters during any off time he had from the tours and/or Mikaela's students' dives for most of the summer.

"Hey, Miks." Shea gave her that psychoanalyst look again, paired with so much disarming compassion. "What's going on?"

"I found you!" Lauren Cahill burst through the growing crowd, camping chair strap slung over her shoulder.

We should have brought chairs. Already, sitting on the ground was starting to hurt, due to the rocks and protruding roots. Maybe she had time to go inside the fudge shop and grab a couple of folding chairs. "Hi, Lauren. Join us." *Please, and keep me from having to answer the ever-insightful Shea. Fixed up in no time, indeed.* "You remember Jenna-Shea?"

"Of course," Hunter's mom said, waving since Shea was still parked on the ground and out of reach. "Good to see you again, Jenna." She got to work unwrapping and unfolding her blue chair. "Are the students joining us?"

"No, they'll be on the lab's float." Although, she didn't know where Pierce might end up. "It's a giant sea urchin design."

Lauren settled next to Mikaela. "I feel badly for sitting up here when you're on the ground." She started to stand.

"Oh, no. Please. I'll be on my feet for most of the parade anyway. Thanks, though."

"Oh, here comes help." Lauren's face glowed with a mother's pride, and Mikaela followed her gaze. *Hunter.* He hiked the hill, wearing his touring business uniform—Dockers and this time a navy polo with their logo. He'd be on duty later today.

Her breath hitched again.

Shea leaned in. "I heard that." She stood, brushing off the seat of her jumper. Mikaela stood too, and Shea leaned in once more as Hunter was still about thirty feet off. "He looks good," she said out of the corner of her mouth.

"Shush."

Hunter arrived, carrying three camping chairs. He stopped in front of her and offered her the most amazing, unguarded smile. He tipped his head toward her towel, which had failed to provide a comfy spot. "I had a feeling."

"Life saver!" Shea gushed. "Good to see you again, Hunt."

Hunt. Even Mikaela hadn't started calling him that again. Might send the wrong message. But now, hearing Shea say it, jealousy burrowed through her heart. Ugh. Here she was, trying to have opposing goals. She couldn't both have *Hunt* and not have him.

She reached for her pendant around her neck but then remembered—the necklace had disappeared. No doubt she'd find it on the floor next to her dresser in the cottage. She'd have to look tonight.

He unwrapped and unfolded two of the chairs and offered them in turn to Mikaela and Shea. "Hey, Mom. Where's Bailey?" Bailey was their family dog. They'd gotten him at six weeks old right before Hunter's graduation, and he'd often joined them for the holiday parade.

"You still have him?" Mikaela hadn't thought of him in years.

"Yeah, but he's been acting strange. I asked our vet about him, and she said he might be going blind. I'm supposed to watch him closely."

"Aw," Shea said.

"Oh, no." Compassion softened her insides, both for Bailey and for Lauren. Hunter's mom didn't need anything happening to her beloved pet this close to Reid's death.

Death. She had tried not to think about the boating accident, about Granddad, about today's anniversary. She would get through this day without going there. She would. There was no reason to bring it up and spoil Hunter's mood, or anyone else's.

They all settled into their canvas chairs, and then Hunter looked around. Funny how he'd set his chair between Lauren's and Mikaela's. They lined up in a row, facing the street, awaiting the start to the parade. "Granny coming?"

"The shop was packed," Mikaela said. "Here's hoping."

"There she is." Hunter jumped up, darting toward the shop to usher Granny into the group.

"I raised that boy right," Lauren said, nodding.

"Yes, you did." Shea elbowed Mikaela who grunted.

Hunter offered his arm and Granny accepted, smiling up at him as if he were a knight. In the distance, the marching band played their pep song. Hunter got Granny settled into his chair and stood on the other side of his mother. Gallant. Chivalrous. Noble.

He'd thought breaking up with her was noble. Setting her free to go find, what had he said, "Captain Stupid"? If she looked at their breakup as a means of letting her choose her future—this island or anywhere in the world—she couldn't remain angry at Hunter for how he'd ended things. In that light, she saw his kindness. And if the exchanges he kept having with her right now—glimpses of that open smile, those shining eyes—were any indication, he'd sacrificed a lot letting her go.

Shoot, but that fact could draw her right back to him.

Everyone chatted, watching for activity. The leaders and marching band should appear soon. Mikaela focused on the route, hoping her students would represent the U of Sea well.

There was Shea's elbow again.

"Girl." Mikaela scowled in her direction. "If you do that one more time . . ." What were they, teenagers?

Shea gave her a look. *We are gonna talk later.*

I'm sure we are.

Snare drum beats echoed off the buildings lining Spring Street, giving an off-beat resonance in town while the crowds cheered. Fitting. Keeping up her façade and distance were wearing on Mikaela. What she needed was a relaxing day to simply enjoy her time with her family and friends. She pulled out her phone and snapped shots of the parade as the floats went by. Shea took a couple of pics as well. They posed for selfies, getting Granny and Lauren into some shots. At one point, they stood and Hunter stepped up behind them as they clicked a selfie—photobombing. Then, Shea asked for a shot of both Hunter and Mikaela together.

He obliged right away, stepping up to her, bringing his clean scent with him. He wrapped an arm around behind her for a side hug, and she caught his warm smile. So much for keeping her distance.

"Get closer together," Shea called over the cheering crowd as another float approached.

Mikaela swallowed but allowed Hunter to tug her toward him, his warm hand at her side. Yeah, she'd kill Shea later. Or she'd tell her everything. Shea only knew half the story. It was time for a heart-to-heart.

The lab's float appeared, and phone in hand—and quite out of character for him—Hunter directed a reverse stance so they could get a selfie with the slow-moving giant sea urchin in the background. Their smiling faces, once Mikaela wiped away her surprise, flashed large and close in his screen. *Click.* The students hooted and somebody whistled, but Mikaela hoped it was all in good fun as she spun and waved at her students and the other lab faculty and students on board. The sea urchin shape bulged on either side with students poking out of the round top.

"Looking good!" She encouraged, and though she couldn't make out everyone in the huddle of people, she hoped Pierce was obeying orders and was somewhere on that truck.

This year, one of the florists' floats came through offering carnations for a small fee. Hunter ran up and quickly paid for several. Then, he returned and handed one first to his mother, then Granny, then Shea, and finally Mikaela. Was he trying to convince Shea they were together? He was only proving her insinuation by all this attention. Not that Mikaela minded. Perhaps she should treat today like she'd treated their first "business" meeting—give herself permission to relax and enjoy the day.

After the parade, Hunter volunteered to haul the chairs to his truck and pick up Granny Belle and his mom on his way back through. Shea and Mikaela would take her car out to Granny's, which meant she'd have alone time with her bestie.

Maybe she'd stop ribbing Mikaela every time Hunter acted, well, like Hunter had started acting lately—attentive, affectionate. Determined.

As if he were on some sort of mission.

CHAPTER TWENTY-FIVE

Shea tossed her long light-brown hair over her shoulder. "I'd forgotten how cute you two are together. No, wait. That's not the right word. It's more like *perfect*." She stood next to Mikaela in the kitchen, dicing dill pickles for the potato salad. Sunlight glinted off the bay outside, shooting a wavy, moving reflection onto Granny's kitchen ceiling. A peaceful sight. Mikaela could watch it for hours. As a child, she'd spent long minutes doing exactly that this time of day during the summer.

She looked around for any sign of Hunter or Lauren. No one yet. They were all still outside, at the table, setting up their picnic, talking and chuckling and hopefully not overhearing through the open window. If she knew Hunter, he was turning chairs over and checking for spiders. She elbowed her best friend this time. "I am going to send you home on the next ferry if you don't let up." She couldn't stay mad, though. Not at Shea.

"Seriously, what's the problem?" she teased. "Have you seen that look in his eyes? *I* was undone, and he's not even aiming that dreamy expression at me."

Mikaela scanned her memory. What was the name of the guy from Jenna-Shea's past? Oh, yeah. "Liam."

Shea tipped her knife toward Mikaela's side of the kitchen island. "Don't you dare."

She resumed her chopping, the knife *thwack*ing the cutting board in time. "You're on thin ice now, Dr. Rhoades. Thin. Ice."

Mikaela leaned forward. "What you need," she whispered, "is some time together—a whole season of nothing but Liam with *that* look in his eye."

"Okay, okay. I give up. Sheesh!"

Finally. Silence.

That tipping knife again. "But I still want answers."

Mikaela grabbed the tray of plates, napkins, plastic ware, and tumblers and moved toward the slider. "Mm-hmm. I know." They needed a few uninterrupted hours.

Granny sat in the chair Hunter held. "Thank you, young man."

"Can I get you anything?" Sure, this was her house, but he'd help where he could.

Her blue eyes glinted up at him in the filtered sunlight of late morning—the trees near the water providing the filter. "I think it's all out here."

Mom sat next to Shea, leaving two chairs open, side by side—one for him, one for Miki. But Miki moved around to the other side. "Do you mind, Shea? You have your sunglasses, and I don't want to get a headache from squinting."

She was back to avoiding him. He'd hoped that after he explained his reasons for letting her go, she'd understand and no longer hold their past against him. But she'd gotten skittish again. Of course she had her obligations, but the chairwoman had hinted the future wasn't as locked up as Miki always implied it was.

And Jenna-Shea. She was giving Miki such a hard time today, which only made Hunter fight a grin. If anyone could figure out Miki's hang-up and help her get past it, it was her best friend.

He hoped.

Flashbacks from their first meeting kept him up at night. She'd fed him fudge, and he'd wanted to lick the chocolate off her fingers. She'd let him hold her in the kitchen, shared how she'd hated missing Dad's funeral. And—smart or not—he'd put his heart out there. But then she mentioned secrets. What secrets?

"Okay." Jenna agreed with Miki's request and scooted toward the seat next to his. She didn't flirt, but she was playful. A fun best friend to Miki since she needed to loosen up. Jenna's parents were loaded and occasionally chartered boats, sailing up from Seattle, dropping off their daughter back in the day, visiting for a short time with Miki's mom and dad, and then sailing off. The only downside had been he'd seen less of Miki when Jenna was on the island because they'd been inseparable. Would that happen on today's charter?

"Jenna, it means a lot to me that your parents hired Cahill for their tour today." Back when they were younger, the Browns hired a Seattle-based operation. Had Shea put in a good word for Cahill? Had Miki?

"We're excited." Next to him, Jenna spread a napkin over her lap, all gracious poise. Across from him, Miki seemed more uncomfortable than she may have been beside him. He didn't mind. This way, he could watch her face, see her flush. He checked another grin.

"They wanted someone to show them whales, and we knew you were the one."

"Since we have several hours, and we're starting in B-ham, we'll have a good chance of locating them. Might even happen on a super pod." He hoped, because having the Browns as repeat customers would help his business. They could write online reviews for him and hopefully refer their well-to-do friends.

"Or minkes." This from Miki who passed potato salad to Granny.

"Oh, that's right," Jenna said. "Your favorite."

He hadn't forgotten. That gave him an idea.

Jenna-Shea's phone buzzed somewhere under the table— probably her pocket. "Oh, I'm sorry. I meant to leave my cell in my bag." She tugged out her phone and read the screen. "Uh-oh." She stood. "I've got a few missed texts, and now my dad's calling. I'll be right back." She excused herself and skipped down the deck stairs toward the lawn. "Hello?" she said, her voice fading as she strode away from the group.

"What do you suppose that's all about?" Miki shifted in her seat, turning toward the table after watching Shea's exit. "I hope everyone's okay."

A breeze blew Granny's wind chimes and rustled small waves out in the bay where white sails dotted the blue seascape. Hunter drew in a deep breath, his fried chicken cooling on his plate. Being here with Miki, her family, and his mom felt right. He didn't deserve a day like this—a morning off. An expensive charter booked for this afternoon with Shea's family. His business picking up. He didn't deserve hope. Maybe that warden wasn't a beast after all. Maybe hope was about to come through on all her promises so he could be free from her prison.

"I love this moment." Mom, who sat at the end of the table, agreed with his thoughts as if she knew them. "The weather, the friends, and family. It's lovely." She raised her glass. "To all of you." She tipped her head toward where Jenna stood on the lawn, down by the dock. "And to Jenna."

Everyone lifted their glasses. "To being together."

A few minutes later Jenna clicked up the steps in her sandals, phone now clutched at her side. "Oh, guys. Bad news."

"What happened?" Miki turned in her swivel chair.

"My little nephew has appendicitis. They're rushing him in for surgery. My parents are staying close to my brother and his wife, which means," she continued, sucking in a deep breath as she took her seat again, "we're not going on a charter this afternoon."

Hunter's gut sank, and he felt his smile and optimism fade. No charter, no afternoon income. Sure he had other private clients lined up in the next few weeks, but he charged extra for holidays, and Shea's family had been happy to add catering and extended hours—the works. Now what? He'd been counting on their charter to help make July's payroll. Plus, he was on the hook for the caterers.

"I'm sorry, Hunter. Miks." Jenna-Shea nodded at each of them. "My dad said to keep the payment. They feel really badly for canceling at the last minute."

Hunter shook his head, mirroring his mother on his right. "No, we'll refund him. You can't anticipate something like emergency surgery." But how would he pay the caterer?

"Hunter's right." Mom didn't quite check a sigh. "I hope he'll be okay."

When Hunter's brother, Jonah, had been a small child, he'd had a serious scare with appendicitis. One Hunter remembered too well. His mother did too, no doubt.

"But it's too late for you to schedule anyone else. We took the holiday slot and then didn't show up, as it were." Jenna's brow wrinkled. "I feel awful for the lost income."

Granny watched everyone and then offered a long exhale. "Listen, I know this was unexpected, but sometimes blessings come from unexpected things. Like Mikaela being here this summer. Some of us didn't expect that." Warmth glinted in her eyes as she attempted to change the subject.

He'd play along, for a moment. Granny was right. Hunter hadn't expected Miki to be here this summer, thanks to, "Mom..." He drew out his mother's name, and she blushed.

"Guilty."

Miki pursed her lips, which did nothing to hide her smile, and lowered her head.

"And you weren't much help with that secret either, Doc," Hunter accused, loving the way her grin grew on her darkening face.

She met his eyes. "Hey, I wasn't keeping it a secret." She shrugged.

"Dr. *M.*" Hunter's eyes went back to Mom.

"Yup, guilty again," Mom conceded.

Jenna laughed. "Well, I think it's hilarious and so like God to let the unexpected bring something good." She gave a pointed look to Miki that Hunter didn't miss. All these matchmakers. Except he didn't want to trap her. He wanted to woo her.

"So, since we have the whole day off, let's take our own boat out and go have fun!" Granny said.

For the second time, Hunter's gut clenched. *Did she mean...?*

"You mean"—Miki gulped—"the *Isabelle*?"

"Of course, why not? I know it still runs well because Hank was over here the other day checking on it."

"He was?" Hunter had waited too long. "Did he ask to borrow it?"

"Nah, he said you had one for him. But if *you* need to borrow it, Hunt, please, please do."

He blinked against the sudden burning behind his eyes. Fifteen years ago today. Across the table, Miki's smile vanished and she met his gaze. She got it.

"Would you mind taking us out on her this afternoon?" Granny's voice had gone soft, emotional, and Hunter felt his heart crack open.

He faced her. "It would be an honor." His voice broke on the last word. That tell-tale burning in his nose sent him scrambling to stand and bolt away from the table. Somehow, thinking of Ben brought up thoughts of Dad, and this was the first Fourth without him.

Once he collected himself, he had a call to make to the caterers.

And somehow, he'd take this group out on the *Isabelle* today. For now, he'd better go see for himself how she looked. He hadn't come face-to-hull with her for a long, long time.

CHAPTER TWENTY-SIX

"Do you think he'll be okay?" Shea all but wrung her hands. For a trained psychoanalyst, she wasn't hiding her angst very well. "I feel responsible."

Mikaela's own heart squeezed. Granny mentioning her boat. Hunter bailing on their brunch. The loss of income. Jaxon's appendicitis. She wouldn't answer, though. She'd let Lauren chime in. She was no longer a spokesperson for him. She'd given up that right for the sake of protecting him.

"He'll be fine." But the way Lauren studied his receding form showed her own concern.

"Oh, it's the boat," Granny said, twisting each ring in turn. "I don't think he's seen it since that day when we put it away in the garage." She didn't mention Granddad, which took courage. But she also didn't mention Reid, which Mikaela thought was merciful.

Lauren glanced at each of them before reaching for her napkin and dabbing her eyes. "I think God's bringing up some things that Hunter needs to deal with, but it's not easy."

No. It wasn't. God was doing the same thing in Mikaela's life, and she didn't like it. They'd gone all this time without going there, but apparently you only got a free pass for so long.

Lauren faced her. "Could you check on him? I have a feeling you'll be more of a comfort than I will right now."

"Of course." Friends comforted friends. Mikaela pushed back her chair and stood. Maybe thinking about her grandfather made him miss his dad? If taking out the *Isabelle* wasn't such a good idea, they should go get *Cahill's Prize* instead. Except, Granny had been the one to suggest her boat. Maybe she felt there'd be healing in the journey for both their families on this anniversary.

Mikaela marched across the lawn, toward the large garage bay. Hunter had already raised the door and now stood there, gazing up at the boat, which sat on a trailer and towered above him—all white and blue hull, in glossy paint.

The breath was sucked from her lungs, and her stride lurched.

The *Isabelle*. The past. Granddad. Yeah, she'd ask Granny if they could change the plan. Mikaela hadn't gotten emotional about Reid's boat. But seeing Granddad's was like seeing his favorite fishing hat or that black vest he used to wear most of the time. Heaviness covered her. She could almost smell him, see his cheerful smile.

"It's smaller than I remember." Hunter's voice sounded scratchy, raw. Pained. Like when they'd talked about his father in his kitchen that night.

She inched closer. *Be a friend.*

The boat didn't look small to her. The high-hulled cabin cruiser loomed before them as she joined Hunter. "It's been a while." Her raw voice matched his.

"Fifteen years today." His head bobbed in successive nods as if the gesture could chase away the emotion of his words. But Granddad hadn't been his relation, not that Hunter hadn't loved him. Was this about Reid?

She still hadn't looked directly at Hunter—couldn't tear her eyes off the *Isabelle*. "I was hoping we could get through the day without reliving it, or remembering it. I'd rather no one hurt today."

He offered her his gaze and seeing him turn, she met it. Nodded. *Me too,* he seemed to say. "But for Granny, I'll do it." He rubbed his chin, and she knew he was barely keeping his emotions in check. On this side of the house, no one could see them. Still he had a thing about keeping himself together, audience or not.

She touched his arm. "I know this is hard. I'm sorry. If you need a shoulder, this friend has two." She pointed at herself and gave him a wobbly smile.

"Friends offer their shoulders too?"

"Yes. Yes, they do."

He reached for her and she moved close, letting him hold her to his side. She nestled against *his* shoulder as if her face were meant to be there. He smelled of sunscreen and Granny's grill where he'd prepped the hotdogs earlier. Something so right about fitting together with him here. He kissed the top of her head, and she held her breath. Though the gesture could be brotherly, she took it as very intimate. The most intimate gesture between them this summer so far. Well, the only one she'd been lucid for.

"Thanks, Miki," he whispered.

She'd let the nickname slide as usual lately. But the kiss? "Was that for old time's sake?" She didn't need any reminders. Not when her heart threw flashbacks into her mind's eye repeatedly lately—dreams, memories, pulse-sparking images of kissing him as a teen. Funny how he'd recently asked her about flashbacks.

"Nope." She could hear the grin in his voice but didn't dare pull back enough to look him in the eye. Why had she asked about his innocent kiss? "It's payment."

She did pull back then. What was he up to? "For what?"

His fingers squeezed her side in a playful way. "You kissed my face when I rescued you, right?" His voice went all tender and gentle. "Well"—he swallowed—"you just rescued me."

Not that she minded him kissing her head. But, if he ever moved around to her face, she'd be in trouble.

"Unless you wanted me to kiss your face."

Standing this close, he could. All he'd have to do is lean down a little. She stepped back. "Is that what friends do?"

He pocketed his hands. "Maybe not." His voice sounded stronger now, like their conversation had strengthened him. Perhaps this outing could work. Maybe all of them could face this anniversary and survive, simply by being together through it.

And maybe she could convince herself she *didn't* want Hunter to kiss her, on any part of her head.

When Mikaela returned to the group, Granny and Lauren had packed up a pile of food to take aboard, which they wheeled toward the garage on a wagon. After finishing a phone call, Hunter set to work backing his truck toward the trailer for transport to the water. No one doubted they'd follow through.

Shea was busily cleaning the table and deck from their meal. Mikaela joined her.

"How is he?" Shea asked, hooking a thumb in the captain's direction.

She reached for the half-empty bowl of baked beans. "Good. We're both good."

Shea studied her. "You sure?"

A breeze tried to carry a napkin away, but Mikaela swiped it up. "Yes. He merely needed a friendly hug."

"I'll bet."

Her teasing tone irritated Mikaela. "Let's talk later. Maybe find a quiet spot on the boat when the others are busy. I need to tell you something."

Shea touched Mikaela's arm. "Sorry, Miks. Did I offend you?"

She hugged her best friend. "Of course not. But I have a heavy secret that needs unpacking. With my BFF."

"Well, now I'm worried."

"Nah, don't be. I'm fine." They each grabbed the last few forks from the table. "And keep us all updated when you hear from your brother, okay?" Thoughts of the little boy's surgery kept flitting into Mikaela's mind.

"Definitely."

Granny's boat launch still worked for getting the *Isabelle* into the bay, at least at high tide. Thankfully the water level had cooperated. But they might have to moor in the harbor later if the tide receded too far.

At the wheel as they set off, Hunter looked like he'd always been there. He was doing a remarkable job of hiding any wayward emotions as he worked the controls and tuned the radio to hear the chatter of local tour guides who didn't take Mondays off, or who generally did, but who worked holidays.

"Think you can find us whales, Captain?" Granny, who was seated in the co-captain's chair, asked over the motor.

He gave her a smile. "That's what I do."

In the chair back on the left side, Lauren smiled. "That's why we named him Hunter."

Shea and Mikaela sat on a bench seat right inside the cabin. All around them, the windows provided a clear view and a wind shield.

"Oh, it all makes sense now," Shea offered. "And don't you have another son named Noah or...?"

"Jonah."

"Ha! Fitting." Shea laughed. "So you and Reid figured one of your sons would run the whale tour business one day?" Shea had such an easy way about her. Normally, Mikaela wouldn't be so forthright about bringing up Reid's name, but Shea's gentle, honoring approach worked and Lauren seemed to unfold from her tense posture of minutes before.

"We hoped." She smiled at her son's back.

"Well, you look good, Hunter. Like a born captain." Granny leaned back in the chair. She'd spent several hours sitting right there during her life on the island's waters with Granddad.

He took his eyes from the waterways for a moment. "Thank you, Granny Belle. And Mom." Mikaela caught something in his posture, as if their support buoyed him. He straightened his shoulders, then resumed working the controls.

They made their way out around Dinner Island and deeper into Griffin Bay.

"Hey, where's the commentary, Captain?" Shea teased him. "Where are we? What are we seeing?"

"Ah, it's going to be that kind of day, huh, Jenna?" But he didn't sound irritated.

"Yes, sir. The full treatment, if you please." Shea snorted. "And whales. Definitely."

Hunter chuckled too. "No problem. I'll simply give them a call."

"You may have to pay him for this 'full treatment,' Shea," Mikaela said. "I mean, you are asking a lot. Usually he has a naturalist announce everything."

"Well, you're trained. C'mere." Shea grabbed her and pointed toward Hunter. "Stand by him and announce everything, Dr. Rhoades."

"Highly overqualified," Lauren said, offering her an out.

"Better than *unqualified*," Granny put in and matched Shea in pointing Mikaela toward the captain.

No getting out of this now. "I'm on it. I'm on it." She shifted past

Shea, a smile on her face. "Sheesh, tough crowd."

Hunter wore a grin when she came up next to him. She parked herself beside him, her back to the front of the boat so she could see the group, but not the view straight ahead.

"Okay, Captain, whenever you need me to announce anything, say the word," she said to him. The noise of the boat and the wind would keep their quiet voices from being heard by the others, most likely. So, Hunter could signal to Mikaela and she could call out the news to the rest.

"Let's start by telling them where we are."

"Okay." She glanced around. "Okay, everyone. We're moving out into Griffin Bay. Straight ahead, we have Lopez Island." She leaned toward Hunter. "Any intel for wildlife sightings?"

He pointed toward the right and upward.

She peeked and announced, "Bald eagles circling off the starboard side."

He nodded toward the left.

She studied the skies. "And ospreys diving for fish on the port side."

Hunter chuckled.

She grinned and added, "Ospreys are also known as sea hawks, like this region's football champions." She scanned the glistening blues of the water on either side of the wake behind them. "If we keep our eyes peeled, we might see sea otters or seals. Or perhaps a sea lion thermoregulating."

Hunter snorted again. "Nice one, Prof."

"You like that?" she asked him quietly. "Watch this," she said, then turned toward the group, feeling herself relax. "Thermoregulation is the sea lion's way of regulating its body temperature by floating, belly up in the water, fore flippers open to the sunshine. Of course, they also do this on land." She grinned and tried to choke back her giggle over everyone's blank expressions as she continued. "The human body thermoregulates as well in order to maintain, or return to, homeostasis."

Hunter reached over and offered her a high five. She slapped his hand, and the others clapped their hands. She bowed. "Thank you. Thank you."

Granny was all grins. "You are a ham, dear. I'd forgotten."

She winked at her grandmother. "Are we having fun?" she asked the group. Happy nods followed. She elbowed Hunter. "We need to give these cheerful passengers a whale sighting, Captain," she said out of the corner of her mouth.

He seemed to fight a loud laugh. She obviously hadn't pushed hard enough because he didn't let it loose. She loved this back and forth. He was game. She was feeling more tranquil as she leaned against the side and kicked out her feet in front of her, crossing them at the ankles.

"Okay, while the captain is busily taking us out to the next exciting tourist attraction, let me tell you part of the history of San Juan Island."

Shea moaned. "I'd rather you not."

Mikaela knew she'd hate it, but she also felt like she had to keep things moving. And she liked provoking folks when she felt comfortable and relaxed. Something about this group, this day, this outing felt right. Absolutely right.

"Psst," Hunter met her eyes when she returned her attention to him.

"Yeah? You don't think we need a history lesson either?"

He nodded toward the front of the boat and raised his brows. "Would you like to tell our passengers what type of creatures those are, Dr. Rhoades?" He kept his voice low.

She scanned the water ahead and locked on creatures surfacing. Short, black dorsals, white streaks down their sides. The small animals moved like dolphins, swimming right alongside the boat. "Ladies, we have a treat for you," she said, sweeping her hand forward. "Please turn your attention to the Dall's porpoise accompanying us today."

The women crowded the plexiglass windows and *ooh*ed.

Mikaela tried to see the bow of the boat, but couldn't from here. "Think they're riding the bow wave?"

"Can't tell from here," Hunter said.

"Let's not mention it then." She didn't want anyone attempting to walk out onto the deck. When the porpoise had moved on and things had settled, she elbowed Hunter. "What else ya got?"

"I have a feeling . . ." He pulled the *Isabelle* in a wide arc to the right. Sure enough—payoff.

"Oh, what a treat! Look!" Mikaela gave up her stuffy naturalist impression and just pointed while everyone gathered to the windows. Hunter cut the engine, and their boat slowed.

"Orcas!" Shea shrieked, pulling out her phone.

Granny and Lauren were calmer, but they both wore big grins.

"You can head out onto the deck, but please be careful," Hunter said.

Mikaela's smile faded as she realized he was worried about a repeat event too. Her breath seized in her chest. Part of her wanted to demand everyone strap on a life vest, even though the waters were calm and the people on board were competent swimmers.

As the others moved out of the cabin and onto the deck, Granny Belle shifted closer to Hunter. "I'll stay here."

"Good thinking," Hunter said. "You already have a front-row seat."

Standing next to him, Granny Belle wrapped her arm around his side, and he returned the gesture. Mikaela watched for a moment before pulling out her phone for a pic. She loved how Hunter was part of her family. And she was a part of his, almost as if they still dated, or had married.

No. As if they were brother and sister.

Well, shoot. That didn't fit no matter what she told herself. Watching him navigate so skillfully, protective of Granny and the others . . . Mikaela's heart fell into a familiar rhythm. This was no sibling sort of reaction.

She shook off the thoughts and reached toward the bench where she pulled up the seat and located the life preservers and a couple of vests. If Lauren or Shea slipped and fell in, they'd have immediate help today.

The sea looked mostly calm, and the temperature was rising as any last trace of marine layer lifted away from the horizon. Shea and Lauren carefully maneuvered out on the perimeter, seeking handholds as they went. This thirty-six-foot cabin cruiser had a mostly level deck, complete with a cable railing. Mostly safe. As long as everyone was careful.

The *Isabelle* slowed to a near stop as the orcas continued playing in front of them. A pod of about five animals seemed content to show off for them. Transients.

"You going out there, or staying in here, Miki?" Hunter faced her, arm still around Granny on his left. If she stayed in here, she'd probably end up against Hunter's other side.

She hooked a thumb. "I'm going for a closer look."

Outside, she navigated around the deck, using the cable for support on the bobbing motorboat. Shea and Lauren were near the stern, and she joined them. Shea shot picture after picture with her cell phone.

"Is it normal for them to stay in one place?" Shea asked, her face lit up.

"I think they're showing off."

Lauren watched with a hand shielding her eyes. "I thought only dolphins did that."

"Same family. All whales—cetaceans."

"Thank you, Professor." Shea gave her *the look*.

Mikaela smirked at her. "What?"

Lauren reached for her arm. "Thanks for making today fun, Mikaela. I'm so grateful."

Indeed. Humor saved the afternoon. Mikaela rested her hand over Lauren's. "My pleasure."

She heard noise behind her and turned. Hunter made his way toward them on the deck. Mikaela peeked behind him into the cabin. Granny sat there, smiling. Content.

"Take a look over there." He pointed.

Mikaela studied him. "Did you drop anchor, or what?"

"We won't drift far. No worries. Calm seas."

Oh, right. The cable wouldn't reach the seafloor here. Too deep. Creepy deep. Down where six gills and wolf eels lived deep. Or giant Pacific octopus.

"Ooooh!" Shea squealed, pointing and aiming her phone. "What are those?"

"Sea otters," Hunter announced.

"We may never have to leave Griffin Bay, Captain Hunter." Mikaela clapped his shoulder. "Good work."

He grinned at her, something sort of stern around his eyes. "You are so asking for it."

She gave him an impish grin, twining her hands together against her front as if she were innocent.

"I'd still like to see gray whales, dear," Lauren said. "I'm always stuck in the office whenever you're out on tour. It's been a very long time." Her gaze went wistful.

"If it's grays you want, Mom, you'll have them." He marched toward the cabin. "C'mon in everyone, and we'll get underway," he called over his shoulder. "Dr. Rhoades, back to your post."

Was it a bad thing that giddiness shivered up her spine and motivated her steps to rush forward?

Friends hurried on request, right?

CHAPTER TWENTY-SEVEN

Later that night, as the sky was beginning to darken, Granny begged off the annual trek to the *Millennium's* deck where—unless they had a private charter booked—the Cahills and guests watched the fireworks, saying she was rather tired. Lauren stayed behind with her. On the Friday Harbor dock, Shea and Mikaela weaved through the waterfront crowds and approached the vessel. They'd have their own private place for viewing on board.

"We didn't get a chance to have our chat," Shea reminded Mikaela.

"You're right. Maybe after the fireworks?" What a pleasure it'd been to have Shea here today. She'd head home tomorrow, back to her work as a psychotherapist in Bremerton. The only issue was whether to tell Shea her big secret, or keep it stuffed inside and live out the consequences alone. Literally. Because her secret dictated her lifestyle—her singlehood.

Yippee.

"I thought you and Hunter might want some alone time tonight."

"Nah, it's not like that this year." Mikaela waved a hand for Shea to precede her onto the boat. She followed. "Hey, Hunter," she called. "You here yet?" No answer. He'd darted home earlier but promised to meet them back here. She locked the cordon clasp and they moved through the indoor salon toward the staircase for the upper outdoor deck, where they could spread out blankets and watch the show.

"Well, let's get set up. It's almost ten." Of course, ten o'clock meant the sky wouldn't be pitch black, but the sun would have set. On clear nights this time of year, the sky only faded to a deep navy blue in Western Washington for much of the night.

They stepped out into the open air at the back of the boat where benches lined the perimeter, and where the Cahills and

Rhoades used to gather and recline on blankets and stare up at the sky over the bay every Fourth.

"I don't get it," Shea said, spreading out her blanket. The *Millennium* pitched a little and the wind brought a chill, not unusual for the Fourth in Washington. "All that flirting on the trip today."

"Flirting?"

"Chemistry, honey. And you must admit you two make an amazing team. And what you did for him, for everyone . . .? You are still all heart, Miks."

"Who wants to be sad all the time? I have a feeling he's still grieving pretty heavily." Her thoughts flashed to their discussion of Reid. "His dad only recently died—several months ago. I was merely trying to keep things light, for him, for Granny. Lauren." *Myself.*

"I understand," Shea said, bending to smooth a corner of her blanket. She straightened her spine. "You enjoyed yourself today. Admit it. And if he hadn't been there, you wouldn't have had as much fun. Am I right?"

Mikaela finished getting her own blanket settled, but she wished for another to wrap around her because the temperature was quickly dropping out here on the water. Shea had asked her about Hunter. Could she admit it?

"I mean, what if it'd been Jonah captaining? Or one of your students?" She patted the metal railing before settling down. "Or ole Sam Kerry who sometimes pilots this boat."

Mikaela joined her on the deck, wrapping her arms around her bent knees. "No, you're right." There, she'd said it. But she'd never admit it to Hunter. "Today—this summer, thank you very much—wouldn't be the same if I were teamed with anyone else."

Shea nodded, pursing her lips. "That's because no one else will do for you. Period."

A deep sense of grief dropped into Mikaela's stomach. She could deny Shea's assessment, but when her bestie was right, she was right. "I like him. Still. A lot." A rush of affection flowed with her words, a rush she couldn't deny any longer. "But none of that changes anything. I can't—"

"Why?" Shea looked around. "He's not here. Talk to me, Miks," she pleaded. In all their phone conversations since Mikaela returned to the island this summer, she'd managed to avoid this conversation.

It was time to unburden herself. She squeezed her knees. "I haven't told you. I haven't told Granny. And, obviously, the Cahills don't know."

"There's a secret even Granny doesn't know?"

"Yes." And to do it again, Mikaela would keep the same confidence. She shivered. The vessel beneath her seeped its cold, metallic chill up through the blanket. Or maybe it was their topic. Really, she had no guarantees. Not with her time bomb.

A noise carried from behind them, and then a voice. "Hi, you two."

Hunter.

"Hey, we were beginning to wonder about you, Captain," Shea said, twisting, like Mikaela, to see him.

He carried a thermos and a stack of Styrofoam cups. "I figured we'd want something hot."

The wind kicked up, and all remnants of the warmth of that day's sun vanished with it. Mikaela jumped to her feet. "Let me help." Their hands brushed, sparking electricity. "Thank you for thinking of this."

"You always were a thoughtful guy, Hunt." There Shea went again, using his nickname. But his eyes stayed locked on Mikaela's.

"It's cocoa, so not much caffeine." He opened the thermos while Mikaela held the white cups for him. "What'd I miss?"

She liked the playfulness in his voice. No sign of the crab lately. She swallowed, hoping her friend would cover for her because words weren't forming at the moment.

"Oh, I was about to update her on my nephew."

Thanks, Shea.

"Good. How is he?" Hunter finished pouring the final serving and set the thermos aside, recapped. Then, he accepted the cup from Mikaela and sipped. He looked warm in his Cahill Touring sweatshirt. Since she wanted to keep her distance, she should probably stop thinking about his shirts and wearing his shirts and smelling his shirts. Instead, she'd stand here shivering.

She sipped her cocoa, letting the hot liquid warm her from the inside. If only drinking this would alleviate her grief. Now that she'd begun realizing all her choices were costing her, sadness robbed her optimism about the future. *Don't think about it.*

"Jaxon came through surgery fine. He's out of recovery. They're watching him closely, though, because his temp is slightly elevated."

"I'll keep praying," Mikaela promised. *Lord, please heal him.*

"Oh, and my folks think they'd like to still come up and tour this summer." She shifted her attention to Hunter. "Though it may have to wait until Labor Day. Any chance Cahill has an opening for a private charter? I know it's really short notice, what with everyone booking ahead."

"I'll check," he answered. "It falls on a Monday, obviously, so no usual tours, but we might have the evening free. Most folks like to sail during the warmest part of the day, especially since by Labor Day the weather might have already turned."

"We're a hardy bunch. We'll bring our parkas and huddle around holding hot cocoa." She lifted her cup. "Cheers."

Hunter zeroed his focus back in on Mikaela. She studied the other boats bobbing in the dim bay, but she could feel his eyes on her. "Miki, are you shivering?"

Why did he have to be so attentive?

A memory flashed of him holding her many a Fourth of July evening during fireworks, arms wrapped around from behind.

Why didn't she carry a coat around with her all the time? Even standing away from the steel hull, her teeth chattered. "M-m-maybe a little." Was this the result of keeping her secret inside so long? Some sort of nervous breakdown? Or the fear of everything coming apart on her? She'd tried for years to hold her life together, to bury her secret. To pretend her decision didn't hurt.

Shea zeroed in, giving her a knowing look as if she knew about the battle and the release of pent-up stuff.

Yeah, I know. I'm a nutcase.

Light flashed off to her right, followed by hissing noises and small explosions before reds and yellows burst into the sky and cascaded down until they faded. Mikaela, Shea, and Hunter turned and faced the bay. Mikaela was determined not to sit because she was colder down on the metal deck than standing up here.

Hunter rested his hand on her shoulder. "Scoot." He gave her a gentle nudge, and she moved off her blanket, which he lifted and shook and settled around her shoulders. She used her free hand to squeeze the corners he handed her. "Warm up or you'll have to go inside the wheelhouse. We have shore power. I can turn on the heat."

"I'll be fine." It'd been so long since someone had taken care of her, she'd forgotten the rush of love—wait. That was too strong a word. The rush of *feelings*—affection, like she'd conceded earlier—that hit her when someone cared about her in tangible acts of kindness.

Shea studied the sky, but a flash of blue light on her face showed her amusement. Mikaela wanted to defend herself, but really, what good were all her defenses lately? Even to herself.

More fireworks, and the crowds on the dock and in neighboring boats cheered and children clapped, shrieking with joy. Shea joined in with oohs and aahs, but Mikaela couldn't stop thinking about her secret. What if she'd divulged it right as Hunter joined them? What if he'd heard? *Had* he heard their conversation? Her confession? Eeks.

She downed the last of her cocoa and reached toward Shea's cup. "Finished?"

She nodded and stacked her cup inside Mikaela's. Hunter grabbed both and set the stack down, lodging the Styrofoam into the framework of the *Millennium* so the cups couldn't blow away.

"You warm enough, Jenna?" Hunter asked. She'd wrapped her blanket around herself too.

"Yeah. Thanks, Hunt." She nodded toward the harbor. "Watching fireworks over the water is magical. All the reflections." Shea probably didn't go to the Space Needle show very often, given the crowds. But, there were likely shows in Bremerton on the

Fourth, given the military presence. Friday Harbor crowds were nothing compared to Seattle's. Mikaela usually watched fireworks from the peacefulness of her high-rise condo.

"Yes, it is magical," he agreed, giving Mikaela a look.

Knowing what she did, Amelia Wren wouldn't judge Mikaela, right? Nor would she divulge Mikaela's secrets. Hopefully. Dr. Wren was living proof that life wasn't a guarantee, that healthy organs could fail. And that you could have a fulfilling life without having a family. Mikaela had modeled her career after the chairwoman, and she'd inadvertently modeled her personal life after her mentor's as well.

Warm breath fanned her ear during the noisy fireworks overhead. Warm breath and a familiar scent. "You're still shivering." Quiet words, imperceptible to anyone but her.

She tucked the blanket closer around shuddering shoulders. "I'm okay," she said, barely keeping her teeth from chattering. Yeah, apparently she *was* having a nervous breakdown. And apparently stuffed anxiety later manifested in uncontrollable shakes.

"May I?" Hunter's gentle appeal came from behind her.

She peeked over her shoulder and saw his open arms, but he kept his distance. Awaiting permission.

"Jenna won't mind, will you, Jenna?"

"Are you kidding me? Warm that girl up!" Shea commanded before returning her gaze to the sky.

I'm gonna get you, my friend. Mikaela aimed her vengeful thoughts toward her bestie, not that she knew it. Hunter still stood behind her. "I guess you'd better do what she says." She yielded as her heart skipped a few beats. He stepped up behind her and brought his arms around her, crossing them against her tummy. Immediately, heat permeated her blanket. Her malfunctioning nervous system was no match. Even her anxiety seemed to melt away in his safe arms.

The display was winding down—with longer breaks between colorful explosions.

As the next rocket shot up, Hunter pressed his face close to her ear. She shuddered again, but not from cold. "I like you too. Still. A lot." His words came out in a husky whisper.

Her breath caught. He'd heard.

"And, as one of your *friends*—who, by the way, are good at helping us warm up—I want you to know that any secret you have would be safe with me." He paused, his breath still warming her ear and sending zinging sensations down to her cold, curled toes. "In fact, as your friend, I can probably help. If you let me." He shifted and once again pressed his face to the side of her head. She pictured him closing his eyes, sniffing her hair, like in that selfie. That image made her breathing go all shallow.

Another loud firework exploded over the water, and Hunter jerked up, his head tipped back. Through her peripheral vision, she watched the flashes light the angles of his face, his lips in silhouette.

She'd told Shea that she liked him. But she didn't. She loved him. Heaven help them both.

Certainty dropped into her gut. She loved him.

Her secret-keeping days were numbered.

CHAPTER TWENTY-EIGHT

Black coffee scalded Hunter's tongue and throat, but he let it burn. Mom's news this morning about the foreclosure proceedings on hers and Dad's house dug around like a clam shovel in his gut. If they didn't get current on both their mortgages, they might have to live at the dock. Except that wasn't possible, or legal. Nor was living on board the *Millennium*.

Mom refused to move in with him and give up the house where she'd shared her life with Dad until she had to. Hunter couldn't blame her for that. If he could make any payments on a mortgage, he'd pay hers. The income lately at Cahill had gone toward running the business. They'd scraped up payroll the past few months. He'd scheduled every extra hour with charters. How could they get caught up if there was never enough money, not to mention more than enough?

Would they have to close the business Dad had worked so hard to build?

"Hey, Hunt. Shoot. Ease up. You're going to burn the skin right off your pipes." Dan had a point, and Hunter set down his coffee cup.

Hunter wasn't the only one suffering. Dan and he sat at Friday Café, customers—mostly locals—tooling around, laughing at adjacent tables as if their lives weren't upside-down like his was. And Dan's. "What's the news on Junior?"

Dan sighed. "Same. We drove down to Seattle yesterday for more tests. They want to monitor the baby closely. Of course, by the time they realize there's a prob—" Dan's eyes widened as if the stakes had just punched him.

Hunter reached out, put a hand on Dan's shoulder. He didn't have much to offer, but he'd listen.

Dan ground his jaw, one fist clenching and unclenching on the table. "She's moving in with her parents in Seattle this weekend."

His voice came out rough.

"Shoot. I know you didn't want to do that—have her be so far away."

"I want her safe." Pain etched Dan's eyes. "She'll be closer to the hospital. I want the baby safe too, but all I can think is she's my top priority." He tilted his face toward the table and shook his head. "That's so wrong."

Hunter tried to put himself in Dan's shoes. "Nah, it's natural. She's your wife." If Miki were in the same situation, how would Hunter react? He valued life, all life, but he didn't want to think about dividing his loyalty between an unborn child and his beloved wife.

Miki. A flash of holding her on the deck of the *Millennium*, her vanilla scent mixing with the salty sea air. She must have been hiding something awful given how much she'd shook. For the first time, he felt fear. What if she hid some kind of horrible news?

Focus on Dan, Cahill.

"Well, either way, this sucks. I hate it. Thought about leaving my job, but I can't because of healthcare. We need this policy more than we ever did." Dan's turn to gulp hot coffee. He grimaced.

"I hear you." Hunter and his mom were barely covered. He prayed she never got really sick. Like Dad had.

He'd been toying with an idea, but he wouldn't be able to offer healthcare benefits. Still, it would let Dan be in Seattle near his wife. "Didn't you mention Beth's parents live in Ballard?"

"Yeah."

"You have your captain's license." Dan had earned his along with Hunter, years ago. "You can pilot vessels. How would you feel about helping expand Cahill Touring?" Maybe this was the answer, if Hunter could afford to branch out.

His brow wrinkled under his dark brown hairline. "Work for you?"

"Yeah. Maybe Hank would give you leeway, given the circumstances."

Dan thought a moment. "He mentioned he needed part-time help handling supplies down in Seattle, but I didn't volunteer because it wasn't enough hours. He *is* offering full medical. And running charters for you would—"

"Fill the extra hours."

"Yeah . . ."

"Cahill could offer charters around Seattle and the area islands—Vashon, Bainbridge, perhaps Fox and Whidbey. It's summer, so there'll be a demand. We would need to get the word out somehow."

Since he'd skipped college, Hunter hadn't taken the business classes he'd planned to. Maybe that's where he was lacking. But, Mom could help with the business side. Either way, you had to market a new venture to gain awareness and to do that effectively, he'd need more money. Maybe he'd line up a few customers from personal contacts to get the ball rolling. Their payments could go back into the satellite and marketing. And they could offer some sort of incentive to get people to leave reviews.

Hope surfaced in Dan's eyes, if those raised brows meant what Hunter figured they did. "I can hire a couple teenagers to cover the off-loading and loading, on Hank's dime. And I could spend any off time with Beth."

Hunter nodded at him.

"Dude." His volume rose. "This might work."

"For local jaunts, we could send Cahill's Prize down there." Of course, they'd have to rent a slip. Another expense. "But for large groups . . . know of any vessels we might use?"

"Hank's forty-nine footer is in dry dock in Anacortes, but you might be able to work out a deal. Plus, this might solve his problem of needing a boat too, which means he may not need to borrow one now."

They'd need a backer, but Hunter would start by contacting Hank. "I'll call him." Pride swelled in his chest. It'd been a long time since he'd helped someone else, because, really, what did he have to offer? Perhaps he should try harder with Carter. The guy needed a worthwhile project. "The thing is, I can't pay much at first. But if we get good business, you'd share in the profits. A fair percentage. Until I can afford a salary." He hated admitting it, but if this helped

Dan, Hunter would swallow his pride and move forward.

"Well, I'll still be working for Hank and have that income if he goes for this idea. And"—Dan's voice cracked—"I'll be with my wife." He blew out a loud breath, collecting himself. "Her folks can help with some of the expenses, and we could either rent or sell the house up here."

This could work. Hope was at it again.

"Beth used to be in PR. She might have a few ideas for inexpensive advertising or using social media to bring in the customers. She has a degree in business."

"Think she can safely offer to help?" The last thing Hunter wanted was to put her at more risk.

"Yeah, she's had to give up her job here. She's been going a little stir-crazy not being able to use her degree. And as long as she's resting most of the time, I think some computer hours couldn't hurt."

Hunter raised his brows at his friend.

"We'll check with her doctor, if that'll make you feel better. You're only asking her for advice—like consulting. It's not like you're asking her to captain vessels or load cargo."

"I'm serious. You need to find out."

"Oh, I know." Dan's face went all soft. "Listen, if this works out, we'll owe you big time."

"Nah, I'll owe you. And believe me, as soon as I'm able, I'll pay Beth for her hours too. Have her track 'em."

"I'll call her right after this." He waved his paper coffee cup.

That settled, ideas churned fast. "I have a few things to set in motion. Know anybody who can update my website?"

"Hmm, maybe Beth does. She doesn't do it. Doesn't like anything super techie." Dan sat back in the wooden chair, much more relaxed than a few minutes ago. "So, you and Miki? How's that going?"

Hunter had been waiting for Dan to dig into his personal life. "She wants 'friendship'."

Dan gave him a knowing look. "Well, friends can be close."

"Right." Hold hands. Hold each other. Share secrets, he hoped.

"Either way, you were right." The confession burned. "I couldn't not try."

As if he'd known all along, which of course he had, Dan grunted. "Well, there's hunting, and then there's wooing. I'm guessing she'll respond more to wooing than hunting."

"I'm trying." Maybe it was time to step up his game. They had another "meeting" planned, but this one would be out on the water.

"Have you told her how you feel?"

"You mean spilled my guts? Not exactly." But he did have proof she felt something toward him. Oh, and he had his own secret he needed to tell her. Now, for a chance to confront her about what he'd discovered.

Dan snorted again. "Well, nothing says wooing like guts."

Hunter choked on his coffee but then sobered.

Dan squinted in Hunter's direction. "What's bugging you?"

"She's gonna leave again." It was the foolishness of this chase that slowed him down, held him back.

"Didn't you say you'd talked to the chairwoman?" Dan was concocting a scheme; Hunter could see it.

"Yes."

"Doesn't the department head decide things like who comes, who goes, who *stays*?" Dan leaned in. "My guess is if this project works, the U will need someone onsite to run it—here. Ongoing." He waved a hand. "Let Hawaii fend for itself."

Hunter backed out of Granny's driveway, her two kayaks latched to his pickup. She'd wished Miki and him well, and then scurried back into the house to catch the oven timer. He gave Miki a glance beside him, then focused on the road. "You're kinda quiet today. You nervous about going back to Haro Strait?"

"What? No. I'm preoccupied. Dr. Wren left a cryptic message and promised a phone call later tonight. Hate when she does that."

"Gotcha. Well, maybe it's good news?"

Miki grimaced at him. "I'm guessing she saw the poor reviews."

He'd been trying not to think about them. "Well, if she did, we'll tell her of our plans to fire Jace and relieve Destinee of her post." No matter how many warnings, those two couldn't get their acts together. Hunter still couldn't believe those reviews though. If his Seattle satellite wasn't coming together so well, he'd be worried about Cahill tanking in the next few weeks as their reputation took these hits. *Please God, help.*

Praying was coming a little easier lately.

"Yeah, she's not going to like that."

Hunter shrugged as he took a left onto Douglas Road. "They brought it on themselves." Still, the betrayal stung. "You okay with me putting Carter on website duty?" Carter's preliminary designs for the redo were far beyond what Hunter could have done.

"Yeah, good thinking. *Pierce* is in the wrong department." She eyed him over that name correction but he stayed focused on the road and grinned.

No doubt.

She fidgeted. "Listen, we need to talk about a couple of things."

After the long stretch on Bailer Hill Road, he pulled the truck into Lime Kiln Point State Park's lot. "Sure thing. But let's get out onto the water first." He had his own agenda tonight, like braving the question of whether she'd forgiven him for leaving last time. If she forgave him, what else could stand in their way, especially if Dr. Wren decided to let her stay? What did she want? And was he courageous enough to walk away again—or rather watch her leave again—if that's what she wanted?

He also wanted to show her what he'd found.

Once parked, she slipped on her light purple sweater before they lowered the kayaks from his truck. His long-sleeved blue-and-yellow plaid shirt was versatile. He didn't expect to be chilled, but he could unroll the sleeves if the wind came up. She hefted her kayak off the ground, grunting. "Okay, maybe we carry these together. Apparently project management hasn't kept me in the best shape."

"Nah, these are older models. Much heavier than nowadays." He grabbed one end of her kayak, and she grabbed the other. "And you might be right, but for the record, I like that you aren't as burly as Uncle Earl was."

"Ha! Right? Or hairy. That guy had a carpet of red hair all over his back." She shuddered as they hauled the vessel to the shore. "A shocking picture of manhood he was, especially for a thirteen-year-old girl. Shirts mandatory!"

"For everyone?" He tugged on his own tee.

She smirked at him, and he laughed outright. They set the kayak down and marched up the hill to get the other one.

Summer evening sunlight glinted off the strait, shooting golden sparks of light into the air. The water lay like glass tonight. Soon they paddled side by side, slicing through the surface. "Well, what's on your mind, Miki?"

She tipped her head his direction, her oar going still. "You're looking a little puffy in your life jacket tonight, Captain."

"Ha!" Was she flirting? Yum. "Am I, Professor? Well, let me say that you look like a blue marshmallow in sunglasses ready for the bonfire."

"You didn't." She sent a spray of saltwater his way.

"Huh. Really?" He made to douse her, but when she cringed, he couldn't follow through.

She opened her eyes and studied him. "You're not going to drench me?"

"Nope." He shook his head. "But I have something to show you." He nodded straight ahead of them, up the channel.

An orca's nose popped up as the killer whale spy-hopped. Onlookers cheered from the shore. "Wow. They're right there." Not far from the first animal, a pair of dorsals arced up before slipping back into the sea. "Such grace," she said, awe in her voice. "I mean, I know we encounter them almost daily on the tours, but this is at eye level. I'd forgotten how much I love seeing them more regularly."

He watched her. "Indeed." Oh, he loved her. Longed for her. But what did she need? What did she want? "You wanna get closer?"

"You bet."

"Let's go. And if they knock you into the water, I'll just rescue you again."

"I'm *not* going to fall in again." She didn't sound as irritated as the words implied. But she seemed worried, burdened. Maybe this evening could help with that. They paddled toward the pod. A few other orcas, all with various sized dorsals, joined those first two. Three males and two females, plus a couple of adolescents. All members of T-pod. Hunter and Miki would have their own private T-party.

He grabbed her kayak, hauled her closer to him. "Hang on." They'd gotten real close now. He glanced into the water, saw the black and white below them. Should they move? No, they'd wait to see what the orcas did.

A tall, sharp-tipped fin sliced the water right beside Miki's kayak, just on the other side of her and she gasped. "Whoa."

He muscled her watercraft even closer to his and took her hand. The dorsal towered out of the water about six feet, if Hunter were to guess.

"So close." From this side angle he could see her wide eyes behind those sunglasses. "Makes me want to jump in and swim with them."

"Except, you dive with them you'll be wishing for scuba gear and a tank of air."

"True." She squeezed his hand watching the show.

And he wanted to give her the world.

A bit farther west into the channel, Hunter saw the familiar spray of a specific animal. "Miki, how about some other types of whales?"

Her attention snapped from the surfacing orca pod, which was now moving away from them, to his face. "What did you see?" She scanned the waters. "Where?"

No large vessels in the channel right now. He jerked his head toward the west. "C'mon."

She paddled to push forward with him. They stroked toward the site, and slightly more north, because if Hunter guessed correctly, the creature would surface again, right about . . .

Miki watched the water in front of them. "I don't see anything."

"Look beside you."

She gasped. "Hunt!"

He urged her to keep moving forward, parallel with it. "Don't scare him away," he said, but his breath evaporated. She hadn't called him Hunt in over a decade. Did that mean she'd forgiven him? She still cared, he had no doubt about that now. Not after what he'd found. But what good was his evidence if she still chose to leave?

A minke whale had joined them and was keeping pace beside her kayak. A pair of blowholes materialized. The spray got her, and she squealed. Stretching to probably thirty-five feet, the dark gray baleen whale stirred something in Hunter. Something he hadn't felt in a while. Awe.

They stroked forward at a steady pace. "It's staying right beside me."

"Hmm. He likes you." He had to tell her tonight. Put his heart out there. And something told him she might not brush him off this time.

"Oh, man, this is amazing." Beside them, the whale came up to breathe once more, making a loud noise from the creature's immense lung capacity. Then the playful whale tucked his blowholes back under. But he didn't leave Miki's side, not that Hunter blamed him for that. Miki met his eyes. "You gave me a whale—my favorite kind. How'd you know there'd be a minke out here tonight?"

Something had told him as he considered what they should do for their meeting. Something. Or someone. Was it crazy to think God had guided him? "Just a hunch." He stared off toward the channel opening where a freighter came into view, the stacked boxcars on board glinting in the sunshine like a stack of metallic building blocks.

The minke dove beside her, fading from view. Probably headed off for food.

"You ready for a late picnic?"

"Sure." They spun their kayaks around and headed back.

As they retraced their earlier path, hauling the kayaks up to the truck, she drew in a deep breath. "So, you think maybe God brought us out here tonight right on time to see the whales up close?"

At the truck, he took over and shoved the first kayak into position, using the bungee cord to secure it. "Actually, yes." When he finished he joined her beside the truck.

"You haven't really mentioned God much lately, except to ask for prayer for Dan and Beth."

"They're doing well, by the way. Getting things underway in Seattle. Keeping Beth close to her new OB."

"I'm glad." She shook her head. Maybe she couldn't imagine the situation either. After all, she hadn't become a mom yet. *Someday.* "But you and God—where are you with Him?"

Hunter considered the prayers he'd prayed. He wouldn't tell her his prayer about tonight, except to say, "I have put in a few requests now and then."

She squinted at him. "You have?" She went still, studying him. "Have you been praying all along?"

"Surprise you?"

"Yeah, a bit." She spun back toward the water's edge where they'd left the other kayak. "Granny Belle has been trying to get me to stop begging God and start asking Him. But ever since . . ."

Hmm. He gently snagged her arm. "Your secret."

"Yeah. And it's time I told you."

He forced a smile. "Well, it's not like you're dying, right?" He hoped. "Why so serious, Prof?"

She stayed silent, that burden looking heavier by the moment given her slumped shoulders. She resumed the trek to the shore.

He marched to the kayak and hefted one end. His heart pounded and not from exertion. Yeah, he may not be as ready as he thought to hear what she'd been keeping from him.

CHAPTER TWENTY-NINE

She could never tell him about her revelation on the *Millennium* on the Fourth. If she did, he'd dive in and she would no longer be able to protect him. So, she'd dump out her other secrets, but that tidbit about her affections? Nope. Locked up tight.

At a picnic table fifteen minutes later, following way too much silence, Mikaela sat across from Hunter as he passed out tinfoil-wrapped egg salad sandwiches Granny had made for them. Sunlight slanted in from the west, but they still had over an hour of daylight left. Her fingertips went numb. *Breathe.* She opened her mouth to speak, but he stopped her with a raised hand.

"Before you start, I need to know how serious this secret is. Because you've gone too quiet on me here."

Her heart thumped. For some reason, shame wrapped her secrets, not that she'd done anything wrong. But, he was right. She should start slow. "Well, it's not exactly a matter of life or death." Mostly.

He sighed as if she'd eased a huge concern. "Still, you look worried, like crazy worried. But, Miki, it's me. Hunt." He reached for her hand on the table between them, and she let him take it. Yeah, she'd called him Hunt earlier. Felt good. Right. "Talk to me."

She sighed. "Okay . . ." Tears burned in her eyes. Crazy. Why was this so hard? She *wasn't* dying, for goodness's sake. Then, it hit her. She'd missed him. Seriously missed him. Painfully. "I am so glad God brought us back . . . here. I'm glad we got to clear the air."

"So, you forgive me?" His voice came out almost too soft, like he was fighting his own battle.

A rush of warmth chased a lump up her throat. "Yes, of course I do. I get it. You thought you were helping me." Plus, it had worked out for the best.

Relief passed over his face again, and he glanced off toward the sky for a few blinks. But then he ground his jaw as if emotions were boiling right below the surface. He zeroed back in on her. "I'd do anything for you, Miki."

Maybe he was a safe place after all. "I inherited kidney disease."

His brow furrowed. "You what?"

"It's a long story, and that's only the first part." She drew a deep breath. *You can do this.* "You wonder why I'm so devoted to Dr. Wren? Well, I'm carrying around one of her kidneys in my body."

He blinked, his brow furrowed. "Since when?"

"Since college. Now she's down to one, and that one is starting to fail."

He shook his head, clearly not understanding.

"Which means, *I'm* a ticking time bomb."

"Not necessarily." This time his head shake was purposeful. "What do your doctors say?"

"They think I'm overly cautious. 'Drink a lot of water.' 'Limit fluid intake.' 'Avoid excessive salt.' 'Watch out for certain produce.' I've heard it all. 'Get married.' 'Don't—'"

"Wait, what do your kidneys have to do with your marital status?"

She squirmed. Here it came—the shameful part. "My next secret." And the reason she'd keep protecting him, even if it cost her a desirable future. Here.

He stood up, moved around the table, and sat beside her like he knew this was big. He wrapped an arm around her, and she leaned in. For one moment, she'd let her guard down. He rubbed her upper arm, but didn't speak, as if waiting for her to decide when she was ready.

Her chest burned. Now or never. "I can't have babies."

He flinched. "What?" He seemed to catch his breath. Then, "Why not?"

"When I started to have weird symptoms a while after the surgery," she began, her voice coming out hoarse. She didn't let herself dwell on this. Kept telling herself her career was enough. Funny how that lie was more believable in Seattle than here on the island with Hunt. "They ran a series of tests. And that's when they diagnosed me as infertile." She gulped against the emotion in her chest. "I know how important kids are to you—and rightly so. They're important to me too." Her breath shuddered out of her. "But I don't get a choice here."

Maybe he'd understand. He'd give her a friendly hug, and they could finish out the summer and move on. Then, he'd go find a wife who could give him the family he'd always wanted.

He was silent. Too silent for too long.

"Say something," she whispered, hiding against his shoulder where he let her stay.

"You thought . . ." he began and then groaned. Was he crying? She tried to pull back, but he tucked her close again like he didn't want her to see his face. "You thought, what? That you were damaged and no one would want you? That—" He sucked air. "That I wouldn't want you?"

She gulped against a sob. "Yeah. I mean, you want your own kids."

His stomach convulsed, and his jaw clicked near her ear. Still, he wouldn't loosen his grip.

She tried to swallow the lump in her throat, but it burned hotter. "I wanted to protect you." She barely got the words out. "I didn't want to hurt you."

His bicep twitched behind her as if gearing up for action. Like he was prepping to go to battle for her. But this news didn't come with a way out or a villain to best. "How long . . . how long ago did they tell you this?"

"Eight years."

He winced. "Eight?" His breath snorted out on what sounded like a disguised sob, and he got to his feet and marched toward the trees. He stood there with his back to her, one hand on his waist, the other running through his hair. His hunched shoulders rose and fell with deep breaths before he strode back over. His reddened eyes flashed in the sunlight like the lighthouse's lens on its rounds. "You thought you were doing me a favor?"

She nodded. Surely he could understand that.

"So, until then there was hope for us?" That look in his eyes said *How could you?* as if he *didn't* understand.

She had to retreat. Get her own bearings. She stood as well, tried to recall the experience of rejection even though it had faded. "Not after you sent me away."

"I didn't 'send you away'." He pointed to himself. "Plus, forgiven, right?"

She nodded, her heart melting. That meant a lot to him, more than she'd thought it would. "Yes, definitely. I'm sorry." She was losing her footing here. She had to make him see. Turn this so he could get her perspective. "After I was back in school, and when I didn't hear from you all that time, well, eventually I came to terms with the fact we wouldn't be together."

"I called you over and over." He tucked his hands into his jeans pockets.

She shrugged. "I didn't have any other solution. I needed to stay in Seattle."

"And I needed to stay here."

"Then, I got sick." She paused. "After the diagnosis of infertility, I told myself it was all for the best. You wanted a family. I assumed you'd moved on."

A couple of steps brought him closer. "You have to know that if you had come back, we would have picked up where we left off. Or if I could've gotten to Seattle . . ."

"But you couldn't move. Your family needed you here."

"And you were chasing your doctorate."

"I know your heart, Hunt." She reached for his arm, determined to treat him like a friend. "But there wasn't a way for it to work. And that's truer now than ever."

"You made that decision for me." A touch of steel reinforced his voice this time.

"We're going in circles. We weren't together."

He shifted and her hand slipped, but he caught it and ran his fingers between hers. "Remember on the *Millennium* when I mentioned that I still like you. That wasn't the whole truth." He stepped even closer. "I love you, Miki. Present tense."

Regret punched her in the stomach. All this time and he wasn't even reacting to her news as she figured he might. Except, he was.

He could overlook any flaw when it came to her, couldn't he? And distance. He conveniently overlooked that too.

"I always have. I never stopped." He gently placed a hand to the side of her face, swiping moisture away with his thumb. "I can't believe you decided this for me." A tear ran down his face, soaking a path through his scruffy whiskers, but he didn't hide. "I can't believe we've lost all this time."

"But nothing's changed. I'm not free to live here." Yet, suddenly, that's all she wanted.

"Do you want to?" His heart rested in his eyes, waiting as he held his breath.

"Aw, Hunt."

"You can't admit it? Even right now?" He reached into his pocket. "Don't tell me you don't have feelings for me."

Uh-oh.

He held up a familiar chain and a pendant fell from his hand, dangling between them. He'd found it. She'd worried it was lost forever.

She cupped the pendant, and he released the chain. "I didn't know where that went," she whispered as her objections evaporated between them. Her final secret—the one relating to her affections—was now exposed.

He dipped his head to meet her eyes. "You wore it back to the island this summer."

"So?" She looked away, shrugged, tried to cover. Disgusted with herself for her immaturity. "Adolescent silliness." Why *had* she worn it back here? She still couldn't answer that for herself. She slipped the chain around her neck and hid the pendant under her shirt.

He grunted. "C'mon Miki. I know the secrets now. And they're no match for me. So, unless you're hiding a husband down in Seattle, you're running out of excuses *and* escapes."

Could she dream about them being together? No. No she couldn't. There were still too many barriers. "My future's still in Hawaii."

"Forget about that."

"I can't."

He took both of her hands. "For one second. Do you . . ." He blew out a breath as if gathering his courage. "Do you love me?"

If her mind ruled, the answer would have to be a resounding no. For too long, that's what she'd done—let her mind rule her life. After her four-year degree, she'd considered coming back to the island. Chatting with Mr. Cahill, getting a naturalist's job on board. Picking up with Hunter again, if possible. But then, the diagnoses. And right now, Hunter was *saying* he didn't care about the infertility. But wouldn't he? Someday?

The sun tilted lower toward Vancouver Island. "Well?"

Maybe it was time for her heart to rule. Maybe it was time for her to risk what she hadn't risked before and— "Yes," she said on a rush of emotion. "I don't think I ever stopped." Which was why she still wore his engagement ring on a chain around her neck.

His mouth opened, and his gaze notched up toward intense. "You do?" His voice faltered.

Joy swirled in her chest, like dancers set loose. "Mm-hmm."

He stepped even closer and drew her to within inches of his face. Her heart thumped. His attention dropped to her lips.

She stepped back, though if her heart could choose, she'd have gone toward him, not away. "But I don't have all the—"

He placed his index finger over her lips. "So, we have some problems to solve. So what?" He turned and started gathering up their picnic foods. "Let's go."

Halfway back to his truck, she caught his free hand. "Hang on. That's it? This is a problem-solving mission now?"

"What's the matter, Prof?" Humor glinted in his eyes. Humor and sparks.

She eyed his lips this time. Crazy. She was thinking crazy. But somehow, he brought out the crazy in her. "I think you know."

"Maybe, but it's not up to me." He marched off toward the pickup where he hefted the cooler in behind the truck seats via the passenger door. Did he have any idea how infuriating he could be? And what did their declaration mean, anyway? Hawaii still waited for her. She still owed her mentor her future. But did Hunter have to look so good with the golden rays of sun pitching color at his scruffy face, making his gray eyes shine?

Her secret hadn't stopped him from loving her. Didn't even faze him. That rush of affection morphed into something stronger. Something more insistent.

He held the passenger door open for her. "Prof," he said, waving her in.

She stepped in front of him but didn't climb up. "When you tell someone you love them, you don't simply jump into the nearest transportation and problem solve."

He gave her that same infuriating grin. "You don't?" Yeah, such innocence.

She clutched his T-shirt and dragged him toward her. She backed toward the outer wall of the truck until she pressed against the metal. "There's something we've left out here."

Slowly, he put his arms on either side of her, over her head, so casually as if he had all evening. "Really?"

"And I'm not in shock this time."

He smiled, and his gaze dipped to her mouth. "You do seem perfectly lucid, Professor."

Another tug brought his face closer to hers. "Will you stop with the professor business?"

He drew closer, his face sobering. "If you say so."

"One more thing."

He swallowed. "Yeah?"

"Please don't turn your face this time." She pushed up toward him and met his lips with hers. He let out a sound and wrapped his arms around her, returning her kiss with determination, his body pressed against hers. But in a moment, his insistence downshifted to tenderness as one of his hands found the back of her head. His gentleness opened a new corridor in her heart. He loved her anyway. Her biggest flaw hadn't stopped him. Tears burned her closed eyes.

He pulled away and rested his forehead against hers. "Miki, I don't want you to leave again."

"I don't want to go." And she didn't. Ever again. But what choice did she have? Also, didn't he care that they could never have their own kids? No little girl to name after Granny Belle? No little boy to name after his father or Granddad? Her chin trembled. "So, you're okay that we can't have children?" Stupid shame.

He ran a thumb over her chin. "I only want you. You're all I need. You willing to give up your studio in Seattle?"

They hadn't addressed all her commitments. She still couldn't let Amelia down. But, wait a minute. "Hey, you knew my condo was tiny?"

He chuckled, tracing his fingers down her arm to take her hand. "Granny showed me pictures."

"Humph." She couldn't stay irritated though. "It is lonely there."

"I can do something about that." He ran a finger under the chain of her necklace to lift the ring. "We'll figure this out. And kids, we'll solve that too."

"You mean adoption?" Her phone buzzed in her pocket.

"Or fostering. I know you love to rescue mammals."

She smiled. "You know it." She yanked her phone out.

He gestured toward the screen. "Chairperson Wren?"

She read the Caller ID. "No." Oh, no. "Dr. Denver Smythe."

CHAPTER THIRTY

Mikaela grabbed her buzzing phone off the nightstand. She'd gotten ready for bed, but didn't expect to get much sleep tonight. Shea's face showed on the screen. Thank goodness. Maybe she could help make sense of the inner battle in Mikaela's heart right then.

She and Hunter had spent a gorgeous evening together, and the kiss kept replaying in her mind, but Mikaela couldn't commit to Hunter. Could not. She'd gotten caught up in their time together—which hadn't been an official meeting. Yes, she still loved him. But now everything might be falling apart.

And surprise, Dr. Smythe was onsite. She had a challenging day ahead, proving her abilities to him tomorrow. *Oh, joy.*

She connected the call with Shea. "I told him," she said. Yeah, Hunter now knew all her secrets. And her darkest one hadn't affected his love for her.

Shea laughed. "Hi to you too. But hold on. What happened? Tell me everything."

Mikaela tucked herself into the soft chair in the corner of her bedroom and curled her legs up beside her, wrapping her summer robe over them. "I shared my secrets: kidney disease and infertility."

"Wait . . . Miks? You never told me about that."

Tears pushed into her eyes. "I know." She explained the whole story to her bestie, finally.

"I'm so sorry." Shea's voice sounded raspy. "I wish I could hug you."

"I was ashamed, you know, but Hunt . . . the news didn't even faze him."

Shea sighed. "I'm not surprised."

"And then, he found the ring." Thinking about it made Mikaela cringe. But she was glad it hadn't been lost. She pulled it over her head and gazed at it, letting the lamp light catch the small diamond's facets.

"Ah, the one you've worn around your neck since forever? Really, girl, you send some mixed messages."

Yeah, she'd beaten herself up about it more than once in the last few weeks. "Well, tonight wasn't much different."

"What happened?"

"He told me he still loves me."

"Ah!" Shea squealed.

"But it doesn't change anything." It couldn't. Right? Ugh, she needed to figure out her life. Get her act together, once and for all. Why did incompetence still plague her? Despite all her preparation, she still didn't have a handle on her life, on her future.

"Wait. He put his heart on the line. Did he ask you how you feel about him? How *do* you feel about him?"

She groaned. Would the fun never end tonight?

"Miks?"

"I love him."

"Ah!" This time Shea's scream was louder and Mikaela pulled her phone away from her ear, glad she lived alone.

"I tried to deny it when he asked. But that ring is a bit of a giveaway." And their kiss hadn't left much of a question. The kiss she initiated and, uh . . . demanded. The kiss he returned with such tenderness. Whoo . . .

"You've pined for him for years," Shea said, her voice gentler.

She shook her head, though of course Shea couldn't see her. If she admitted it, she'd have to admit she'd failed here too. "Nah, I've pined for the life I can never have."

"No. It's much more personal than that. You know you wouldn't be happy marrying anyone else."

"Shea, it doesn't change anything."

"You have a second chance. It changes *everything*."

Mikaela smoothed the robe over her legs. "Well, I still have to show up in Hawaii. I have to finish this, for Amelia."

"Tell me something, Miks. What exactly are you afraid of?"

Mikaela swallowed hard.

"Fear has you by the neck. It's a tough taskmaster and an

insistent motivator. But God's not in it. So, let's expose it. What are you afraid of?"

"Shoot, girl. That's insightful." Leave it to the psychologist to know how to locate Mikaela's hang-up.

"Uh-uh. No diverting. Spill it."

"Right. Um, fear. I guess I'm afraid of being abandoned again. Or rejected." The words didn't bring any sort of sting. Maybe they weren't accurate anymore.

"You give Hunt a second chance, and there is no way he is going to reject you."

The truth in those words hit like a dart in the bullseye, landing with assurance in Mikaela's heart. She knew it.

"I think there's something more," Shea said.

Insight punched Mikaela in the stomach, and she gasped. "I'm afraid I'll fail him, like I failed"—she sucked in a sob—"Granddad."

"So," Shea began after a few quiet moments, "the way you protect those you love is by keeping your distance. That's a lonely existence. Quite a price to pay for one moment in your past. Hon, you were fifteen."

Mikaela sobbed again and reached for a tissue from the box on the nightstand. That's exactly what she'd been doing. Exactly what she'd believed since the fallout of that awful day half her life ago: that because of her failure that day, she deserved to be alone.

"We nailed it," Shea said, her voice soft. "Brought it out into the light so it can't harass you so much in the dark anymore."

"You're good at this," Mikaela said, letting herself chuckle. "You should be a counselor."

"Heh!" Shea snorted. "Good idea. But seriously, have you asked Amelia what you should do? I mean, the woman's your mentor. I would think you could seek her . . . I don't know, mentoring."

"Denver said she's in the hospital, and I should give her space so she has the resources to heal."

"Her kidney?"

"Yeah, which is another of my worries."

"Worry when the doctors tell you to. Don't borrow anxiety from the future. Terrible banker."

"Humph, right?"

"Seriously, Miks. Don't break his heart again."

Her lungs squeezed. She couldn't see a way around it. "I don't think I have a choice," she whispered.

"What do you want?"

The second person to ask her that tonight. "I want this—a life here." She looked around at her bedroom in the cottage—the nautical décor. Heard the waves crashing through the open windows. Smelled the salty air. "I want to be a highly overqualified naturalist for Cahill Touring and Charters." Like she'd joked with them on the Fourth.

"Then, Dr. Rhoades, find a way."

Early the next morning, Hunter sat on the dock at his place, feet above the water as the tide crept higher. God had come through for him. Again.

Hunter used to chat with Him a lot, back before the losses. Somehow God had faded from his life after Miki left, not that He had made some decree that sent her away. Funny the connection between opening his heart to Miki and how that seemed to open him to God. But after she left, Hunter closed down, pushed God away.

That fleece Hunter had asked for a few weeks ago—that token—to let Miki stay? He'd come through for him. And tonight, she'd confirmed she'd forgiven him for breaking up with her—another miracle.

God felt close. As if the I AM sat beside him, dipping His toes into the bay like Hunter. Immediate. Present. And Hunter's heart stirred, like the moving pebbles under the incoming waves. Shifted. Polished. Shining. Refreshed.

Jesus . . .

His presence pressed even closer as Hunter thought the Name. "Jesus . . ." he whispered, closing his eyes and breathing in the salty breeze. A sense of assurance swept over him. "Thank You for answering, for hearing." For years he'd thought God wasn't listening. But this summer, He'd shown Himself. *You hear me.*

Hunter's problems were far from solved. He'd felt comfortable enough to pray about Miki, then his dad's business, and more recently about this new Seattle endeavor. So far, Dan reported progress. Their calendar was filling up. Hope. Or maybe, hope rewarded.

Not that Hunter deserved to hope, or to ask for help. But . . .

See, the thing about opening his heart—that left him exposed to getting hurt. And it'd kill him if Miki left again. Or if Dad's business failed despite all this effort.

With each hand on the deck beside him, he rocked back and forth. She'd kissed him. Initiated that kiss. Grabbed his shirt. Didn't let him refuse—not that he would've turned this face this time. Man . . .

It worked, Dad.

And that ring? She still had it. And still wore it, though on a chain. Now to get it back on her finger.

His phone buzzed against his leg. *Lord, I know it's still impossible. So much is out of our hands.* Another buzz as he held the phone in his hand. *Could You make a way for us?* His thumb hovered over the image of Miki on the screen as warmth spread through his chest. *Would You let us be married, have a family, somehow?*

He pressed to accept the call. "Hey, Miki," he kept his tone low, as if she were next to him. That whole "unable to have kids" thing didn't change how he felt about her one bit. How could it? She had his heart.

"We've got a situation." She sounded serious and professional, no hint of intimacy in her voice like he'd used in his own. "Could you meet Dr. Smythe and me at the dock?"

He was already standing. "Absolutely. So, he's on the island?"

"Yes, Captain. And he has brought some information that requires our immediate attention." Her nerves were breaking through the façade of professionalism, and he wished he could hold her hand, ease her anxiety.

"Don't worry, Miki. I'll be right there." He darted into the house and donned his Cahill garb. Before he climbed from his truck in town, he'd also don his professional persona. Anything to make Miki look good to this Smythe guy. She should finish strong, this assignment. And he'd do what he could to make that happen. Then, she'd be released—miracles could happen, right?—and decide to stay.

Then he could marry her.

Finally.

CHAPTER THIRTY-ONE

When Hunter strode into the touring office, Mom's expression confirmed his fears. No sign of Miki or the bigwig—the funding rep, as she'd explained—from Seattle. Mom's face told him this visiting doc from the U of Sea wasn't pleased. Carter came around the corner from the bathrooms down the hall, a strange look on his face. Why was *he* here?

"Did you finish the web redesign?" Let there be good news today.

Carter seemed startled by the question, then he shrugged. "Sure, it's ready."

Hunter glanced between Mom and Carter.

Carter shifted as if realizing Hunter's unspoken question. "I'm here at my uncle's request. They're waiting out near the *Millennium* for you."

Oh, that was right. Carter was this visiting doc's nephew.

"Got it." He pointed Carter toward the exit. "Be right out." After Carter stepped through the doorway, Hunter approached his mother. He hooked a thumb toward the dock. "Any idea what happened?"

Mom wrung her hands. "None . . . Mikaela looks pretty worried, like something's gone very wrong."

That's what he feared. No matter how badly Hunter wanted Miki to stay, to build a life here, he still didn't want her to fail or leave the U of Sea on bad terms—if she did eventually have to part ways with them. Hunter reached for his mom's hand. "I'll take care of it." He offered her a smile, and she seemed immediately buoyed as if she had no doubt he could solve this.

He marched out the door and down the dock toward his family's vessel. Clouds pushed in on a marine layer, making the air moist and tangy with salt. The three of them—Miki, the doc, and Carter—clustered, though Miki stood a bit apart. Oh, she looked good. Strong. Capable. Determined. That fierce spirit he loved. And, she was covering her anxiety rather well. He straightened his own spine, put on a professional smile, and geared up for a strong handshake as he drew near.

"Good morning, Professor," he said to Miki first, and she drew a long breath as if relieved he'd arrived. Her eyes smiled at him while her mouth remained neutral.

"Good morning, Captain. I'd like you to meet Dr. Denver Smythe, a fellow professor in my department from the University of Seattle. As I mentioned, he's the funding representative for the new launch in Hawaii. Currently, he is acting chair of the marine biology department." Her shoulders trembled.

Didn't that role belong to Dr. Wren?

Hunter shook his hand. The man had a regal bearing, as if he was some type of royalty who condescended to consort with the likes of them. He had a headful of white hair as if the follicles were afraid to cross him and give up their hold, though they had given up their pigment.

"Captain, I'm glad you're here," Smythe said, his voice strong. "We have some issues to discuss. Is there a private place where we could continue this meeting?" The man's bearing went toward stern now. Did this "acting chair" have the authority to fire Miki? No wonder she seemed worried underneath the surface. Every now and then she shook her hands at her sides as if they were numbing from her holding her breath.

"Pierce," Hunter began, remembering to call Carter by his first name. "Please take your uncle aboard."

Carter led the way onto the *Millennium*, followed by Smythe. When they were safely inside the main salon, Hunter whispered to Miki, "Breathe. It'll work out."

Maybe it was the peace of knowing God had this situation, and that He cared, like He'd proven this summer already. Nothing could shake Hunter's calm. Not after Miki had confessed to still loving him. They'd figure this out. God was finally on Hunter's side.

"Right," she nodded. "I'm glad we're in this together. I feel like he's got some sort of huge proclamation. And we're not going to like it."

"Maybe." He reached for her hand, but she tipped her head toward the vessel and their visitors, and Hunter nodded understanding. The way his eyes crinkled at the corners all tender like that made her believe him. But really, she'd come to a decision last night, even after telling her bestie that she wanted to stay. Fact was, she couldn't. She had to see this through for Amelia.

Hunter's unconditional acceptance melted her, but it'd be selfish of her to stay here when Amelia had sacrificed so much for her and was counting on her to see both this project through, as well as the launch in Hawaii. Then, she'd be expected to stay there and run the program. Once again, she couldn't see a way around leaving this island for the next.

But that expression in Hunter's eyes? Hope. Drat.

So, one problem at a time. She motioned toward Interim Chair Dr. Smythe and Carter and strode toward the dangling cordon.

Hunter was right behind her. "Let's do this."

They found uncle and nephew with heads bowed, sitting in the main salon on the bench seating that lined the walls. As Mikaela and Hunter approached, they both stood.

"Welcome aboard, Dr. Smythe," Hunter said. "You seem to have something on your mind." The *Millennium* swayed on the water, but the air was warmer on board, given the windows' protection.

"Yes, please tell us what brings you here." Amelia had been unreachable. But for Dr. Smythe to assume the role of acting chair, Amelia had to have vacated her seat. Why hadn't she told Mikaela? Was she hospitalized again? Some sort of emergency?

If she were, that was a confirmation that Mikaela had chosen correctly and should follow through on her commitments. The ring pendant against her chest seemed to burn her skin. Not *that* commitment . . .

She shook her head and refocused. *Stuff everything else down.*

Do what must be done.

Dr. Smythe inhaled deeply, his back straightening. He was a bit taller than her, but no match for Hunter's height. "It has come to my attention that this trial isn't running as smoothly as we'd hoped."

"I can assure you that the captain and I have addressed every situation as each arose." Including firing Jace and reassigning Destinee, but Mikaela wouldn't highlight their shenanigans. Plus, the way Destinee was blowing off her new assignment at the lab, she may not last the summer quarter.

"I've been sending updates to the department chair, Dr. Wren, regularly," Hunter said, and Mikaela noticed his formal speech. He was really trying here. He'd always supported her. Her heart squeezed with the thought that he didn't know she still planned to leave. "Dr. Wren hasn't seemed overly concerned."

"Well," Dr. Smythe began, "she is suddenly incapacitated and I have needed to step in. Just in time, it seems." He raised a hand when Mikaela was about to ask for details. "I am not at liberty to divulge her situation. All you need to know is that I have taken over. And when I learned"—he glanced at Pierce, and Mikaela had a sinking feeling in her stomach like an anchor tossed overboard—"of certain *issues* here, I knew that there hadn't been proper oversight."

Beside her, Hunter shifted. He seemed to be gearing up to defend Mikaela, but she didn't need his help. Before she could speak, Dr. Smythe waved her off and a look passed between Hunt and him.

"I've seen those e-mails you mentioned." Dr. Smythe scowled. "That's one of the reasons I'm here today."

What did *that* mean? She glanced between them and they locked horns, but no one explained. Maybe Mikaela should have asked to be cc'd on Hunter's back-and-forth with Dr. Wren. Why hadn't she? Another *oversight* on her part. Great.

"I'm sure we can put your mind at ease, Dr. Smythe," Mikaela said when neither of them explained. Why did she suddenly feel there was some sort of conspiracy—of a personal nature—between her mentor and Hunt? "What, exactly, is it that concerns you?"

He gave one nod to his nephew. "Show them."

Pierce seemed to hesitate, as if he didn't agree with whatever it was his uncle was up to. But he produced his phone and flashed Hunter and Mikaela photos, one after another, of the two of them in—

"What is—" Mikaela reached for the phone, somehow remembering politeness. "May I?" she asked Pierce. He handed it off and Hunt moved closer, peering over her shoulder.

She held her breath. How had Pierce gotten these shots? They were current photos of rather romantic moments between Mikaela and Hunter this summer. That first dive when they thought the new guy was seasick. Other rendezvous moments, some on board the *Millennium.* Thankfully no kissing. But still, the poses looked far from professional. And Dr. Smythe had seen them?

Why would Pierce betray them? Hunter had gone out of his way to find a task for Pierce to do that drew on his strengths. The new guy had changed in the few weeks he'd been here. Had he been faking the seasickness in order to spy on them? She cast a look at him, but he hunched his shoulders and wouldn't meet her gaze. Okay, there was more to the story there. Still, his betrayal hurt.

Dr. Smythe shifted on his feet. "Well? Do I get an explanation? I mean, Dr. Wren and I have specific expectations." He drilled his gaze into Mikaela's, and she forced herself to breathe. Her fingertips went tingly, and she opened and closed her fists at her sides. "Now, my nephew brings me these—this *evidence* of something far from fitting conduct." The man's face was growing red. He produced his own phone and after a few swipes flashed messages toward Mikaela. "I'm curious about your response to these e-mails. I noticed you weren't cc'd."

Mikaela reached for the phone.

Hunt blew out a loud breath beside her. "I can assure you, Dr. Smythe, we were professional when on duty."

From the corner of her eye, as she read the e-mails between Amelia and Hunter, Mikaela saw Dr. Smythe shake his head. "Those exchanges do not read that way to me, *Captain* Cahill." So formal. No one called Hunter "Captain Cahill."

The condescension in his tone registered in a faraway part of Mikaela's mind, the forefront of which was caught up in phrases like:

How are things going with our project, Hunter? From Amelia.

She's slow to warm up to me this summer.

She's driven. And lonely.

I might be able to do something about that.

Well, with the history between you, you're the man for the job.

But why would Amelia want Mikaela distracted? Maybe that's why Dr. Smythe felt the chairwoman had failed and that he needed to come rescue the project. Over the years, her mentor had hinted that Mikaela needed a family so she didn't end up like Amelia—alone for a lifetime. So, she'd teamed up with Hunter this summer? Seriously? Without telling Mikaela? That stung.

Not to mention she'd implicated herself by pointing Hunter toward a personal relationship while on the job. That couldn't reflect well on the chairwoman.

Mikaela sought Hunter's eyes. His brow furrowed, his eyes crinkled, but with worry this time.

How could you?

She faced Dr. Smythe, formal façade back in place. She'd cry later. In fact, with Dr. Smythe onsite, she might even excuse herself from this island for a while and track Amelia down. They'd made her personal life their mission. Ugh. How pathetic did that make her?

Did that mean Hunter was putting on this whole wooing thing all summer? That he didn't mean what he'd said? Did he get extra points from Amelia for getting Mikaela to kiss him? This time her fists clenched at her sides for another reason. No lack of oxygen now. These thoughts weren't even logical, but she'd have to sort them out later.

She faced the interim chair. "Dr. Smythe, I can assure you I had no idea of these *exchanges* as you put it. No one likes to be used as a pawn, maneuvered and positioned by people they trusted." One quick glance at Hunter who winced. "But know that from now on, we will conduct shore dives, which will not require the captain's involvement, and I will keep my distance from the captain on the tours except when the students are concerned. There will be no more after-hours meetings. The summer is winding down, and September is coming." She handed his phone back to him.

"I am so relieved to hear you say that. But I have a more certain way of ensuring this program finishes strong next month."

Pierce grabbed his uncle's suit-jacket covered arm. "Wait."

Dr. Smythe stilled. "What is it?"

"Don't send Dr. Rhoades away."

Send her away?!

Hunter jolted. "Excuse—"

Pierce pulled out his phone again and tapped the screen, then showed something to his uncle. "She and the captain have been great this summer. Captain Hunter had me redesign his website. They figured out what I was good at and had me doing related jobs." He peeked at Mikaela, an apology in his eyes, but she was still stuck on those words: *don't send her away*. "If you make her leave now, well, I don't think anyone else could do a better job of running things here than these two."

Dr. Smythe shoved the phone back toward Pierce and peered down his nose at his nephew. "That is not up to you. Now," he said, facing Mikaela while Hunter seemed coiled and barely contained beside her. "As I was saying, given this conflict of interest here,"— he gestured between Hunter and Mikaela—"I'm going to assign my associate, a Dr. Conrad Jessup, to finish the summer." Dr. Conrad was a retired U of Sea professor who'd settled locally. Mikaela had seen him around the labs a few times this summer.

Maybe this was for the best. Not seeing Hunter every day, and sometimes evenings too, would give her some time to process what happened. Right now, it looked like he'd conspired to trick her. Her shoulders slumped, but she straightened them. No. No self-pity. Only forward momentum. Ignore the pain in her chest. Block out the flashbacks of their history, Hunter's professions of love, and that kiss.

"I understand, Dr. Smythe." Her throat closed as the finality hit her, and she paused to collect herself. "I'll pack and head back to

Seattle." Where she could have a nice long chat with Amelia, provided her mentor was up to talking. Mikaela had failed again. Hopefully Amelia could help her salvage what was left of her career—guide her to the right path after this. Because, like before, her career was all she'd have.

"No—" Hunter said, reaching for her arm, but not touching her. Yeah, they'd come full circle.

She took one step back, distancing herself. Met his worried gray eyes. "Not to worry, Captain. I'm certain Dr. Jessup will competently assume my role." Without any conflicts of interest.

"I'm afraid you misunderstood me, Dr. Rhoades." Dr. Smythe carried himself with so much authority. Even his voice demanded attention. No doubt he wasn't full of incompetence like she was. Maybe one day she'd fail less often. Except she was already trying as hard as she could.

Hunter sighed as if relieved. But, she was still leaving. One way or another. Dr. Smythe had given her a way out—a graceful escape. She'd take it. If Amelia was seriously ill right now—and Mikaela planned to find out right away—she'd need Mikaela to carry on more than ever.

"I want you to begin your time in Hawaii early. Over there, you won't face any conflicts of interest. Plus, the team there needs your reassurance. You'll begin the work there onsite, then I'll find a suitable replacement."

There went her oxygen. "Replacement, sir? But Dr. Wren is relying on me. We share the same vision." Surely he wasn't firing her for a few e-mails outside her control.

He crossed his arms. "No. I have someone else in mind." *And now that the chairwoman is no longer in charge, it's time for my choice to move into position.* He didn't add those words, but Mikaela still heard them.

"Is this candidate someone I know?"

"No. He's a returning faculty member. He's been overseas for a while."

Pierce went all fidgety. He certainly wasn't the new assignee. But what about his father?

Mikaela faced her assistant. "Pierce, do you know the returning faculty member?"

Dr. Smythe puffed out his chest. "You have a right to know. It's Dr. Jonathan Carter, my brother-in-law."

Pierce's father.

Hunter grunted beside her, and she met his eyes. He seemed torn. Irritated, definitely. But not quite ready to condemn the senior Dr. Smythe. Did he think that if she were relieved of all her duties, she'd simply leave the U of Sea and settle down in Friday Harbor? That this made the decision for her? Yeah, there'd be no shame in that path now.

Not to mention all her hard work to get to the position of assistant professor—all the research and teaching and publishing and traveling. All lost because of one "conflict of interest"? She'd been trying to help! And now, she was drowning.

"I see." Nepotism—the same beast that assigned Pierce to her team, though he had no interest in marine bio or oceanography— would now seal her future. She'd fight it if she weren't so concerned about withdrawing from this island in favor of the next. "Do you . . ." She paused to inhale. "Do you know when Dr. Jessup will assume the new role here?" She'd take up the next battle with Amelia. One crisis at a time before she cracked in half.

"He's standing by and awaiting word from me. Don't worry," he said, waving her off, "I'll inform your students and make sure all is in place after you leave and before I turn things over to Dr. Jessup."

"What about after this season is over? I was hoping the chairperson would see fit to continue to have a working rapport with Captain Hunter and his enterprise. In fact"—though he'd betrayed her, she'd still pitch his company. No reason they should both fail—"Cahill Touring has recently launched a new chartering service in Puget Sound, out of Seattle. Perhaps the U of Sea would have need of their services there."

"Perhaps," Dr. Smythe muttered, noncommittal. "For now, thank you for your time. I'm assuming I won't have to concern myself with your conduct in Hawaii?"

"Of course not." She never should have gotten off track, allowed

241

Hunter to distract her. But he wouldn't be in Hawaii, so she could refocus on her career and make Amelia proud. "I'll be on the next plane out."

Hunter made a sound, and she turned to him. *Don't leave.*

She nudged past him. "Excuse me." She just wanted to get away from here—the *Millennium*, the memories, the betrayers. Keep herself together until she could fall apart.

"Dr. Rhoades," Hunter called after her and because Dr. Smythe was present, she turned. "What about"—he cast a glance at their visitor and then back to her—"what about your students? They'll . . . miss you."

"They're in good hands with Drs. Smythe and Jessup. I wish you well, Captain." She spun and retreated down the boarded dock.

CHAPTER THIRTY-TWO

"Thought I'd better check in, boss."

His best friend shouldn't have to treat him any differently. So, Hunter was Dan's boss; Dan didn't have to keep reminding him of it. "Stop calling me that."

Hunter pulled the phone from his ear and rolled his tight shoulders. He pounded toward his truck. Mom had waved him out when he'd brought the duo into the office. She could entertain them, answer more of Smythe's questions. Then, Hunter had called his first mate, checked if he could run today's tour. Hunter needed to catch up with Miki, apologize. Try to fix this. She didn't understand. "How's business down there?" He trusted Dan, but it didn't hurt to get an update.

"Better every day. We've gotten on the radar of some local well-paid athletes. They like to entertain guests from out of town, and this affords them privacy."

"Wow, how did we—?"

"My wife knows people."

"Sweet." So, the new venture was growing. Hope. "How is your wife, and how's Princess?" Dan had finally shared they were expecting a daughter come November. They'd dubbed her Princess in lieu of her upcoming name.

"Beth's good, and so is Princess, so far." Dan inhaled, and the sound carried through the phone. Hunter climbed into his truck and waited him out. He had a ton of things on his mind, but this needed his attention too. "Listen, Hunt, I can't thank you enough for making this happen."

"Are you kidding? *You're* making it happen."

"Dude, listen. Thank you."

Hunter allowed himself a small smile though Dan couldn't see it. "Take care of your family." He liked how it felt to do something for a friend.

"I've gotta run. But first, what's happening with you and Operation Woo Mikaela?"

Hunter snorted. "Well, she kissed me." His chest caved in as the memory replayed in his mind.

"That's moving things in the right direction."

"Then, she left." And that was why he hadn't started the truck, hadn't chased her. She was still determined to leave.

"Wha—?"

"For good. Apparently, I'm still not enough of a draw to keep her in Friday Harbor." He rubbed the back of his neck. Yeah, this didn't hurt at all. It's not as if his guts were lying in the open or anything.

And there was the issue of his own collaboration with Dr. Wren . . . Shoot.

"You know, last time you didn't go after her."

Hunter scoffed again. "You don't remember? Dad needed me. And yeah, he's not here, but he still needs me. On *this* island."

"He told you to romance Mikaela. You think he'd have a problem with you chasing her in order to make that happen?"

"What about Mom? And Cahill Touring?" He couldn't leave now. Not with Smythe breathing down his neck and sending a retired sea dog to him after all. They'd analyze his every move, probably point out all his failures. Fantastic.

"Same's true of your mom. She's a determined matchmaker."

Couldn't argue with that.

"Hunter, do not let Miki get away this time."

"She's ticked at me anyway."

Dan grunted. "What happened?"

"Don't you have to get to work?"

"My boss'll understand." Hunter could hear Dan's grin in his voice.

"She found out I've been chatting it up with her boss in Seattle—the chairwoman—and that we were conspiring together for me to romance her. So, yeah."

"It seems to me there were a lot of things conspiring for you to romance her this summer."

"Humph."

"She didn't stand a chance."

Courage fled him as he played out possible scenes in his head—track her down at her rented cottage. Explain. Ask forgiveness—once more. And watch her still drive away. He groaned and gripped the steering wheel. "I can't do this again." Had he said that out loud? Losing her after this summer would kill him. A gaping wound opened up in his chest. He'd failed. Apparently, that was his destiny.

"So do the opposite as last time."

The opposite. Last time he'd let her leave, had tried his best to wish her well as she went off without him. Did Dan mean for him to follow her this time? "I can't leave now. I certainly can't fly off to Hawaii."

"Nah, you have to. Find a way, Hunt, or miss your last chance."

"You're right." Miki would probably never be back. "Thanks." They hung up. He pulled the truck out onto the road.

Was this how God rewarded hope? "Is this what You planned all along?" He spoke toward the cab's ceiling. "To break my heart like last time?"

CHAPTER THIRTY-THREE

"Pick up. Pick up." Mikaela threw her clothes into the open bag on her bed. She'd box any leftover personal items. The cottage's owner had graciously agreed to mail them to her place in Seattle where her house sitter could handle them. They'd hash out the lease issue for this cottage later. Right now, she had a plane to make. A few planes, actually. First to Sea-Tac via a seaplane and a shuttle, then the Hawaiian Islands and a puddle jumper to get her to the lab base there.

Still no Amelia. What, had someone confiscated her phone? She'd try every Seattle hospital until she reached her, telling the staff she was Amelia's daughter if she had to. She was like the daughter Amelia never had.

Oh no. What if the chairwoman were purposely refusing to take Mikaela's calls? What if she was so frustrated with how Mikaela had failed on this assignment, that she was testing her and letting her figure out her own path through the marsh? Except, if that were true, wouldn't Amelia have let her know she was disappointed? And why hadn't she warned Mikaela that Dr. Smythe was en route, that he was now the acting chair? She pocketed her phone and yanked the charger from the wall so she could throw it into her shoulder bag.

She'd trusted her mentor. And Hunter. And they'd ganged up on her. That tortured look on his face made her question everything. Had he meant any of it? All that lovesickness . . . But what motive would he have? And Amelia. Had she only wanted to pawn Mikaela off on the nearest prospect? Of course not. Still, the humiliation stung. All those meetings were a farce. And she was the fool.

But, that lovesick expression . . . her heart teetered on the edge while reason took more cracks at knocking it off. She should let him explain, not that it would change her plans.

A seaplane awaited her, ready to buzz her up off this island. She couldn't imagine returning. Before she left, she owed Granny a face-to-face. She had half an hour. She'd finish packing here and head over to say goodbye-for-now.

Granny was in the backyard, clippers in hand as she stood next to her huge hydrangea bushes. She smiled as Mikaela approached. "Hey, sweetheart. What brings you over in the middle of the day?"

Mikaela tucked her sunglasses atop her head as she entered the shade. "Long story." She walked up and hugged Granny Belle. "Have a few minutes?"

"Let's get some ice water and have a seat."

Soon, they settled on the deck at the round table. "I'm headed to Hawaii early. One of the professors from the U showed up and has reassigned me. My boss isn't answering her phone—I think she's in the hospital. And Hunter and she were in cahoots to get me married off by Christmas." Well, okay, that might be taking it a little far, but their scheming hurt somewhere down deep that Mikaela hadn't let herself admit still existed.

"Wait a second." Granny's blue eyes shone with a touch of humor over Mikaela's fast speech. "Start at the beginning."

Mikaela filled her in on the photos Pierce had taken and the e-mails Hunter and Amelia had exchanged. "Worst part? I'm still not good enough. I tried to exceed expectations, to make Amelia proud. To show them I could do this." She rubbed her throat. "I guess I'm not ready. I should probably resign from the Hawaii post too." Except Dr. Carter was due to relieve her there, so it didn't matter now.

"'Still not good enough'?"

How much of this should she share? After all, the root lay with Granddad. "All my life, well since I was a teen, I've let people down by not being competent. Didn't matter how badly I wanted to succeed or how much I wanted to please those authority figures." She was still that fifteen-year-old, frantically pushing buttons on the marine radio and getting nowhere.

"You may not want to hear this, but again, what is God saying?"

"You assume He's talking to me about this."

Granny covered her hand with her own. "Well, hon, I assume

you're at least asking Him to."

"What if He doesn't want any of the things I want?" Oops, that sounded whiney.

"So, you're trying to outrun Him? Hide from Him? The God whose thoughts toward you outnumber the grains of sand?"

Mikaela took a long drink from her ice water glass. The liquid cooled her aching throat.

"'If I take the wings of the morning, and dwell in the uttermost parts of the sea, even there Your hand shall lead me, and Your right hand shall hold me.' That's from Psalm 139. You know it?"

"Sure." She had some recollection.

"The same passage that says His thoughts about you outnumber the grains of sand."

She considered the beaches, and then the sea bottom. And the world's desserts. All over the world—so much sand. "Surely, that's an exaggeration. I don't warrant that much attention." Who could handle a love that big?

"If you think that way," Granny began, her voice gentle, "no wonder you don't ask Him about your life and trust Him to answer."

"He didn't help that day." Her voice box clogged.

Granny set down her water glass. "What day?"

Oh, she hadn't planned to go here . . . "When Granddad died. Or when I got the diagnoses."

"First of all, you are *not* to blame for my dear Ben's death. And hear this—neither is God."

Even talking this out with Hunter hadn't eased all of Mikaela's guilt apparently, because the wound opened up again. She still blamed herself. Wait. She wasn't the only person she blamed. She *did* blame God.

Shoot.

No wonder she didn't talk over the details of her life with Him.

"And what's this about diagnoses? As in more than one?"

That was right. Granny didn't know the second one. "You knew about my kidney problems."

"Of course. Past tense, I hope, now that they found you a donor and the transplant was successful all those years ago."

"Yes, thankfully. Fact is, I'm also infertile." See, if she said it fast, she could brush over the stabbing pain. Not that she was ready for kids right now. But she'd always assumed someday she'd have them—that when she was ready she'd be . . . able.

"What? I had no idea." Granny squeezed her hand. "That's difficult news."

"I told Hunter the other night."

Oddly, Granny's face spread into a smile. "Let me guess, the news didn't faze him?"

Mikaela couldn't hold back a grunt. "Not one bit."

"I'm not surprised. That man is smitten with you. Fully."

"Those e-mails, you know where my boss is telling him to date me under the guise of check-in meetings, made me rethink all of that." But part of her knew. Didn't it? Knew he cared. Hoped desperately that he hadn't been faking that lovesickness.

"Nah, he's a goner. No question. But you're leaving again?"

"I don't have much of a choice. Plus, I'm hurt. They both lied to me."

"Okay, let's table that." Granny spread the vinyl cloth over the deck table as if to demonstrate. "Back to the diagnosis. Have you talked to God about that? I mean, you mentioned being hurt and that it made you question Him. How did He answer those accusations?"

She shrunk in her chair. "I haven't brought that up either." But then it hit her. He'd allowed it, knowing her hopes for one day and her silly fantasy that went along with wearing that ring on a chain all these years.

"Afraid of what He'll say? Or that He won't answer?"

"Honestly? I didn't think it'd make a difference to bring it up."

"Honey, He named every star and tells the sea where to stop. You don't think He might be able to do something about your diagnosis?"

"What if . . . what if He doesn't want to?"

Granny's warm smile came with tears. "Then, you ask Him what else He has for you. Because He will always have something for you.

He can't help Himself. It's His nature as the ultimate giver. Take a look at Ephesians, chapter one." She reached for Mikaela's face. "Plus, I doubt that He means to sentence you to a life of solitude only because He may never give you a pregnancy and a baby. You are worth loving. And you are loved."

A flash of Hunter's unconditional acceptance brought more tears to her eyes. She tried to catch the sob, but it spasmed out of her. Granny had found the root. Since her diagnosis, Mikaela hadn't felt lovable. Worthwhile. Not that her worth or life's purpose were entirely tied up in one day bearing children. But had she swung too far the other way and made her sense of self-worth all about her career? And if so, now that her career teetered on the cliff, where would she find value next?

Granny scooted indoors and returned, handing her a tissue. Then, she let the silence carry healing. Finally, she leaned forward. "Your worth isn't connected to anything you can or cannot do, nor does something you've done reduce your value."

Tears spilled out. "I hated that Granddad died that day, and I couldn't help him."

Granny's blue eyes teared up. "It wasn't your fault. You couldn't have kept him from walking the deck of our boat and falling in. And it's not your job to protect Hunter, to try to keep him from giving his heart away, even to you."

Was that what she'd done? Why she always felt compelled to leave? "I did make a kind of mental pact to protect those I love and to always be prepared." Not that she hadn't failed over and over.

Granny nodded as if Mikaela had landed on a key point and solved a mystery Granny had wondered about, or confirmed her suspicion. "Is it possible your anxieties cause you to try to control everything, when really it's God's job to oversee everything? He's the only one who is sovereign."

She barely caught another sob. "It's wearing me out."

"I'm sure it is, honey. You've taken on a task God didn't give you."

"So, He wants me to be passive about my future?"

"No. He has the answers you're looking for."

"Doesn't it bother you that God didn't protect Granddad? Give us some help that day?"

"Oh, sweetheart. He *did* help. Hunter and Reid came back alive from the stormy sea that afternoon. You did too."

Simply thinking about Hunter possibly dying that day made Mikaela shudder. "I didn't look at it like that." If neither Reid nor Hunt had made it back on the boat, what would she have done? She'd already proven she couldn't work the radio, and she certainly couldn't have motored the *Isabelle* back to Granny's dock. "You're right. Things could have been even more tragic."

Granny's face was full of compassion. "I think you've misinterpreted a few things from your past and based the rest of your life on those interpretations. Right now, God's unraveling all that, bringing up questions. It's a good thing. Go with it. Talk to Him about it."

Mikaela sighed. "Thanks, Granny. I've got a long night of flying ahead. And now I have some talking points for prayer."

"So, you're still going?"

"Yeah. Dr. Smythe implied they're expecting me." She stood, brushed her jeans free of pine needles from the stately firs.

Granny stood too. "Will you be back?" Her voice sounded quiet, as if she were afraid to hear the answer.

"I have no idea."

Herschfields' cottage lay in speckled sunlight, deserted. No sign of Miki. Hunter checked his watch. He hadn't hesitated that long back at the dock. Surely it'd take longer than fifteen minutes to pack up and find a flight. Where was she? Smythe had sent her to Hawaii. Would she take a ferry back to the mainland and then fly from Sea-Tac, or drive north to Bellingham and fly from there? Had she even found an upcoming flight that worked? Would she charter a seaplane down to Puget Sound?

He dialed her phone before he backed out of the driveway. Still no answer. Maybe she'd gone to her grandmother's to update her in person before leaving. He'd try there. But first, he'd drive by the ferry line.

Felt like déjà vu, heading toward the terminal. If he saw her car, would he park and run over to the waiting vehicles and ask if he could climb into hers? His stomach clenched.

See, this was the problem last time. He couldn't stop her. His love wasn't enough. *He* wasn't enough. So, he'd ended up "setting her free." Only because he'd learned he couldn't win. Her car wasn't in the lanes that he could see as he approached from up the hill and drove by. So, maybe she wasn't using the ferry this time. Would she leave her car on the island and head off via seaplane?

He dialed Granny's number.

"Hey, Hunt." Granny sounded tired, which wasn't like her.

"Granny, any sign of Miki?"

"She left a little bit ago. She's taking a seaplane from the harbor. You might catch her."

"Thanks!"

"Check in later?"

"You bet."

He parked in a stall at the Port of Friday Harbor and jumped from his truck. Would she have parked here? He should have asked Granny. No sign of her car in the lot.

That's when he heard the plane engine.

"Hey, Captain. What brings you over here today?"

Hunter swung around as the seaplane lifted off in his peripheral vision. Bill Kyle stood there—one of the pilots for this local seaplane operation. He was in his mid-fifties and had been friends with Dad. "Oh, looking for . . . someone." Hunter's throat tightened. He glanced back and saw the plane banking right.

"That professor lady?" Bill nodded his graying head toward the bay. "You just missed her. I passed her on my way back up the dock."

Of course. Of course he had. She hadn't even touched base this time. He ground his jaw, held himself together. "Thanks," he said, pretending it didn't matter.

"You okay? How's your mom?" Bill's voice carried the usual compassion of folks in town, people who had known and admired Dad.

"She's okay. Thanks."

"I've said it before, but it bears repeating. If you need anything, son, let me know." He nodded toward the town, tucked into the hillside overlooking the marina. "We're all in this together."

No doubt the flight operation had known some hard times too. "Thanks, Bill." He reached over and shook the man's hand. "Appreciate it."

Then he strode back toward his car. May as well have been out on the tour today for all the good it had done to chase Miki around town.

You just missed her.

That was why this whole thing—a summer of fulfilling his promise to Dad, of wooing Miki—had been a fool's errand.

He climbed into his truck, blinking fast. Shoving the emotions down, he threw the truck into gear. Some choice words eked through his clenched jaw.

This was the price he paid for being an idiot—for believing this time might be different. For hoping. For risking opening up again.

His phone buzzed, and he yanked it out of his pocket. Stupid hope, bullying him to even check. But what if Miki had somehow been cleared to use her phone in flight? He saw the screen. Not Miki. Granny Belle.

As much as he'd prefer to protect her from his anger, he couldn't not answer. "Hey, Granny." He ground out.

"Hey Hunter, if you have a minute, I could use your help at my shop. We need to move the old fridge out to make way for the next one. Could you pop in for a second?"

Yeah, because the people delivering the new fridge wouldn't see that whole move-the-old-one-out thing as part of their job. Sure. But this was Granny. "You got it. I'm not far away now."

"Great. Thanks, Hunter!" She sounded too chipper, like she knew everything and she was trying to cheer him up. Too late for that.

253

CHAPTER THIRTY-FOUR

Granny met him at the back door to her fudge shop, which she held open. On the way up the hill, he'd told himself to lock his emotions away. Caring meant towing his heart too close to the motorboat's propeller blades.

When it came to guarding his heart, God had encouraged him to open up. And, sure, he'd felt good for a while—better than he had in a long time. Like God wasn't out to get him and that maybe he could have the life he'd always wanted. But right now his shredded heart was leaking pain all over. His chest burned where his heart used to be. His eyes stung.

He stepped into the shop's kitchen and saw no one else around besides himself and Isabelle, no moving crew. The industrial-sized fridge hummed as usual, like it had since before Ben died. That thing was going to last forever, which meant Granny had drawn him here with a made-up story. She handed him a heavy chunk of chocolate peanut butter fudge wrapped in wax paper and pointed toward a stool she'd set up next to her long, wooden work table.

If he gulped enough of this fudge would his throat stop burning? He gnawed off a huge bite. She turned to the working-and-in-good-condition fridge and lugged out a gallon of milk, then poured him about ten ounces. Yeah, that'd help too. He accepted the glass and averted his gaze. But Granny sat down right across from him.

"One question, Hunt, because I know she's gone." She didn't even bring up the fridge.

Keep chewing. Don't feel. It's best if you don't feel.

She put a hand on his arm. "Did God turn things around for you?"

He scowled over that question, met her gaze for a flash. Gulped milk. Sure, He'd turned things around—all the way around to where they'd started the summer. Life, or God, had kicked him back into his cell. He'd spend the rest of his life there—a lonely failure who kept his head down and found some way to help his mom.

"You've been in a pit since, well, since Mikaela left the first time. Have you had any joy this season? Any peace? Any healing?"

His chest burned too much to speak. He'd just answered those questions for himself. The only reason he stayed was because he respected Granny. He'd hear her out. Then, he'd head back to his dungeon.

"You've been chasing Mikaela, but God's been chasing you. All summer, all your life." She nodded her head as if to confirm her own speech. "He wants you to have love, a fulfilling life, peace, joy. Healing. All of it."

Oh, what a cost.

I miss you, and I haven't gone anywhere.

Those words stabbed a different ache, and from a deep, lonely place in his chest, Hunter let himself answer: *I miss You too. Help me.* Because right now, he was sailing in a storm, and he had no idea which way was which, given these deep troughs and towering waves. And he did not want to go back to his prison cell.

"You can keep running after her, or you can run to Him. Let God fill up the empty places. Let Him be your joy, your life. Your peace." She shrugged her shoulders. "Your home."

The fudge felt like a rock in his gut. He set the wedge on the table. Was that what this was about? He'd replaced God with Miki?

The idea clicked in like truth, sinking and locking into place. He had. In fact, not only this summer, but maybe most of his life . . . Those Sundays she was in town, he only went to church when she did—*because* she did.

And if God really had given him those things—peace, healing, a new zeal for life—this season, maybe He wasn't the mean, disinterested villain Hunter now thought He was.

"God is for you."

Like she'd heard his thoughts. If all this was true, Hunter needed to put God in first place. He scraped up his voice. "You're right, Granny." He swallowed the burning lump. "I . . ." He closed his eyes, sucked in a long breath, tipped his head back. "I'm sorry,

Lord."

Her warm hand covered his on the table, but he didn't open his eyes. He simply sat there a minute. A sense of rightness swept into him, as if he'd finally landed on the biggest tripping hazard in his life. And peace. Peace washed over him. He winced, letting it inside.

I am here.

Thank You.

God did hear. He did care. He knew. And somehow Hunter knew He'd act. He opened his eyes to find Granny's blues sparkling back at him.

"I don't deserve it," he whispered. He'd bounced back and forth even today—yes, God hears! No God doesn't!

"None of us deserves it."

"I still don't have the answers."

She shrugged. "Me either."

He snorted and wished he hadn't. But that only made him chuckle.

Granny laughed too. "It's going to be okay."

When he hinged all his life around Miki and her choices, nothing was ever right. But hinging his life on God . . . well, that made him wonder if, no matter what happened, maybe everything really would be okay.

No matter what travel brochures would have you believe, Sea-Tac Airport and downtown Seattle were in two very different locations.

Mikaela stood in the long taxi queue in Sea-Tac's parking structure and awaited her turn. She'd head north into the city and check with the nursing staff at Bayview Hospital. Amelia still wouldn't pick up. But Mikaela knew where she was now. Was it possible her mentor was in for emergency surgery and hadn't been able to make or receive calls due to being under anesthesia and then in recovery? And if she were dealing with a health crisis, as Dr. Smythe intimated, shouldn't someone be beside her, like a daughter stand-in?

But, no matter what her health crisis right now, she was counting on Mikaela to follow through on her assignment. So, maybe Mikaela should leave this line and get on that flight to Hawaii. Dr. Smythe was in charge now, and he'd sent her to the tropical islands. But this whole situation didn't add up. Why would Amelia risk her own job and Mikaela's by making those e-mails the official check-in, knowing Dr. Smythe might see them? Why not text Hunter from her private phone, if they were going to scheme? She wouldn't want to sabotage Mikaela, or the program, right? She'd been friends with Reid Cahill. There's no way she would risk sabotaging Cahill Touring.

Mikaela had stayed analytical for the last two flights, barring off the emotions, distracting herself. The buzz of this international airport around her, the traffic, the smog, the people rushing everywhere, the lines . . . she didn't want this city life.

And though she could, in theory, walk away from everything she'd worked so hard for all these years, she could *not* let her mentor down. Not after everything she'd done for her.

Which was why she'd go to Hawaii and make every effort. And try to forget she'd left Hunter standing at the Port of Friday Harbor dock, watching her seaplane lift into the sky.

She yanked her luggage along behind her and left the growing taxi queue.

Here she was, again, making her own decisions without praying first. Rushing off, and then standing indecisive at every fork in the road. She marched back toward the elevators and took one up a floor to the Sky Bridge and back into the terminal. Inside, she found a sunny window without too much commotion around her.

Simply rest. Oh, His voice. And she hadn't even started talking. He'd been waiting to talk to her.

Her heart thudded, her fingertips were numb.

Breathe.

She inhaled, her lungs expanding. *I thought I was past this.* She checked but saw no one nearby. Keeping her hand on her luggage handle, she closed her eyes into the sunlight. *I didn't anticipate going to Hawaii early. Tell me again, what do I do about Hunter? I was trying to help him.*

You did.

Images flashed through her mind of Hunter's smiling eyes, his laughter. His letting loose as they took the family on the Fourth cruise and teamed up to give everyone a memorable private tour. His earnest expression when he'd told her he still loved her. Those thoughts could warm her if she weren't angry at him. *I didn't like being made a project.*

Isn't that what you made of Hunter? Wasn't Cahill a project?

She swallowed, and her eyes snapped open. Traffic buzzed past below outside, people rushing, cars honking and dodging. She *had* treated Hunter like a project. A sick feeling filled her empty stomach, and she laid a hand on her tight abdomen. *I'm sorry, Lord. I did.* Now she knew how he must have felt that day she'd arrived all "Here I am to fix everything!"

Ugh.

You need to tell him that. You need to talk to him.

A child squealed somewhere nearby, and Mikaela glanced at the clock on her phone. Time to catch that flight to Hawaii.

But she would talk to Hunter. Sometime. And she'd hear him out, because that's what friends did. Even friends like her with a messiah complex who only wanted to help.

She advanced toward the long security lines. Yeah, it'd take a miracle to make her flight now. *So, Lord, I need to leave all of this in Your hands.* If she made this flight, she'd trust that it was God's will. No matter how much it hurt.

CHAPTER THIRTY-FIVE

As soon as Mikaela took her phone off airplane mode on the ground in Hawaii, an e-mail, several text messages, and a few voice mails awaited.

According to the e-mail from her local contact here, there'd been a change of plans. Rather than meet on the Big Island, she was to remain on Oahu and meet her team in Honolulu the following morning. They'd booked her into a local hotel and had sent transportation to collect her from the airport. Nice of them to give her one day to recover from flying overnight.

Balmy morning breezes whispered around her as she slugged through the open-air walkways in the airport. No morning chill of summer days like in Friday Harbor. She'd flown the red-eye and desperately needed rest. At baggage claim, a driver held a sign that read, "Dr. Rhoades." He'd get her to the hotel.

In the town car, her phone buzzed again, reminding her that in her busy arrival she hadn't checked all those texts and voice mails. An incoming call. From Amelia.

She scrambled to accept, almost dropping the phone. "Amelia! Are you all right?"

"Oh, good. I finally reached you." She sounded weak, but determined. "I'm fine. Listen, where are you?"

"Heading to my hotel in Honolulu. Why?" Surely she'd been updated about the new plans, and this wouldn't surprise her.

Her mentor groaned into the phone. "That's what I was afraid of."

"Why? What am I missing?" Hadn't God wanted Mikaela to come here? For once, she'd prayed ahead and not solely pleaded that God would bless her endeavors. Instead, she'd trusted that He'd show her what to do.

"Dr. Smythe," Amelia began, "did not have the authority to force you to abandon your summer assignment early."

"What? But he's the interim chair now that you're . . . uh, sick?"

"I didn't want to worry you. I had a kidney transplant. It's been a battle for a few months. But they finally found me a match. And, as you recall, the pace rushes when everything comes together."

Mikaela pressed against the back seat of the town car, sighing deeply. *Thank You, God.*

"I have been out of the office more than usual. And of course, for the surgery. But Denver had no right to charge up to Friday Harbor and kick you out."

"Do you know why he did it?"

"Yes, something about pictures of you and the captain flirting. Or that's what he said. Nonsense."

Mikaela chortled. "Well, he didn't seem to think so."

"Unbelievable. I go under anesthesia and need a couple of weeks to recover, and he sees it as a license to book a seaplane and invade the islands."

Mikaela laughed aloud, shaking her head. Amelia hadn't lost any of her sense of humor. "Well, what now? The local team is expecting me."

"So, take a few meetings, look around. Make sure everything is in place there as much as possible. Your replacement will appreciate it."

Mikaela stilled. "My replacement? So, Dr. Smythe's brother-in-law will still take over here?" Her thoughts circled while exhaustion weighed her down.

"Yes." Amelia drew a deep breath as Mikaela's town car arrived at the hotel—another open-air building with no street-level front wall before the stairs that led up to the check-in desk from the sidewalk. "I don't want you to worry about any of this. Tell me something."

"Sure. Hang on one second." She tried to pay the driver, but he waved her hand away saying the fare had been covered. He brought her luggage around from the trunk and smiled before driving off. Standing on the sidewalk, Mikaela focused again on Amelia. Morning sunshine warmed her shoulders. "Sorry. Go ahead."

"Where do you want to be? I remember years ago you said Hawaii would be a great place to settle down. Lots of opportunity for a marine biologist. But what does your current dream look like?"

Hunter's smile flashed into her mind. That lovesick gaze that undid her and practically coerced her into wanting to kiss him.

Amelia was still waiting. "Where's home? Because I'm guessing things might have changed."

Should she share the truth? Tell her honestly what she thought? How to explain herself without sounding like a martyr. "Several years ago, my mentor—

"And friend."

Mikaela smiled as people moved around her on the sidewalk. "Yes, and friend, heard about my hereditary kidney disease. She willingly went in to be tested as a possible match. And we matched."

"Yes, we did."

Mikaela's eyes stung. "You've been such a gift to me, all this time—professionally, personally . . . medically."

"Heh!" Dr. Wren sounded stronger as the conversation progressed.

"So, let me see this through—this launch out here in Hawaii where you've always wanted to live. Let me do this for you."

"No."

Like in Washington, Mikaela gripped her luggage and closed her eyes. *No.* She'd failed so badly that even though the chairwoman loved her as a friend, she didn't trust her as a professional.

"You still haven't answered my question," Amelia pressed.

"All cards on the table?"

"Every last one."

"Friday Harbor. That's home." She sucked a breath, willing oxygen to her fingertips. "Always has been." Her heart had never really left.

"Then this is my latest gift to you, as benevolent as I am—ha!—move back to Friday Harbor. Run the new program there. Remain a part of the U of Sea. Or . . . don't. Maybe you want to finally go into marine animal rescue. Do what makes you happy. And grow a family. Trust me. Don't miss out on that like I did." Amelia's voice grew small. Mikaela wouldn't tell her the final secret—her infertility. Maybe during a later conversation.

Dr. Wren wasn't condemning her for failing once again. Instead, she was releasing her to pursue her current dreams. To pursue Hunter. Speaking of which . . . "I hope this isn't overstepping, but I didn't like being your project."

"Hunter's in the same boat." Amelia laughed at her pun. "So that makes you a good pair, doesn't it? Now all you need is close proximity. Think you can fix that?"

Mikaela strode toward the hotel's check-in desk, unable to stop her smile. "Yes, Dr. Wren, that's something I can absolutely do."

CHAPTER THIRTY-SIX

When the charter schedule had already been booked for Labor Day, Jenna-Shea Brown's family had chosen this Monday in mid-September as their charter day. The weather was cooperating. And instead of tooling around Bellingham Bay, they wanted to explore the San Juans, without the crowds of a regular tour. Hunter and his first mate, Sam Kerry, would take the *Millennium* down to Anacortes on Fidalgo Island and pick them up. Oh, how he wished Miki were here today. Not that he was centering his life around her anymore, but Jenna-Shea was her dear friend and ... well, Miki belonged here. He missed her.

Whataya say, God? Hunter climbed up from the galley after ensuring the caterers, who would sail with them today, had what they needed. The galley smelled of garlic and vinegar from the Greek salad, and of roasted meat from the souvlaki. Several kabobs lined with lamb and chicken tempted him almost too far. But he hadn't paid for this food. His customers had. He'd eat leftovers. In about seven hours when he brought the *Millennium* back to dock in Friday Harbor.

The engines hummed along without hiccups. *I know I put her first. I'm trying not to do that anymore.* Hunter would trust Him because that was the only way of life where he'd finally found ongoing peace. And occasionally hope, the old cruel master. Except hope had given him some happiness this summer. "Your will, God."

His baristas—there were two on board today—were dusting the vinyl benches in the salon while sunshine poured in. No sign of a marine layer today. The naturalist who had replaced Jace Jones shuffled around, seemingly unsure of what to do until the tour began. "See if Sam needs anything on the bridge, Kurt."

"Sure, Cap'n."

Apparently Jace and Destinee had run off together right after being let go. The rest of the students weren't here today—probably finishing up their summer projects over at the lab with Dr. Jessup. Dr. Stuffy was back in Seattle, and his nephew had gone with him.

Carter hadn't wanted to look Hunter in the eye after his deception came out. Not only had he taken the pictures, he'd posted negative reviews for Cahill Touring under a few different names online. But he had, with his head down and his feet shuffling, come to Hunter and his mother, and explained he hadn't meant to get them in trouble or risk the business. His uncle had coerced him into testing Mikaela and Hunter and trying to catch them doing things wrong. He was determined, from the outset, to ensure his brother-in-law had a place to land when he returned from Europe.

Carter had insisted he really was seasick on smaller boats. He apologized, and though it hurt that Miki had had to leave because of Carter's hijinks, Hunter couldn't really hold anything against him. Meanwhile, the website redesign was getting lots of attention, and Carter had gotten commissions to build sites for other local businesses. He'd seemed like a new person before he left.

"Hellooo!"

What in the worl— His mind flashed back to earlier this summer, and he stepped away from the stairs where he'd been about to join Kurt and Sam on the bridge. Sounded like . . . *Miki?* He spun and saw her standing on the dock, a long summer dress teasing her legs over strappy sandals. Her golden hair hung in wide curls over her bronze shoulders. He liked this déjà vu.

The smell of diesel from running engines soured the air as he walked toward the cordon, still in place.

"Permission to come aboard, Captain?" Her grin could yank his heart out of his chest.

Was this possible? "Why aren't you in Hawaii?"

She snorted and crossed her arms. "Some welcome."

He released the cordon and lifted a hand toward her to help her board. Then he went all formal. "Oh, excuse me, Professor. Welcome back."

She stopped in front of him, and Hunter could feel his baristas' eyes on them, but he didn't care. He lowered his voice. "Tell me you're really here."

Her eyes sparkled with a smile. "I'm really here."

"For how long?" *Please, God . . .*

"Let me answer that this way: perhaps you shouldn't say 'welcome back' so much as 'welcome home'."

His breath caught. "Yeah?" *Oh, Jesus.* Sometimes Hunter's prayers were simply that, lately—two words to the Lover of his soul.

She stepped right into his space then, and her vanilla scent overpowered all other aromas. "We have some things to talk about."

He grinned down at her. So much spunk. "Do we?"

She pressed her lips together, a delicious grin hiding there somewhere. But then she went serious. "Yeah, like why you and the department chair would team up about me."

"You and Mom teamed up about me, Professor M." He took her hand to show he wasn't angry.

"Best thing I ever did."

"So you're the prof who'll be sailing with us today?"

She laughed. "From now on, if I may, Captain." She stilled, and her attention lowered to his mouth.

See, now he had a decision to make. Here on board, he was supposed to be all professional and keep the biz's reputation aboveboard. But if she wanted a kiss, there was no way he'd deny her. His breath went choppy merely thinking about that.

"Is all forgiven, Hunt?"

He cupped her elbows now, and she rested her hands against his chest. "Yes. And can you forgive me?"

She studied his eyes. "Something's different."

"You didn't answer my question."

"No. I mean, yes. Yes, I forgive you for anything and everything I need to. But you're different somehow."

He tipped his head. "No more Captain Crabby?" Hopefully for good this time.

She eyed him, smiling. "Yeah, though I have been known to kiss a few crabs in my day."

He chuckled deep. A sense of rightness, of *home*, like Granny said, stirred inside.

One of her hands slid up his chest, over his shoulder, to the back of his neck and he bent to help her reach, which put his face very close to hers. When she opened her mouth, he took that as permission and closed the gap bringing his lips to hers.

"Hey, Cap'n—" Sam's voice behind him.

Hunter pulled back, taking Miki's hand, not sorry one bit. "Sam, look who's joining us."

"Mikaela Rhoades." He smiled like a caring grandfather. "How long will you be with us?"

Hunter tilted his head to catch her answer, still not ready to risk believing she was back for good.

"For as long as Captain Hunter will have me." She brought her free hand into Hunter's view and opened her fist. The chain and gold ring glittered in the light. She dropped the combo into his hand, and his heart thumped. Was this the moment? Should he wait until Shea was on board? Talk to Miki's father again?

Lord . . .?

No answer, except a feeling inside that this *wasn't* the moment. He pocketed the handful of gold. "For safekeeping."

She smiled at him, swinging their hands between them.

"Well, I guess that answers that." Sam faced Hunter, a big dopey grin on his face. "We have some paying customers waiting in Anacortes."

"Yes, we do." He pulled Miki toward the stairs leading up to the bridge. "Let's go pick up your friends, Professor."

At the dock in Anacortes, Hunter and Mikaela welcomed Shea, her sister and family, and Shea's parents aboard. In all, six guests plus the crew members and caterers, including Mikaela. But she was beginning to see herself as more of a crewmember.

During her flight back from Hawaii to Seattle and then the shuttle and seaplane trip to Friday Harbor, she'd pondered her future—well, prayed and pondered. What did she want? She wanted a future with Hunter, in Friday Harbor, working out on the water. If she continued in her role at the U of Sea, she'd be required to attend and conduct quarterly meetings in Seattle, keep up with her researching and pursuit of publishing, not to mention several trips a year to meet with fellow experts in her field. Her time would be divided. But was she ready to leave the university and walk away from what she'd built there?

On her Facebook feed, halfway across the Pacific on the plane's Wi-Fi service, she'd seen a meme with this verse: "Delight yourself also in the LORD, and He shall give you the desires of your heart . . ." Was delighting related to talking to Him more often? Maybe it was a small start, but she'd at least finally begun to ask Him about her hopes and dreams.

And look what had happened. Granny had said God was generous. Perhaps, even though Mikaela didn't have everything figured out, her weak attempts still mattered to Him. Maybe, though she hadn't made all the best decisions, He was honoring her latest ones. He was already giving her the desires of her heart. And that made her grateful to Him, which felt a lot like delight.

As Hunter shook hands with Shea's father, Stephen Brown, pride welled up in Mikaela. Hunter was a good man. Something was definitely different about him since she'd been away. She hadn't known what to expect when she returned. But he'd been warm, content like she'd never seen him. And it made her respect and admire him more.

He caught her gaze and welcomed her beside him. No more standing on opposite ends of the boat. Shea gave her a knowing look as Mikaela settled against Hunter's side with a smile. Shea raised her eyebrows and Mikaela nodded, grinning like a fool, no doubt. Must have answered several of her BFF's questions.

From beside Hunter, Mikaela greeted Stephen next, and then his wife, Delores. "Welcome." Something so right about being tight against Hunter's side. Wanted. Cherished. Home. She could decide her future later. Today those unknowns could wait. Maybe she'd grown because now she didn't have to be prepared for everything.

Jenna-Shea's sister, Jewel-Kate, climbed aboard in front of her husband, Andrew, who carried their recently recovered son, Jaxon.

"Hey you guys!" Mikaela hugged Jewel. "How's your little guy?" She tweaked Jaxon's bare knee. He wore shorts and a T-shirt.

"All better now," Andrew said. "Captain," he greeted Hunter. Jaxon squirmed to get down.

"Feel free to call me Hunter. We're probably about the same age."

"Ah, but I could never sail something like this." He gestured around them at the large vessel. "I would like a peek at the bridge, though. Always have been fascinated by the romance of the sea." He elbowed his wife, who smiled up at him.

Jewel gave Hunter a mock scowl. "Don't encourage him or next thing I know we'll be living on a houseboat and tooling around Elliott Bay every afternoon."

Mikaela laughed aloud before hugging Shea, who'd hung back. "Hey, girl. How are things?"

"What's going on, Miks? Something you need to share with the class?" Despite her words, she kept her voice low.

Mikaela shrugged. "We're together." Could she help it if her face glowed like fireworks on the Fourth?

Shea's brown eyes lit up. "When we get a second, you're going to have to tell me everything."

"Absolutely." Such freedom in having all her secrets out now.

Jaxon took off running through the salon as soon as Andrew let him down. Hunter put on his captain's hat and squatted. "Hey, Jax!" The boy turned and stopped, eyed Hunter and his hat. "Do you know who I am?"

Once shy Jaxon approached and stood straight and tall. "Yes, sir." He saluted. "You're the captain."

"Yes." Hunter returned the salute. "I'm Captain Hunter. And I need to tell you about some rules we have on board the *Millennium*—that's the name of this ship."

"The '*Millen-ni-num*?'"

"Close enough. We have some very important rules here. First, we don't run."

The boy nodded, looking serious but not ashamed.

"One of the rules is so important it only applies to you." He pointed at Jaxon and earned a grin.

Mikaela's heart melted at the way Hunter interacted with him. He'd make a fantastic father. *Please, God.* But she didn't have to beg Him. He already knew. And somehow she knew He cared. Peace flooded over her at those thoughts.

Hunter turned toward the naturalist, Kurt, as he approached carrying a miniature life jacket. "As long as you're on board, you need to wear this." Hunter held it up before the boy. "Got it?"

Jaxon nodded, sober-faced. "Yes, sir."

"This is a special vest. Do you mind if I put it on you?" Hunter sought permission from Jaxon and both of the kid's parents, who consented.

"That's fine." Jaxon seemed eager to cooperate with this special rule. Mikaela wanted to hug Hunter for how he'd talked the squirming boy into obliging.

Hunter tightened the straps. "Now, I need to tell you something else."

Jaxon's eyes went wide. Hunt had his undivided attention.

"If, and I say if because we're hoping this is never needed, but *if* you were to be in the water out there"—Hunter pointed toward the harbor and all that deep blue—"here's what you do: turn your face toward the sky and this vest will help you float up so you can breathe air." Hunter peered up again at Jewel-Kate and Andrew. "Does he know how to swim?"

Jewel grimaced. "We've only had a couple of classes."

Hunt refocused on the kiddo. "Okay, then, do you know how to hold your breath if the water covers your face?"

Jaxon nodded vigorously. "Yes, sir!" He puffed out his cheeks and held his breath.

"Good job! Now, breathe."

Jaxon complied.

"If you are surrounded by water, tip your face toward the sky. If your face is *in* the water, hold your—what?"

"Breath!"

Hunter high-fived him. "And if your face is outside the water, even if your face is still wet, do what?"

"Breathe all I want!"

"Yes!" Another high five, and Mikaela's heart fell deeper for the handsome captain who'd made sure their precious cargo knew the rules and had strategies if anything were to happen. Not that anything would. As far as Mikaela knew, no one had ever fallen off the *Millennium* during their trips.

"Excuse me, am I in the right place?" A dark-haired, tall, fit man of about thirty stood on the dock. "I'm meeting Stephen Brown here."

Beside Mikaela, as everyone stood around in the salon, Shea gasped while her father, Stephen, stepped from behind Kurt. "Liam, you made it!" They shook hands, and Liam climbed aboard.

Liam? Liam Barrett? Shea's onetime boyfriend from college? They hadn't dated very long, and Mikaela had never gotten the whole story. She eyed her bestie and read so much discomfort, she almost laughed. Ah, the tables had turned.

"Captain Hunter, I hope you don't mind," Stephen began, "I've asked a family friend to join us for the sail today. This is Liam Barrett, he's the handyman for our properties down on Bainbridge Island."

While everyone greeted Liam, Mikaela pulled Shea away from the group. "What's *he* doing here?"

Shea cast glances over Mikaela's shoulder. "I don't know. My parents keep trying to play matchmaker. My mom's all about my bio clock."

"Speaking of babies, why isn't he married with a bunch of them?" The guy was sure handsome enough to attract a woman's attention.

"I don't know." Shea crossed her tan arms over her sundress. "I haven't asked him. Do me a favor and run interference. I'm on a break from dating. And why are you grinning?"

"Because I like that we're talking about *your* romantic life for once and not mine."

"There is nothing romant—"

"Jenna-Shea, dear, come say hello to Liam," Shea's mother, Delores, called from the huddle of family and friends.

Shea groaned and complied, but she grabbed Mikaela's hand and dragged her along behind.

CHAPTER THIRTY-SEVEN

A little longer and they'd arrive in Anacortes and drop off the Browns and the Mills, and that Liam guy. Shea seemed uncomfortable around him. Must be a story there. Hunter was proud of their success today. The Browns and their guests had seen orcas, harbor seals, bow-riding Dall's porpoise, a nest of bald eagles, and even some humpback whales, which had appeared in greater numbers this year out here in the Salish Sea.

"Captain!" Kurt yelled up from the bottom of the stairs. "Child overboard!"

Hunter's heart stopped. "Take the wheel, Sam. Call the Coast Guard!"

"Sure thing, Cap'n." Sam turned off the engine, and Hunter bolted down the stairs. In all the years Dad had run the tours, they'd never had a person go overboard. Obviously Hunter had failed again.

He arrived at the bottom of the steps to engine silence—ominous. He dumped his cell and his keys on the barista's counter and kicked off his shoes. On his way to prep the rescue raft, he called to the clustering group in the main salon who were pointing toward the water. "Keep an eye on him. Tell me what happened."

Miki appeared at his side and helped him unlatch the raft. She'd already removed her sandals.

Jewel-Kate and Andrew were frantic. "He got away from us," Andrew said. "And the current pulled him one way while we kept going the other." At least he hadn't jumped in too—an often fatal mistake.

"Don't lose sight of him." Hunter stared at their backs while they pointed. "Stay on board. I'll get him."

Delores cried and clung to Stephen. "He's drifting away fast!"

Frantic splashing caught Hunter's eye off the starboard side, but Jaxon was too far for the roped life ring to reach him from here.

Plus, Hunter hadn't covered what Jaxon should do with the life ring. So, the first two steps in *Reach, throw, row, and go* were moot. *Oh, Lord, I've failed again.* This was why he'd never measure up. But maybe he didn't need to be perfect. Maybe simply being a dependent son was enough. *Father, please help us get him safely back.* Now that his own dad was gone, he'd found comfort in addressing God this way—the Father to the fatherless.

He hauled on a life jacket and tightened the strap. Miki returned to his side with a portable life ring, rope coiled. She'd also pulled on a life jacket. "I'm going with you."

"No, stay here. Keep an eye on him." Images of her grandfather, Ben, in the water flooded his mind. Nope. He wouldn't risk her life. "Miki, I don't want to worry about you too."

She breathed fast, and a battle waged in her eyes. "I'm coming." *Let me do this.* Maybe she needed to prove herself. If he couldn't use the help, he'd tell her to stay on board.

"Okay. Kurt. Gear up." Thank God, quite literally, that they'd trained the newbie for this.

"Yes, sir."

Hunter faced the families. "Keep pointing. Sam's already calling for help, and I heard the anchor drop." *Things will* not *end like last time.*

He and Miki got the raft into position. Hunter rechecked and got another visual on Jaxon. He was drifting fast, like something stronger than the current was pulling him. *What in the world?*

He and Kurt dropped the rescue raft into the water and fired up the engine. They couldn't maneuver the *Millennium* closer without serious risk, and the propellers on this little boat would need to be stilled when they got close. But first, they had to get close. *Hang on, Jaxon.*

Beside him, Miki braced herself, leaning into the waves' impacts like he was doing. Kurt steered. One of the reasons Hunter had hired him was his extensive experience on the water.

They drew closer to the splashing, and Miki pointed. "I see him!"

"Whoa!" Kurt yelled. Three orca fins surfaced, surrounding

Jaxon. Hunter knew they never attacked humans, so were they trying to help him?

"Cut the engine, Kurt." Hunter tried to stay calm. In the middle of the low swells and members of the K-pod floated Jaxon. No longer splashing and waving his arms. He was head-up in the water, but his eyes were closed. Had he inhaled seawater? Were they already too late?

"Please, God. I know You hear us. You're with us. You care. Don't let Jaxon drown today." Miki's prayer brought a lump to Hunter's throat.

One of the orcas surfaced again, and Hunt couldn't miss the fishing net over its dorsal. The same netting that was wrapped around Jaxon's foot. "Oh, Lord . . ." He prayed aloud this time. "There's fishing net. You two stay here." He dove into the cold water pushing against his body's reaction to the intense temperature change. He hadn't swum with orcas before and hadn't ever planned to. But the animals didn't seem to mind his presence. In fact, they seemed to make a pathway for him to get through and reach Jaxon.

"Hey Jax," Hunter said as he came next to him, kicking as he tread water. "It's Captain Hunter." The boy was breathing. "Thank You, God. Listen, Jax, I'm going to get you back on our ship." He worked to unwrap the netting from the kid's foot, and then brought Jaxon close to pull him back to the raft. He heard a splash nearby and glanced up to see Miki swimming toward the orcas. What was she doing? He'd already safely gotten to Jax.

He couldn't worry about both of them. She was a good swimmer. So long as she hadn't injured herself going in, she'd be fine. He pushed toward the raft, and Kurt reached down to pull Jaxon aboard. Once the boy was safely on board, Kurt started first aid measures to get the kid to expel any water he'd swallowed.

Hunter spun in the water, kicking to push himself higher and see over the swells. Where was Miki? His heart stopped. Then he saw her swimming back to him, a look of triumph on her face. He handed her into the raft and then dragged himself in as well. "What happened?"

Shivering, she wrung out her long hair and began to weave it into a side braid. "That orca knew the fishing net was also wrapped around Jaxon. That's why she stayed close to him. I couldn't leave her like that. So, I set her free."

He reached for her hand. "Thank God she didn't dive."

Jaxon was coming around. "Thank God for a lot of things today," Miki said.

He met her eyes. *We did it.*

The triumph in her eyes said, *Yes, we did!*

EPILOGUE

Two Months Later

Hunter paced, waiting for the ferry to dock. Wind whipped against him in gusts this November day. Salty spray from the whitecaps in the bay tanged the air. He hunched his shoulders and dug his hands into his jacket pockets. He'd wait inside the touring office if he wasn't bursting to see Miki. She'd been gone two months, selling her condo in Seattle, tying up loose ends at the U.

From the bridge of the *Millennium*, he'd watched the ferry approach for the last twenty minutes as it eased into the harbor. If Miki hadn't driven onto the boat, he'd wait for her over at the terminal, despite the biting wind. Mom scurried around inside the shop, all nervous excitement. Hunter shook his head, smiling. She'd grown more lighthearted lately, a new spring in her step.

Since they'd launched the Seattle satellite and gotten good word-of-mouth among some of the elite there, business had increased so much Dan was now working full time for Hunter. They had hired a complete staff, and leased a small office in the south end. Dan and Beth's baby girl was thriving and due any day now. Local tours had stopped at the end of the peak season—September. But they still did private charters, including weddings and anniversary parties. Business was successful. He'd done it—saved Cahill Touring.

Mom insisted Dad would be proud. Hunter didn't fight the smile right then. Really, he couldn't take much credit. Like Granny said, God had turned things around. Astonishingly—from losing the business, and their homes, to a new idea and a growing business and getting caught up on their mortgage payments. He'd given his mother a raise and even discussed her taking more time for herself. She'd found some new hobbies and joined a women's group. She seemed to be healing more and grieving less these days.

Dr. Amelia Wren had chatted with Hunter a few times this season while Miki had been away, settling things in Seattle. Yes, they wanted to carry on with the program. Next year, they'd add spring quarter, along with a new faculty member from the U of Sea. Miki had changed gears. She'd be the advisor, but after rescuing the orca from the fishing net that day last September, the local whale rescue team had been in contact. They wondered if she would consider working with them part time. And, of course, Cahill Touring had an immediate opening for an overqualified naturalist on all their tours and charters.

He missed last summer's crop of students—Seth, Anya, and Kristopher. They'd cheered for Miki and him when they'd seen them together, and Hunter had almost regretted that Destinee hadn't still been here. She'd always teased that Hunter and Miki belonged together, and with good reason.

A little blue Kia zipped into the small parking lot. *Miki.* Hunter stepped forward and pointed her into his empty parking stall. She wore a big grin as she parked. He met her at her door, opening it for her, blocking what wind he could. "Are you really here for good?"

She climbed from the car wearing black leggings with boots and a long, brown coat. She looked adorable all bundled up. Standing in front of him, she said, "I sure am, Captain."

He wrapped her in his arms. "The harbor's a little less hospitable this time of year."

"I don't care. I'm warm."

"You're *home.*" He leaned down for a kiss.

After a moment, she shivered and he tugged her toward the office.

"Granny's here!" Miki said as he held the door open for her. Inside, holiday music played and candles burned on the counter. Miki hugged Granny Belle and Hunter's mom.

"Welcome back!"

"I'm so glad you're here to stay!" Granny said, hugging her twice.

Could either of these two matchmakers grin any wider? Miki

slipped off her gloves. The ring in his pocket seemed to burn against his leg. "Miki?" he said, getting her attention so she turned toward him. He lowered himself to one knee, and she gasped and walked closer. "I have a question for you." Mom and Granny Belle huddled together, big smiles behind raised hands. Suddenly his lungs tightened. She was really here. Finally.

Thank You, God.

He shot a glance at Mom whose eyes said, *Your dad would be so proud.* He swallowed and refocused on Miki. Pinching the ring with his fingers, he lifted it to her—the same ring he'd proposed with last time up over the San Juan Islands. Tears filled her eyes as she gazed down at him, and he could hardly contain the love flooding his heart. "Will you marry me?" He'd hoped to say more, but those were the only words he could manage.

Her chin quivered. "Yes!" She reached her trembling left hand toward him, and he slipped the ring onto her finger. Then, she took hold of his hand and pulled him to his feet while Mom and Granny Belle whooped from the sidelines.

He stood and stepped close, taking her face gently in his hands. "I love you." He thumbed away a tear that slipped down her cheek.

She caught a sob and another tear slipped down while he tried to rein in his own emotions.

"My Miki."

"I love you too, Hunt. I always have."

He bent his head and kissed her again, as if their family members weren't in the room. Considering all the clapping and cheering, they didn't seem to mind.

Afterward...

Now for a Sneak Peek at book two
Finding Love on Bainbridge Island
As well as an Author Note and contact info

Finding Love on Bainbridge Island

CHAPTER ONE

Liam Barrett could use some fresh air.

This red-eye from Hawaii to Seattle seemed unending, especially with this snoring guy next to him smelling of curry. Before the flight crew demanded he pocket his phone, he wanted to check on his aunt. So long as she kept uploading pictures of her pets or the stormy June weather on Puget Sound, he knew she was okay. But any lag in her online activity and he got worried. His zany great-aunt Matilda was a social butterfly, but she could also be a bit . . . eccentric. The shorter her leash—and his absences from her vicinity—the better.

A vintage photo of a father, mother, and children was captioned in Auntie Mat's latest upload: *Family is everything. Make peace.* He shook his head, though it wasn't surprising she would post something odd. The point was—he had confirmation she was fine. A relief after everything she'd done for him.

The phone buzzed in his hand as another FB notification popped up: *New friend request from Jack Barrett.*

His heart thumped. Wha—?

A flash in his mind of his mother, alone, crying and not stopping. Preschooler Liam standing at her bedroom doorway, watching. *"You okay, Mommy?"* He'd rubbed his stomach where it hurt. Should he run to her? Hold her hand? Could he hug her and make it better like she did for him? He darted to her side. *"Mommy, are you broken?"*

Now at almost thirty, his thumb shook as he pressed the power button and turned off his phone. He should've deleted the request immediately. Blocked him. Rejection would send a message without Liam having to send a message. He wanted to throw his cell. Or maybe hurl himself off something. How soon could he and his buddies schedule another getaway full of daredevil stunts?

"We are now beginning our descent into Seattle-Tacoma International Airport. Local weather in Seattle is fifty-six degrees and cloudy with a 70 percent chance of rain this afternoon. Local time is 6:35 a.m." The flight attendant went on to list the various end-of-flight things, like raised tray tables and final trash collection, and Liam tuned him out.

Jack Barrett.

Liam hadn't seen that name for at least two years. Back then, he'd run an online search, as if compelled to track down the man and prove Liam was no longer helpless. Half hating his own curiosity, he'd scrolled links. He hadn't done this research as a child, hadn't asked his mom any questions so he wouldn't upset her. The name *Jack Barrett* wasn't uncommon in the Northwest. But, heart thumping, Liam had narrowed it down to those born in Bremerton, Washington, around fifty years ago.

Best match for the Jack Liam researched? A felon, busted for armed robbery, grand theft auto, drug possession, and several DUIs. No wonder Mom never mentioned him. Stellar guy. Role model material. Liam didn't drink, didn't use drugs. *He'd* never chased the next high—outside of adrenaline. Or been pulled over by the police. Not even so much as a parking ticket. No, in those ways he was nothing like Jack.

It was the similarities that troubled Liam.

Shake it off, dude.

The plane touched down and most passengers squeezed into the aisle as soon as the fasten seat belt light went out. Liam let the guy in his row pass, glad to put some distance between them. As much as he wanted to bail, he'd be last off today. He and his three buddies would exit after the final passenger—one member of the group moving much slower since the "incident." Poor Hitch.

Liam had a role with his buddies—easygoing. Jack Barrett's name could cancel that part of Liam. The part that had learned to move forward, avoid being too serious.

Around him, his buddies roused. Across the aisle, Isaac "Jinx" Tabor stood and reached overhead. Liam bumped him, though he had plenty of room above his own seat. "Hurry up, Jinx."

Jinx laughed and reached into the compartment. "Shoot, Liam, hang on! I'm grabbing our newly disabled guy's bag too."

"Disabled? Thanks for that. It's only a broken bone." Clark Branson, known to the group as Hitch since he'd recently gotten married, waited behind them near the lav doors, crutches rammed under his pits. "Flying was sure easier before I needed these." He nodded toward the new accessories.

"We didn't tell you to break your ankle." Liam tugged down his duffel bag. This was good. Forget the notification.

"Get a move on, will you?" This from Dylan "Burr" Burgess at the tail of the plane.

Liam marched toward the now-open cockpit. Another adventure in the books. They'd dived with sharks and tried cliff diving for the first time.

Out in the concourse, the four of them lined up. Hitch hobbled along and without him even asking, the others slowed their pace. The guy's foot must be throbbing after the several-hour flight with no way to elevate it. Still, the guys teased him about the new *hitch* in his step.

"You're all gonna get it. Line up, and I'll whack you with my crutch!"

"Who knew those things made good weapons? Maybe we should alert security." Liam laughed. "You know your wife is going to kill you, right?" Heaven help Liam, but having a wife who could insist he avoid adventures wasn't for him. *Good luck, Hitch, and no thanks.*

Liam caught his sheepish expression before Hitch answered. "Yup."

"See, that's why I'm not getting married," Burr said, yanking his duffel strap higher up his shoulder.

"Nah," Jinx joked, "no one'll have you!" He darted away before Burr could punch him. "There's a reason we call you *Burr*."

This earned him a scowl.

The troop went quiet while they waited for the elevator to take them to baggage claim where Hitch's wife and father would meet them. Soon, Jinx and Burr would head back to the Eastside, and

Liam would return to Bainbridge Island—something his buddies would never forgive for how posh the island was. Didn't matter that Liam lived in a tiny house—not the cool kind—inland, which meant no water view. Or that the roof leaked after the last rainstorm.

At baggage claim, gorgeous Fiona Branson approached the group. Hitch wore the dopiest of grins. She beelined to him as if she didn't want him to take another step and break something else. "Oh, Clark! Are you all right?" The guys elbowed each other over that name, while Fiona examined him, probably looking for more injuries.

All that fussing—Hitch could keep it. Except, what would it be like to come home to someone? He had a sudden image of Jenna-Shea Brown, the only person he'd ever wanted to come home to. But, she'd made it clear long ago that he'd blown his one chance with her.

All her fuss aside, no one had ever looked at Liam like Fiona looked at Hitch.

"Hey, everyone!" Hitch's dad stepped into the group. Elijah Branson was a solid guy. He'd personally taken them up in his plane for a few skydives over the years. Seeing Hitch like this, Elijah didn't fret over his son, merely patted his shoulder. "Glad to see you're still with us."

"Hey, Dad," Hitch tilted his head down, but then he raised it and met his father's eyes, as if seeking approval or something, even though he was a grown man. But the looks they exchanged—silent communication from knowing each other so well. Shoot. What was that like? To have someone trustworthy who worked to protect you and build you up?

A dad. Not that Liam would know much about that dynamic.

Eli eyed his son's gimpy limb—the cast the Hawaiian doc had put on him, anchoring his ankle to his shin. "You're okay?"

Hitch nodded. "Yup."

"Good. Let's get you home. I'm here to carry this." He reached toward the duffel bag Fiona held, which she happily handed over with a "thanks." Fiona smiled at her father-in-law. Yeah, everyone got along well with Eli. The rest of the guys greeted him, shaking his hand and guy-hugging him with their other arms. He brought respect out of you, and you couldn't object to his warmth, or the way he genuinely cared for his son and his family, but also this foursome who grew up raising Cain together.

They still enjoyed their adventures. But the clock was ticking for Hitch. His days of cliff diving, skydiving, and shark diving were about to end.

A few see-ya-laters after that, and Hitch hobbled off with his wife and dad while Liam watched them.

"You coming, Liam?" Jinx asked from several feet away.

He meandered in his direction. "How's your beach house project?" Jinx fell into step next to Liam—a faster pace now.

Cold, moist air hit as soon as they entered the sky bridge that led to Sea-Tac's parking structure and the taxi line. Raindrops streaked the tinted plexiglass, rushing down the sides of the elevated and transparent tunnel perched over the harried traffic below. Yeah, Hawaii in June beat Seattle hands down.

"Electrical this week. Glad the Browns don't need the house for another few weeks. It's been one thing after another."

Burr nudged Jinx. "Yeah, we feel sorry for you. All that suffering at the beach."

"I don't live at the beach, Burr." *He* could volunteer to trek over and help, but nope. Whatever it was Burr did all day kept him too busy to lend a hand.

Burr grunted again.

For once, Liam was fighting to succeed at something, but all Burr could do was badger him. Enough. "No, I get it. You don't have your life together, so you can't respect that that's what I'm trying to do." Ever since Liam had learned of Jack Barrett's criminal record, he'd determined not to be like him. To avoid brushes with the law, but also to thrive at work, be dependable.

At the walk-up parking payment booths, Burr stopped. "Yeah? Is that what you think? Working on my sobriety doesn't matter?"

"Dude, it matters." Jinx spoke up—ever the peacemaker. "C'mon, Liam."

Liam ground his jaw. No matter what he did, Burr always seemed ticked at him, which pushed Liam's buttons and made him overreact. "Knock it off, Burr." Everyone had seen him their last night in Hawaii. Nobody said anything, but everybody saw. The guy was spiraling again, without a chute. It wasn't like the four of them to sit around in a circle and spill their guts to each other. So no one really knew what was eating Burr—what secret, or regret, or whatever. The way Burr could push Liam's hot buttons made Liam keep his distance.

Except Liam did owe him.

Burr pivoted away. "See ya, Islander."

There it was. His nickname. Liam clenched his jaw. He didn't hate the nickname, but he knew Burr meant it as a dig—implying Liam was always on vacation or that he was lazy. Burr stalked off. Liam looked at Jinx. "Keep an eye on him, okay?"

A fast sigh. "Yeah. I always do." Jinx lived near Burr, so it fell to him to play babysitter of the tribe's weakest member.

"Jinx!" Burr called from the elevator bank, elbow locked while he held the door.

He jumped, but then shifted into the put-together façade no one ever bought. Jinx was not only the peacemaker, he was the klutz. Eccentric himself in some ways. "Gotta run. Give your auntie Mat a kiss for me!" Because he tried so hard to fake competence in everyday life, he often tripped or sabotaged himself—thus the name Jinx.

But if anyone could figure out what was up with Burr, it was Jinx. For some reason Burr didn't bark at him, most of the time.

Liam watched him lope off toward the brooding Burr and felt that sense of aloneness that always followed the high of the guys' getaways. Hitch with his family, Jinx and Burr driving back to the Eastside, and Liam stuffing his parking stub into the automated booth, followed by his credit card, before scuffing toward his parked truck. It was cheaper to leave his beat-up truck here for a few days than to pay a ride service the fare both ways for the distance to Bainbridge from this airport.

He'd head back to his house—alone—and try not to think of

how good Hitch had it.

Oh, and Jack Barrett. Liam would rather not think of him ever again.

Liam was going to kill her.

Matilda Hartwell clicked on the active message box in Facebook. *I THINK HE MIGHT BE READY TO AT LEAST LISTEN TO WHAT YOU HAVE TO SAY.*

The response was quick. *ALL I CAN DO IS HOPE.*

AND PRAY.

Their conversation went still for several moments, and Matilda wondered if the other writer had stopped to do just that. She'd heard he'd changed, but what if he wasn't a good guy, even now? She wanted to write a new message immediately and demand to know if he'd truly changed. Get him to promise only good would come of this contact attempt. Thing was—Liam was no longer a child under her protection. Not that she'd ever put him in harm's way, of course, not even emotionally. Not after all Liam had been through.

Honestly, she wouldn't even consider messaging this man today if she wasn't utterly convinced this road was best for Liam. Her nephew carried too much baggage from the past. Too much hurt—and anger, probably—though he covered it pretty well.

Minutes had passed now, and still no activity on the other message-sender's end. Matilda clicked into the message box once more and typed: *ALL YOU CAN DO IS TRY.* Gulp. *SEND HIM A FRIEND REQUEST. SEE WHAT HAPPENS.*

Again, silence. Had he left his computer, or pocketed his phone? The site's note said he'd "seen" it, but that notification could result from an open computer. No guarantees he was there.

She'd take a break and see if her gull friend was back on her water-side deck. Perhaps he was hungry. She kept old bread only for him. Sure, part of her knew she should let him fend for himself, but he kept her company while she gardened. For that, he deserved a treat. Plus, she enjoyed singing with him.

Ten minutes later, she returned to her laptop. Still nothing. And then, motion. He was typing.

ALREADY DONE . . .

Matilda's nails clicked as she responded: THEN, WE WAIT.

TERRIFYING.

I KNOW.

Liam would have a few choices when he found the friend request. He could delete it right away. He could block the sender. And if God was working miracles at this moment, Liam could accept. Matilda pressed her lips together. No doubt God *was* working miracles somewhere, but Liam had some decisions to make and God wouldn't force him.

For as long as Matilda had been Liam's guardian, and even before, she'd tried to teach him the freedom of forgiveness, and how not forgiving brought regret, anger, even rage to the surface. Hopefully he'd keep those truths in mind when he saw the name pop up in his friend requests.

When Liam returned from his latest adventure, she'd ask him. In the meantime, she clicked back over to the genealogy site. She knew the details around Liam's generation and some of the previous generation, but the one before that—almost nothing. Today, she'd try to find Liam's paternal grandparents' names. But for now . . . She clicked into the family tree she was creating and pressed Liam's name. Then she clicked on Add Father.

There she typed: *Jack Barrett.*

Author Note

Dear friends, I took some artistic license throughout this story—from the setting, to the touring company, to the school's pilot program. I even invented a university. If you're familiar with the settings, I hope you'll find some great moments here. I wanted to write a series that transported readers to the sea, to the beach, because I am an incurable beach lover!

Large marine animals and bodies of water have fascinated me most of my life. Our family took a vacation to Michigan's Lake Superior when I was a tween, and I remember the boulders and tall, fresh-water waves and how the huge freighters terrified me; but I also recall enjoying the mystery of the deep water. Later, I moved to the Pacific Northwest and got to enjoy saltwater up close. What a treat! All the sea life and mystery—exactly what does lie in the deep? I still can't get enough.

I've been an avid reader of Christian fiction for well over twenty years. Several years ago, I browsed a Christian bookstore looking for a novella collection of beach-based fiction, something set along the Pacific Coast, that I could read during the warm summer months. I couldn't find any such collection, so I decided to write a novella myself. Fast-forward through time and the novella grew into the full-length story you now hold in your hands.

Now for some fudge. My kiddos will tell you, whenever we take family vacations to the beach, I always find the nearest fudge shop and pick up a bit to share. This once-a-year sweet is such a treat. So, I had to include that dessert in this beachy story.

And finally, I enjoyed exploring the aspect of God wooing people in this novel. I know God woos us because He's done this with me, and I'm so grateful. He sees, He knows, He cares, He rescues, and He is working on our behalf. This is our God.

Many blessings, dear readers!

I'd love to connect with you if you have a question or want to make a comment. Also, I love reviews, so if you enjoyed this book, would you consider leaving a review on Amazon, Goodreads, BarnesandNoble.com, etc.? Thank you!

You can connect with me at the following places:

www.AnnetteIrby.com

https://twitter.com/AnnetteMIrby
(or @AnnetteMIrby)

www.SeriouslyWrite.blogspot.com

www.AnnetteIrbyReviews.blogspot.com

Facebook: Annette M. Irby Reader Friends
https://www.facebook.com/groups/252272708574760

Made in the USA
Lexington, KY
01 October 2017